PROMISE ME THIS

PROMISE ME THIS

CHRISTY AWARD–WINNING AUTHOR

CATHY GOHLKE

Tyndale House Publishers, Inc.

CAROL STREAM, ILLINOIS

Visit Tyndale online at www.tyndale.com.

Visit Cathy Gohlke's website at www.cathygohlke.com.

TYNDALE and Tyndale's quill logo are registered trademarks of Tyndale House Publishers, Inc.

Promise Me This

Copyright © 2012 by Cathy Gohlke. All rights reserved.

Cover photograph of woman taken by Stephen Vosloo. Copyright © by Tyndale House Publishers, Inc. All rights reserved.

Cover photograph of coastline copyright © PeteRyan/National Geographic/Getty Images. All rights reserved.

The *Titanic* at the moment of its Departure from Southampton Harbour on 10th April, 1912 (litho), /Private Collection/Archives Charmet/The Bridgeman Art Library International.

Designed by Ron Kaufmann

Edited by Sarah Mason

Published in association with the literary agency of Natasha Kern Literary Agency, Inc., P.O. Box 1069, White Salmon, WA 98672.

Unless otherwise indicated, all Scripture quotations are taken from the *Holy Bible*, King James Version.

Scripture quotations marked NIV are taken from the Holy Bible, *New International Version,*® *NIV.*® Copyright © 1973, 1978, 1984, 2011 by Biblica, Inc.™ Used by permission of Zondervan. All rights reserved worldwide. www.zondervan.com.

Library of Congress Cataloging-in-Publication Data

Gohlke, Cathy.
    Promise me this / Cathy Gohlke.
      p. cm.
    ISBN 978-1-4143-5307-4 (softcover)
    I. Title.
    PS3607.O3448P76 2012
    813'.6—dc23   2011034977

Printed in the United States of America

18   17   16   15   14   13   12
7   6   5   4   3   2   1

A Wedding Gift
For Tim and Elisabeth Gardiner
Welcome Son and Precious Daughter
Loved Beyond Measure

"See! The winter is past; the rains are over and gone.
Flowers appear on the earth; the season of singing has
come, the cooing of doves is heard in our land."

SONG OF SONGS 2:11-12 (NIV)

ACKNOWLEDGMENTS

This story and its themes are offered with thanksgiving, as a picture of Christ's love story to the world—His gift by grace that forever changed and made possible all that we are and hope to be.

I am deeply grateful to . . .

—my husband, Dan, for donning your chauffeur cap and sharing research adventures for this book throughout England, France, and Germany, and for your insights on this manuscript. You bless me with your love.

—my son, Daniel, for traipsing the hills and dales of France and Germany with me, for interpreting and translating among the people, museums, and books found in lovely France and in my manuscript. Your companionship is joy to me.

—my daughter, Elisabeth, for sharing research treks through Berlin and Oranienburg, and for the inspiration of your loving nature. This book is dedicated to you and to your new husband, Timothy Neil Gardiner—a man of God and most welcome family member. May God bless your life together.

—Natasha Kern, my agent, for loving this story enough to challenge me, for wise counsel through new territory, and for finding its publishing home.

—Stephanie Broene and Sarah Mason, my insightful and gifted editors, for working with me to bring to print what lay on my heart; Babette Rea, my innovative marketing manager; Christy Stroud, my publicist; the wonderfully creative design, PR, and sales teams, and all at Tyndale House Publishers who worked to bring this book to life.

—the generous and diligent team of family, friends, and colleagues who shared my vision for this story, read, or critiqued this book in its early stages: Gloria Bernice Goforth Lemons, Gloria Delk, Dan Lounsbury, Reverend Karen Bunnell, Carrie Turansky, Terri Gillespie, and Tracy Leinberger-Leonardi.

—my families of origin and marriage, friends, church family of Elkton United Methodist Church, and writing colleagues who regularly pray for and encourage me in this journey. I know that I do not travel alone, and I am so very grateful.

—Marge and Henry Jacobs, for sharing your fathers' war photos, family heirlooms, and history from WWI.

—Debbie and Dominique Desmettre, for opening your home to weary travelers and for recommending WWI research sites in France.

—historian Somers Carston, the enthusiastic volunteers of the Cape May County Historical Society, and the wonderfully helpful staff of the Cape May Courthouse Library in New Jersey. You brought Cape May County, NJ, (1912–1919) to life for me.

—the owners and creators of Leaming's Run Gardens in Swainton, NJ, just outside Cape May Courthouse. Allen's Run Gardens are based on your lovely gardens, graciously open to the public.

—the curators of the Southampton, England, Maritime Museum for your fine *Titanic* collection and many books; the groundskeeper in Bunhill Fields cemetery, London, for patiently answering my questions; the many museums, new and used bookstores, and helpful staff in London, Dover, and Lincoln, England; the museum staff and helpful people of Calais, Verdun, Colmar, Reims, Lyon, and in the countryside of France; the many tour guides, museum staff, and bookstores in Berlin, Germany, and the gracious German families who opened their homes to an inquisitive American.

—Charles Haas for his excellent books on *Titanic*, Lyn MacDonald, for her extensive interviews of WWI medical and military personnel, and Arlen Hansen for his research on the ambulance drivers of WWI.

And thank you, always, Uncle Wilbur, for reminding me that a sure way to know if I'm working in the will of God is to ask, "Do I have joy? Is this yoke easy? Is this burden light?"

PART ONE

≋ CHAPTER ONE ≋

THE GREAT SHIP RETURNED late from her sea trials beyond the shores of Carrickfergus, needing only her sea papers, a last-minute load of supplies, and the Belfast mail before racing to Southampton.

But in that rush to ferry supplies, a dockworker's hand was crushed beneath two heavy crates carelessly dropped. The fury and swearing that followed reddened the neck of the toughest man aboard the sturdy supply boat.

Michael Dunnagan's eyes and ears spread wide with all the fascination of his fifteen years.

"You there! Lad! Do you want to make a shilling?"

Michael, who'd stolen the last two hours of the day from his sweep's work to run home and scrub before seeing *Titanic* off, turned at the gruff offer, certain he'd not heard with both ears.

"Are you deaf, lad? Do you want to make a shilling, I say!" the mate aboard the supply craft called again.

"I do, sir! I do!" Michael vowed, propelled by wonder and a fear the man might change his mind.

"Give us a hand, then. My man's smashed his paw, and we've got to get these supplies aboard *Titanic*. She's late from her trials and wants to be under way!"

Michael could not move his feet from the splintered dock. For months he'd slipped from work to steal glimpses of the lady's growing. He'd spied three years ago as her magnificent keel was laid and had checked week by week as ribs grew into skeleton, as metal plates formed sinew and muscle to strengthen her frame, as decks and funnels fleshed her out. He'd speculated on her finishing, the sure beauty and mystery of her insides. He had cheered,

3

with most of Belfast, as she'd been gently pulled from her berth that morning by tugboats so small with names so mighty that the contrast was laughable.

To stand on the dock and see her sitting low in the water, her sleek lines lit by electric lights against the cold spring twilight, was a wonder of its own. The idea of stepping onto her polished deck—and being paid to do it—was joyous beyond anything in Michael's ken.

But his uncle Tom was aboard *Titanic* in the stoker hole, shoveling coal for her mighty engines. Michael had snuck to the docks to celebrate the parting from his uncle's angry fists and lashing belt as much as he'd come to see *Titanic* herself. He'd never dared to defend himself against the hateful man twice his size, but Michael surely meant to spit a final good-bye.

"Are you coming or not?" the dockhand barked.

"Aye!" Michael dared the risk and jumped aboard the supply boat, trying for the nimble footing of a sailor rather than the clunky feet of a sweep. Orders were shouted from every direction. Fancy chairs, crates of food, and kitchen supplies were stowed in every conceivable space. Mailbags flew from hands on dock to hands on deck. As soon as the lines were tossed aboard, the supply craft fairly flew through the harbor.

Staff of Harland and Wolff—the ship's designers and builders—firemen, and yard workers not sailing to Southampton stood on *Titanic*'s deck, ready to be lightered ashore. The supply boat pulled alongside her.

Michael bent his head, just in case Uncle Tom was among those sent ashore, though he figured it unlikely. He hefted the low end of a kitchen crate and followed it aboard *Titanic*, repeating in his mind the two words of the only prayer he remembered: *Sweet Jesus. Sweet Jesus. Sweet Jesus.*

"Don't be leaving them there!" An authoritarian sort in blue uniform bellowed at the load of chairs set squarely on the deck. "Bring those along to the first-class reception room!"

Michael dropped the kitchen crate where he stood. Sweeping a wicker chair clumsily beneath each arm, he followed the corridor-winding trail blazed by the man ahead of him.

He clamped his mouth to keep it from trailing his toes. Golden oak, carved and scrolled, waxed to a high sheen, swept past him. Fancy patterned carpeting in colors he would have wagered grew only in flowers along the River Shannon made him whistle low. Mahogany steps, grand beyond words, swept up, up to he didn't know where.

He caught his breath at the domed skylight above it all.

Lights, so high he had to crane his neck to see, and spread wider than a man could stretch, looked for all the world to Michael like layers of icicles and stars, twinkling, dangling one set upon the other.

But Michael gasped as his eyes traveled downward again. He turned away from the center railing, feeling heat creep up his neck. Why the masters of *Titanic* wanted a statue of a winged and naked child to hold a lamp was more than he could imagine.

"Oy! Mind what you're about, lad!" A deckhand wheeled a skid of crates, barely missing Michael's back. "If we scrape these bulkheads, we're done for. I'll not be wanting my pay docked because a gutter rat can't keep his head."

"I'll mind, sir. I will, sir." Michael took no offense. He considered himself a class of vermin somewhat lower than a gutter rat. He swallowed and thought, *But the luckiest vermin that ever lived!*

"Set them round here," the fussy man ordered. Immediately the first-class reception room was filled with men and chairs and confounding directions. A disagreement over the placement of chairs broke out between two argumentative types in crisp uniforms.

The man who'd followed close on Michael's heels stepped back, muttering beneath his breath, "Young bucks busting their britches." A minute passed before he shook his head and spoke from the side of his mouth. "Come, me boyo. We'll fetch another load. Blathering still, they'll be."

But as they turned, the men in uniform forged an agreement and called for Michael to rearrange the chairs. Michael stepped lively, moved each one willingly, deliberately, and moved a couple again, only to stay longer in the wondrous room.

But as quickly as the cavernous room had filled, it emptied. The last of the uniformed men was summoned to the dining room next door, and Michael stood alone in the vast hall.

He started for the passageway, then stopped. He knew he should return to the deck with the other hands and finish loading supplies. But what if he didn't? What if he just sat down and took his ease? What if he dared stay in the fine room until *Titanic* reached Southampton? What if he then walked off the ship—simply walked into England?

Michael's brow creased in consternation. He sucked in his breath, nearly giddy at the notion: to leave Belfast and Ireland for good and all, never again to feel Uncle Tom's belt or buckle lashed across his face or shoulders.

And there was Jack Deegan to consider. When Deegan had injured his back aboard his last ship, he'd struck a bargain with Uncle Tom. Deegan had eagerly traded his discharge book—a stoker's ticket aboard one of the big liners—for Uncle Tom's flat and Michael's sweep wages for twelve months. As cruel as his uncle had always been, experience made Michael fear being left alone with Jack Deegan even more.

To walk away from Uncle Tom, from Jack Deegan, from the memory of these miserable six years past, and even from the guilt and shame of failing Megan Marie—it was a dream, complex and startling. And it flashed through Michael's mind in a moment.

He swallowed. Uncle Tom would be in the stoker hole or firemen's quarters while aboard ship. Once in Southampton he would surely spend his shore leave at the pubs. Michael could avoid him for this short voyage.

"Sweet Jesus," Michael whispered again, his heart drumming a beat until it pounded the walls of his chest. He had begged for years, never believing his prayers had been heard or would be answered.

Michael waited half a minute. When no one came, he crept cautiously across the room, far from the main entry, and slid, the back side of a whisper, beneath the table nearest the wall.

What's the worst they could do to me? he wondered. *Send me back? Throw me to the sharks?* He winced. It was a fair trade.

Minutes passed and still no one came. Shrill whistle blasts signaled *Titanic*'s departure from the harbor. Michael wondered if the mate who'd hired him had missed him, or if he'd counted himself lucky to be saved the bargained shilling. He wondered if Uncle Tom or Jack Deegan would figure out what he'd done, hunt him down, and drag him back. He wondered if it was possible the Sweet Jesus listened to the prayers of creatures lower than gutter rats after all.

≋ CHAPTER TWO ≋

"I SIMPLY CANNOT KEEP the child alone with me any longer," Eleanor Hargrave insisted, stabbing her silver-handled cane into the pile of the Persian carpet spread across her drawing room floor. "While I am yet able to travel, I am determined to tour the Continent. My dear cousins in Berlin have been so very patient, awaiting my visit while I served my father, then raised your father's orphaned child."

It was the story of martyrdom Owen had heard from his spinster aunt month after month, year after year, designed and never failing to induce guilt. It was the story of her life of sacrifice and grueling servitude, first to her widowed and demanding father, whom her younger sister had self-ishly deserted, and then to the orphaned children of that sister and her husband. His aunt constantly referred to that sacrifice as her gift to his poor departed father, though no mention was ever made of her own sister, Owen and Annie's mother. Owen tried to listen patiently.

"It is unfair of either of you to presume upon me any longer. You simply must take the girl and provide for her or return here to help me look after her. If you do not, I shall be forced to send her away to school—Scotland, I should think."

"I agree, Aunt. I'll see to it immediately."

"You cannot know the worry and vexation caused me by—" His aunt stopped her litany midsentence. "What did you say?"

"I said that I agree. You've been most patient and generous with Annie and with me—a saint." What Owen did not say was that he, too, was aware that his sister grew each day to look more like their beautiful mother—the sister Aunt Eleanor despised. It was little wonder she wanted Annie out of his sight.

"You will return here, then?"

He heard the hope in his aunt's voice.

"I've made arrangements for Annie to begin boarding school in Southampton."

"Southampton? You mean you will not . . ." She stopped, folded her hands, and lifted her chin. "No one of consequence attends school in Southampton."

"We are not people of financial consequence, Aunt. We are hardworking people of substantial character, as were our parents." Owen had yearned to say that to his aunt for years.

Her eyes flashed. "Your pride is up, young man. My father would say, 'Your Allen Irish is showing.'"

Owen felt his jaw tighten.

And then his aunt smiled—a thing so rare that Owen's eyebrows rose in return.

She leaned forward to stroke his cheek. "Impetuous. So like Mackenzie. You grow more like him—in looks and demeanor—each time I see you."

Owen pulled back. He'd never liked the possessiveness of his aunt's touch, nor the way she constantly likened him to his father. And now that he'd set his sights on the beautiful, widowed Lucy Snape, whose toddler needed a financially stable father, it was essential that he establish his independence.

Eleanor sniffed and sat back. "It is impossible. Elisabeth Anne must remain in London. It is the only suitable society for a young lady. You will return to Hargrave House." She took a sip of tea, then replaced her teacup firmly in its saucer. "Your room stands ready."

"Not this time, Aunt." Owen spoke quietly, leaning forward to replace his own cup, willing it not to rattle. "I will support Annie from now on."

"On gardener's wages. And send her to a boarding school—in a shipping town!" She laughed.

"A convenient location for those going to sea." Owen paused, debating how to proceed. "Or those crossing the sea."

"The sea?" His aunt's voice took on the suspicion, even the menace, that Owen feared. But he would do this, afraid or not.

Owen leaned forward again, breathing the prayer that never failed him. "Do you remember Uncle Sean Allen, in America?"

She stiffened.

"He and Aunt Maggie offered Father half of their landscaping business in New Jersey after Mother died."

"A foolish proposition—a child's dream! The idea of whisking two motherless children to a godforsaken—"

"It was a proposition that might have saved him from the grief that took his life—if you hadn't interfered!" Owen stopped, horrified that he'd spoken aloud the words harbored in his heart these four years but delighted that at last he'd mustered the courage.

She drew herself up. "If it was not an accident that sent him to his grave, it was his own ridiculous pining for a woman too silly to help him manage his business! I offered your father everything—this home, my inheritance, introduction to the finest families. He needn't have worked at all, and if he had insisted, I could have procured any business connections he dreamed of in England. I can do all of that for you, Owen. I offer all of that to you."

And it would be the death of all my hopes for Lucy—or even someone like her—just as you were the death of Father's hopes and dreams. "I'm grateful for the roof you've given Annie and me these four years, Aunt. But it's time for us to go. Uncle Sean has made to me the same offer he made to Father, and I've accepted. I sail Easter week."

"Easter!" she gasped.

"As soon as we turn a profit, I'll send for Annie."

"He has been in that business these many years and not succeeded?" She snorted scornfully, but the fear that he meant to go did not leave her eyes.

He leaned forward. "Do you not see, Aunt? Do you not see this is a chance of a lifetime—for Annie and for me?"

"What I see is that you are foolish and ungrateful, with no more common sense than your father! I see that you are willing to throw away your life on a silly scheme that will come to nothing and that you intend to drag the child down beside you!" Her voice rose with each word, piercing the air.

Owen drew back. He'd not hurt Annie for the world. At fourteen, she was not a child in his eyes; that she remained so in Aunt Eleanor's estimation was reason enough to get her away from Hargrave House.

Eleanor's face fell to pleading, her demands to wheedling. "Owen, stay here. I can set you up in your own gardening business, if that is what you want. You can experiment with whatever you like in our own greenhouses. They will be entirely at your disposal."

Owen folded his serviette and placed it on the tea tray. The action gave him peace, finality. "I'm sorry you cannot be happy for us, Aunt. But it is the solution to our mutual dilemmas."

A minute of silence passed between them, but Owen's heart did not slow.

"Leave me, Owen, and I will strike you from my will." The words came softly, a Judas kiss.

Owen stood and bowed.

"My estate means nothing to you?"

"It comes at too high a price, Aunt." Owen breathed, relieved that the deed was done. "I'll stay the night and then must get back to Southampton. I'll return to collect Annie and her things early next week." He bowed again and walked away.

"There is something more. I had not intended to tell you—not yet."

Owen turned.

His aunt folded her hands in her lap. "It was your grandfather's doing."

Annie knelt beside the stair rail, her nerves taut, her eyes stretched wide in worry. When at last Owen stepped through the parlor door, she let out the breath she hadn't realized she was holding.

But Owen didn't move. Annie leaned over the railing for a better look at her brother. His hands covered his head, pressed against the doorframe, and she was certain he moaned. She stood back, biting her lower lip. She'd never heard such a sound from her older brother. "Owen? Owen!" she whispered loudly into the hallway below.

At last he climbed, two stairs at a time, but she'd never seen him look so weary.

"I could hear her shouting all the way up here. What has happened?" Annie met him at the landing and rushed into his arms.

"Come, close the door, Annie." Owen spoke low, pulling her into her room. "Pack your things, everything you want to keep. We'll not be back."

"Pack my things? Why? Where are we going?"

But her brother would not meet her eyes. He pulled her carpetbag from the top of the cupboard and spread it open. He picked up their parents' wedding photograph from her bedside table. "You'll want this."

"Whatever are you doing?"

Owen wrapped the frame in the linen it sat upon and placed it in the bottom of her bag. "I'll tell you when we've settled for the night. Now you must pack, and quickly."

"Am I going to live with you?"

He shook his head. "Pack, Annie."

"Is Aunt Eleanor sending me away?"

"She knows we're going. She—"

They both started when Annie's door swung wide.

"Jamison!" Annie gasped.

The old butler's bent frame filled the low doorway. He looked over his shoulder, put a finger to his lips, and motioned Owen closer. "Do you have a place for Miss Annie, sir?"

Owen ran his fingers through his hair. "In Southampton, as soon as I can arrange it. I don't know what we shall do tonight."

Jamison nodded and pushed a crumpled paper into Owen's hand.

"Jamison!" Eleanor Hargrave bellowed from the first floor.

"What's going on?" Annie begged.

"Take this round to my old sister, Nellie Woodward. Her address is on the bottom. She will do right by you for the night," the butler whispered.

"Jamison! Come—at once!" Annie heard their aunt rap her cane against the parlor doorframe.

"Good-bye, Miss Annie." Jamison's ever-formal voice caught in his throat.

"No." Annie shook her head, confused, disbelieving, and reached for Jamison. "I can't say good-bye like this!" Her eyes filled. "Someone tell me what's happening!"

The butler took her hands in his for the briefest moment, coughed, and stepped back. "God take care of you both, Mr. Owen. Write to us when you get to America. Let us know you are well, and Miss Annie, too." He nodded. "You can send a letter to my Nellie. She'll see that I get it."

"America?" Annie gasped. "We're going to America?"

Jamison caught Owen's eye, clearly sorry he'd said so much, and looked away. But Owen wrung the butler's withered hand. "Thank you, old friend."

Jamison turned quickly and crept down the polished stairs.

"Owen," Annie began, hope rising in her chest.

"Don't stop to talk now, Annie! Hurry, before Aunt Eleanor sends you off with nothing!"

Annie whirled. "America! Where to begin?" She plucked her Sunday frock from the cupboard; Owen grabbed her most serviceable. She tucked in stationery and coloring pencils; Owen packed her Bible, *The Pilgrim's Progress*, and the few books of poetry their mother had loved.

"You must wear your spring and winter cloaks. Layer everything you can."

"It isn't that cold!" Annie sputtered.

"Do it," Owen insisted.

They stuffed all they could into her carpetbag and a pillow slip. Ten minutes later they turned down the lamp, slipped down the servants' stairs, and closed the back kitchen door softly behind them.

CHAPTER THREE

"WELL, THEN—" the widow Woodward clucked her tongue—"you're away for good and all to America, are you, Miss Annie?"

Annie drew in her breath, looked helplessly toward her brother, desperate for an explanation, and finally shrugged. "Yes, I think we are."

But Owen turned away.

Nellie Woodward raised her brows as she poured their tea. "Her ladyship won't like that, now will she?"

Forty-five years Jamison had worked for the Hargraves. Annie knew there was little the butler did not know about their sad and wealthy family, and she suspected there was nothing he'd not told his sister over Sunday-afternoon tea those many years. Still, she was not at all certain where confidence ended and propriety began. She kept her peace.

The moment the widow left the room for plates and scones, Annie pressed her brother. "When do we leave for America?"

Owen slowly set his cup in its saucer and covered Annie's fingers with his hand. Annie saw the lump in his throat go up and down as he swallowed, then swallowed again.

"Do you remember Father talking about his brother, Uncle Sean—Uncle Sean and Aunt Maggie, in America?"

Annie nearly laughed out loud. "Surely! They invited us to join them in America after Mother died." She clasped her hands. "So that's where we're going!"

"That is where I'm going."

Annie's laughter died in midair. "You?"

He nodded.

She flicked her head, positive he jested. "That's not funny, Owen."

"I'll send for you as soon as I possibly can."

Annie felt the floor drop beneath her. She stared blankly at her brother.

"I must make certain this is a good move for us before I take you across the world. Aunt Maggie wrote that Uncle Sean is not well; they need my help. I know every bit of gardening that Father ever taught me, and I've learned a great deal more these last years, even developed my own strains of Old World flowers and roses. I'm certain I can help them."

"I can help too! I'm a hard worker!"

Owen cupped her face in his hands. "You're the hardest worker I know, Little Sister. But you must finish your education. I promised Father, on his grave, that I would take care of you."

"How can you take care of me from across a vast ocean?" Annie pushed him away, her voice rising.

"By making certain you're safe here." He took her hands again and spoke quietly. "Father believed Uncle Sean had a fine venture started, that he only needed more help from his family to make a go of it. I want to believe all that Father told me. I want to get our own piece of what they call 'the American dream.' But I need to make certain it's more than a dream before I plop us both down in the middle of it."

"Don't do this, Owen. Take me now. Please, please take me now."

"Six months—a year at most—and I'll send for you. Just as soon as I know the business can turn a profit."

"But—"

"I've enrolled you in a boarding school in Southampton with a good lady—Miss Hopkins. She'll watch over you just as she does all her young ladies."

"Southampton? I'll be near you, then?" The first flicker of hope sprang in Annie's chest.

"Until I sail. Until Easter week."

"Easter!"

"The important thing is that you'll be away from Aunt Eleanor. I cannot leave England knowing you're trapped in her house."

Annie sat back, refusing to believe him, desperate to give his words some other meaning, unable to imagine being left on the same island, alone, with Aunt Eleanor. "You can't just go," she whispered.

Owen spread his hands.

Annie saw the pain in his eyes—pain she could not bear . . . or bear to cause. "She's worse of late."

"Jamison wrote me as much." Owen seemed relieved, if only to divert the conversation. "I'm sorry. I should never have left you with her."

Annie drew a ragged breath. "It couldn't be helped. But she dotes on you so. Still, she's hateful to me when you're not there." Annie shook her head, bewildered. "I don't know what makes her so. I don't do anything to her."

"Grandfather modeled hatred. It's all she's ever known."

"But Mother wasn't like that."

"No, Mother was love itself. It was something she and Father shared. Aunt Eleanor despised her for leaving, for finding happiness with Father— courage and happiness she couldn't begin to understand."

Annie picked at her serviette. "Last week she called me by Mother's name. She did not say it kindly."

"That's why you can't stay, either." Owen pushed a stray wisp from her forehead.

"I don't wish to stay. I only wish you would take me with you." Annie's eyes filled again.

"Soon, Annie," Owen vowed but turned away. "Just as soon as I can."

The next morning Annie placed her hairbrush inside her carpetbag. She'd long dreamed of going away with Owen, of leaving Aunt Eleanor and Hargrave House forever. But she'd wanted a new life, not an enforced holiday with strangers. There had to be a way to make Owen stay until he could afford for them both to go. And if it required every ounce of tears and wheedling she possessed, she would use it to change his mind. She'd seen Aunt Eleanor use those feminine tools with great success.

But when she descended the stairs, she overheard the widow's whispers.

"I'd offer you to leave the darling girl here, Mr. Owen, but you know it might get back to Miss Hargrave, and then where would my brother be? No one can tell her mind till she's spoken it, and it ain't always laced with kindness, now is it?"

"No, Mrs. Woodward. I'm sorry to say it is not." Annie heard Owen's sigh beyond the wall. "I hope our being here overnight does not cause either of you trouble."

The widow clucked her tongue. "She'll never know that much."

"I hope I'm doing the right thing." Annie could hear Owen tapping a pewter spoon against the table. She crouched on the stairs and leaned her head against the railing to better listen.

"Of course you are, sir! You can't be staying there, stuck up like her pretty plaything, can you? It ain't fitting for a man, is it?" Annie heard the widow's crumb brush swat table crumbs onto her tray. "I seen it with your old dad, God rest his soul. I don't mean to speak ill of the dead; no, I don't. But he should have done just what you've done and, better yet, what you're fixing to do. He should have up and left the old—!" The widow Woodward stopped abruptly. "I didn't mean that, sir. At least I didn't mean it unkindly as it sounds."

Annie smiled in spite of herself.

"No offense is taken, Mrs. Woodward. I needed to hear someone say it aloud." Still Owen tapped his spoon.

"That's all right, then." The widow plunked dishes onto her tray. Annie heard her totter toward the kitchen. She must have turned. "If you don't go now, Mr. Owen, you'll be stuck here forever—you and Miss Annie, too. It would suffocate the life out of you, just like it did your poor father. And you'd not be wanting that old spinster's life for your darling sister. That's just what she'd make her into—a miniature of her mean and miserable self. Mark my words."

Annie felt the heat rise up her neck and face. She grasped the stair railing and pulled herself to her feet as the kitchen door swung closed, swatting at tears that insisted on coming, tears that had nothing to do with feminine ploys. She could not ruin Owen's life by guilting him into staying in England. An ocean was little enough to separate him from Aunt Eleanor. She could not do to him what Aunt Eleanor had done to Father. How she would manage with her beloved brother an ocean away, she didn't know. But creeping back up the stairs, she determined to try, for his sake.

≋ CHAPTER FOUR ≋

"Owen?" Annie stood an hour later, carpetbag in hand, outside the widow's gate. Determined to retain her composure, she lifted her chin. "Who will tend their graves when we've gone?"

Owen smiled, and his smile lifted Annie's heart. He took the carpetbag from her, then dug into his pocket. "This very morning we shall pull the weeds and cultivate the tops of the mounds. We'll sow all the seeds we have." He cupped Annie's palm and trickled tiny seeds of promise into its curve. "We've more than enough to cover both. They'll bloom this summer, then come again next year, and every year, even without us."

"Won't they be lonely?" Annie knew her chin quivered, but she blinked back tears.

"I believe Mother and Father are dancing this day in heaven, if truly they can see us." Owen clasped her shoulders. "They never would have wanted either of us in that house. You know that."

Annie nodded, determined to smile.

"We've a new life to build, and we shall need every bit of English pluck and Irish grit to get us through."

Annie nodded again. She wondered if Owen had any idea what pluck and grit it would take for her to see him off.

By midmorning Annie's skirt was soiled. She and Owen had weeded, scraped, turned, and sifted the topsoil of their parents' plots in the midst of Bunhill Fields cemetery. They had hoed shallow ditches, spaced close enough to crowd out the most persistent weeds, and sprinkled seeds, sparingly, down their rows.

"Mother loved these blue spikes." Owen smiled, brushing the earth from his fingers. "Father always said they were the color of her eyes."

"Like mine," Annie said, smiling faintly.

"That they are. Blue as the bluest lobelia England ever grew!"

Annie sat close to Owen but could not look at him. "But Father . . ."

"What about Father?"

"I heard you and Aunt Eleanor arguing. What did she mean when she said that it was no accident that sent Father to his grave? That it was his own ridiculous pining for a woman too silly to help him manage his business?"

Owen did not answer but stiffened and sat back on his heels.

"She meant Mother, didn't she?" Annie held her breath.

Owen stood and dusted off the soil from the knees of his trousers. He picked up the pocket rake and spade he carried with him everywhere, wiped them on the grass, and polished them with his handkerchief.

"Owen?" Annie persisted.

Still he did not answer, did not look at her, but packed the tools away and reached for her hand.

Annie stood, brushing her skirt, and stared at her brother until he spoke.

"Did you read the book I sent you?"

"I began, but I'm not fascinated by it. And what has that to do with my question?"

The corners of his lips lifted slightly. "You do not have to be fascinated by it."

"It was written so dreadfully long ago, Owen. Couldn't you find me something amusing?"

"The writer is one I hope will become your friend. He's a neighbor of Mother and Father's."

"A neighbor? How silly! He's been dead for ages."

Owen grinned. "He might have lived before them, but his work and writings were very much a part of their lives." He tweaked her honey-colored curls. "I remember Mother reading his book to me when I was younger than you are now."

"Well—" Annie placed her hands on her hips—"perhaps if I had you or Mother reading it aloud to me, I could take more pleasure in it."

Owen laughed aloud. "You've got me there!" He pulled her aside. "Here, our friend and neighbor—come take a look at his stone." Owen spread his coat on the ground before Annie. He traced the outlined relief on the side of John Bunyan's tomb with his finger, as if he had memorized the sculptor's movements. "This is a picture of the pilgrim, called Christian, from the book. See how he's weighed down, carrying that heavy load upon his back? He can hardly bear it, and the way is steep and rough."

"Yes, but you've still not answered my question about Father." Annie tugged her brother's sleeve.

But Owen seemed to ignore her. "That's the way of our lives—all of us. We're loaded down with burdens too heavy to bear—disappointments, losses, sin. Even guilt about our inability to overcome the burdens that bend us low. The longer we tread with that heavy load on our backs, the more we are likely to despair."

A full minute passed before Annie reached out and tentatively touched the stone. "Father was terribly sad after Mother died, wasn't he?"

Owen's eyes met Annie's at last. "She was the light of his life. Losing her took everything from him. A year passed and he could not let go of his grief."

Annie narrowed her eyes, concentrating on the shapes in the stone. "Father was caught by the Giant Despair." She bit her lip. "Do you think his death . . ." Annie could not make herself form the words. "Do you think it was not an accident?"

"I don't know. Only God and Father know that." Owen clasped her hands between his palms. "I only know that despondency, even despair, is not the end of the story. I want you to know that too. No matter what pain, what hard things come to us in life—and pain and trouble come to all of us—no matter what dark roads we walk or poor choices we make, it is not the end of the story." He stood and pulled her to her feet. "Come see."

Annie grabbed Owen's coat from the ground.

He pulled her to the opposite side of the tomb and spread his coat again, then tugged her down beside him. "Look here, at the picture." He pointed to the tomb's relief. "Do you see?"

"He's no longer burdened!"

"No, his load—his guilt and sin—have all been cast aside."

"He's not weary-looking or sad," Annie said in wonder, tracing the lines of Christian's burden-free back. "Because he's reached the cross?"

"Because he has reached the cross and taken hold of it. See how he grasps it, how he clings to it—a living relationship with the One who bore it! It is all in all to him. He kneels upon the solid rock and is looking up—not down at his burden!"

"It's the entire book in a picture—in two pictures!"

"But there's so much more in the book. Christian's long journey is a companion for our life's journey. Promise me you'll read it—all of it—then read it again. And write to me of what you think as you read, just as we write of everything."

"I promise." Annie tucked her skirt beneath her feet. "It won't be the same as having you here, but . . ."

"But you'll not be alone. You are loved far better than I can love you, Annie."

"Sometimes I need arms," she whispered, leaning against her brother's back, willing him to wrap his arms around her.

Owen drew her round from behind him, and she buried her head in his chest. "Of course you do. We all need arms about us. We shall trust the Lord to watch between us until we meet again. It won't be long—not a minute longer than I can manage."

≋ CHAPTER FIVE ≋

THROUGH THE NIGHT and the long next day, Michael skittered from pillar to post, from deck to stateroom, and finally climbed into a freezing lifeboat hanging from its davit—anywhere he might dodge the crew and builders' representatives as they tested, measured, and tested again each small device aboard the wondrous ship, finally put to sea.

Shy of midnight he started, waking to the shrill whistles of the tugs. Michael knew without seeing that *Titanic* neared its mooring. The great engines stopped. He'd have to find the right moment to steal ashore.

By the time pink stained the sky, men worked quickly to close and cover ventilators and louvers, sealing doors.

"Finished," exclaimed a voice too nearby.

"For now, you mean." A second voice spoke. "We'd best take our tea while they're coaling her. We'll be cleaning stem to stern soon as they've finished."

Michael knew the coaling of a vessel could take hours. He also knew that in the careful cleaning of the fine layer of coal dust it left behind, and in the final inspection, even a lifeboat would be no safe place to hide.

He did not want to be anywhere near the ship when the stokers finally filed ashore, lest he be caught by his uncle Tom. Dozens of men came and went on a dozen different errands. It was no small feat for Michael to slip from his hiding place and blend into those hastening to and fro. But amid the general bustling, drifting away along the dock was child's play.

Chilled to the bone, Michael searched till he found a pub with a back alley. He'd learned long ago that even pubs that bolted their doors did not always bolt their windows. Some did not wash their glasses before closing up late at night. Drops from a dozen glasses could send a warm stream down his throat and build a weak fire in his belly.

Michael spied the sign of a fish-and-chips shop in the next block. He waited. No dog cried the alarm. Michael's tongue ran over chapped lips. His mouth watered at the thought of fried-fish grease soaked into the pages of newsprint wrappers. If lucky, he'd find bits, remnants stuck to the paper, crumpled in the dustbin. Fish heads weren't to everyone's liking, Michael knew, but he'd seen the wharf rats eat them, and they surely thrived. It could keep him in body for another day. But even those pickings ran slim this morning.

Michael's stomach rumbled, angry at the waking that offered no real satisfaction. Cold and hungry as he was, he was more than weary after two nights of half waking, half sleeping, ever dodging and fearing discovery.

Farther into town Michael came upon a stone building. The morning light showed the garden torn apart, bricks and flagstones askew, tarps strewn over building and gardening supplies. Small shrubs, draped, stood sentinel against the stone wall.

Michael blew on his hands to warm them, stomped his feet to feel his toes. He pulled the tarps from the shrubs, thinking they couldn't be as cold as he, and dragged one over wooden planks. Stretched along the plank bed, Michael pulled his thin coat tight about his aching ribs, wound himself head to toe inside the second tarp, and sank into a deep sleep.

≋ CHAPTER SIX ≋

MICHAEL DREAMED AGAIN of Megan Marie—of soft black ringlets framing her pale face, her wide blue orbs growing wider still as they stood alone on the dock, nearly swamped in the early-morning fog. Her small fingers curled around Michael's larger ones, warm and trusting, and he wrapped his arm around his sister.

And then Jack Deegan and Uncle Tom stumbled toward them, down the thudding planks, arguing, deep in their cups. Someone else—a man with a tall black hat and coat and a silver stick—walked up to Megan Marie and Michael. He twisted their faces first one way and then another. He frowned and narrowed his eyes. When he let them go, Megan Marie clung harder to Michael, whimpering, her face buried in his sleeve. The man pulled from his pocket the biggest wad of pound notes Michael had ever seen and shoved them into Jack Deegan's hands. Then he knelt before Megan Marie and Michael with a peppermint stick in each hand, holding one close to draw Megan Marie near him and extending the other to keep Michael at arm's length.

Hungry, they were both so hungry. Megan Marie let go of Michael's sleeve to reach for the peppermint stick, but Michael did not notice, for he reached toward the other. In a sudden swoop the man lifted Megan Marie from the dock, and Uncle Tom raised Michael by his collar, his feet dangling in the air, and punched him in the stomach.

Megan Marie screamed Michael's name, but all Michael could see was the back of the stranger's cape, running, running down the dock, Megan Marie's small hand raised in her pleas. "Michael! Michael!"

Michael squirmed, bit Uncle Tom, and dropped to the dock. But before he could race after Megan Marie, Jack Deegan lifted him by his britches and threadbare coat and threw him into the sea. Michael thrashed and thrashed, not knowing how to swim, and all the while the cries of Megan Marie pierced his soul.

And then he was lifted, lifted, and tumbled again. Only he wasn't fighting, scrabbling against the water; he was clawing the bare, hard ground.

Gasping, still half-asleep, Michael sprang to his feet and staggered backward, covering his face with his arm to stave off the beating.

"Whoa, lad! Whoa!" A man reached for Michael, but Michael tripped and fell.

Now fully awake, he scrambled, crab-walking backward. "Leave her! Leave her alone!" Michael shouted.

The man before him stepped back, raising his hands, surely as astonished as Michael himself. "Leave who? You're caught in the dreaming, lad."

Michael's chest heaved. He couldn't get his breath or stop his heart from pounding against his ribs. The tall young man before him looked nothing like the man in the dream, nothing like Uncle Tom or Jack Deegan.

"Get off!" Michael spat.

"Steady, lad. Steady on, now." The man spread his hands as though gentling a wild beast. He raised the tarp. "Have you slept here the whole night, then? Out here in the cold?"

Michael couldn't get his bearings, couldn't answer for the rattling of his teeth.

"The shrubs will do. It didn't freeze last night. We're lucky, that way." The man's frown deepened. "But surely you're nigh frozen!"

Michael looked from the man to the tarp, to the bushes, back to the tarp, and then to the man. "I . . . I'm sorry, sir," he chattered. "I didn't know it was wanted. I didn't take it all the night. Just after midnight—not even all of that." He stood, edged along the wall, one eye on the man, one eye on his route of escape. "I'll be going now. Begging your pardon for the trouble, sir."

But he tripped over the man's lunch pail and sent the precious contents skittering along the ground. It was too much. "Ach! I'm sorry." Michael stooped to pick up the buttered bread, the cheese tossed from its

26

cloth, but the moment he leaned over, his eyes spun back in his head and he dropped to one side.

Strong fingers grabbed him before he slumped to the ground.

"Wake up, lad! Wake up!"

A burning shot through Michael's limbs and chest as the man lifted him upright by his armpits. He cried out.

The man nearly dropped him.

Michael felt himself drowning, drowning, but forced his eyes open, willed them to focus.

The man shoved his face close to Michael's but turned away in a grimace. "Have you been after the drink, then? And here you've come to sleep it off!"

Michael swiped his lips with his sleeve. Anger swelled in his chest—to be accused of following in Uncle Tom's footsteps by a stranger! "I never—!" And then he caught himself. "I took a drop but only to warm me through. Let go of me now. I'll be on my way."

But Michael stopped, looked down at the ground at the man's lunch still spread across the soil, and groaned. "I am sorry for your lunch, sir. I never meant . . ."

The man stood back, considered Michael. He frowned and rubbed his chin. "Well, it's more than I can eat, anyhow, and it's no good shoving it back in the pail now it's soiled. I'll have to toss it away."

Michael's panic brought a light to the man's eyes.

"If you can use it, take it up. But sit yourself down on this slab to eat it."

Michael's mouth watered at the thought. "I've nothing to pay you for it, sir." It was more a plea than an apology.

"No need to pay me—"

Before the words were fully spoken, Michael had grabbed the bread and torn into it with fervor.

The man's jaw dropped, but he turned away and busied himself with the righting of the tarps.

Michael gulped the smooth cheese until he choked, and when he couldn't seem to get hold of himself, the man turned and slapped him on the back until the bulge of bread and cheese dislodged itself from his throat.

Michael knew he meant it kindly, but it didn't keep him from crying aloud—just as if the man had clubbed him.

"Take it easy, lad. The bread's not walking away. You've all the time in the world to eat it."

Michael tried to nod, to reassure the man he was all right.

"Just off a ship, are you?" the man asked.

Michael nodded, never slowing his chew, but cast the man a worried glance. He couldn't afford so many questions. He cursed his Irish brogue.

"And do you have family here?" The man asked casually enough, but Michael knew he was curious.

He swallowed, wiped his sleeve across his mouth again. "Me granddad's off to London. I'm waiting for him to come back."

It was a pitiful lie. Michael knew by the tilt of the man's head that he didn't believe him. But he chewed on, barely slowing for air.

The man, tall and broad of shoulder, sat down next to Michael. He tossed a stone from hand to hand and stared into the distance. "I suppose you'll be needing a place to stay until then."

Michael stopped his eating, sure he hadn't heard rightly. He looked at the man, taking his measure in half a moment. "I will, sir."

"And I suppose you'll be needing food and a job to earn your way— just until your granddad returns."

Michael nearly choked again. "I will, sir. I'm a good worker, sir. I've swept chimneys and hauled coke for years, sir!"

The man nodded again, his eyes on Michael's calloused hands. Grime under broken nails surely showed he was fit for hard labor.

"Do you know of anyone needing a hand, sir?" Michael tried not to hope.

The man stood. "Well, I might. But it's sober work and hard. I can give you no wages, but I could share my lunch and the room where I board."

Michael stared at the man, not quite believing he was real. "Do you mean it, sir?"

"I do." The man looked away. "But you must work hard, and it's only for the week. I'll be sailing on *Titanic*, come 10 April."

Michael gasped. "*Titanic*? You're sailing on *Titanic*?"

"I am," the man replied, frank as a butcher.

Michael blinked. "To America?"

"Yes, I've work in New Jersey. Why do—?"

"She's a lovely ship, governor," Michael interrupted. "You'll have a wondrous sail; I'm sure of it."

The man half smiled, his brow furrowed in question. "So you've seen the grand lady, have you?" He tossed his stone to the ground. "I thought she'd only docked."

Now Michael looked away. "Yes, sir. Well, you hear things—don't you, sir?"

"That you do. My name's Owen Allen, and I'm pleased to meet you." The man extended a strong hand. "What is your name, lad, and do you go to school?"

Michael swallowed hard, wiped his hand on his britches, and clasped Owen's hand in return. "Me name's Tim, sir—Tim Delaney. And I have gone to school, when I get the chance. But I'm smart enough—reading and writing and all of that—if you're worried. I'll not be slack on the job!"

Owen shook his head. "I'm not worried, Tim. The job doesn't require it. You just seem an odd mix."

"Oh, I'm a veritable prodigal with the books and ciphers, sir!"

"A prodigal?" Owen puzzled, then nodded, clearly amused. "A prodigy, perhaps?"

"Yes, sir! That, sir! I learned to read at me mother's knee when I was just a lad."

"Well then, young prodigy—" Owen straightened his grin—"if you've finished eating my lunch, what do you say we remove the rest of these tarps and set to work?"

"Yes, sir!" Michael wiped his mouth a final time and set the lunch pail carefully against the wall.

All morning the two worked a steady pace. By noon the sun shone bright. They'd dug holes, finished planting and watering the shrubs, and had piled the extra planks next to the road to be collected by the rags-and-bones wagon the next day. Michael knew his work had pleased Owen. He could see it in the grin Owen gave him from time to time, hear it in the ragtime tunes he whistled.

When Owen tugged a handkerchief from his back pocket and wiped his brow, Michael laid down his spade.

"Do you think you could stomach a bite to eat, then, Mr. Tim?"

Michael dragged the last of the unwanted roots to the rubbish heap and pulled his sleeve across his forehead. "I could, sir." His stomach rumbled. "Only I've eaten your lunch, sir."

Owen took coins from his vest pocket. "I believe I've enough for two cups of tea and the sharing of a fish pie, God bless us. What do you say?"

Michael felt his eyes widen in disbelief. "I say that's a wonder, sir!"

Owen laughed out loud. "All the world's a wonder!" He cuffed Michael gently on the back.

Michael winced and pulled away.

Rebuked, Owen stood back, cocked his head, and squinted. But he asked no questions, and Michael was glad to follow behind.

⪼ CHAPTER SEVEN ⪻

THE MOMENT OWEN STEPPED into the boarding school kitchen, Annie pulled him to the table and sat him down across from her. Carefully she set a pot of steaming tea, her plate of warm orange-and-currant scones, and crocks of marmalade and Devonshire cream between them.

"Cook said my first batch came out 'rather like chimney bricks—'" Annie imitated the gruff lady, wagging her finger in Owen's face—"and that they were 'a waste of good ingredients, those.'"

Owen burst into a fit of laughter. "Well, you've certainly put your brick-making days behind you, my lady." He bit into the buttery warmth. "Mmm. The best I've ever tasted."

Annie smiled, and her pink cheeks dimpled. "Well, Cook helped me some with the second batch." *Once she understood that I was baking them for the "handsome rose gardener," she couldn't bring the butter and sugar out fast enough.*

Owen winked. "God bless her, then."

"What did you say is his name, Owen?" Annie poured milk for her brother's tea. She didn't know whether to be pleased that Owen had finished work early the night before and had more time for her or to be annoyed that all he could speak of was some new boy who had helped him all day in the town hall gardens.

"He says his name is Tim—Tim Delaney." Owen hesitated. "But I don't believe him."

"Why should he lie about such a thing?" *And why would you bother with such a boy?*

Owen furrowed his brow. "I don't know, really. I'm thinking he's run away." He pushed his chair from the table. "All I know for certain is that I called him by name a couple of times . . . and he never even looked up. Makes me think Tim is not likely his name."

"Maybe he's deaf or simply not paying attention."

Owen looked at her. "That sounds like something Aunt Eleanor would say."

She colored. She was tempted to "harrumph" him but realized that, too, was something Aunt Eleanor would do. The thought made her shudder.

"Now, I didn't mean that so unkindly as it sounds, Annie. It's just that we should do all we can for this boy while we're able. You'll feel the same once you meet him."

"But you're leaving in a few days, Owen. We need our time together. And what good will a week's worth of work do him? He needs a steady job, doesn't he? You cannot supply that."

"I'll see if Bealing's can use him, once we've finished the town hall gardens. With the coal strike over, they'll have steady work again supplying the liners with potted plants and fresh flowers. And spring brings more outdoor work in the fields." Owen rapped the table. "I'll speak with Mr. Bealing today. I think they'll take him on."

He crammed the last of his scone into his mouth and stood, pulling his coat over his shirtsleeves. "I'll bring him round before services tomorrow morning so you can meet him. He can join us for Easter Day."

"But, Owen, he's a stranger—and these are our last holy days together!" Annie could not escape the desperation in her voice any more than she could stop the passing of the days. *He acts as though he sees neither.*

He bent to kiss her cheek and slapped his cap atop his head, all in one quick motion.

She turned her face away.

"That he is—a stranger—and we took him in." Owen playfully pinched her cheek, winked, and walked through the door into the morning. "Be ready by nine!" he called over his shoulder. "We'll come round for you, love!"

Annie slammed the kitchen door behind him and threw her carefully ironed apron to the table. *He'll be laughing all the way to the town hall!*

"Well, I'm not sorry he didn't come, Owen." Annie tucked her arm through Owen's as they strolled along the quay. "It may be selfish and wicked of me, but I'm glad to have you to myself this Easter Sunday." Annie saw that her confession grieved Owen. She stopped and asked quietly, "Are you really so very vexed with me?"

"Not vexed. Certainly not with you." Owen dropped her arm, pushed back his cap, and smiled—almost—as he tugged a long ringlet of her hair. "I am worried for the lad. He's terribly afraid of something. I don't know what." Owen kicked a stone with his boot. "When I asked him to join us, he made up some cock-and-bull story about his old priest—a Father Boyd—forbidding him to step foot into a Protestant church. Said he'd called it a 'den of vipers.'"

"The idea!" The flush in Annie's cheek rose, nearly as bright as the nosegay she carried.

"He said 'consorting with the devil church' was the reason his mam had been excommunicated from the Holy Roman church—that, and for marrying a Scots-Irish Presbyterian." He shrugged. "I can't make him out, but I pity the lad."

Annie sighed. "I'm sorry for him, Owen—truly I am. But what more can you do? You've talked to Mr. Bealing. He's agreed to give him a try in his nurseries." She smoothed her skirt and looked away. "I do think the boy brings his sufferings on himself. You saw how he stood across the street from the church and stared at us. Even when you called him, he turned away—and on Easter Sunday! Beastly manners!"

"Annie!" Owen said more sharply than was his habit. "You're talking like Aunt Eleanor again."

Annie lifted her chin.

"And what appears poor manners might be something more kindly explained." Owen tipped his hat to a lady in passing. "You saw the anguish on his face. He refused to join us, but there's something more behind it; I'm sure of it."

"I suppose. But, Owen, please let's not quarrel. You promised we would spend the afternoon together." Her moments with her brother were fleeing—an india-rubber ball racing downhill. She could not spare one in regret.

Owen straightened and pushed his frown away. "I did, indeed. And so we shall." He offered Annie his arm again. "May I introduce you to the town hall gardens and your brother's handiwork, my lady?" He winked.

She nodded eagerly, glad for Owen's jest.

"There's a bench there. I'll show you how to run your fingers beneath its seat and feel the carving of our names. No one else will know they're there, but you will know."

He smiled so kindly Annie thought her heart might burst.

"And when you touch our names, you'll remember that I'm here with you in every way I can be. Visit the bench on your birthday—your fifteenth." He smiled. "I'll be thinking of you the same day. Let those carved letters be my promise to send for you the moment I'm able."

Annie nodded. She swallowed the burning in her throat and clung the tighter to Owen's strong arm, determined not to cry outright. "I hold you to that promise, Brother."

≋ CHAPTER EIGHT ≋

MICHAEL SPENT TUESDAY AFTERNOON waiting and dreading the setting of the sun, waiting and dreading to meet Owen at the docks. One last job with the only friend he could claim before that friend sailed away. And what a fool he'd made of himself—refusing Owen's invitation to Easter services with him and his sister, then spying on them from behind a lamppost. Michael clapped his cap against his knee and groaned aloud. *A fool!*

He would have been fearful of running into his uncle by the quay, except that he knew the ship's crew—certainly the stokers—would be drowning in ale as long as their fists could grasp a glass in local pubs that night. The "no drinking at sea" rule for crew members boosted the business of port pubs the night before a sailing. Still, just to be certain, Michael pulled up his jacket collar and tugged his cap down.

Mule-drawn carts, loaded and heaping with pots and plants, trundled down the dock just before dusk, and Owen behind them.

"Tim! You're here, lad. I want you to meet Mr. Bealing." Owen bent down to whisper, "Stand straight, Tim. This is your chance for a new beginning."

The idea shot through Michael in a rush. This was what he'd long told himself he wanted—a new beginning.

Michael, Owen, Frank Bealing Sr., Frank Bealing Jr., and a strong Bill Geapin hauled load after load of potted palms, plants, and cut flowers in every variety aboard the great ship. Michael had never seen so many thousands of flowers, nor could he guess their names. They set all on a great tarpaulin in the foyer, just long enough for some of Mr. Bealing's party and *Titanic*'s crew members to catch them up and deliver them hither and yon the length of the ship. Michael couldn't imagine where so many plants and flowers might find homes—and still they carried more aboard.

"Owen Allen," Mr. Bealing Sr. shouted above the din, "carry this group to the reception room outside the first-class dining saloon."

Michael trailed behind with another load.

"And you, lad, take that big palm along and lend him a hand."

"Yes, sir." Michael stepped smartly toward the dining saloon, hoping Mr. Bealing noticed how quickly he responded to an order.

"Whoa, Tim!" Owen turned around. "Where are you going?"

Mr. Bealing called over his shoulder. "Follow the lad, Owen. He's headed in the proper direction."

Owen stepped lively, but Michael outdistanced him. Owen caught up, panting, "Tim—did you not hear me calling? How in the world do you know where you're going, lad? It's as though you're a homing pigeon aboard this ship!"

Michael slowed abruptly. "Lucky guess, I'm thinking."

"I'm thinking it's something more." But there was no time for questions.

The hours slipped by one by one. Fragrant flowers in every color of the rainbow, those grown in season and unseasonable varieties forced in hothouses, were piled into Michael's arms. Together, he and Owen delivered cut flowers to the cooling room, small plants to tables and corners, to the Parisian café, everywhere they were directed. Before the night ended, they'd been over a fair portion of *Titanic*'s public areas and staterooms. They'd watched the Bealings create displays so large that each one looked an entire garden to Michael.

"A fair floating Eden!" Owen exclaimed when at last they set their feet upon the dock.

"You've done well." Mr. Bealing shook Owen's hand. "I wish you weren't off to America, Mr. Allen. I could use you in the nurseries. Still, I wish you Godspeed."

"Thank you, sir." Owen doffed his cap. "I've appreciated the extra work, sir, and I thank you for the opportunity you're giving my young friend." He set his hand on Michael's shoulder. For the first time Michael didn't shudder at the weight of Owen's hand—a clasp and not the clamp he was used to from his uncle Tom. "He's a good worker, God bless him; I can vouch for that."

"Yes, well . . ." Mr. Bealing's gaze fell upon Michael. "We'll give you a try, lad. You've no experience, but I can see you're a willing worker. Be at the nursery at 7 a.m. sharp tomorrow. We'll see how things go along."

"Yes, sir," Michael said, but he couldn't muster the enthusiasm such an opportunity warranted.

Mr. Bealing frowned but nodded, then looked back at the ship. "*Titanic*'s dressed for the ball, so I'm off." He stopped, kneaded the back of his neck, and turned again to Michael. "You'll be wanting to clean up a bit before we load another ship. Use your first wages wisely."

"Yes, sir." Michael looked at his broken shoes, feeling his neck and face flame. He knew what he looked like but for the first time considered that he might stink as a gutter rat as well. When he looked up, Mr. Bealing had moved along, busied himself with the mules and their drivers.

"It's all right, Tim," Owen whispered. "All things in time."

But Michael knew the time was gone. It wasn't that he cared overmuch for the rebuke he'd been given by Mr. Bealing. Michael had known worse all his life. But the spreading of this new path before him reminded him that in a very few hours Owen would be gone from England forever. Michael had never even told Owen his name—at least not his full and proper name. He'd lied outright about having a granddad, about his priest, about a dozen things. But what mattered, all that mattered, was that Owen had called him his friend. And he'd been a friend—the only friend Michael could remember having.

Owen squeezed Michael's shoulder, trying to shake him from his reverie. And Michael bolted.

He couldn't say good-bye to Owen, dared not try to thank him in a voice that would surely break. Michael could not sleep another night on the floor of his friend's room, could not accept another morsel of food or drink, not a pitying or encouraging word from this man who'd given him in six days more kindness than Michael had known in the six years since his parents' death.

Without a word or a backward glance, Michael ran. Fiercely pounding the planks of the dock with his broken hobnails, he tore through the gates, then pounded the cobbles of the darkened street. He pushed back tears that threatened and oozed, unwanted, from the corners of his eyes. Those rebel, unfamiliar streams served only to anger him. Why was kindness so hard to bear, so foreign that it could not be endured?

Michael couldn't think it through, refused to think, but set his face to run until he was spent. Too late he saw the three men, twice his size and more, stumbling from the Grapes Pub swearing, singing, bent over in their raucous laughter. But when the collision came, knocking all four to their knees, Michael smelled the sour and familiar stench of ale-soaked breath and bodies.

The beefy hand that grabbed Michael's jacket collar, yanking him to the ground, was no stranger, either, and Michael's heart heaved, broken, to the pit of his stomach. He dared not speak. But the word echoed and reechoed through his brain, *Betrayed! Betrayed! Betrayed!* It was a joke too cruel.

"Fool!" Uncle Tom swung a fist toward Michael's face, then another that found its mark. As the punches landed, Michael slammed shut the door in his mind, turning the key in the lock, retreating to the familiar dark and secret place inside himself, a place where he could not hear or see or feel or know—a place to wait until the beating stopped, however long that took. Another punch knocked the breath from Michael's lungs.

And then there was an unexpected tussle of arms and legs. One of the men stood, stumbled across Michael's feet, and fell face forward into his uncle, knocking the three of them to the ground again. For a moment, a brief and precious moment, Tom Auld lost his grasp on Michael's jacket. Already tasting the blood from his split lip, Michael jerked away, rolling into the lane.

Before any of the men could rise, Michael scrabbled backward, found his feet, and sprang through the alley, through the next garden, and over a low gate. Two blocks away he could hear his uncle rage—the memory it conjured a garden claw torn down Michael's spine. He waited until the cursing ran its long and heated course.

Michael sat long minutes hugging the shadows, his back pressed against a cold iron gate, willing his breath to slow, his heartbeat to stop pulsing in his eyes.

He couldn't say what drew him back to the cobbles outside the Grapes half an hour later. He didn't want to go, yet couldn't keep himself away.

The pub stood dark, locked against the night, and the lane, blessedly empty. Only the gaslight of the lamppost shone a pool in the street. Michael slumped against a garden wall and drew a sharp breath. Had his uncle recognized him, or was that a beating he awarded a stranger in his path? Either way, it had been a close shave.

That was when Michael's eyes narrowed to take in the dark lump in the gutter where they'd fought. It looked for all the world like the kit of a ship's crew member. *There'll be a purse!* Hope tripped his heart. A purse could mean a new shirt and trousers, a room with a meal and a bath.

A sudden gritty determination for Mr. Bealing's steady job fought for attention in his brain. He could imagine the weight of the pound notes and coppers sagging against the leather as he reached into the gutter and rummaged through the kit. A shirt, a coat, to be sure, but what he had hoped was a purse was flat and hard and held no notes at all.

Michael's throat thickened. It was nothing but a book. What use had he for a book? He opened it beneath the gaslight and frowned. In the yellow glow he read the letters slowly—the name, the occupation. He tried to grasp what he held in his hands.

Not a wallet filled with pound notes to set him on his new road in England, but a stoker's fair lifeline lay in Michael's hands. A seaman's book—a "Certificate of Continuous Discharge" belonging to one Mr. Hart, assigned to *Titanic*.

≋ CHAPTER NINE ≋

MICHAEL TACKED LAYERS OF CORK to the soles of his hobnails and padded their heels with the same, adding two inches to his height. He stuffed the shoulders and sleeves of the coat he'd pulled from the crewman's kit with newspapers scavenged from a rubbish bin. Michael pulled his cap low and his collar high. If anyone clapped a hand on his back, he'd be done for, but from a distance and in the dim light before dawn, he looked the part of any fireman or trimmer boarding *Titanic*.

Michael knew his uncle Tom would be one of the last to head for the ship after his hours in the pub. By boarding and unloading his gear before the other crewmen, he gambled that he could stow away somewhere in the ship's dark bowels—maybe find a hiding place in the cargo area—long before the eight o'clock muster.

He dared press his luck no further. His disguise would never make it through the ship's medical inspection. By leaving the seaman's discharge book on a bunk with Mr. Hart's gear, Michael figured it more a case of borrowing than stealing. It would surely make its way back to him someday. Michael pushed back the nagging guilt of such a notion.

How he'd manage for food or water during the voyage Michael didn't know, but he would sort that out as it came. He figured that since he'd stolen aboard in Ireland and walked ashore in England, he could surely find his way ashore in New York.

The trick was to avoid Owen until they docked. But if he could find Owen once they'd landed, if he followed him to the place called New Jersey, maybe Owen would give him a job in his family's gardens. If not . . . well, he'd be no worse off than he was now. And wasn't America the "golden land of opportunity"?

The bells had not tolled five o'clock when Michael followed the first man aboard who looked a member of the black gang. He kept his face low and trailed slowly through the mess, the stokers' general room, and into a large cabin lined with bunks. As the seaman stowed his gear, Michael tossed his kit and discharge book onto the nearest bunk, as though he'd done it every working day of his life, then disappeared down the first stairwell he found.

※ ※

Annie stood at her dormitory window and swiped tears from her eyes with her apron.

Owen had taken his last good-byes before breakfast. He'd told her to stay behind with Miss Hopkins, to help in any way she could during the days before school resumed, then to faithfully attend classes, to mind her studies.

She'd begged and wheedled to go to the docks to wave him off, but Owen had held firm.

"It's hard to leave you, Little Sister. I need to know you are safe and warm and cared for. I need to go with this picture of you in my mind—here, with Miss Hopkins—not shivering and tearful at the docks. Do this for me, Annie."

Unhappily, Annie had finally agreed, though only to bring peace to Owen's brow. He'd kissed her good-bye so tenderly. She'd bitten her lip to keep from crying, for love of Owen. Still, her body had shuddered, and he'd held her until she breathed evenly. And then he had walked away.

Annie had watched the clock tick off its painfully slow minutes, then wished them back. Red-eyed, she'd toyed with her breakfast, excusing herself from Miss Hopkins at last on the pretense of not feeling well.

I cannot polish woodwork or read novels and pretend nothing is different about this day. I cannot!

Annie let the window curtain fall into place. She untied her apron and threw it upon her bed, grabbed her wrap, and snuck down the back stairs and out the door.

Miss Hopkins would scold her, surely, by every right. But Annie would have her way in this one thing. If lucky, she'd not only see *Titanic* leave port but catch a parting glimpse of Owen.

Annie reached the docks at last and headed directly toward the four gigantic funnels that towered above *Titanic*. She dodged a thousand waving handkerchiefs as she wove through laughter, squeals, and cheers that rippled the crowd. Well-wishers of every class and station swarmed the quays to see the magnificent ship set sail. And though she could not see the band, a ragtime tune, cheerful and snappy, charged the event.

Annie scanned the hundreds of faces lining *Titanic's* decks, desperate to find Owen's. But he must not see her—she'd never have him believe that she counted his wishes as unimportant.

She jumped at the ship's triple whistle blast, signaling its departure. Then ugly shouting cut in—not from passengers or well-wishers, but from what looked to her like a gang of angry crew members. The gangway had been lowered and swung away. But a cluster of rough crewmen, apparently late and stranded on the docks, raised their fists and bellowed to be let onto the ship. Clearly the officer saw them but refused to send the gangway back and let them board. The men continued to rage and curse, some running the length of the dock, though it did them no good.

One of the stranded men stopped short, gaping at something or someone on board the ship. From where Annie stood, she saw the brute of a man rage purple and thunder with both fists, shouting words she'd never heard in all her life, words that made her insides quiver.

Her eyes followed the brute's tirade to a teen who leaned against the railing. Frozen to the spot, he looked for all the world like the dark-haired boy Owen had helped, the one he'd said had run off last night without a word. What was his name? Annie tried to remember. His eyes spread wide and skin wrapped tight round his skull. He stepped sharply back into the throng of passengers. "Tim," Annie whispered, "what are you doing . . . ?"

Titanic's blue peter flew up the mast; her whistle triple-blasted again; her forward funnels belched steam, as her tugs, belching smoke, made taut their hawsers. *Titanic's* mooring lines fell away, hauled ashore by dockhands, and the liner, intent on her maiden voyage, was pulled slowly, carefully from her berth.

Annie forgot Tim and pushed along the dock, twisting between elbows and shoulders, between ladies' hats and feathers, between umbrellas and walking canes, purses and packages, between small children and their parents, frantically searching for a glimpse of Owen. At last she spotted a brown leather cap lifted high in farewell along the railing—a strong arm and a cap that might have been Owen's.

In that moment a hundred thousand flowers filled the air, a joyous farewell from the passengers aboard *Titanic*. But for Annie, the shower of Bealing's buttonholes and pert nosegays—so many lovingly grown and tended by her brother—beat against her face in a stinging rain, a million petal tears to mingle with her own, flung high and swept into the sea.

CHAPTER TEN

No sooner had Michael found refuge in the driver's seat of a fine new automobile in the hold than a steward spied him and unceremoniously shoved him up the stairwell. "If I find you here again, I'll throw you to the sharks! Now get back to your parents and be quick about it!"

Michael had raced to the deck, mingling with third-class passengers, just in time to stare into the purple face and fists of Uncle Tom, stranded opposite the gangway.

Breathless, Michael stumbled back into the cheering throng, clutching both arms to stop the tremors running the length of his limbs. *But now I'm sailing—and Tom Auld is left standing on the docks of England.* Michael shook his head and drew a breath, intent on steadying his nerves, unable to fathom the luck or the wonder of it—to be rid of his uncle forever.

As he wove through the jumping, waving crowd, a sharp cracking broke the revelry on ship and dock. A thousand heads swiveled toward the commotion. Sturdy lines from the ship *New York* snapped free of their moorings in its sudden struggle with the portside backwash from *Titanic's* gigantic propellers.

Titanic, ordered full astern, turned its mighty bow slightly but was too slow to steer quickly from the path of the smaller ship. A cry swelled from the docks.

Michael couldn't see, but he could imagine that the heavy, snapping lines from the *New York* had lashed among the crowd, and he winced to think of the sting.

He could not hear the directions of the ship's officers, but the clamor and gasps of passengers ran the length of the ship. Most stepped back, but a few surged forward, craning their necks far over the railings.

"She's broken loose! She'll smack us broadside!" A young man swore.

"A collision," whimpered a woman from the deck above Michael, "and we're not even clear of port!"

"Don't be an alarmist, Isabella," the man beside her chided. "She's only drifting. They'll pull her out before she hits."

"But that ship is headed straight for us!" And she was. The smaller ship looked like a match coming to strike *Titanic*'s stone.

Michael squirmed a path across the deck in time to see a small tug toss its lines to the seamen of the *New York*. The first line snapped again, but the second held and the little tug valiantly pulled the *New York* from *Titanic*'s path, with only feet to spare. A collective cheer went up from the deck. Whistles and waves from ships and shore responded.

"A bad omen, that," a man on the deck above Michael vowed. "A bad omen, indeed." He turned to the woman beside him. "Do you love life?"

"I love it!" she responded.

"Then get off this ship at Cherbourg. That's what I'm going to do."

The man moved along the deck, and Michael could hear no more.

But a woman beside him took up the pace, speaking to no one in particular. "I overheard a man, a respectable gentleman, say this very morning that God Himself could not sink this ship!"

Michael stepped back. The pit of his stomach churned. He didn't know if he believed in omens or premonitions, but he knew better than to challenge the abilities and sovereignty of the almighty God.

Titanic had not cleared Southampton Water before her passengers' heads turned to better hear and see the ship's bugler as he roamed the decks, bugle lifted.

"'The Roast Beef of Old England'!" shouted a boy not much older than Michael on the deck above.

"The call for midday meal." A woman Michael took to be the boy's mother linked his arm. "Have your ticket at the ready, Teddy. No ticket, no seating!"

Passengers hurried to separate themselves into decks and dining halls according to class, eager for their first meal aboard the lavish ship. Michael, having no ticket and careful to avoid running into Owen, sauntered a few steps behind a group of seasoned travelers who remained on deck, sentimentally pointing out the disappearing sights until they'd passed the Isle of Wight.

Michael wondered, a bit surprised, if leaving England was the best plan, after all. But he'd cast his boat upon the sea and could not pull it back.

≋ CHAPTER ELEVEN ≋

"RICE SOUP, corned beef and cabbage, boiled potatoes, and, oh—that tasty peach dessert! Never was a ship so grand—even in steerage! Why, it's as posh as second class!" a Yorkshire woman broadly proclaimed.

Michael wondered how she knew, doubted if she'd ever made a voyage besides this one. He closed his eyes. His stomach groaned again as he listened to the satisfied moans of diners who, willing at last to leave their tables, straggled to the deck in groups of common language.

Despite the rising breeze, a mix of families, young men playing cards in the sunshine, two pretty girls—arms linked—out for a stroll, and couples, clearly courting, took up posts along the deck and up and down the promenade.

Michael eyed the families with envy and watched the girls with shy appreciation. What it would be to attach himself to such a group—to be smiled upon and wanted and cared for. Then he turned away. Such a fancy did not belong to him.

As *Titanic* neared Cherbourg, the sun splayed its late-afternoon rays—amber, orange, and copper—across the water. It might be his only chance to see the coast of France. But he'd have to watch from someplace Owen would not.

Michael climbed the stairwell to the deck above. Keeping his cap pulled low and eyes upon his shoes, he made his way toward the new deck.

"A moment, young man!"

Michael started, nearly colliding with a young woman in uniform—a woman who looked for all the world to Michael like a flame-haired sergeant major, backlit and haloed by the late-day sun. He turned to bolt, but she grabbed him by the nape of his neck.

"Let me go!" Michael squealed. Nimble and quick, he yanked away. But the sergeant major, fully his match, reeled him in.

"And have you pilfering from the café the moment my back is turned?" The woman lowered her voice to something less than a howl. "Just what do you think you're doing here, anyway, and how did you get up here? These are first-class quarters! Where are your parents?"

Michael felt as much as saw the dozens of pairs of eyes riveted on the commotion, peering at him with curiosity, amusement, and finally disgust. He jerked away. "I haven't any."

"No parents?" The woman momentarily relaxed her hold. "Who are you traveling with, lad?" She twisted Michael round to face her.

And Michael's eyes locked on Owen's, his jaw agape, on the deck below.

"Answer me!" the woman demanded.

Owen turned away, and Michael saw him flee toward the stairwell. *He must hate me—be ashamed to know me.* Michael could feel the heat begin in his toes, race up his legs and torso to the tip of his head. *Why, why didn't I go back to the hold?*

"Answer me, I said!" The woman, every bit a White Star Line stewardess, shook Michael until he thought his teeth might rattle right out of his head.

Michael could not think up a lie quick enough but stared helplessly at the deck between his shoes.

"A stowaway, then," she pronounced.

"No!" he fairly shrieked, the fear of God rising within. *We're not really to sea—not to Cherbourg, let alone Queenstown! Will they dump me—send me ashore?*

A gentleman, just exiting the Palm Court, turned raised eyebrows toward the scene.

The stewardess, with a firm hold on Michael's elbow, led him nearer the railing. "Calm down, lad! I'll not eat you. What is your name?"

"Lucy!" Owen called, and Michael's heart sank lower yet at the sound of his friend's voice. Owen crossed the deck in long strides, bound directly for them.

The sergeant major stewardess straightened, tugging the hem of her jacket. "Your name!" she insisted.

Michael felt his features crumple, every light within him dimmed. "Michael. Michael Dunnagan," he whispered as Owen reached his shoulder.

"There you are, Tim! Where have you been, Cousin? I've been searching the decks high and low for you! Look at you! Filthy!" he charged. "You've not been larking about the stoker hole, have you? How many times have I told you it's dangerous down there?"

And then Owen urged, "Remove your cap when speaking to a lady—such a charming lady. Mrs. Lucy Snape, I believe." With one flick of the wrist Owen knocked the cap from Michael's head, flipping it through the air and landing it neatly in his trembling hands, then swept a fine bow and a wink before the stewardess.

The fire in the young stewardess's hair paled beside the fire in her cheek.

Michael blinked, uncertain.

"You are the . . . Here, now, what are you doing here? Do you know this boy?" she sputtered but loosed her grip on Michael's collar and smoothed her skirt.

"Indeed, Mrs. Snape. And I thank you for finding and keeping my adventurous young cousin safe."

"Your cousin? I did not know you had a cousin."

"Most of us have cousins tucked away here and there, Mrs. Snape."

She colored all the more. "You called him Tim. He said his name is Michael—Michael Dunnagan, did you say?"

"Well, of course it is! Some call him Tim; some call him Michael. Isn't that so, Timothy Michael Dunnagan?" Owen, all six feet and fourteen stone of him, turned and winked at Michael.

Michael nodded vigorously even as he swallowed convulsively.

"Timothy Michael Dunnagan." The stewardess chanted the mouthful and tipped her head to one side, clearly not believing. "And where do you hail from, Timothy Michael Dunnagan?"

"Southampton," Owen said, but not fast enough to drown out Michael's feeble "Belfast, mum."

Now we'll both be caught lying!

"Belfast or Southampton? Which is it, Mr. Allen?" She turned to Owen, frowning.

"Owen George Allen, at your service, mum. I'm flattered you remember me."

"I have seen you every week in Southampton these past months, as you well know. But how is it I did not see you with your Irish cousin, Mr. Allen?"

He ignored the question. "Ah—the lad needs a fresh start in a fresh country. Born wrong side of the blanket," he whispered to the fiercely blushing Lucy. "Nothing to be proud of, surely, but just as surely not the boy's doing."

Lucy bristled, tugging the hem of her uniform jacket again, but stepped back. "I shall check the passenger list. In the meantime, Mr. Allen, please keep your cousin on the decks to which you are assigned. This—" she pointed to the deck—"is first class." She lifted a pert nose. "He's old enough to know better."

"Absolutely, mum, and my sincere apologies. It's a trouble with growing boys—always famished and in search of a bite to eat. But you needn't worry. I shall deal with him directly." Owen bowed again. "I'm ever so glad you've been promoted to first class, Mrs. Snape. God bless you."

Lucy's color burned, and even Michael realized that she, too, was not in the place assigned her. Owen grinned, grabbed Michael by the ear, and led him away.

"Ow! Let go!" Michael whimpered.

"Walk with me, Tim lad, or you'll likely walk the plank," Owen whispered cheerily, directing them rapidly to the deck below. Michael felt Lucy Snape's eyes boring into the backs of their heads. "So how did you get here and what the devil do you think you're doing?"

"I'm not stowing away. I'm—"

But Owen raised a brow and tugged the harder.

"All right!" Michael sputtered, pulling back. "I'm going to America—like you. There's nothing for me, not in Belfast and not in England."

"Nothing but a job you promised to do for Mr. Bealing—a job I've staked my reputation on, not to mention the grandfather you were wait-ing for—or more likely a mother and father somewhere, worried out of their skins!"

"Dead," Michael shot back. "Both dead of the fever, six years past."

Owen stopped short and frowned. But Michael saw no anger in his eyes. "Do you mean to tell me you've fended for yourself these six years? Truth, lad."

"No." Michael hesitated. "I mean, no, I've not fended for myself alto-gether. I lived with my uncle Tom in Belfast since. But he's gone away to sea—sort of."

"Sort of—is he here? You followed him on *Titanic*, then?" Owen pushed.

"No." Michael turned away in pain and frustration. He did not want to tell Owen he'd been bullied and beaten for years on end. He would not say aloud that he was no better than a wharf rat.

"They've Marconi operators aboard. We can send word wherever he is."

"No!" Michael grabbed Owen's sleeve. "I'm running away for good and all. I can't go back. You don't know what it's like!"

Michael felt Owen stiffen and followed his eyes to the deck above, where Lucy Snape beckoned. But Owen turned, rubbing the late-day stubble on his jaw, and Michael knew he pretended not to have seen her. When Owen pulled Michael from the railing and led him toward a far stairwell, Michael followed meekly. Running would do no good, and hadn't Owen just saved him—again? Still, he dared not hope.

"Suppose you tell me exactly what it is like, then. And suppose you begin by telling me your real name—the truth this time!"

They traveled stairwells and corridors until they reached the door of a third-class cabin.

"In here—my cabin." Owen pushed open the door. "I share with a Swede—doesn't speak a word of English. While he's out, I want an expla-nation. From the beginning." Owen closed the door and crossed his arms.

"Michael. Michael Timothy Dunnagan. That's my name."

Owen's chin rose.

"God's truth."

Owen's mouth formed a grim line. "I don't know if you would recognize God's truth if it jumped up and chomped your mutton. How old are you?"

"Fifteen. I'll be sixteen on Michaelmas."

"You don't look a day over twelve, thirteen at best."

Michael looked down. He felt the weariness of the world weigh upon his chest. Truth or lie, what did it matter? Owen would never believe him now.

Owen sighed. "So. Michael, is it? Why didn't you tell me the truth from the beginning?" His tone had lost some of its gruffness.

"I was afraid," Michael confessed. "Afraid you'd send for my uncle Tom, afraid you'd turn me over to the constable."

"I'm thinking that's where you belong."

Panic fought pain for the upper hand in Michael's chest. But he set his jaw.

Owen tilted his head. Michael knew he was being weighed in the balances.

"Did your uncle do this?" Owen traced a line across his own cheek to mirror the scar on Michael's, an old scar, but long.

Michael felt the familiar heat run up his neck and looked away. A minute passed before he said, "Sometimes when he's so drunk he can't stand up in his shoes, he . . ." Michael couldn't finish.

Still, Owen did not speak.

"Uncle Tom left Ireland on a trade. He as good as sold me to Jack Deegan. I didn't know what to do. And then, at the last moment, I was helping load chairs on *Titanic*, and suddenly there I was, standing alone."

Michael rambled on with his long and convoluted story of hiding in the lifeboat, of sneaking off the ship in Southampton, of climbing through a pub window in search of warmth from a drop of ale in a glass, and the greater blessing of fish heads discovered in the rubbish bin.

"You offered me food and a job, Mr. Owen. It was the best I've had since Mam and Da."

"So you thought you would follow me to America?"

Michael shrugged helplessly.

"How did you get aboard?" When Michael looked away, Owen grasped his shoulder. "Answer me."

Michael gasped, winced, and cringed.

"Are you hurt, lad?" Owen's voice lowered.

Michael would not answer but felt the blood drain from his face; he swayed.

"Steady." Owen guided him to the bunk. "Have you slept or eaten?"

"When I stayed with you."

"That's nearly two days, man! No wonder you're off your kilter." Owen dug through his pockets and pulled out a handkerchief, spreading its contents of bread and cabin biscuits before Michael. "Eat these and sleep awhile. When they call for tea, I'll fill my pockets and bring all I can."

Michael tore into the bread and biscuits as though he'd not eaten in a month. Owen lifted Michael's feet to the bed and tugged his boots from his feet even as he ate, then pulled the red-and-white coverlet over him.

It was the most wondrous soft and clean bed Michael had ever lain upon, and he sank gratefully into the pillow, licking the last of the crumbs from his fingers and shirtfront. Whatever lay ahead, he could better face it now.

"Thank you, Mr. Owen. Thank you." Michael was sincere, but a taint of panic rose in his heart. "Will ya be turning me over, sir?"

Owen shook his head. "Ease your mind, lad, and sleep awhile. I'll not be turning you in, God bless you. But I don't know what we will do, what we can do." He dimmed the light. "We'll talk later. I'll be out in the general room. I've a letter to write to Annie before we reach Queenstown."

Michael nodded, and it was the last he saw or heard. Even before Owen closed the cabin door behind him, Michael had fallen into a deep and much-needed slumber.

※ ※

Owen closed the door. He made his way to the general room and, finding as quiet a spot as was to be found, sat down with his pen and tablet. He stared at the white enamel walls as if they might offer a solution.

Owen sighed. *What Pandora's box have I opened? Will the authorities allow Michael into New York? What will become of him if they don't?*

And supposing they do let him enter America, dare I take him on to New Jersey? Will Uncle Sean and Aunt Maggie have room? Will they be willing to make room? Owen shook his head just thinking of the audacity and trust of the lad.

At length a slow grin began in one corner of his mouth and worked itself into half a chuckle. Well, why wouldn't it work? Michael would be an extra pair of hands, and God knew He had put the boy in Owen's way time and enough. It was stumble over him again and again or pick him up and walk together. *What a sense of humor You have about You, Lord. I didn't mean to be so daft. I'll do all You show me for the lad.* It wasn't exactly a prayer but more of a communion.

The room filled as those on deck were driven in by the cold of the darkening sky. Owen realized that the ship must have departed Cherbourg, though he'd not noticed when.

Queenstown, Ireland, would be the last port of call and his last opportunity to post mail before *Titanic* crossed the Atlantic. He had promised Annie a letter. Owen chuckled softly. There was so much more to write her now.

For the first time in years Michael dreamed of his mam and da. He was six again, and Megan Marie was a babe in their mother's arms. Mam had spread an embroidered cloth over the summer grass, a picnic of cheese and jam and currant buns—Michael's favorite in all the world. She was just pouring the tea when Da pulled off both his shoes, hoisted Michael upon his great shoulders, and charged down the bank of the River Shannon into the glistening water, both of them laughing and shouting at the top of their lungs for the joy of being alive and together in the late-afternoon sunshine.

Michael caught his mam's twinkling eye and the sharp dimple in her left cheek. She tried to fuss at her men acting the fool, romping and splashing to high heaven, but she could not keep her mouth grim. Her laughter rang like church bells.

Megan Marie kicked up a fuss from her blanket in the sun, and Mam scooped her babe in one arm and hiked her skirt over the other. Gingerly she made her way down the bank, testing the water's edge with her bare toes. Da dropped his tomfoolery in an instant. With Michael still on his shoulders, he waded through the current and swept his two favorite women into his arms and above the water. It was the happiest moment of Michael's memory, one he'd long forgotten. To dream of it was bliss and peace, a gift beyond measure.

When Michael woke, the light in the room was still dim. A snoring giant of a man lay in the bunk across the narrow aisle. Two currant buns, a pat of butter and one of jam cupped in a folded paper, and a fine slab of cheese stowed between two slices of fresh bread, all wrapped in a napkin, sat atop Michael's pillow. A mug of half-warm milk stood inside his boot. Wells, silent and sacred, gathered in Michael's eyes.

He wondered as he ate where the good man Owen was and where he slept while Michael remained in his bed. But the wondering stopped before the last mouthful. Michael slept again, a warm and dreamless sleep, until morning.

≋ CHAPTER TWELVE ≋

"MICHAEL, MICHAEL." Owen shook the boy's shoulder gently. "You need to wake up, lad."

Michael pried open heavy lids, then shielded his eyes against the lamp. "What, then? Mr. Owen?"

"I'm here, lad. I want you to wake up and wash. I'll give you a clean shirt. They'll be blowing the bugle for breakfast directly. You're to take my meal ticket and go to the dining hall. I want you to eat your fill."

"But that's for you, Mr. Owen. I'll not be taking your meal ticket."

"You will if I say so, Michael Dunnagan. If you're to be in my employ, I'll want some meat on those bones. How do I know you won't faint dead away in the middle of a job?"

"I'd never!" Michael vowed. "I'm a good worker, sir!" And then Owen's words seeped into Michael's sleepy brain. "Your employ, sir?"

Owen smiled. "You are a good worker, lad. And we'll talk more about your employment, if the Americans let you into New York. Ellis Island's not particularly noted for its ease on immigrants—let alone stowaways. But now I want you to eat and I want this bunk. We'll take turns for meals and sleep and won't annoy our Swedish friend lest he complain to the steward. So step lively."

Michael scrambled from the bunk. "Yes, sir. I will, sir."

"You'll like the breakfast," Owen whispered. "There's rashers and eggs and potatoes in their jackets."

Michael felt his eyes grow in their sockets. "And tea, sir?"

"All the tea in China," Owen laughed. "Eat and drink your fill, God bless you. If you're able, slip some bread and cheese in your pocket for later. But if the waiters mark their eye upon you, don't try it. Don't draw attention to yourself. If anyone asks your name, give them mine."

"But you'll be hungry, sir."

"I'll be sleeping. Wake me when you spy Ireland's shore. I'll not want to miss that. I'll take the midday meal. Now, take this ticket and be off."

Michael was halfway through the door when Owen called him back. "You must wash and change your shirt first. You look every bit the stowaway you are."

"But—"

"No buts, Michael. Do as you're told." Owen pulled a spotless shirt from his pack.

"Yes, sir." Michael's heart sank.

"What's that on the bottom of your shoes?"

"Me shoes?" Michael looked down. "It's cork, sir. To make me taller."

Owen shook his head. "I don't think I want to know any more. Pull it off. It looks sloppy."

"Yes, sir." Michael pulled the cork from his shoes without a moment's hesitation, but changing his shirt was something altogether different. How could he manage with Owen there? Michael kept his back to the sleeping Swede, marking a fierce stance toward Owen.

The room was too small to maneuver with two of them standing, so Owen sat on the bunk to remove his shoes. When he glanced up, he looked beyond Michael to give the boy his privacy.

But the mirror above the washstand drew his eye. Orange and yellow bruises and variegated scars—those healed over white and those half-raw still an angry red—crossed and crossed again the length of Michael's back. Owen turned away, both because the bile rose in his throat at such a sight and because he knew the boy had done all he could to hide them. He would not shame Michael.

Owen lay on the bunk with his face to the wall, knowing he could not look on the boy without pity. He feigned sleep as Michael scrubbed. When he heard the door of their cabin close, Owen opened his eyes.

He was tired and had looked forward to a good long sleep. But now he slid to his knees, locked his hands across the bunk, and poured out his heart to almighty God, beseeching on behalf of his young friend, begging for wisdom.

Half an hour went by as Owen prayed. When he stood, he understood exactly what the Lord would have him do, though he could not see the outcome. Owen pulled his journal from his bag and began to write.

Michael roused Owen late in the morning as the gray-green mountains of Cork rose ever so surely from St. George's Channel.

"I've wanted to see these shores since I was a lad." Owen drank in the shoreline with a delight Michael could not understand. "My father longed to return to his home in County Clare. He talked of taking Mother and me before Annie was born. And he wanted us to see the Cliffs of Moher. He talked and talked of them, high and sharp and glistening in the sunlight. But it never came to pass. I envy that you know this land, Michael."

But Michael knew nothing of the Cliffs of Moher and could not muster a kindred enthusiasm for Ireland.

Titanic stopped her engines and anchored a good two miles from the Queenstown shore. She waited as tenders, loaded mostly with third-class passengers, chugged toward her. Sellers of Irish lace and linen, of pipes and canes and shawls were allowed aboard to hawk their wares. Women and even men from first class pored over the craftsmanship and never blinked at the laying down of pounds and dollars, enough to keep Owen and Michael in food and shoes for months.

"Ah," Owen whispered, "I'd like to get some of that Irish lace for Annie and a woolen shawl for Aunt Maggie . . . something delicate for Lu—" He stopped.

Michael looked at him quizzically. "Lucy? Do you mean the sergeant major?"

Owen blushed but did not answer; it was the first time Michael had seen any sign of embarrassment in his friend. He looked at his shoes, then leaned farther out over the railing, his face turned from Michael.

"You're sweet on her, Mr. Owen!" It was a statement of fact and a great astonishment to Michael. Try as he might, he could not catch Owen's eye.

"Yes, I'm glad to see these shores. Father pined after Ireland, I think— second only to his pining for my mother, once she died."

Michael was not about to let Owen change the subject. "You *are* sweet on her!"

Owen hesitated. "I met Mrs. Snape and her parents in Southampton. She is a fine lady and a good mother to her young daughter."

"The sergeant major is *married?*"

"Widowed," Owen said simply. He turned with unaccustomed sharpness to Michael. "Her name is Mrs. Snape, Michael, and you are to speak of her and to her with the utmost respect, should your paths cross again."

"Yes, sir." Michael feigned humility even as a grin crept across his face.

Owen saw it and gave a good-natured, gentle jab to the boy's arm. "You've seen through me, lad."

"Are you courting her, then, sir?"

Owen sighed. "If she'd have me. Not that I have anything to offer her—not yet." He straightened. "But I will. If hard work and determination can make such a thing happen, I will."

They stood, shoulder to shoulder, watching the loading of new passengers—perhaps 150 or so—onto *Titanic.* They saw hefty bags of mail exchanged, and with it Owen's letter to his sister.

Finally *Titanic's* three deep whistles sounded. The tenders, carrying their hawkers and mail and those few passengers bound for Ireland, cast off. *Titanic's* starboard anchor was raised.

"Good-bye, sweet Annie," Owen said.

"Good-bye, sweet Megan Marie," Michael whispered in turn.

"And who is Megan Marie?" Owen grinned at Michael. "The lady of your heart, young sir?"

Michael felt his blood drain. He didn't need a looking glass to know it. He'd not meant to speak aloud.

"Michael?" Owen reached a hand toward the boy. "What is it? What is this pain?"

Michael could not answer. He could not look at Owen, fearful that what he had done and what he'd failed to do in protecting his sister might show in his face.

"Whatever it is, Michael, you must leave it behind. Think of it only to forgive or to ask forgiveness. You've a new life ahead of you in America. We both have. We are bound to look ahead."

As if on cue, *Titanic*, beauty of the sea and ship of dreams, having secured her full complement of first-class highbrows and second-class working folk, her steerage bowels stuffed with immigrants who dared hope for new work and new lives in a new world, glided from Queenstown Harbor and set her bow for the western sea. Strains of "Erin's Lament" piped sorrowfully from the stern of the ship—fitting and poignant for the departure, but a sharp contrast to the bustle of newly boarded passengers.

Owen and Michael leaned against the railing, separated by their own memories. They watched the dance of sunlight and shadow as clouds played across the shrinking hills of Ireland. They watched as *Titanic* turned and sailed toward the red and gold of the setting sun. They watched until there was nothing but sea.

☀ CHAPTER THIRTEEN ☀

"Three cups of tea I drank with sugar and cream, and they'd have given me more for the asking! Two helpings of bangers and mash and all the rice and apples I wanted. Can you believe it?" Michael's spirits had clearly soared since their afternoon on deck, and Owen was glad of it.

"I brought you some bread and butter, and here." Michael pulled a mug filled with dry hash and sausages from beneath his coat. "There's more where that came from."

Owen laughed. "I'm sure that's quite enough."

"There's to be dancing tonight," Michael confided breathlessly, sounding for the world like a young man about to attend his first dance.

Perhaps, Owen thought, *he is.* "You go, then, lad, and I'll sleep a bit more. When you've had your fill of revelry, you can take the bunk, and I'll see what's abroad."

"You don't mind?"

Owen laughed. He'd no desire to dance with anyone but Lucy, and she wasn't likely to be kicking up her heels in steerage. "Go on with you and God bless you, lad. Just don't call so much attention to yourself that we're given the plank to walk."

Michael pulled a sober face. "I won't, sir. I'll likely just watch, sir." Then he dashed from the room.

When Michael had gone, Owen pulled his satchel from its storage. He spread its contents across his bunk, fingering each packet of seeds, each dry shoot carefully wrapped in brown paper. He pulled out the roots of his favorite roses, the double white ones he had propagated and the two his father had developed, naming them for his wife and daughter, the Lady Helen Cathleen and the Elisabeth Anne. They were promises, needing only a bit of earth, a gracious sun, and the bountiful rains of heaven to make them root and grow and flourish. He shook his head to think that a man's future lay in things so small as those spread before him.

Owen knew each seed by name and each root, each shoot, for the flower that it was. He knew the Latin and the common names. He understood their weaknesses, their strengths, their susceptibilities. He knew what each particularly craved in nourishment, what made each one flourish. He understood what was spread before him better than he hoped to understand most humans.

Owen had not labeled the packets. There was no need when a man knew their names and properties as well as he knew himself. But that evening he took a pencil from his pocket and labeled each one. On the back he listed the date he would have sown the seeds in England, the height they were bred to achieve, the amount of sunlight they required each day, the best mix of soil and sand and peat and fertilizer, whether they would show best in a border or a bed, and the names of plants they were happy to grow beside.

"I'll teach him, Lord—all I am able." Owen scarcely realized he'd spoken aloud or that two hours had passed since he'd begun his task.

Before Owen finished his prayer, the Swede had broken into the room, eyes glazed and bearing the rank smell of vodka. He gestured toward Owen, then turned his back and ripped apart his duffel, strewing its contents across his bunk. Owen wondered if the man was sober enough to find whatever it was he sought. At last the Swede raised a bottle high and turned to Owen in jubilation. Though his eyes shone bright with drink, his brows peaked in curiosity at Owen's packets and notes. The man's eyes narrowed in puzzlement, then opened wide.

Owen pulled together his packets, feeling strangely exposed with the Swede staring down on him. He knew his bag held not only his future, but that of Annie, of Uncle Sean, Aunt Maggie, and now of Michael. It held his hopes for Lucy, or for someone like her, someday.

He knew, too, that there were dozens of farmers headed for the fertile soil in America, possibly the Swede among them. Any one of them would find a select stock of seed, free for the taking, a temptation. They would have no way of knowing the difference between common seed stock and the results of four years plus his father's life work.

Owen's bag no longer felt a secure hold for his precious cargo. It was not as though he could take his lot to the purser's office and ask that his valuables be locked in the safe. He would be laughed from the cabin.

He turned his back on the Swede, hoping the man would return to his drinking, but it seemed to Owen that he dallied. Owen tucked the bag between himself and the wall, lay the full length of the bunk, and made as if to go to sleep. Still the Swede stayed, and it felt to Owen like waiting.

The minutes ticked by and Owen found himself struggling to keep awake after a long day and precious little sleep the night before. He'd nearly dropped off when he felt the man's presence too near. He opened his eyes to find the Swede standing above him. The man stepped back. Owen sat up and stared as the big man fumbled for his coat sleeves and stomped from the room, color in his cheeks.

As soon as the Swede's footsteps died down the corridor, Owen pulled a sewing kit and linen nightshirt from his bag. Ripping the shirt into a dozen pieces, he began to stitch pockets, deep and wide, to the inside of his jacket and more along the inner front of his heavy coat.

Owen was still sewing when Michael burst in. "You're awake, Mr. Owen! Do you want to have a go at the dancing?"

"No, I don't. I want you to put my jacket on and keep it on."

"Your jacket? But why, sir?"

"Because I said so," Owen snapped.

Michael waited.

Owen tossed the hair out of his strained eyes and cracked the tension from his neck. He jabbed the needle sideways through his coat and all but swore at the tenth bloodied prick of his fingers.

"Do you want me to sew that for you, Mr. Owen?"

"Can you run a stitch?"

"Aye, I can, sir. I've had some practice on my own shirts. Mrs. Cairn taught me."

Owen didn't know who Mrs. Cairn was, but he blessed her and gladly turned the needle over to Michael.

"But why am I sewing patches inside your coat, sir?"

"Pockets, not patches—to hold the seeds and roots and shoots I've collected from my flowers and roses in England. They're the beginning of our Old World garden for America. Without these my help won't mean much to Uncle Sean."

"Are you afraid someone might pinch them? Is that why we're sewing them inside?"

"You're quick."

Michael shook his head and bit off the end of thread. "Experienced, sir. Experienced."

Owen tried not to smile. "Good, then. You understand."

"It's the Swede, ain't it? He's a shifty-looking fellow. I don't trust him, not from the minute I laid eyes on him."

Owen raised his brows.

Michael shrugged. "Just a feeling come over me."

"Always listen to those feelings, Michael, those instincts. They'll not mislead you." Owen filled the pockets as Michael fashioned the remaining pieces of linen into safe havens.

When they'd finished, Owen hefted the overcoat for inspection. "A bit heavier, certainly, but it doesn't look too bulky. I don't think anyone will suspect as long as I don't button it—let it hang loose." He picked up the jacket. "This is all right too. You're a good man to have in a pinch, Michael Dunnagan. Well done."

Michael beamed.

Owen considered. "I was going to wait until morning, but I think now is a good time to have a bit of a talk."

"Yes, sir?"

Owen wished Michael did not eye him so anxiously. "You've done nothing wrong, Michael. I only wish to form our plans, to make certain we are agreed."

Michael let out his breath. "Yes, sir."

"It's about the gardens I've planned. In the remaining days of our voyage I mean to teach you what I can about the seeds and roots we carry—which is which, how to care for them. And I want to begin working on some garden designs together."

Owen spread the coats across his bunk. "Planting time will go quickly when we get to Uncle Sean's. We'll need to get these beauties in the ground right away. The roses will take a couple of years to develop enough to propagate, but most of the flower seeds ought to bring fine, big blossoms and new seeds the first year."

"You really mean this, don't you, sir?"

"Mean what?"

"For me to work with you and with your uncle, to try and make a go of it all."

"We must make a go of it; our lives—and Annie's—depend on it."

Owen sat beside Michael. He spread his palms before him. "Do you see these? These are green fingers to match my green thumbs. Everything I touch grows and thrives. And now I've touched you, Michael Dunnagan." He smiled. "So you've no choice but to grow and thrive as well. And if I have it my way, Uncle Sean and Aunt Maggie will welcome you not only into the business but into the family. Would you like that?"

Michael stopped breathing. It was plain.

"Michael? Is that not what you want?"

Michael began to speak, stopped, and began again. Owen saw the pleading in his eyes. "Please don't say it, sir, 'less you mean it."

Owen knew to keep his voice steady. "I mean it 100 percent. We cannot know what will happen in New York, what will happen with the authorities there. But I shall do all in my power to get them to release you, into my care if necessary. And I do mean it about working together. I've no doubt Uncle Sean will welcome us as a team. I cannot speak for them for the family part, though I cannot doubt it. But I can speak for me, Michael Dunnagan. And if you are willing, and if you are wanting it, we shall be always as brothers." He gave his hand in promise.

Michael stared, his eyes wide, at the hand offered him.

Owen pulled his hand back. "There is only one thing, and that is Annie."

"Annie?"

"My sister."

"Yes, Annie." Michael's face fell.

"Annie must come first, before either of us take a penny from the business. I've given her my word to bring her to America just as soon as the business is stable and as soon as I raise funds. Every penny of our earnings must go first to bring her to join us in New Jersey. Do you understand?" Owen offered his hand again.

"Yes, sir. I do, sir. Annie must come to America." His hand remained by his side, but Owen lifted and pumped it.

"And we are both bound to protect and care for Annie."

※ ※

Owen's words seared Michael's heart, made it race. He tugged his hand away, but Owen caught it and would not let go.

"There's no pulling back once you've put your hand to the plow, Michael. This is a free gift, with no strings attached, save our bond for Annie. I see the man you are, the man you're working to become, and that is what matters."

You don't know what I've done to my own sister, what I let be done. You can't trust me with yours.

"Mr. Owen—"

"Don't call me 'Mr. Owen' anymore. I'm now your elder brother, Michael. We've shaken on it."

Michael struggled between the joy of obtaining in a moment more than he'd hoped and dreamed, all that he'd ever wanted—a brother, a family—and the shameful, hungry cries of his past. "I'm grateful; it's just that I don't deserve this."

Owen smiled. "What do any of us deserve?" He tilted his head. "Do you know the Lord Jesus, Michael?"

Michael didn't understand the question. "He's dead, sir. They killed Him." It was what he thought whenever he heard people talk about the Sweet Jesus as if He were the neighbor next door.

"No, He's very much alive, and He wants to know you."

Michael frowned. He found himself crying out sometimes, crying the

"Sweet Jesus" prayer, though he did not expect an answer. He shook his head. "I just don't understand that, sir."

"You don't have to. Our knowledge is not needed, only our belief, our faith. He knew we could never earn our way before almighty God, so He gave His life as an atonement for our sins. That atonement is free for the taking, an unmerited gift."

"Unmerited." Michael repeated the word, tasting it in his mouth.

"It means we've done nothing to deserve it. It's grace. Jesus said, 'I am the resurrection, and the life: he that believeth in me, though he were dead, yet shall he live: And whosoever liveth and believeth in me shall never die.'"

Michael could not stop the ache in his throat. He could believe in such a gift for Mr. Owen and Miss Annie, for his mam and da. But he could not doubt that the Good Lord Jesus, the Sweet Lord Jesus, despised him.

He'd visited a church once on the sly from his uncle Tom and had seen the preacher pound the pulpit, had heard him shout eternal damnation, hellfire, and brimstone to sinners. Michael knew he was a sinner. That was one of the few things of which he was absolutely certain. Why else had he had to live through such hellfire and damnation from Uncle Tom?

But he couldn't reconcile those ideas with the goodness of Mr. Owen and this notion of grace for the taking.

"Jesus said, 'Come unto me, all ye that labour and are heavy laden, and I will give you rest. Take my yoke upon you, and learn of me; for I am meek and lowly in heart: and ye shall find rest unto your souls. For my yoke is easy, and my burden is light.'

"Think of it, Michael. Do you labor? Do you feel the weight of something, of anything in your life?"

Michael's breath caught. *Please don't ask!*

"You needn't tell me anything, Michael." Owen placed his hand on Michael's shoulder. "But tell the Lord Jesus. Whatever you've done, whatever has been done by others to you. Ask His forgiveness for your own sins, and lay down the hurt done you. Know that He wants to take all that burden from you. He will bear it. He offers rest for your soul."

A sob escaped Michael's throat. *Rest for my soul. Oh, God, what would that be like? Could I lay down my hate, my fear of Uncle Tom and Jack Deegan? Could I ask forgiveness for me?*

Michael could not speak. He wanted what Owen offered, but he could not believe in such a Jesus. It went against every voice of shame he carried.

At last Owen lifted his hand. "It's waiting for you, Michael. Like anything we're offered, we must reach out our hand to grasp it. And if it feels beyond your reach right now, it will remain just where it's always been . . . right there for your asking."

Michael did not trust himself to answer.

"So," Owen continued as though he'd not just told Michael the most astonishing thing he'd ever heard, "first thing tomorrow we shall begin your gardening lessons. By the time we reach America, you'll know more than one end of a spade from the other. We need to convince Uncle Sean that you've an Allen thumb with a Dunnagan name."

✺ CHAPTER FOURTEEN ✺

Friday dawned fair and full of promise. Owen and Michael pored over seed packets and roots whenever they found a quiet corner in the general room or a spot along the poop deck. Michael learned the names and properties of each seed. His brow furrowed in attempts to bring to life the image of the blooming flowers that Owen sketched, but he committed to memory everything his mentor said.

Owen ripped pages from his journal and scribbled lists for Michael to study—mixtures of soil and fertilizers, everything he could detail concerning propagation. "I don't know what garden pests New Jersey battles. Uncle Sean will tell us that."

Finally Michael held his head.

"It's overmuch," Owen sympathized. "It will go better once we're working, once you feel the earth in your palms and hold new shoots between your fingers."

"There's a lot to remember."

Owen smiled. "At last. You've dropped the *sir*—you were making me feel an old man." He gave Michael's shoulder a gentle shove. "Anyway, it will all come in time." Owen folded the lists and stowed them in the back of his journal. "Let's plot some gardens. Uncle Sean and Aunt Maggie have thirty acres. Uncle wrote that they use ten for nursery plantings, nearly an acre for greenhouses, and an acre or so for their home and storage sheds. The rest of the land is still wooded."

On a fresh page Owen sketched serpentine paths and half-moons and crescents. He drew circles and ovals and rectangular plots. "There doesn't seem to be enough business to support the nursery alone, and Uncle Sean and his hired man haven't been able to keep up with the landscaping jobs they've been offered—not enough manpower. You and I will come in handy there." Owen continued to sketch.

"But I've been thinking: what if we clear large plots through the remaining wooded acreage and plant small gardens—a different variety of flowers and roses in each plot, a different name and theme? What if we connect the small gardens with trails through the woodland, forming a long path to wind and twist and turn throughout the property—perhaps add a pond with water flowers and, in time, a fountain maybe, or even a small waterfall?"

Michael's head spun as Owen dreamed aloud.

"Uncle Sean wrote that the land in New Jersey is flat, that the summers are longer than in England. We could open the gardens to the public and charge admission. Aunt Maggie could sell cut flowers to customers from her own shop, right there in the midst of the gardens, and over the winters we'd all make dried flower bouquets and wreaths and swags for decorating, and any number of savory herb bundles for cooks."

Michael caught the fever. "And benches in the gardens for sitting, and those things that flowers grow over to cover a pathway."

Owen laughed. "Excellent! Trellises and arbors! And even gazebos!"

"Mam had one in her garden, one of those over-the-path things." Michael formed the shape with his hands and looked up but did not see Owen. "I'd forgotten till now."

"We'll grow all the American varieties we can, but we shall specialize in Old World flowers and roses."

"And we'll bring Annie to America soon," Michael vowed.

"Yes, Michael, we will. Just as soon as we're able." Owen turned serious. "I feel the rightness of all that lies ahead."

And so did Michael.

On and on they talked, Friday into Saturday. They took turns sleeping and eating and sharing the food one saved from his meal for the other.

Nothing in all of Michael's life had prepared him for the joy of those days. To imagine that they would continue for the remainder of his life was sometimes too precious to bear, too wonderful to believe. And so he tucked that great hope away in the smallest corner of his heart, where it grew and grew—where, for the first time in six long years, light bloomed.

⁂ CHAPTER FIFTEEN ⁂

Dearest Owen,

Your letter, sent from Ireland, arrived by this afternoon's post. It is so good to hear from you, and to think that it came all the way from Father's homeland! These have been the longest three days in my memory, and I am glad to have your letter to carry in my pocket. Everything is still so new here.

Miss Hopkins is very nice and not so stern as Aunt Eleanor. She became a bit cross with me the day you left. I shall confess it now—I ran down to the docks to see you off. I was not there long, just at the end, when Titanic *pulled away, nearly colliding with that ship, the* New York. *But I had to see you one last time! Six months or a year is a dreadfully long time to be separated. I think I caught sight of your cap raised in farewell—at least I want to imagine it was you.*

Was Ireland so beautiful as Father said? Were the hills as green? But then, how much could you see from the deck of a ship?

As you may suppose, I am not terribly thrilled that that boy—Tim or Michael or whoever he truly is—found his way on board to you. Stowing away is frightfully bold of him! I think you are much too forgiving and generous, Owen. If anyone was to accompany you to America, it should have been me.

I suppose what's done is done, though it fuels my fire. I know you mean well and good, but I do not want to "adopt him as our brother," as you say in your letter. You are the only brother I have ever known or ever want. We are enough for each other. I think you should send him packing. Besides, they probably won't let him into New York. I wouldn't.

The only good I can see from it is if he works twice as hard as he looks like he can—scrawny boy that he is—and can help you make a quicker go of Uncle Sean's landscaping business. Then you can send for me in three months, rather than six!

All the girls will return to school from their Easter holiday soon. Classes begin Monday morning. I suppose I am glad to have had this time alone with Miss Hopkins. It helps me to know her better. Did you know that her first name is Annie?

I am a bit frightened of so many girls coming at once. I am used to being tutored—first by Mother and then by the tutors Aunt Eleanor hired. I don't know what to say to so many girls, and I do not want to stand out as odd. I fear I may. You had best pray for me, Owen.

Please write very soon. This will be your first letter in America!

Your sister, ever so truly,
Elisabeth Anne Allen

Annie carefully folded the thin pages of her letter, tucked them into an envelope, and sealed it. She penned the address of her aunt and uncle in her best hand and placed a stamp in the corner.

It felt a sacred mission, walking out the door and down the cobbled street to post her first letter to America. Annie pictured her wonderfully tall and handsome brother opening her letter and imagined how he would read it, miss her, and surely remember where his first sibling loyalties lay. At least she hoped he would see her words that way and not compare her jealousies to those of Aunt Eleanor. Annie sighed, kissed Owen's name once, then dropped her envelope through the slot of the mailbox. "What's done is done," she whispered, lifted her head, then returned to the school.

≋ CHAPTER SIXTEEN ≋

CAPTAIN SMITH conducted Sunday morning's divine services from the White Star Line's own prayer book, with all classes invited to attend in the first-class dining saloon.

It was the first church service Michael had been to in a long, long time.

He and Owen exchanged a grin over the urgent whispers and awed nudges of the third-class passengers close about them.

"The room's a grand sight, ain't it, Owen?" Michael jabbed Owen and pointed to the palms they'd helped place the night before sailing day. Owen smiled and nodded, then pointed again to the hymnbook from which they sang.

> O God, our help in ages past,
> Our hope for years to come,
> Our shelter from the stormy blast,
> And our eternal home!

Could there truly be an "eternal home"? Michael sang the words true and clear, but he wondered.

"You ought to sing more often. You've a fine instrument in your chest and a voice made for praise, Michael Dunnagan." Owen spoke as they left the services.

Michael remembered his mam saying much the same to him as a child when they stood together, all as a family, in church. It seemed everywhere he turned, Owen opened old memories for him. So many all at once were both a treasure and an ache in his heart. How could he contain such joy and pain all mingled together? Would the dam burst inside him?

"I see you are training your young cousin in the ways of the Lord, Owen Allen."

Michael had been so lost in his thoughts that he'd not seen Lucy Snape match their pace.

Owen, clearly caught off guard, stumbled before he bowed. "Mrs. Snape."

Michael felt the helpless quickening in Owen's manner. He owned that Lucy Snape was a beautiful woman.

Lucy lowered her voice. "There is no Tim or Michael Dunnagan listed among the passengers."

Owen paled and blinked.

"I do not know what you are about, but I have seen how you care for the boy, and certainly he looks as if he needs it."

"It's my fault, Mrs. Snape. I—" Michael began, but Owen cut him off with a hand on his arm.

"I take full responsibility for the boy, Mrs. Snape. I—"

"Hush, the two of you!" She turned aside and walked with them. "I do not know what you will do in New York. I assume you've figured that out. But I have watched you these days past, and I know that whatever the boy is to you, you are good to him." She toyed with her purse strings. "It is the sort of kindness I want for my daughter, Margaret."

Michael brightened. "You'll not turn us in, then?"

"No." She laughed nervously. "Though I should! If they realize I've known what you're about and did not report you, I shall lose my position, surely."

"You are a good woman, Lucy Snape." Owen spoke softly and reached for her hand. And then, boldly, "May . . . may I write you once we've settled in New Jersey?"

"I hope you will, Owen Allen. I hope our paths will cross again." She blushed, withdrawing her hand, and placed small papers, folded, into Owen's.

"Your address?"

"No." She blushed, prettier than before. "I imagined the two of you could use some extra meal tickets. This boy needs fattening up."

"How did you—?"

"There are advantages to being a White Star Line stewardess, at least if you are friendly with the right staff." She smiled. "I must go. If I do not see you again to speak, I wish you well in your ventures, Mr. Allen."

"Owen."

"Owen, then," she replied.

Their eyes caught, and Michael wondered at the current that passed between the two. He fancied he could wave his hand between their faces and they would never notice.

Lucy made as if to go, then turned to Owen again. "RMS *Titanic*—write me there," she whispered and was gone.

Owen stood, staring after her.

"We're a knot in the aisle, Owen," Michael whispered as passengers worked their way around them. But Owen was clearly lost in the wonder of Lucy Snape. Michael took him by the coat sleeve and guided him back to third class.

Mr. Fletcher, the bugler, played the call for dinner. Michael pried the crunched tickets from Owen's hand. "Here, wake up now, Owen. We can go into dinner together, thanks to your ladylove."

At that Owen smiled all the broader till he chuckled and laughed out loud.

Michael would have been content with the vegetable soup served. But the roast pork with sage and onions, the boiled potatoes and green peas, the fresh bread and butter and cabin biscuits filled every corner of his frame. When the waiter brought in plum pudding with sauces and topped the dinner with bright oranges, Michael decided there really must be a heaven after all and that he and Owen had just feasted at its banquet.

Though they sat side by side eating their fill, Michael wagered Owen could not have told him half of what he had stuffed in his mouth. *It's a shame not to notice a fine dinner like this. Love might be grand, but it seems a mite hard on the digestion.*

After dinner they strolled the deck in the cold sunshine, took turns sleeping, then walked again.

Owen's plans seemed to have taken on a new urgency since their encounter with Lucy Snape. He seemed wound like one of the tops Michael had seen a child from second class spinning on their way back from morning services.

"Our gardens will be for Lucy and little Margaret, as well, by and by. Our family is growing by leaps and bounds!"

Michael was glad for Owen's happiness and hoped that all of his grand dreams would come true. If anybody deserved them, Owen did. But Michael knew that happiness and dreams could be swept away in a moment, and he feared to believe before they'd begun, before there was something he could hang on to. "Do you truly think we can do all of it?"

"We've each two hands, Michael," Owen chided. "As long as a man has two hands and a strong back, he can make things happen. It's no good being fearful. Worry won't change the future a whit, and it misses the joy of this glad day."

Michael wanted to believe it.

※ ※

By late afternoon they could feel the temperature drop. They enjoyed the best tea they'd had aboard ship and relished how it warmed them through. Michael devoured his favorite currant buns, which Owen, too, favored, washed down with cup after cup of sweet and steaming tea.

They raised their voices that chilly evening—Owen a strong baritone and Michael a clear tenor—in a hymn sing organized by one of the passengers, a pastor.

They'd planned a late, brisk walk along the deck. The brightened stars spread thick above and the sea below lay still, calm as plate glass. But the biting cold drove them indoors to blow on their numbed hands, to stamp and shiver in their coats and boots.

Because they had both pocketed meal tickets, they agreed to alternate sleep, four hours on and four hours off, then meet for Monday-morning breakfast. Michael, worn from the sea air and barely able to prop his eyes open, took the early sleeping shift.

When he entered the cabin, the Swede was not there, but Owen's bunk was rumpled. His bag was not properly stowed. Michael thought that odd and set to putting things to rights. But he saw that the latch was broken, and inside he found all of Owen's belongings torn helter-skelter. He knew Owen would not have left them so.

Michael buttoned his jacket—Owen's jacket—securely and adjusted the packets of seeds before he lay down, pulling the coverlet to his throat. He hefted himself on elbows and leaned against the wall, determined to wait for the Swede. *I'll throw that rascal over for the thief that he is, the thievery he intended. Then I'll get Owen and we'll call for the master-at-arms. We'll* . . . But the thought was not formed before Michael's eyes drooped and he fell fast asleep.

≋ CHAPTER ʃEVENTEEN ≋

"DID YOU HEAR THAT, Michael?" Owen's plea raked the remnants of Michael's dream. "Wake up, then. Wake up!"

Michael fought the stifling weight in his chest, tried to push back the fog that plagued his mind.

"Are you all right, lad?"

The beam of Owen's torch blinded Michael's eyes until he pushed the light away.

"A dream—I think," Michael stammered.

"Well, it was enough to rock *Titanic*," Owen jested. "It sounds as though the engines have stopped."

"Stopped?"

"For the night, I'd wager. There's a great deal of ice about." Owen loosened his tie. "But there was some odd grinding noise a bit ago. I heard a steward say that one of the propellers likely dropped. I don't like the sound of that, but he seemed to think it would make no difference to our getting into New York on time." Owen waited. "Sure you're all right, then? You look a bit gray."

Michael tried to sit up. "I get so tired."

"The sea air, that's all. Everyone sleeps at sea."

Michael pushed away the coverlet and pulled his feet over the bunk's side.

"Here, lad." Owen poured some water in the bowl. "Wash your face and clear your head."

Michael dutifully splashed the cold water on his face and up his neck but dallied at the washbowl.

"Are you up to sitting in the general room?"

"It's my turn."

Owen rubbed the back of his neck and stretched. "No matter. Are you under the weather, feeling feverish?"

"No," Michael said. "No, I'm all right. Just foggy in my head."

"A walk on deck will bring you round. The air is bracing, right enough." Owen pulled off his boots and stowed them in the corner. "I'm hoping for spring in New York. It certainly isn't here." The Swede's snoring nearly drowned Owen's last words.

"That Swede." Michael remembered. "I think he rooted through your bag. The latch was broken—everything helter-skelter when I came in."

Owen stared at the gape-mouthed man. "Never mind. I expected as much. He's drunk enough to sleep through the day and be no bother to us now. We're wearing everything important." He pulled his coat around him and lay carefully on his back. "The main thing is that I do not crush these roots. Call me before the bugler comes round. I shall be ready for a hot meal."

"Right." Still Michael lingered. He brushed his jacket—Owen's jacket—and buffed his shoes. He dug the dirt from his nails with Owen's penknife and combed his hair with Owen's comb.

When he could think of no reason to stay longer in the warm cabin, Michael forced himself to open the door, only to find a steward ready to pound it with his fist.

"Life belts. Life belts, everyone. A precaution; captain's orders."

"Life belts?" Michael stared after the man as he made his way from one cabin to another, banging on doors, delivering his short speech but offering no explanation.

"Did he say life belts?" Owen was beside him now.

"H-he did," Michael stuttered. "Why do we want life belts?"

"I don't know." Owen frowned. "Wonder if it's anything to do with that grinding noise I heard just before the engines stopped, just before I woke you."

Michael remembered the woman on the deck in Southampton. "God Himself can't sink this ship," he mumbled.

Owen did not respond, but Michael was certain the bare electric bulb from the hallway could not account for the color of his friend's face.

Owen turned up the lamp in the cabin, quickly pulling on his boots. "Probably a drill of some sort. I'll find out. We'll be wanting to do as we're told." On the way out, he paused without looking back. "Wake our snoring friend." He closed the door behind him.

Michael's throat tightened. He pulled a life belt from the top of the cupboard and set it at the Swede's feet, then sat on Owen's bunk to wait. Still the Swede snored, but Michael, nearly afraid to breathe, did not go near him.

It seemed an hour before Owen pushed open the door, took the second life belt from the cupboard, and threw it toward Michael. "Put that on," he ordered, grabbing the life belt at the Swede's feet. He jostled the man's beefy hands, his shoulders. "Wake up. Wake up, man."

But the big man snorted, groaned, and rolled over, waving him away.

Owen grimaced and shook the man roughly. "For God's sake, man, get your life belt on and get above deck!" He threw the man's jacket across his chest, jerked him up by his shoulders, and pointed toward the door. But the Swede, bleary eyed and still the worse for drink, made sounds of foreign swearing. He hauled back his fist and swung, grazing Owen's jaw and opening his lip.

Michael, numbed through, did not react to Owen's split lip but asked, almost idly, "Why does the lamp cord hang askew like that?"

Owen swiped blood from his lip. "She's beginning to list."

Michael shook his head. He knew such a ship should not list. It was as though his body understood that a nightmare brewed, but his brain refused to listen.

Owen pushed wide the cabin door.

Michael watched as anxious men and women gathered and filled the white enameled hallway, holding sleepy small children towing stocking dolls and blankets, and some with babes swaddled in shawls across their chests. They mingled, some half-dressed in nightgowns, others in thin or woolen wrappers or layers of day clothes, coats upon greatcoats.

Michael stood with great effort and stared as if from a distance. He might have laughed at the odd combination of worn brogans at the end of hairy legs peeking from nightshirts. He might have chuckled at the congregation of woolen and flannel sleeping caps pulled low over ears if not for the frantic current that sped through their owners' speech. Mixtures of English and Gaelic, of French and of languages Michael did not know filled the shrinking air. He could not understand their questions, their prattle, but fear and confusion communicated clearly in every language.

"Gather your wits, Michael!" Owen had layered his warmest clothing and was trying to tie something round Michael.

Michael looked down to see life belt straps bandaged across his chest—the same canvas-covered life belts that armored the huddled mass of men, women, and children outside their door. The fog in his brain thinned. He tugged, ripping at the life belt even as Owen tied him in. But Owen's strength of purpose was no match for Michael's fury.

"I'll not wear your life belt! I won't, Owen!" Michael pulled free of his friend and jerked the belt over his head, shoving it back into Owen's chest.

"You must, Michael!" Owen stood close and spoke low. "*Titanic's* hit a berg. I stopped alongside a crewmen's stairway and overheard two officers. She's making water fast. The mail hold is already awash. They've moved the mail higher, but it's no good. The water keeps coming. I don't like it. I don't like it at all."

Michael shook his head as though the shaking could stop time. *No, not now—not this!*

"They're calling for women and children above deck. They're loading first class into lifeboats now. Women and children only, Michael!"

Owen pulled Michael by the sleeve, and Michael let himself be threaded through the crowd of third-class passengers until they reached the nearest stairwell. But the stairs were packed and blocked by something or someone ahead that Michael could not see.

"What is it?" Owen grabbed the shoulder of the man ahead of them. "What is the holdup?"

But the man shook his head at Owen and repeated again and again, "No Engleesh. No Engleesh."

"They won't let us through!" an Irishman behind Michael shouted to those still crowding the passageway behind him. "Is it locked? Is the gate locked?" he demanded.

"I can't see," Owen shouted. "We can't stand here waiting." He turned Michael round, then pushed past him. "Come!"

Michael followed as Owen elbowed and plowed their way back through the thickening crowd. By the time they reached their cabin corridor, water had begun to puddle round their feet as if someone had overflowed a bath.

"He's gone," Michael said of the Swede as they passed their cabin door. But Owen did not pause, and Michael, the fog in his head finally gone, trailed his friend through a maze of corridors.

But they could not outrun the freezing water. The icy puddle had grown to a rising creek and seeped through the soles of their shoes. They reached the general room from an angle new to Michael. Steerage passengers by the dozens clustered anxiously, apparently waiting for direction; they huddled, talking, kneeling, praying through rosaries.

Owen dragged Michael on, twisting and turning through corridors until they reached another stairwell, then shoved him up the stairs. They were nearly to the top when they saw a lock upon the gate. Owen groaned but Michael gasped. "A key! There's a key!"

"Thank You, Lord Jesus!" Owen whispered. And then louder, "God is with us, Michael."

Michael twisted the key in its lock, hoping with all his heart that God was with Owen. He trusted God for Owen's sake, though not for his own. And he trusted in the giant ship herself. "*Titanic* cannot sink. She was the talk of Belfast—they built her unsinkable."

Owen snorted. "She is wood and metal, Michael. She can surely sink. Hurry now!"

They climbed to the next landing and the next before coming upon another locked gate. This time there was no key, no crowd, and no steward.

"There's got to be another way. Think," Owen ordered. "When we delivered the flowers and palms, which way did we come to reach this deck?"

Michael knew. Not from their delivery of Bealing's flowers and palms but from the night he spent dodging crewmen when he'd stowed away from Belfast to Southampton. "This way." Michael, sure of his route, dashed through a labyrinth of corridors and wound up stairways. Owen matched him step for step.

They raced the length of the broad hallway along E deck, the crew's quick route from one end of the ship to the other. *Scotland Road,* Michael remembered. *They call this Scotland Road.*

Their pounding boots formed a rhythm. They whipped round a corner, nearly colliding with the back of a steward withdrawing his key from a cabin door. A knocking sound startled all three, and a woman's shrill scream from inside. "Let me out! Do not lock me in!"

The flustered steward fumbled his keys, dropped them, retrieved the ring, and set to unlocking the door. "I'm sorry, miss—terribly sorry. I thought this floor was empty. My orders are to lock everything—a safeguard against looting."

The pale young woman did not speak but threw a heavy cloak over her shoulders and flew past him.

Michael felt Owen's jab to his arm, and the two of them shadowed the woman up the stairs. But something was the matter with the stairs. Michael's feet did not fall where he placed them and he wondered if that was what it was like to be drunk—only it was the ship that swayed and not him. He steadied himself against the railing.

Michael smelled the sea before he saw it. As he stepped on deck, the frigid night air pierced his trousers and jacket as though he wore nothing at all.

The night sky, alive with millions of stars, close enough to touch, suddenly exploded. Rockets burst into white flame, trailing long and sparkling tails into the black sea below. Michael knew they signaled distress—he'd heard seamen talk of such—but they looked to him like the kind he'd seen burst over Belfast at the new year. *Rockets should signal celebration,* he thought, *and not the end of the world.*

"I don't want to go into the boat without Papa!" a small tousle-headed boy shrieked and made every attempt to squirm from his mother's arms. But the man—his father, Michael thought—pushed him back toward his mother. Tearfully, she pulled the child close. "Why can't Papa come now?" the child whined.

But the proper British officer standing near the lifeboat was firm. "Women and children only. Women and children. Sir, you must step back."

Michael watched as the officer took the boy, now screaming mightily for his father, and handed him again to the mother once she had stepped into the lifeboat.

Michael heard the father's feeble assurance. "I shall see you in the morning, Robbie. Be good for Mother. It's just a precaution. You will go for a little ride, and then we shall all be together in the morning."

Had he not known what was happening, he would have imagined they were all waiting for a train. But Michael knew it was a train that only some would catch that night. It reminded him of the night after Mam and Da's burial, the night the village midwife—the lusty woman who'd delivered him and most of their village into this world—stood on the platform, waving him and Megan Marie off in the pouring rain, keening all the while.

Little Megan Marie had keened back. She had pounded the window of the train with her tiny fist and wailed for all the fear of what lay ahead, for the loss of all that was known, and for knowing, just as Michael did, that their parents were locked in boxes in the cold ground. How would they ever find them?

Michael had looked, he knew, just as that father on the deck. No amount of crying would bring their parents back. So Michael had not cried. And neither did the tousle-headed boy's father. He simply stepped back and raised his hand in farewell.

Michael could tell by the long fur coats and formal evening dress of those nearby that most of the passengers boarding lifeboats came from first class. He cringed in the face of spasms of anguish and tears but could not look upon the strong, stoic faces of the men who stayed behind—their jaws set firmly in place.

And all the while music played—jaunty ragtime airs that Michael knew had to be coming from the ship's orchestra, though he could not see them. Somehow it kept the general calm, and even though he knew better, he could almost believe things would come right after all. Why else would the band still play?

In the glow of the ship's electric lights, Michael could see a collection of lifeboats already spread across the glassy sea as though a few adventurous souls had decided to take a holiday row in the dark, perhaps to enjoy *Titanic*'s electric lights and music from afar. Michael pushed his imagination to the limits, if only to shut out what might lie ahead.

Owen stepped aside and spoke to an officer. Michael momentarily forgot his certainty that the Almighty despised him and prayed that the officer might let Owen aboard, perhaps let him row one of the boats. *He's strong from all his years of gardening; he'll make a strong rower. He's a good man, Sweet Jesus. Let them take him.* It was the best Michael knew to pray, but any attention he brought from the Almighty, he suddenly feared, might not be in Owen's favor. *For his sake and Miss Annie's, Sweet Jesus—not mine.*

"I won't leave without my husband!" a young woman shrieked. "We've only just married. You must let him come!"

"Ruth, you must go. I'll join you as soon as I can. Do it. Go on—be brave . . . for me," the man pleaded, then kissed her long and warmly, leading her all the while, as in a dance, toward an opening in the railing, toward a lifeboat.

How can they part from one another? But how can they refuse to part—to give up their chance of escape? And then, *I'll never kiss a woman. I'll die never having kissed so much as a lass.*

An older woman, a raised voice Michael recognized as cultured and perhaps American, insisted, "No! I'll not be separated from my husband. As we have lived, so will we die. Together." Her silvering hair shone softly in the electric lights as she stepped away from the small boats.

Though no longer young, she was beautiful, holding tightly to her husband, refusing the officer. Who was she? Michael fancied such a woman might be royalty. Weaving through the crowd, he leaned closer to her, thinking he would like to touch a queen, once, at this, the end of his life.

"I think, with respect to your years, Mr. Straus, that no one will object if you accompany your wife," the officer said quietly.

But the bewhiskered gentleman raised his chin and straightened his spine, despite his wife's hold on his arm. "Not while there are others. I do not wish any distinction in my favor which is not granted to others."

The officer spoke again, but the two turned away. The beautiful lady smiled into her husband's eyes and pulled his scarf snug about his neck. He stroked her lined cheek.

"We are old people, Isidor," she said, "and we will die together."

A chill swept through Michael's bones and he turned away, knowing he had glimpsed an intimacy too personal. Still, mesmerized, he peeked again and watched as the couple walked back to a glassed-in part of the deck, watched as they sat, side by side, in steamer chairs. He watched them watch as the world fell apart around them, as though sitting down aboard a sinking ship was something they had done before. And he wondered if he could make his heart so calm as they appeared.

≋ CHAPTER EIGHTEEN ≋

A SHRILL WHISTLE fired into the sky and another distress rocket flared. *Titanic*'s funnels belched steam through a hideous roar. Owen was shouting something only an arm's length from Michael's face, but in the noise and confusion Michael could not hear him.

A man in evening dress, glassy eyed and still parading a brandy, turned at Owen's shouting and scolded, "What are you doing in first class?"

That brought the officer's narrowed eye around.

A woman wrapped in a long fur coat and heavy muff slapped the drunkard. She said something, her expression high and haughty, but no one heard her words, for another long blast drowned her out.

The officer turned back to his duties.

The challenger tipped his hat and moved on.

When the man had disappeared into the crowd, Owen shouted, "God bless you, mum!"

"God bless and help us all," the woman shouted back. "You had best get this boy in a boat!"

"My brother needs a savior tonight," Owen replied. "He's just a lad. Won't you take him with you?"

"I'm not going. I am not married. I have no children."

"You have now, mum." And Owen clasped Michael's hand in hers. The woman wavered, clearly taken aback.

"No!" Michael jerked away. "I'll stay with you, Owen. We'll wait and go together."

"I'll come later. It's women and children only for now." He turned again to the woman. "Please, mum."

93

"I won't go without you!" Michael shouted, as near hysterics as he had ever been.

Owen gripped Michael's shoulders. "You must, Michael; you must. You're the key to keeping our dream alive and dry now. I'll join you as soon as I'm able. But if I must swim for a time, our roots and seeds will freeze and there will be nothing for us—nothing for Annie."

"I won't leave you!" Michael's tears threatened, came very near escape.

"If we're separated, you go to New Jersey, to Uncle Sean, and wait for me there. His address is in my journal, in my coat pocket." Owen unbuttoned his greatcoat.

Michael's head would not stop its vehement shaking. "No! I won't take your coat! I won't go, Owen! I won't!"

Owen pulled his coat off and wrapped it round Michael, forcefully shoving Michael's hands and arms through the sleeves, even as Michael fought him. He shook Michael, suddenly stern. "You promised me. You promised that you would not let me down and that you would do all in your power to protect and provide for Annie. I hold you to it!"

Michael's head stopped moving. The mention of Annie's name brought visions of Megan Marie. "You go instead of me, Owen. Annie needs you. She doesn't need me."

Owen buttoned his coat with its treasure-laden pockets around Michael. He fastened the life belt Michael had struggled against around the boy's chest. The fight was gone. "They won't let me go, not now. And I've got to find Lucy. I've got to make sure she's in a lifeboat. Be a man, a brother I am proud of this night, Michael Dunnagan!" And then, softly, "I'm a strong swimmer. God bless you, Michael. Carry our dreams to safety." He squared Michael's shoulders. "What are we without our dreams?"

Michael could not refuse Owen, could not refuse the carrying of his friend's dreams, could not deny his plea for Annie's sake. He ignored the prickles taunting his eyes and threw his arms around Owen.

"Women and children? Are there any more women and children?" the officer called.

"Here! One here!" Owen cried, pushing Michael and the lady who had already rescued them once toward the lifeboat. The woman hesitated.

The officer stepped between them and the lifeboat. "Women and children only, please. This boy is not a child. He must stay. Step this way, madam."

But the woman froze, staring at the officer as if she did not understand.

"Please, madam. Step this way quickly."

The woman looked at Owen and Michael, then back at the officer. "He is just a child. He's barely twelve."

Michael grimaced at the lie.

"We can make no exceptions, madam."

"These lifeboats are not full, Officer, and he is my only son!" she cried, and heads turned. "If you refuse my child, I'll go down with this ship! And I will scream my way to the bottom of the ocean!"

"Madam, please—"

But the woman was as good as her word, and locking her arm with Michael's, she began to scream at the top of her lungs. The officer abruptly passed both the woman in her heavy fur and Michael, bundled in Owen's greatcoat, into the lifeboat, then gave the signal to lower away.

"No more boys!" the officer ordered. "Women and children. Women and children!"

Already swung from its davit, the lifeboat jerked awkwardly and repeatedly as it was lowered toward the inky sea.

"Tell Annie that I love her, that I pray for her," Owen called to Michael.

"Owen, Owen." Michael repeated his friend's name, desperate to make the frenzy stop. But it did not stop, and the madness, the flaring rockets, the rollicking music, the disappearing lifeboats, the calm but stern judging over who lived and who died, who grasped at life and who sacrificed, who remained at their stations and who sought a means of escape, went on.

The sea was still, so flat that no swell came to lift the small boat.

"Pull clear!" The call rang from above.

But the boat tottered while a man at the tiller struggled to saw the ropes with his pocketknife, then to loose the oars' lashings.

Water sloshed over Michael's ankles as the oarsmen pushed from the ship's side, then pulled away with all the strength they could command. Michael did not notice the water until later. He wanted only to see Owen's face. But when the boat gained enough distance to view the deck, Owen was not there.

Michael knew that he'd gone in search of Lucy Snape, and he could only imagine Owen running, running back down the stairs, back along Scotland Road, back to wherever he believed Lucy might be.

But, Owen, Lucy is a stewardess! They won't allow crew into the lifeboats when they've first- and second-class passengers waiting!

But Owen had fashioned a miracle for him. Michael determined to believe that he would find a way for Lucy, if a way could be found.

The temperature dropped sharply as the boat pulled away. Someone near the tiller kept shouting, "Row! Row!" Those stationed by the oars pulled clumsily through the glassy water. Another rocket burst the sky, dragging its sparkling white tail into the sea.

"Why doesn't someone come?" a woman cried. "Can't they see our rockets?"

But no ship came, and the precious minutes passed.

Michael looked around them. Boats, perhaps a dozen or so like theirs, were scattered across the water, and he thought again of a daring midnight picnic on the sea, made visible by a million heavenly lanterns, serenaded by ragtime music. "It isn't real," he whispered. "Let it not be real."

Titanic dipped her bow like a great whale preparing to submerge, her lines still lit by electric lights. Deck chairs, tables, all manner of things were thrown from the deck.

"Are they trying to lighten the load?" a woman asked, incredulous.

"Sending things out what can float, mum."

"Rafts," a voice echoed.

"We need more distance," the voice at the tiller charged. "When she goes down, those boilers will blow and everything will be sucked in for miles. Row! Row!"

"No," Michael whispered. And then, louder, "Don't go so far! We'll need to go back—we must get Owen!" But no one paid him any heed.

The orchestra changed its tune. No more ragtime. No more waltz.

But a solemn piece swelled from the deck, a hymn, long and beautiful and plaintive. And though Michael did not know the name or the words, he sensed, young as he was, that all of life came down to this, and that perhaps there were no words.

The bow dipped lower. The stern began to lift. The giant forward funnel strained toward the sinking bow. When the funnel's first guy wire snapped and then another, Michael jerked in response. He watched in horror as the massive black funnel tipped forward, slowly fell, and crashed into the sea, shattering the starboard bridge and every helpless swimmer in its path. Those left on deck raced uphill, toward the stern, pulling themselves up and along by railings and ropes, anything within their grasp.

And then there came a great clatter, a smashing and a growing, grinding noise, a terrible belching and hideous roar from the dying beast. "It's the boilers and everything in her!" the doomsday man at the tiller cried. "Row!"

"It's the end of everything," the woman who had saved Michael whispered.

The bow disappeared beneath the water. It seemed the great ship broke in two and parted, one end from the other. The stern lifted, slowly at first, exposing *Titanic*'s black keel. She rose and rose until her giant propellers cleared the water and hung, poised and dripping, high in the air. She held for moments as hundreds—groping for a line, for a rail, for anything—fell, screaming, to their deaths. She hovered just long enough to breed false hope, settled back, blinked her lights once, and all was dark. Down she plunged, and all the people with her—like an elevator in a mine shaft—and the sea closed over her.

"Dear God!" a woman screamed.

"She's gone," a man whispered, then checked his watch in the light of a torch. "2:20."

The suction predicted by the man at the tiller did not reach Michael's boat. But the piercing screams, the heartrending, desperate cries and prayers begging for help and salvation from over a thousand people futilely beating the waves—the swimmers and those who could not swim—rent the night.

"Row back!" Michael screamed. "Row back and pick them up!"

But the man at the tiller stared, and the oarsmen, leaning on their oars, stared, stunned, at the place where the ship had been. Desperate, Michael climbed over the woman in front of him to get to an oar.

"Sit down, boy!" An oarsman shoved him back.

"Row back!" Michael begged, trying to regain his balance. He shook the lady who had helped him. "Make them row back!"

She whispered, her voice shaking, "For God's sake, can't you hear them? Row back! We've room for more."

"Shut up!" the man at the tiller hissed. And then louder, before anyone spoke again, "We'd be swamped. Do you want to drown, woman?"

"It ain't safe. They'll be clambering aboard and we'd capsize. We'll all drown!" a gruff voice echoed.

"We must try!" another pleaded.

"We can't help them and save ourselves too. They'd capsize us."

The arguing went back and forth, as absurd as dickering for peaches on market day, but no one moved.

And still, from the vast emptiness where *Titanic* had been, the begging, the screaming, the dying, went on. Michael could not have said if twenty minutes or twenty years passed as they all waited, waited, and did nothing.

"Go back now," Michael begged again, more quietly. "Please. Go back for Owen." But no one seemed to hear.

"We should go back," another woman said, this time without conviction. No one responded. And no one challenged the silence, not even Michael.

Minutes passed. Gradually the screams thinned—not so many, not so shrill. A whistle blasted from a lifeboat far away. It blasted and blasted, and from the feeble light of a lantern that shone in one of the boats, Michael could see that two or perhaps three boats pulled and tied together. Apparitions climbed from one boat to another.

Finally a lone boat rowed back toward the place where the great ship had been swallowed. Michael's eyes clung desperately to the lamp in the rescue boat. He hoped and prayed before realizing that the cries in the sea had died out completely.

"Owen," Michael whispered. Again and again he repeated his friend's name. "Owen . . ."

"Hush now," chided the woman beside Michael, the woman who had saved him.

And then, after long minutes, long minutes of mournful, shameful silence, a woman near the stern began talking of the fine grand piano in one of the saloons, of the mahogany writing desks and all that lovely, barely used china, smashed. "What a pity," she lamented. No one answered her.

Michael tried to comprehend what the woman had said. He cocked his head, but as he grasped her words, his breath came hard. He spun round in the small space, groped for the seat behind him, ready to scramble roughshod over every passenger between him and the woman. He would punch her in her stupid mouth, he would shout in her stupid face and rip her foolish hat from her foolish head and throw it into the sea. And then he would make the oarsmen row back until they'd turned every life belt, propped like pillows, round, until they found Owen—the thing he should have done in the first place.

But the woman beside Michael grabbed him by his waist and jerked him, tumbling, back into his seat. She forced him round and clasped his hands firmly between hers, then shoved them with an iron grip into the muff she'd cast aside, locking them away from the bitter cold, away from every temptation.

Hot tears Michael had never shed—not for his mam or da, not for sweet Megan Marie—coursed over his cheeks. He prayed that Owen had not been hit by the "fine grand piano" or cut by the "lovely smashed china." He begged again that somehow Owen had found Lucy and gotten them both, miraculously, into a lifeboat. From his cold plank seat in the lifeboat, a pinprick on the dark sea, Michael vowed outrageous oaths, if only Owen might live.

The minutes wore on. A woman cried that she spied a ship in the distance. Even the brooding man at the tiller shouted that he saw the light of a masthead and commanded that they "Pull for the light!"

They pulled and pulled, but there was no masthead, no ship, and at length the light disappeared. Someone ordered they turn back to be nearer the other lifeboats, seeking whatever safety numbers might provide.

Michael breathed, relieved, and then gasped, ashamed that he counted his own life dear. He took his turn at the oars and found that it warmed him. The mindless rhythm of the strokes helped numb his brain.

Shooting stars broke the endless night and bitter cold. Michael's head and throat ached as he alternately shivered and sweated. His feet and legs tingled, then grew numb.

Finally, black sky gave way to darkest blue. Michael forced himself to focus on the changing colors, to shut out the moans, the hum of grumbles and complaints around him, and to think once more of Owen, to believe that Owen had been saved, that he'd found his way into one of the lifeboats. Owen had promised he was a strong swimmer. Michael gritted his teeth and held him to it.

"I will find him," he whispered over and over. "When morning comes and all the lifeboats gather, I will find him." A ship would come, Michael told himself, and he and Owen would make their way to New York and New Jersey, to Owen's uncle Sean. They would plant their seeds and shoots and do all the things Owen had planned. They would send for Annie within the year.

Michael played the details through his mind, recounted the dreams he and Owen had stitched into a mental quilt over the last few days—the gardens, the serpentine paths, the gazebos they would build.

He shivered against the bitter cold and pulled the hem of Owen's greatcoat free from the water that sloshed over the tops of his brogans. He cradled their dreams, sewn carefully inside Owen's coat and jacket. He had been charged to keep their treasures safe and dry and to be a man, a brother Owen could be proud of; he would do that for Owen—for Owen and Annie.

Yes, they would talk it all over, Michael vowed, in the morning.

≋ CHAPTER NINETEEN ≋

GRAY DAWN CAME AT LAST. Red streaks brushed the stars away and painted pink the ice mountains towering over their valley of sea. But dawn also brought a stiff breeze, a low morning fog, and choppy waters.

At length, a distant booming and a faraway crackle of light scraped the far horizon, rousing even those who'd fallen asleep.

"Another star," a sleepy woman near the bow proclaimed.

"A storm. A storm's brewing!" An oarsman cursed.

"No. It's a falling star," countered the woman near the bow.

"We'll not survive a storm in this boat. Water's coming over the gunwales now." Michael recognized the voice of the doomsayer at the tiller.

The booming grew louder.

"It's a ship! There's a ship!" a woman in the nearest lifeboat called. Michael, still shivering, still sweating, his throat on fire, did not believe her, did not bother to look. But the chorus was taken up by others, and a ripple of hope swept through the small boats. Michael rubbed his eyes and spied a black speck growing steadily on the horizon. Rockets—not lightning—shot from the speck, the ship, into the sky, declaring she was on her way.

"She'll be coming to take up the stiffs," the man from the tiller prophesied.

Waves of remembered guilt for surviving, of anguish for the loss of loved ones who did not, washed over the small boat, wringing their hope as surely as if she had been swamped.

A woman pleaded sanity. "Surely they'll take the living as well."

A lifeboat over a mile away set off green flares. Michael wondered if the faraway ship could see such a small light in the midst of the ocean. But the ship slowed and altered her course. A cheer went up from the ragged fleet of lifeboats as the one stark funnel, black and red against a rising sun of molten fire, grew and grew, making short the distance between them. She stopped her engines near the first lifeboat.

"Row! Row toward the ship!" an oarsman called. Every oar dipped in the swelling ocean with a will. Even the doomsayer hushed his tirade.

Carpathia—even the name lettered on the ship's side was beautiful. By the time they reached the black cliff of the ship's hull, the sea had grown perilously choppy; every rower was spent. But the good *Carpathia* had flushed oil into the sea, creating calmer waters and a lee for the incoming boats.

Michael, unsteady though he was, helped the lady beside him, the lady who had saved his life, into a boatswain's chair, and then two little mites into ash bags that were hauled up the side. He even handed the shallow woman who had spoken of lovely smashed china into a sling. But when the wind lifted her feathered hat and carried it, by his ear, into the oiled sea, he did nothing to catch it.

Once the women and children were raised, Michael and every man who was able climbed the rope ladders and netting let down from above. Twice Michael slipped, his feet still numb from the freezing water.

Once he reached the railing, Michael was pulled to the deck of the ship by strong arms. A woolen steamer rug was thrown round his shoulders and a cup of coffee, laced with something stronger, was thrust into his trembling hands.

"Owen?" he begged the steward who handed him a sandwich.

"I don't know, sir. I don't know if anyone by that name is here or not. Lists are being formed."

Michael refused to go below, to lie down. He ate the offered sandwich at the rail, determined to stand, to search every boat as it came in. He and Owen would go below together.

When the last lifeboat emptied, Michael still stood sentinel at the railing with a hundred women or more, women who had waited in silence for husbands or fathers or sons or brothers or friends, for whole families still missing.

"He might have been picked up by another ship! Can't you send a Marconigram?" Woman after woman pleaded with stewards, with crewmen, with Captain Rostron himself.

Only there were no other ships, and all the lifeboats had been accounted for.

In a search for other survivors, Captain Rostron wove *Carpathia* through the flotilla of ice, circling the area where *Titanic* had gone down. Michael and hundreds of others from *Titanic* gripped the railings, hoping against hope and reason. Passengers from *Carpathia* joined them and hoped and prayed by their sides. But no more survivors were found. Michael thought it devilish that the deadly bergs and growlers could sparkle like golden pyramids in the risen sun. Some resembled ships fully rigged—a ghastly reminder of *Titanic* and her precious human cargo.

Captain Rostron ordered their flag lowered to half-mast and a service in the first-class saloon, conducted by Father Anderson, a passenger and Episcopal priest. He offered thanksgiving and gratitude for those who'd been saved and a memorial service for all who had perished.

At length hope gave way to grief and grief to despair. Women, tense but brave before, sobbed in open anguish for their lost. Tears streamed down the drawn and haggard faces of men. And still Michael could not believe that Owen was gone. He would not believe.

Carpathia circled the site once more. Michael searched the waters frantically. When a uniformed man, ledger in hand, asked Michael for a name, Michael blurted, "Owen, please, sir. Owen."

"Last name?" the man asked.

"Allen. Owen Allen." Michael breathed, relieved, certain the man meant to help him. But the crewman walked away and began talking to another survivor. Michael could not understand why the man did not search the waters for Owen with him, why he didn't run to Captain Rostron and tell him that Owen was waiting—out there.

And then it dawned on Michael that perhaps he had missed Owen at the service or that Owen had not been well enough to attend. Perhaps the man taking names would find Owen somewhere else on the ship and let Michael know later. Michael rubbed his temples. If only his head did not ache so. If only his throat didn't burn, he could think more clearly. Panic crept into his chest even as his lungs tightened.

When the sun sank, he still stood at the railing, searching the sea, just in case Owen had caught a bed board or tabletop or any one of a thousand pieces of *Titanic*'s debris that might float—just in case he had drifted far from *Titanic*'s grave.

"Here, here, young man," an older gentleman pressed when Michael, driven in at last by the cold, burst into the first-class saloon, shivering and panting. The clean-shaven man with unruly white hair made Michael think for all the world of Father Boyd back in Belfast. "What is the trouble?"

"Owen? Owen?" Michael could form no other words. *Father Boyd will understand. He will know what to do.*

"What's that you say? What is your name, lad? Are you with someone?"

"Owen?" Michael repeated. He was looking for Owen, wasn't he? Michael struggled against the voices inside his head, the voices that told him he had lost Owen, or perhaps that he had failed Owen. Michael could not remember. And if he had failed Owen, he would surely fail Owen's sister. *What is her name? Annie. It is Annie. Owen, Annie, Megan Marie—I've failed them all.* The list was too long; the names beat against Michael's brain.

"Why, you're burning up, my boy! Have you seen the ship's doctor?"

Michael had not thought of that. The doctor might know Owen, might have seen him, might have talked with him.

"Steward!" the gentleman called. "Help us, will you? This lad needs medical attention. He's burning with fever. I believe he is one of *Titanic*'s lot. Said his name is Owen."

≋ CHAPTER TWENTY ≋

THE NEWS BROKE in London. It crept into Southampton on Monday's morning fog, in the form of a midmorning notice posted in the window of the *Times* building.

Rumors ran that *Titanic* had struck an iceberg, was sinking, and that women and children were being put into lifeboats. A rescue ship, perhaps *Virginian*, was on its way, all would be saved, and the magnificent steamer, foundered on its maiden voyage, would be towed into Halifax.

But old shipmates and the wives and families of those who made their living on ships—nearly all of Southampton—trusted neither the rumors nor the sea.

By midafternoon a number of girls had returned home from Miss Hopkins's school to await further news with their families. Those who remained at their desks wept quietly, twisted strands of hair round their fingers in distraction, bit their lips, or chewed their nails—waiting, simply waiting.

Annie did not see the words on the page of the lesson book before her and made no pretense of studying. She fingered Owen's letter in her pinafore pocket, reminding herself again and again that Owen had written; Owen was all right; Owen would send for her soon.

On Tuesday morning, just before breakfast, the girls heard whispered words, whimpers, and low moans beyond the door of Miss Hopkins's office. Minutes later a woman in kitchen dress and apron, the mother of one of the girls enrolled, crept from the room. With handkerchief pressed against her swollen eyes and shoulders slumped, she hurried down the hallway and out the door.

Annie pulled back the window shade and watched her go, bare of wrap and apparently unmindful of the cold. The knot that had been growing in her stomach since yesterday twisted and tightened. What could be so dreadful as to make a grown woman cry in public, let alone forget her wrap the day after an untimely spring snow?

When she looked through the window again, Annie saw more women and older men emerge, one by one, from their homes, then huddle and cluster in the street. And then came men of all ages in caps and coats, walking rapidly, heads bent, downhill. A few women followed, mostly dressed in black.

Annie could not swallow the fire lodged in her throat. "Where are they going?" she whispered.

"To the docks, to the White Star Line offices in Canute Street," whispered Katie, Annie's schoolmate, as she too peeked through the shade.

Annie simply stared at her.

"To . . . you know . . . see the lists."

"The lists?" Annie did not understand.

"Surely. Of them that's saved and them that's lost. That's where the lists will be posted."

Annie's breath came in tight little gulps. All this time she could have checked, could have known. She pushed the girl aside, grabbed her coat, and raced for the stairs but ran headlong into Miss Hopkins.

"Annie! Where are you going in such a state?"

But Annie did not stop to answer. She could not speak, dared not open the dam lest it burst. She rushed with the tide of men and women toward the sea, right to the gates of the White Star Line offices in Canute Street, just as the girl had said. She pressed through the crowd but could not see over the heads of the adults.

"Please, mum," Annie begged of a lady taller than herself, "can you see? Is the name of Owen Allen on the list?"

The lady shook her head. "There are no lists yet, dearie. We're waiting. We've been waiting all the morning and some since last night."

"It's the waiting—the not knowing—what's so hard," another woman turned and said.

"No news yet," another voice added. "They said the signal's weak, though how that can be after all this time, I don't know."

"Just the news that for sure and certain she's gone down," chimed in a man standing near Annie. "A gentleman came out and said there's been loss of life and some saved, picked up from lifeboats by *Carpathia*. She's turned round, taking survivors to New York. No names as yet."

Annie felt her knees buckling and clutched the sleeve of the lady beside her.

"Here, missy, it won't do to give way. We don't know anything yet. The White Star Line says they'll post the names of those saved soon as they get them."

Annie did not remember Miss Hopkins pulling her from the crowd or walking her back to the school. She could never have said if she had been scolded for running to the docks. But she remembered the moment of realization, the sudden knowing that her brother would not have taken a seat in a lifeboat before every woman and child was saved. She doubted if he would go before any other man. And the knowledge felt like drowning.

On Wednesday the first survivor lists were posted outside the Canute Street offices. But Annie stayed inside the school, staring hour after hour at the window—not through the window but only at her own reflection. Somehow she felt that if she did not look at the lists, if she stared only at the glass between herself and the world outside, she could hold the end at bay.

Miss Hopkins gave up trying to hold back the children or their tears. "They need to be with their families," Annie heard her say to one of the cooks. Annie turned away. She had no family but Owen.

Flags flew at half-mast. Men, and even women, appeared with mourning bands tied round their arms. Women dressed from head to toe in black. Buildings of business draped black crepe across their windows. Between the town and the docks, the trail of those seeking news remained steady.

Even grown men who had determined to keep watch until all the names were posted sometimes found the vigil too hard. They walked home for a cup of tea or to the pub for a pint. But the uncertainty, the very suspense, drew them back.

≋ CHAPTER TWENTY-ONE ≋

WHEN MICHAEL WOKE, he sensed first that the ship's engines had stopped. Yes, he remembered Owen waking him, telling him that the engines had stopped. Owen would walk through the door of their cabin any moment for his turn in the bunk and tell him about the engines.

But that wasn't right; he should not be awake before Owen walked in, and why did it feel as though it had all happened before? Michael ran his tongue over crusted teeth. He rubbed his forehead, pushed back his matted hair, tried to push the fuzzy feeling from his brain.

"So you're awake, young man." A kindly voice with a thick accent spoke. "Three days is a long sleep."

Michael opened his eyes, blinking against the light. It wasn't Owen. He tried to focus on the drawn and swarthy face above him, tried to concentrate on the man's words.

"You gave us something of a scare, but I'd say you're coming round." The man turned away, busy with things Michael could not see.

The room wasn't right. It was not Owen's cabin. The Swede was not in the bunk opposite. The red-and-white White Star Line coverlet was gone, and in its place lay a blue woolen blanket.

Was he dreaming? His head hurt, but it didn't feel like a dream. He remembered the seeds he should protect from the nosy Swede and ran his hand over his chest, over the pockets he and Owen had sewn inside the jacket he'd promised to wear, to never take off. But he was not wearing the jacket—only the shirt Owen had loaned him. Nearing panic, Michael tried to think—had he taken off the jacket? Where?

And then, in a rush, it all came back—Owen pulling off his greatcoat and fastening it and his life belt around Michael, Owen sending him off in a boat, Owen running to find Lucy Snape, *Titanic* plunging headlong to the bottom of the sea. No more lifeboats. No more ships.

"We've docked in New York. First class is unloading now. It will be a while yet before you can go. I've kept you away from the other passengers. I wanted to keep an eye on that fever. Exhaustion, most likely—but stay and rest a bit. I'd like you to try to eat something." The man smiled. "A little hot food can do a world of good."

The man rang a buzzer, and in a very few moments a steward came running. "Yes, Doctor?"

"A little hot broth for my patient, if you will."

"Right away, sir." And the weary steward was gone.

"We found your New Jersey address in your pocketbook."

Michael stared at the man, not comprehending.

"In your coat pocket. Mr. and Mrs. Sean Allen of Swainton, New Jersey. Are they coming to meet you? Are they your parents, Owen?"

Still Michael did not answer. His heart raced, but he shook his head.

"You are Owen Allen, are you not? Are these not your things?" The man looked more concerned than suspicious. Michael did not know what to say. If Owen had not come to claim his coats or to claim Michael, it meant that he was nowhere on the ship. Reality bludgeoned the door of his brain, but Michael could go no further in his thinking.

"This is your coat?"

"Yes, sir," Michael managed, relieved to see both the greatcoat and jacket.

"Are your parents meeting you? Do you need someone to contact them?"

Michael could not answer.

"Are you traveling with anyone?"

"No, sir. Not now."

"Ah, I see." The man looked all the more concerned. "I'm sorry, son."

Michael could not hold back the pools behind his eyelids or the truth from his mind.

"The American Red Cross will assist in every way possible. I believe I heard some talk of one of the lines offering railway fare." The doctor's unexpected kindness threatened to break Michael's reserve.

Michael forced his thoughts to a different path. Railway fare. *Owen said to go to New Jersey—that he would meet me there if we were separated.*

The good doctor turned his eyes away. "Let me see what I can do." He stopped at the door. "There are ambulances waiting to transport survivors to St. Luke's and St. Vincent's hospitals. It might be a good idea for you to be checked further—it would at least give you a longer rest before journeying on."

Michael knew nothing of hospitals except that more questions would be asked of him. The doctor seemed to think he was Owen, and perhaps that was good; perhaps if the authorities believed that, they would let him into America.

When the doctor had gone, Michael wondered what would happen if he just got up and walked out. The doctor had said they were docked in New York. Could it be harder than walking onto *Titanic* in Belfast or off into Southampton? What was Owen's worry about the officials in New York? Something about Ellis Island? He couldn't remember.

Michael tried to sit up but felt the trembling weakness in his arms and legs, the buzzing in his head. He'd not heard or seen the steward come and go, but he drank every bit of hot broth the man had left. Michael's throat still burned, but the hearty broth warmed him through and set his stomach to growling.

He stuffed the bread from the tray into his trouser pocket and rummaged through the cupboard for his boots. The room would not stand still. Michael wanted to lie back down, to sleep another day or two or three, but he had no such luxury. The sooner he disappeared into the streets of New York, the sooner he'd be forgotten.

Buttoning Owen's jacket across his chest, then Owen's greatcoat, he slipped from the cabin, softly closing the door behind him. He passed through the dining saloon, now empty. A clock bonged ten. He trekked hallways, breathing harder and heavier than he would have wished, holding the wall to steady the spin in his head.

Somewhere not far ahead, he could smell the night air. He heard voices and followed their twisted trail until he found himself edging a milling group of passengers.

"At least they're not putting us through the rigors of Ellis Island," a woman remarked.

"I'd trade this freedom for twenty interrogations and medical checks," another replied, "if only my Harry was with me." She choked back a sob, and the other woman wrapped her arm around her.

Michael swallowed the bile from his mingled broth and weak stomach, then filtered into their ranks. He walked, unnoticed, down the gangway of pier 54.

Relatives, held back by ropes and low fences, rushed the survivors, weeping in relief and weeping in anguish.

Michael felt lost and very much alone amid the confusing joy of reunions and the blatant outpouring of grief. He wormed his way to the street exit and finally toward the pier's entrance.

But he was not prepared to step into the bewildering bombardment of newspaper reporters' questions or the startling explosions of photographers' magnesium flares.

"Ah. Why don't they all just go home and leave us be? Haven't we been through enough?" a sympathetic soul beside him offered.

Michael had no idea. He only knew he needed to find the railway the doctor had talked about. "Excuse me, sir. There's a railway, someone said. Do you know of it, sir?"

"Yes. Yes, I do and am going to take it myself to Philadelphia. The Pennsylvania Railroad is offering free passage for us from Pennsylvania Station. Taxis should be waiting just ahead. As soon as the ambulances go, they'll transport us. Is anyone with you, young man?"

"No, sir."

The man nodded sympathetically. "Nor with me." He pulled his collar about his neck. "Irish—I can tell by your speech. A long way from home, isn't it?"

Michael looked away. He wasn't certain where home was now, nor how that was different than it had been a month ago.

"Where is it you're going?"

"New Jersey, sir."

The man smiled patiently. "New Jersey's a big place. Any more information than that?"

What had the doctor said? Michael closed his eyes, trying to remember. "Swainton, it is. Swainton in New Jersey, sir."

"Yes. Near the seashore. You need a train to Philadelphia and then one on to Swainton." Michael felt the man's eyes upon him. "You'll have to mind the stations. Don't sleep through them or you'll miss it."

"No, sir. I won't, sir." Michael followed the man through the crowd and into the last of a line of taxicabs pulled to the curb. Gratefully he slumped against the door, his forehead pressed to the cold window, as the cab bumped and jostled its way through Manhattan.

CHAPTER TWENTY-TWO

MICHAEL REACHED PHILADELPHIA in the wee hours of the morning. His New Jersey–bound train did not depart until nine thirty. By the time it pulled to the Swainton stop, the morning fog had nearly burned away and the sun rose high in a cold, gray New Jersey sky. The ache in Michael's head swelled and throbbed, and he could not swallow past the knot in his throat. His fever continued to climb.

"Just down the road, a half mile or so, you'll find the post office and general store. Someone there will know the Allen nurseries, young man."

Surely the conductor had been kind and helpful, but Michael dreaded finding Owen's family. What would they think of him? Why was he showing up in Owen's clothes with Owen's dreams tucked in his pockets and Owen dead at the bottom of the sea?

What would they think when they learned he was nothing but a Belfast gutter rat and stowaway their Owen had taken pity upon? And yet he had been saved—saved by Owen, when he and so many worthy men and boys, and even women and children, had died.

The half mile of winding trail passed too quickly, despite the lead in Michael's feet. He turned away from the bursting crocuses and budding daffodils splashed before the few and far-between houses. He closed his ears to scolding squirrels—creatures similar to but somehow different from those he had seen before—and the noisy mating rituals of red-breasted birds, a variety altogether new to him. The symphony of life grated, sprang before Michael in colors bright and garish against the black backdrop of his brain.

"Oh, about two miles, I'd say, down the road what passes the front of this store," the postmaster replied to his questions. "But I doubt as they'll be home just yet. They're down to the church for the funeral. I 'spect you know that. I 'spect that's why you've come. You might just be in time for the burying."

Michael did not ask or offer more. He didn't wonder how it was that they had learned so quickly of Owen's death. It must be some strange American ritual, to hold a funeral even though there was no body. He shuddered and shook his head at such a notion. It was just as well he'd missed it. Michael had no heart for more services, and the family would not want him anyway, once he told them all there was to tell.

The two miles had nearly come and gone when Michael stopped beside Asbury Meeting House. The doors were closed and the churchyard empty. But over in the cemetery, beneath the limbs of an old tree, two gravediggers shoveled heaps of sandy soil into a pit. A path littered with bits of flowers and worn by feet led to the road. Michael did not stop. His mind and feet no longer connected.

He meant to get things over with quickly. He would deliver Owen's coats and journal and pocketbook. He would urge them, as Owen had, to get the seeds and roots in the ground as quickly as possible. He would tell them all they wanted to know about . . . about everything.

I'll beg them to write to Annie, to send for her. I'll tell them that is the most important thing. I'll tell them I will find a job—somewhere. I'll save every penny for Annie—to bring her to America. I vow it on my life.

And then he would go. He did not know where.

The sign was plain enough: Allen's Run Gardens. The door and windows of the paint-peeled, two-story frame house stood shrouded, draped in black.

A tall gentlewoman dressed in drab mourning opened the door. Her green eyes widened, standing bright against her black collar and the grayed auburn hair that strayed from her loose bun.

"Mrs. Allen?" He'd barely spoken, barely lifted his eyes to her, before she reached out to take him in her arms.

"Owen? Is it you, my darling boy?" she asked, looking bewildered but smiling the saddest, dearest smile Michael had ever seen. "We feared we'd lost you."

PART TWO

KATIE BURST INTO THE DORMITORY Friday morning. "What do you think, Annie? My dad is saved! I don't know how, for he's one of the firemen, and they all said the firemen and trimmers were surely doomed. But he's saved!"

Annie tried to speak, tried to be glad for her, but the words would not come.

"We waited ever so long. The docks were packed with men and mothers with babies, and those White Star men just kept shaking their heads and saying, 'No news yet, nothing further.' They even sent out coffee to everybody waiting—Dolly Curry, the manager's own daughter, with trays and trays of coffee with cream!"

Annie did not want to listen.

"But finally they posted the crew lists. Mum says it's not right they made us wait so long, when those first-class passenger lists were posted in the papers right off. But I don't care now. I don't care now because Dad's saved!" Katie crowed.

Annie flung an arm over her eyes, wishing Katie would leave her alone.

"And do you know what else?" The girl shook Annie by the arm, pulled her from her bed. "Sit up, Annie! Do you know what else, I say?"

Annie had no choice but to shake her head.

"I saw your brother's name—your Owen Allen. He was on the third-class passenger list!"

"Which list?" Annie whispered.

"The saved list—he was on the saved list, Annie! Do you hear me?"

Annie heard, and the miracle of it washed over her, first in little lapping breaths and then in torrential waves. She wept aloud in joy and relief and threw her arms around Katie.

Annie dressed but did not bother to comb her hair. She grabbed her wrap. The girls, hand in hand, snuck down the back stairs, through the kitchen, and to the White Star Line offices, where Annie could see Owen's name written in giant blue letters for herself. The joy and the ache of seeing his name in print was nearly more than her heart could bear. She could not understand the miracle, but she loved it just the same.

❈ ❈

Every blind and every drape was drawn in the streets surrounding the school. Not a street was spared of loss and scarcely a household. A memorial service was held at St. Mary's Church on Saturday, 20 April, and Annie watched with hundreds of others from Southampton as the men and uniformed officers of the White Star company filed in long rows through the streets and into the church. *A polished, bleak parade,* she thought, *for the dead.*

Most of seafaring Southampton's men earned their living either on the docks or on the ships that sailed regularly from her port. Because the long coal strike had laid so many ships idle, a greater number than usual of fathers, husbands, uncles, brothers, and cousins had signed on with *Titanic.* Family members knew that those who labored in the bowels of a ship would not likely find seats in the too-few lifeboats of a luxury liner.

Pay for crew members stopped immediately with the sinking of the ship. Widows with families of three or six or eleven children and aged parents with no other support than their hardworking, missing sons were left destitute. Relief funds and collections began soon after.

Annie had no money to contribute to the widows and orphans, but she longed to help, and she knew who did have money—more than one person would ever need. She wrote her aunt Eleanor, sharing her joy of Owen's survival with one who loved him too, albeit strangely, and entreated her help for those who'd lost everything.

After Annie posted the letter, she wondered if writing her aunt was a mistake, but she couldn't see how. She was so very thankful and eager to express her thankfulness by helping and urging others to help in some way.

It felt disloyal to Annie to rejoice aloud, even to sing in her heart, when so many around her grieved openly. But sing she must, so she poured out her heart to Owen. She wrote three letters within the next week, using her allotment of writing paper and postage intended to last the month. She waited day by day for a letter from her brother. She was certain he would write as soon as he stepped ashore in America, telling her of the tragedy, telling her that he was safe, telling her not to worry.

She rationalized the delay by assuring herself that Owen was worn and weary, that he had lost his writing paper and pen and ink in the sinking, that he needed to get to New Jersey as soon as possible. Surely then he would write.

Another week passed, and the town flooded with the homecoming of *Titanic*'s surviving crew, fresh from the port of Plymouth. The joyful hurrahs, the glad tears, the thankful and open-armed welcome of all those beloved heroes who'd fought the sea and won were raised by hundreds at Southampton's train station and carried through the streets of the town.

Annie was glad for those who returned to their families and cheered for her friend as Katie's father whisked his daughter into his arms. But she felt keenly the lack of arms about her and viewed her sorrow as one standing outside herself. She'd not been able to grieve openly while waiting for news of Owen's fate. She'd not felt free to rejoice openly when she saw his name among the saved. And now, with many services past and services yet to come, she felt oddly incomplete.

If only Owen would write, then all would be well. I promise I'll not ask for more. Annie must have written the lines in her diary six times each day. When at last a letter came from America, it was not from Owen.

My darling Annie,

By now you have heard all about the terrible tragedy and surely know for yourself that our dear Owen was among those saved, thank the Lord Jesus. He arrived on my doorstep at the end of that black week of worry. Never was a sight better to behold. That is the best of my news, dear Annie.

I am sorry to share my burden with you, child. My dear Sean, your good uncle, God rest his soul, suffers no more, and suffer he did these five years past. His great, loving heart simply gave out. We buried him the very day Owen crossed our threshold.

Your uncle's fondest wish was to bring you and Owen here, to give you all the love of home and family, to give Owen our landscaping business to secure its future and his own. And your presence would have given us children—a gift we craved but were denied, only God knows why.

And now I do not know what will come, darling Annie, only that I do not have the home to offer you that I once did, and I may not have any before long. We held such hopes for Owen's help and the new roots and seeds he promised to bring. He'd sewn those treasures inside his coat to keep them safe and dry, clever boy.

But we did not understand that Owen is still quite a boy and not the strapping young man we expected. How such a lad could have done the things he and even his father, God rest his soul, wrote us about is beyond my ken. And so, though I am relying on our hired man, Daniel, to continue to work the gardens, I do not know how we shall manage even with Owen's help, if we shall be able to keep the land, or what the future holds.

Owen will surely write you as soon as he is able, but I did not want you to worry for him. He fell upon our doorstep, exhausted and nearly delirious in his fever—no doubt from the bitter cold and soaking of the shipwreck—and with a throat so swollen he could not speak or swallow had he been conscious. Two days have passed. Just this morning his fever broke, thank the Lord. Dr. McGreavy said that though he is still sleeping and needs more rest, Owen will surely waken and fully recover before so very long.

Your brother has been ill-used. I don't know by whom. I fear for and pray that is not also true for you, dear Annie. If there is any means by which I can send for you, I will, just as soon as I'm able. Trust that.

God bless and keep you, my niece. Owen and I will write again soon.

Lovingly,
Your aunt Maggie

"You should be glad that your aunt wrote, Annie," Katie admonished. "Owen found his way to New Jersey. He'll be writing himself, soon as he's well."

But there was something terribly wrong. By anyone's standards Owen was a grown man and strong as the day was long. And what did Aunt Maggie mean that he'd "been ill-used"? Annie wrapped her arms about her and shivered, though the day was warm.

≋ CHAPTER TWENTY-FOUR ≋

MICHAEL HEARD THE MUSIC, the far-off humming, broken occasionally by lyrics he recognized from childhood.

"Have you ever heard the story of how Ireland got its name?
Well, I'll tell you so you'll understand from whence old Ireland came. . . ."

It was the lullaby his mam sang to little Megan Marie; perhaps she had sung it to him, if only he could remember.

"Sure, a little bit o' heaven fell from out the sky one day,
and nestled on the ocean in a spot so far away.
When the angels found it, it looked so sweet and fair,
they said, 'Suppose we leave it, for it looks so peaceful there.'"

But Michael dared not dwell on the music. The music, he knew, would call him, wake him, and if he woke, he would have to face the singer. By peeking ever so slightly through his lashes, Michael saw the blurred singer bathed in candlelight, sitting by an open window, absently holding a book. It was the woman with the graying auburn bun, the woman who had answered the Allen door, the woman who'd called him Owen.

Michael closed his eyes, willing himself to fall off the edge of sleep. But the music, sad and sweet and lovely, so full of longing, remained.

"So they sprinkled it with stardust, just to make the shamrocks grow.
'Tis the only place you'll find them, no matter where you go.

And they dotted it with silver to make its lakes so grand.

And when they had it finished, sure, they called it Ireland."

Lyrics faded into humming. The humming wove a siren song, drawing Michael down, slipping him beneath blue-black waves of sleep, down into the land of dreams.

Fish, lit from within, in contrasts brilliant and softly hued, swam, gently floating round Michael's head. As he sank, a pale-pink light flooded the depths until he could see the ocean floor beneath him, littered with outlines oddly familiar—telltale shapes of broken shoes, chipped porcelain doll faces, and dented pocket watches.

He glanced up as the blue and green and yellow iridescent fish of the sea began to hum in their goitered throats, to swirl a tight knot around and between his legs and arms, to melt his throbbing torso into new music—a grinding, pumping tempo that raced Michael's heart and drew his breath.

The pulsating fish grew round. Stretched and stretched, their colors faded and finally paled to enameled white. Their beaded, glossy eyes wept blood, only to emerge as images of red flags. Michael recognized the new eyes as the White Star Line emblems stamped on each piece of third-class china—the first real china he'd ever eaten from.

Suddenly the heavens and the atmosphere and all the ocean itself were flooded with the fish-turned-china, falling, swimming, swarming around him. The grand piano, playing ragtime, the hundreds of bed linens that had never been used, and the thousand potted palms raced past him. Grains of sea salt, so small they could not be seen, magnified into millions of Bealing's buttonholes—flowers picked and pricked to begin a journey—until they formed a liquid drape and filled his nostrils, sucking his breath.

The temperature dropped steadily. The pink light dimmed, and the cold of the ocean's current seeped into Michael's bones as a shadow passed overhead. Without looking, he knew *Titanic*'s great black keel swam above him.

Michael swore he would not look up but could not resist the pull of what he knew. He watched as the underbelly of the keel cracked—again—and as the forward funnel smashed into the water—again. He watched through the waves as a thousand souls leaped and fell and soared through the night sky into the waves, all over again.

Michael crouched and sprang, desperate to climb the rungs of china fish and grab the bodies, desperate to pull them down to safety beside him. But his fingers could not reach even the hems of their garments; the bodies, frosted, crusting in ice, could not sink for their bobbing atop the ocean.

"Owen," he whimpered. "Owen."

"Shh." Cool fingers stole across Michael's brow, through his hair, pulling him up through the liquid drapery of flowers, up beyond the grand piano that still played ragtime, up to the surface of the ocean, where the red morning sun glowered across an icy field to flash off the red-and-black funnel of a looming *Carpathia*.

Michael wrestled his head against the pillow, unable to push the images, the vivid colors, beyond his dreams.

"Wake up. Wake up, dear boy," the singer whispered.

The music in her siren voice and the "dear boy" caught his brain off guard. Michael opened his eyes.

※ CHAPTER TWENTY-FIVE ※

IT WAS A WEEK before Michael regained consciousness and another day before he had the courage to confess to Maggie Allen his true identity.

But Maggie already knew. In her worry and confusion, in her fear that she must soon bury another Allen before the earth had settled over the one she'd loved best, she had washed and ironed her patient's clothes. In so doing she'd found Owen's seeds and slips and roots, his notes and journal. And though she felt intrusive, she could not resist.

As she read, her dismay grew to alarm; alarm poured grief. Grief grew into anger and frustration. But by the end of Owen's story—his precious story cut far too short—Maggie had grown not only to wonder over the nephew-man she'd never set eyes upon, but to love the pitiable boy he had saved. She prayed that Annie, by reading the journal in Owen's dear hand, would come to love, or at least forgive, the boy too.

"I am glad you're here, Michael. I would have hated setting only two plates at my table," Maggie said while stirring the morning porridge.

"It should be Owen here, Mrs. Allen." The misery Michael carried— for being alive, for bearing the dreams and wearing the clothes of his savior, while that savior, so needed and wanted, lay white in the deep— gnawed through his soul and bled from his eyes.

"Aye. Owen should be here; that is true," Maggie Allen owned. "But not instead of you, Michael. He should have come with you." She spooned porridge into a bowl and set it before him at the kitchen table. "See if you can manage this."

She tipped her head to one side, critically observing the scrawny specimen before her. "But Owen did not come. And that was the Lord's doing if it was anybody's." She straightened. "I do not understand it any more than I understand why my Sean should have gone when we loved and need him so. We need them both. No doubt there's a reason for the way of things, though I make no pretense of knowing it . . . and neither should you." She knocked her wooden spoon against the pot.

It can't be that easy. It can't be that whatever happens, you just keep going. Michael was sure of it.

"That's all there is to it," she said as if she'd heard his thoughts. "Each morning, when we wake—if we wake—we pick up whatever it is we've been given to carry for that day, with the sweet Lord Jesus in the yoke beside us to tote the load. Each night we lay it down, giving it into God's hands. If it's still there in the morning, we pick it up and begin again. If the burden is gone or if there is something different, we know where to start."

Michael did not answer, did not know how to answer, and was grateful when a man, tall and lean, strode in, puffing his pipe like the chimneys of Belfast.

"She's an opinionated old thing, but only half a lioness, just the same. The other half is mother duck." He nodded toward Michael. "Glad to see you in the land of the living, young man."

"This is Daniel McKenica." Maggie Allen ignored the man's tease. "He's hired man for Allen's Run Gardens, and too much bluster by far and away. Still—" she straightened her apron—"he's the oldest and dearest friend my Sean and I laid claim to, even if he does smoke his pipe where it is not wanted."

Daniel McKenica passed the shade of a grin behind his mustache.

"Mr. McKenica." Michael nodded.

"For a woman who's never nursed a babe, she makes a good old hen, don't she?" Daniel remarked with a twinkle in his eye and a *puff, puff* on his pipe.

Michael was confused by the good-natured banter that pranced and danced between the two. If he'd taken such a tone with Uncle Tom, he would have found himself staring into the hobnails of his uncle's boots. But Maggie Allen didn't seem to mind; she seemed to relish it.

Another week passed before Michael owned, just to himself, that he loved Maggie Allen. She was more mother than he'd known since childhood. Even when Michael's feet found solid ground, when he was up and able to fetch water and carry wood, to sweep the porch and feed the chickens, Maggie continued to fuss. She poured into his thin body all the wholesome nourishment her garden and dairy could provide.

She handed him a glass of cold sassafras tea and told him to rest a moment just when he was working the hardest, but she chided him each time his weariness gave way to gloom. It was as though she could read his mind. Once he passed his hand across his forehead, wondering if his thoughts had somehow printed themselves there for all to see.

"There'll be no wallowing about on this farm, Michael Dunnagan—not for me, who's lost my dearest friend and husband of thirty-seven years and the golden nephew who was to work wonders for my heart and this land—and not for you, though you've lost your dearest friend and brother. There is no time and there is no gift in it."

"Work wonders for the land, indeed! Save the farm, don't you mean?" Daniel walked into the kitchen at that moment, pulling up his suspenders. Michael was glad for the interruption to another of Maggie's sermons.

"Well, I don't deny the farm and all there is be at risk. Without Sean and Owen, I do not know how we'll make do." Maggie sighed and looked, for the briefest moment, the picture of worry and despair. "But it simply means there's a bigger, broader plan." She held up her hand. "I know, Daniel McKenica, that you think my spectacles are rose colored—"

"No, Maggie Allen, I don't think that at all," Daniel protested, sitting down to the table. "I think you're balmy and fooling yourself to high heaven! Just don't be fooling this scrawny Belfast youngster along with you."

"Shannon," Michael said, wanting to defend Maggie, though he did not understand her. "And I'm fifteen, sixteen in September."

"What's that you say?" Daniel looked up from the newspaper he'd just opened.

"I come from along the River Shannon, not from Belfast. I only lived in Belfast with my uncle Tom." He looked away. "And I'm nearly sixteen."

"There, you see!" Maggie crowed. "A nearly sixteen-year-old lad from the River Shannon is worth ten of those from Belfast when it comes to growing a garden-and-landscaping business! You just put that in your pipe and smoke it, Daniel McKenica!"

Daniel snorted, but Michael thought he looked pleased.

After breakfast Daniel paused briefly by the open door. "If you've strength in your legs for it, we'll walk the boundaries of the land today, Michael. I've been lookin' over Owen's plans. We'll need to get crackin'."

He was gone in a moment. Michael looked at Maggie, who raised her brow. "Well, you weren't planning on deserting us, now were you?"

"N-no, mum," Michael stuttered. "But I didn't know as you'd want me . . . want me to stay."

Maggie placed her hand on Michael's shoulder. "We have need of you, Michael. And I believe you have need of us. If we care for and look to one another, we three souls can grow our own family."

"And Annie," Michael ventured. "I promised Owen that I would work to bring Annie to America."

"And Annie." Maggie half smiled—tentatively, Michael thought. "As soon as we can. And as soon as she's ready, if she's willing." She brushed away whatever seemed to worry her, then smiled again. "Our Owen chose his friends wisely. We shall sink or swim together."

Michael squeezed Maggie's hand, the first impulsive human touch he could remember giving since he was little, since Megan Marie. Something swelled in his heart that he could not name, but it carried him through the long morning, through his long trek with Daniel around the perimeter of Allen's Run Gardens.

"You can fish in this creek if you like. Maggie likes fresh fish, so it's a good cause to take the time now and again."

As near the docks in Belfast as Michael had lived, he had not fished. Uncle Tom thought fishing a lark and made certain Michael had enough work and chores to keep him from larking about. But Michael remembered his da angling along the Shannon and thought it a glad thing.

Together Michael and Daniel walked the thirty acres of Allen land. Daniel ticked off the plans Sean Allen had detailed before he died, the things they had tried that worked and the things they had tried that had not.

The more Daniel showed Michael and the more Michael felt the strong New Jersey sunshine on his face and inhaled the freshly turned earth, the more he felt as though he'd been there before. He knew that was impossible. But it seemed as if sometime long, long ago, before the time of his remembering, he'd felt just this way, just this warm and safe. It was something akin to the way he'd felt with Owen.

Half the morning passed before a stitch caught in Michael's side, before a sudden shortness of breath and weakness in his legs took him by surprise. In that weariness, the shaming voice of Uncle Tom crept into his heart, and the familiar regret for losing Megan Marie washed over him. Raw grief for Owen flooded his soul.

Michael could not understand himself or his sudden swing of emotions.

Daniel appeared to take no notice but guided their steps back to the house. "A good idea to rest awhile before dinner. Maggie Allen will blame me fierce if you've no appetite for her cooking."

"I'll be able to work by tomorrow, Mr. McKenica. I'm sure of it." Michael did not want to disappoint or vex the man who'd acted so kindly toward him.

"Not tomorrow, Michael, but soon," Daniel McKenica answered. "You and your strength will grow into it, by and by. You'll see." He picked up a hoe leaning against the back porch and started away, then called over his shoulder, "You'll be needing to call me Daniel. I'm Mr. McKenica to them I don't care to know better."

CHAPTER TWENTY-SIX

APRIL TURNED INTO MAY. Even as the British inquiry into the *Titanic* disaster was called in London, Southampton continued to mourn its dead and rallied to aid those left behind. Benefit concerts, fund-raising sporting events, and collections of every sort—public and private—raised money for families of the tragedy. Even memoriam postcards were sold, though the sight of them turned Annie's stomach inside out. She couldn't imagine who would treasure the picture of a ship that had killed their father, son, or brother.

As Annie heard nothing from Aunt Eleanor and nothing more from America, the foreboding and numbness she'd hardly noticed growing inside her began to take focus. She thought a good deal about the cost of independent living—apart from fund-raisers and memoriam postcards—and how one might go about it. She watched girls and other young ladies—one only a couple of years older than herself—who walked to work at the tea shop Owen had frequented, and another who fairly flew to and from the milliner's shop down the road, always late, going and coming. She tried to imagine herself in their circumstances, and she wondered what she might do to earn her own living, if ever she needed to do so.

She was wondering just that when Miss Hopkins sent word that after Annie's French class, she should stop in her study.

Annie could not think what she'd done to be called into the headmistress's office. She'd not snuck out to the docks since Aunt Maggie's letter arrived. She had faithfully conjugated her French verbs and done all the sums required of her by the mathematics teacher. Her copybook was clean; she'd swept the dormitory floor and made her bed with tidy corners.

Annie was still ticking off her "well-done" list, hoping to discover her own infraction, when Miss Hopkins's office door opened.

"Come in, dear. I have wanted to see you, to have a little talk alone," the headmistress began.

Annie was not at all certain she wanted to have this talk with Miss Hopkins, though she could not—or would not—own why. *Let me have done something silly—something genuinely stupid. Let it be that!*

Miss Hopkins drew Annie to the horsehair sofa beside her low tea table. "I have received a letter from your aunt in America, Annie."

Annie's breath caught. *Why would Aunt Maggie write Miss Hopkins?* She was certain that she didn't want to know. *Stop time. Stop time. Stop time.* The words rattled through Annie's mind.

"It seems there has been some sort of mix-up." Miss Hopkins appeared distressed, though trying very hard not to show it. "I have tried to contact your aunt, Miss Hargrave, in London, to learn if she has heard any news or to know how I should proceed, but I have received no response."

Annie sat very still, except for a slow, almost-imperceptible turning of her head from side to side. A whirring began in the tiniest part of her brain, spinning faster and faster, until the noise was a great, pummeling grindstone wearing grooves in her temples.

Miss Hopkins knelt on the floor in front of her, taking both of Annie's hands in her own. "Your aunt Margaret Allen wrote to me that the young man who appeared at her home in the days after . . . after the ship went down . . . was not your brother. He was wearing Owen's coat and he had, indeed, been with Owen on board, but—"

Annie jerked her hands away. She stood, shaking her head vehemently, and covered her ears. *Lies! Lies! Lies!* But she could not say the words.

"Annie." Miss Hopkins's voice was firm but gentle, and she pulled Annie's hands from her ears and held them at her sides. "Your aunt sent this. She wanted me to give it to you. She wrote that she explained everything in a letter tucked inside, but she did not wish you to be alone when you opened it."

Breakfast rose in Annie's throat. She knew what the book-shaped package held before she tore the brown paper wrapping free. It matched the size and weight of the book she wrote in every day, the journal she'd promised to share with Owen when they were together again at last. Owen would never have taken his journal from his coat pocket—not willingly. He carried it there always, just as surely as he carried his small rake and spade in his trouser pocket and his watch in his vest.

Annie closed her eyes tight against the world. "It's a mistake," she whispered, hoarse. "Owen is in Halifax or New York—another ship found him. He is all right. He will come for me. He will come for me."

Miss Hopkins took Annie in her arms as the girl's insistence turned to trembling and the trembling to wracking sobs.

※ ※

Annie did not remember how she found her way to bed that night. But she woke the next morning, her face damp against a tearstained pillow, Owen's precious journal pressed tight to her chest.

She remembered only that she'd read Aunt Maggie's letter, alone, by dim lamplight. The letter told the story Annie had already known in some part of her mind—a door she had quietly locked against the truth: It was not Owen but Michael who had survived *Titanic*'s foundering. It was not Owen but Michael who had made his way to the Allens in New Jersey. It was not Owen but Michael who was sick and now recovering. It was not Owen but Michael who lived and breathed and would surely one day laugh and sing again—though Aunt Maggie wrote that he mourned deeply for his friend.

> *Michael blames himself for living, and I think he would rather not except that he made a vow to Owen to bring his life's work to us, to forge new life in these weak gardens, and to bring you, dear Annie, to America and safety.*

"It isn't fair," Annie cried, "that Owen gave his life, while Michael, nothing but a foundling and a stowaway, lives!" She knew it was Owen's doing that Michael wore his coat, carried his dreams. She knew it because she knew Owen. *But why? Did it have to be a trade? One life for another?*

Annie beat her fist into her pillow, shook and crumpled it. She clung to the tear-wet pillow slip.

Near dawn Annie dressed by the light of the half-moon shining through her window. She tucked Owen's journal into her cloak pocket, tiptoed down the back stairs and out the door. Not even Cook was up.

She walked to the last gardens Owen had created, the lovely gardens surrounding the town hall, and sat on the bench they had shared as the sun set on Easter Sunday.

Annie watched, all around her, as morning dawned on Owen's garden. Chilled, she pulled her cloak tight about her. When the sun rose just enough to read by, Annie opened Owen's journal.

The town clock struck seven by the time she'd finished reading. Miss Hopkins would be calling the girls to rise for prayers and breakfast. She would discover Annie missing. Annie wondered idly if it mattered.

She read of all that Owen had thought and prayed in the days before his death. She knew that he had loved her, that he'd wanted her to be safe and happy. It warmed Annie to see it written in his own hand. She knew now that he had also loved Lucy Snape and had vowed in his heart to love her child. She knew he had claimed Michael as his younger brother and that he'd pledged himself a son to Aunt Maggie and Uncle Sean, to do all for them that he could no longer do for his own parents. Owen had planned a life for all of them in America, as one great and happy family.

But none of it would be, because Owen was dead and Lucy Snape was dead. She had seen Lucy's mother at church, dressed in mourning. Baby Margaret would go on living with her grandparents, and Michael would live in New Jersey, and Annie would . . . Annie did not know what she would do. *What will become of me when this school term ends? When Owen's funds are gone?*

The rising sea breeze dried the tears on Annie's face. She didn't know how she would go on, only that she must. Owen would have insisted.

Annie ran her fingers beneath the bench, searching for the letters Owen had carved there—their own sweet secret, their special place: *Owen & Annie Allen.* The indentations in the wood were precious to

Annie, and she loved them. She swept her hand the length of the bench and was surprised to find something more on the far, far edge.

Annie knelt on the ground and peeked beneath the bench. She read Owen's neat carving of their names within an oval. Beyond it she saw crude letters scratched: *MICHAEL*.

Annie fell back from the bench as if she'd been scorched. She stood and stared at the bench that had been sacred to her, trying all the while to steady the ramming of her heart against its cage. So low was her whisper that not even the wren perched on the nearest shrub heard. "I hate you, Michael Dunnagan! I shall hate you till the day I die."

Annie was not surprised when she was summoned again, two days later, to Miss Hopkins's study and found Jamison, Aunt Eleanor's lifetime butler, waiting. It seemed to Annie that a long play, a tragedy, had been set in motion and that she was simply waiting, day by day, for each cue to her next scene. *I've lived this before,* Annie thought, *but have forgotten my lines.*

Miss Hopkins must have explained to Jamison what Annie already knew, for he simply opened his arms, and Annie, her heart a leaden weight so heavy it slowed her steps, walked into them.

Miss Hopkins encouraged Jamison to talk to Miss Hargrave about allowing Annie to remain at school, to finish the term, to think of enrolling her for the following school year. Annie ignored her. She had no heart for school. Once Jamison told her all he knew, she had no heart for anything.

"The first week of this month, Miss Hargrave received a telegram from the White Star Line in Halifax." Jamison ran the brim of his hat through his fingers again and again. "They said the ship—the *Mackay-Bennett*—the ship sent out to . . . to pick up the bodies had brought their cargo into port. They'd found a man with Mr. Owen's passage ticket in his pocket."

Annie's brain resisted. *That means nothing! Anyone could have picked up his ticket.*

"They asked for someone to come to identify the body," Jamison continued, stealing defeated glances at Annie. "Miss Hargrave said it was ridiculous, that Mr. Owen was listed among those saved. But she'd heard nothing from Mr. Owen in America, you see, and her solicitor, Mr. Sprague, said she must go or send someone to be sure. Something to do with a trust, he said."

"Sit down, Mr. Jamison," Miss Hopkins offered. It was the first time Annie realized the headmistress was still in the room or that she and Jamison, who looked weary and pale beyond his advanced years, still stood.

"Thank you, mum." Jamison sat heavily beside Annie on the settee.

Annie rubbed the tiny nubs of coarse black horsehair back and forth, needing to feel, to focus on something.

"So she sent me. She called it a fool's errand and declared she'd not go herself." Jamison inhaled slowly, then exhaled wearily.

"You couldn't be certain it was Owen." Annie had not meant to say the words aloud. They stole from her lips beyond her will.

"They brought us into a large rink, where all the bod—the people . . ." Jamison stopped, dipped his head, and waited until his voice steadied. "Some in coffins and some in canvas bags, some laid out on stretchers—just as the sea left them. They required identification that we were related to or acted on behalf of someone related to the decea—to the person. Then they took us in to identify them." Jamison looked away, swiping at the tears that puddled in his eyes.

"But they'd all been in the sea," Annie said, staring straight ahead. "They would not have looked the same." *Perhaps they could not be certain it was Owen. And if they could not be certain, then maybe he . . .*

Jamison withdrew from his coat pocket a packet wrapped in a hand-kerchief, which he unfolded and set on Annie's lap. He picked up the small rake and spade, laid them in Annie's hand, and closed her fingers round their handles. He took from his vest pocket the gunmetal watch that Annie had loved to flip open when she was little—the one that had been her father's and then Owen's. "These were in his pockets."

Annie automatically flipped the case, and there was her picture opposite the clock face, her picture with Owen and their parents, taken when Annie was barely six. Time frozen. No sound escaped Annie's lips.

"After I identified . . . Mr. Owen, I telegraphed Miss Hargrave, asking her what I should do. I heard nothing for two days, so I telegraphed again. That is when I learned from Solicitor Sprague that Miss Hargrave had taken a turn at the bad news. He told me to bring Mr. Owen home, to be buried in Bunhill with the mister and missus." Jamison choked, coughing into his handkerchief. At last he straightened. "I beg your pardon, Miss Hopkins. This family has been my own."

"There is no need, Mr. Jamison." Miss Hopkins spoke softly.

Annie would have slipped her hand into Jamison's if she could have lifted it.

"When I got back to London, I found Miss Hargrave had suffered a stroke. She's taken to her bed, and the doctor does not know if she is likely to recover." Jamison drew a deep breath.

"And she has asked for Annie to come home?" Miss Hopkins asked.

Jamison shifted in his seat and blinked his eyes. "Well, not exactly, mum. She cannot speak, as yet." He looked at Annie. "Solicitor Sprague sent me to let Miss Annie know how things stand. He's taken Miss Hargrave's affairs in hand, you see, and . . . and he's arranged services for Mr. Owen for tomorrow morning. He thought Miss Annie would want to know . . . would want to come back to London with me and attend." Jamison waited. "And he wants to speak with Miss Annie directly."

Miss Hopkins searched Annie's face but asked the question of Jamison. "Does Annie need a place to live?"

Jamison let out a relieved sigh. "Mr. Sprague says Annie has a home in London always, as long as ever she wants—a home at Hargrave House."

Annie stood. She might have laughed if she could have remembered how. It was exactly what she did not want—what she and Owen had never wanted—and now it was all she had.

"Annie?" Miss Hopkins lifted Annie's chin and searched her face.

"I'll pack my things," Annie whispered, and fled.

CHAPTER TWENTY-SEVEN

Fog and torrents of rain sheeted their railway car windows all the way to London. It poured again the next morning through Owen's service. Annie thought that the most fitting thing of all.

She was not permitted to view Owen's body. Solicitor Sprague said that time and the sea had done their work. She thought it just as well, what little she could think. She wanted to remember her brother strong and handsome, as he had been on Easter Sunday. She wanted to remember him as when, arm in arm, they'd talked and laughed, strolling the streets of Southampton.

What she could not remember, could not feel, no matter how hard she tried, was the warmth of Owen's arms about her or how it felt to lean her head against his chest and sense the beating of his heart through his woolen vest. That horrid emptiness, that inability to remember, to feel, made Annie shiver, standing by his grave in the pouring rain beneath her black umbrella.

The minister spoke—words, prayers, and a benediction—but Annie closed her eyes and ears. What could he say to bring her comfort when the person she loved most and last in all the world had been so violently taken from it?

When Annie finally blinked, her eyes wandered to her parents' graves beside Owen's, stark proof that she was truly and completely orphaned.

The smallest green sprouts pushed through the black, rain-wet earth, testimony of the gardening she and Owen had done when last they visited Bunhill Fields cemetery, such a little while ago. She idly thought to return later, alone, and continue the garden by planting those same flowers for Owen. Then she remembered that she had no more seeds. She would have to wait another year until the blossoms of her parents' flowers had gone to seed.

She closed her eyes. *Another year or more—what does it matter?*

When she turned from the graves, Annie's eyes caught the image that Owen had pointed out to her on John Bunyan's gravestone—Christian, loaded down by his heavy burden. *That's me,* Annie thought. *That will forever be me. Owen was wrong; I shall never reach the other side.*

Solicitor Sprague spoke as they walked the cobbled pathway back to their waiting cars. "I suppose you have seen and comprehended the situation with your aunt, Miss Allen."

Annie was not used to being called by her formal name. It sounded to her as though he spoke to someone else.

"Elisabeth Anne?" The solicitor spoke again.

"No, sir. No, I've not seen her." The effort to speak felt very great and roused the weight in Annie's chest. "When we returned to London last night, it was quite late. This morning . . . I did not want . . . We simply came here." She turned away. Annie did not want to explain that she dreaded seeing her aunt, that she had no desire to ever see her aunt.

The solicitor nodded. "When you have settled, I should like to speak with you."

In all the years Mr. Sprague had come and gone from her aunt's study, he'd rarely acknowledged her or Owen except to nod in passing through the hallway to the great front door.

"Shall we say ten o'clock tomorrow, at my home?"

"Your home?" It was all the speech Annie could make. What could he want?

Mr. Sprague eyed her keenly. "Yes. Mr. Jamison might accompany you. I have taken the liberty of giving him my card."

Annie knew that was out of the ordinary. But then, everything was upside down. She nodded, aware that she should respond more appropriately and not caring in the least.

"Very well." The solicitor seemed satisfied. Still he hesitated. "I think it best that you do not mention our visit to your aunt for now—should she regain consciousness."

That did raise Annie from her stupor. "If you think that is best, sir."

"I do. Tomorrow I shall explain why." And then, pressing her elbow, he lost his matter-of-fact business tone. "For today, Annie, go home and rest. You have experienced quite enough." He tipped his hat and was gone.

Annie was not prepared for his small kindness or for his use of her childhood name. She blinked back the hot tears that sprang so easily.

Jamison held the car door for her, retrieving her umbrella as she stepped in. "He'll be a friend to you now, Miss Annie."

"Who?"

"Solicitor Sprague. It was he who arranged everything for Mr. Owen—bringing him back to England; 'twas he who insisted I go to the school to fetch you in time for services. He didn't want you to hear about it from a stranger."

"Oh" was all Annie could manage. She frowned. Had Aunt Eleanor been well, might she not have sent for her? Might Annie not have been invited to her brother's funeral?

"He's taken over Miss Hargrave's affairs, you see. It was an arrangement your grandfather made—in case she was ever incapacitated, which she is . . . at least for now." Jamison looked to Annie as if he meant to convey more than his words allowed.

But Annie could not sort it through—not what Solicitor Sprague might want, nor how Jamison knew so much more of her family's affairs than she. She had, as Solicitor Sprague remarked, "experienced quite enough."

CHAPTER TWENTY-EIGHT

ANNIE CHECKED the face of her brooch watch: ten minutes before the hour.

Jamison fussed with his gloves as he pulled the doorbell of Solicitor Sprague's home. "Nurse Sise said Miss Hargrave stirred in her sleep last night, not like she was out cold, as she's been this past week."

"Is that a good sign?" Annie asked.

Jamison eyed her curiously. "It all depends on what you hope for, Miss Annie."

A butler opened the door just then and, stepping back, bowed. "Miss Allen. Mr. Jamison. Mr. Sprague is expecting you."

Annie was not used to being treated so formally. Until she had traveled to Southampton with Owen, she'd been kept very much in the rooms abovestairs at Hargrave House in London. Aunt Eleanor had never taken her to make calls upon friends. But that was normal for a girl of her age and station. Six weeks ago she'd longed for adventure and, though frightened at the thought of Owen's leaving, had thrilled when she and Owen tore away on the train to Southampton. It was the most adventurous thing she'd ever done.

But now, with Owen gone, she wanted nothing more than to be quiet and left alone. Enduring her days in the seclusion of the upstairs rooms in the house on Old Street seemed challenging enough. What did it matter whether or not Aunt Eleanor regained consciousness? What more could her aunt do or take away from her now that she'd lost Owen?

"Your coat, miss." The butler assisted Annie. "This way, please, miss."

Annie and Jamison followed the butler down the hallway, waiting while he opened a heavy oak door. The two men stood aside.

"Ah, Miss Allen." Solicitor Sprague rose from his desk and held a chair for Annie. "Come right in."

"Jamison?" Annie was not at all certain she wanted to be left alone with Mr. Sprague. Until yesterday he had always seemed fierce and formal.

"I'll be just outside the door, Miss Annie, whenever you need me," Jamison replied, not seeming concerned in the least and smiling, much to Annie's consternation.

"Gregory, bring tea for Miss Allen and see that Mr. Jamison has whatever he would like."

"Very good, sir." The butler bowed again, stirred the fire in the grate to a rousing blaze, and disappeared.

Mr. Sprague closed the study door and returned to his desk. He waited until he'd seated himself, folded his hands across the blotter, then looked evenly at Annie.

Annie clasped her hands and swallowed the small lump in her throat.

"I have been the Hargrave family solicitor for twenty-seven years, Miss Allen. Mr. Winston Hargrave, your grandfather, and I attended Oxford together."

"Yes, sir." She had known that much.

"When your mother married Mackenzie Allen, then employed as the Hargrave family gardener, Mr. Hargrave vowed to strike his daughter from his will."

Annie had heard it all before. It reminded her of Aunt Eleanor's repeated threats to Owen. "It seems to be the family way," she whispered wryly, much to her surprise.

Mr. Sprague half smiled. "My sentiments exactly, Miss Allen."

"Yours, sir?"

"I am the family solicitor, Miss Allen. It does not mean that I have always approved of the legal terms I have been required to uphold." Mr. Sprague's forehead creased. "Though I daresay if your grandfather knew before he died how your mother would suffer, he would have made arrangements for whatever medical services she required. He loved your mother, in his way."

Annie stiffened, thinking such words were easily spoken. She could only think of her mother's racking cough before baby William was delivered stillborn, of the nights that she refused a doctor for lack of means to pay, of the piles of money her grandfather surely possessed.

Mr. Sprague hesitated. "I have always regretted that I did not more carefully counsel your grandfather before he died. I thought there would be time to make amends."

"Grandfather was an unforgiving man." Annie was astonished once again at her own frankness, saying aloud the things she had so often thought. What on earth had happened to her tongue? It was as if it knew no discretion. But Annie didn't care. She felt wretchedly weary and such boldness suited her.

"Well said." Mr. Sprague nodded. "Unforgiving and vengeful. Do not follow in his steps, my dear."

"I shall try not to, sir," Annie returned.

"There will be much to try you on that point in future."

Annie blinked. *Much to try me? How could he know about Michael Dunnagan? Surely I've not mentioned him in my grief.*

"Were your aunt in possession of her faculties, I would not be free to divulge the information I am about to share with you, Miss Allen. Mr. Hargrave gave me strict orders to act as your aunt's guardian until she turned twenty-one. From that time forward she would become fully responsible for herself and her affairs, with one stipulation."

Annie straightened.

"If at any time she became incapacitated with no legal guardian of her welfare—if she had no husband—then all of her affairs would come under my guardianship until such time as she recovers or until her death."

"Does that mean I must leave Hargrave House?" Annie could imagine no other reason for her summons.

"No, no, my dear!" Mr. Sprague sounded truly distressed. "It means that at long last I am able to use my best judgment in addressing your aunt's affairs."

"Oh." Annie nodded, though she did not understand how it concerned her.

"When your grandfather Hargrave struck your mother from his will, he made provision for your mother's future children in terms of a trust, payable on their twenty-first birthday. Your aunt Eleanor was made guardian of that trust." Mr. Sprague looked as though he was trying to pour understanding into Annie.

She, in turn, tried to push aside the fog in her head and oblige.

"Your grandfather did not want your mother or father to know of this arrangement. He hoped the realization of poverty would force your mother to return home to him."

"Leave Father? She would never." Annie was sure of it.

"No, she would not. However, before the breach could be healed, your grandfather died in a seizure—apoplexy—leaving intact my instructions not to reveal the terms of his will to your mother, her husband, or to your mother's future children until their twenty-first birthday." Mr. Sprague waited for Annie to absorb his words.

"Does that mean," Annie began, "that there is an inheritance for Owen and me?"

"For you, upon turning twenty-one. And all that would have gone to Owen will now go to you upon your eighteenth birthday—together, that is nearly half of the Hargrave estate. You will want for nothing."

Annie turned her head slowly, trying to comprehend. It could not be true, surely. All the months Owen had scrimped and saved, the twelve months they had been separated while he gardened in Southampton—he would have turned twenty-one in July.

If only he'd waited three months, he could have sailed to America first class with Annie by his side. He could have had all he wanted to pour into Uncle Sean's business in New Jersey. "Owen need not have sailed on *Titanic* at all."

"No." Mr. Sprague studied his hands, his fingers still locked. "I urged him to wait until summer, though I was not at liberty to say why. Owen insisted that he needed to reach New Jersey in time for this year's spring planting. He said your uncle was not well."

"Uncle Sean died; Aunt Maggie wrote me." Annie felt as though the blood had drained from her head.

"I am so sorry, my dear. Grief upon grief."

"Aunt Eleanor threatened to strike Owen from her will if he left for America, if he left London," Annie remembered. "Did she not know that Owen stood to inherit a sum of his own within a few months?"

"She knew; she has always known, and was under no obligation to withhold that information—a freedom I did not possess."

The years of Aunt Eleanor's threats and manipulations, both to her father and to Owen, chased one another through Annie's mind, a snowball running downhill, gathering speed. She calculated the years between her grandfather's death and her brother's birth, then added all the years that followed. "Do you mean, sir—is it true to say—that Aunt Eleanor knew that Owen and I would be provided for by Grandfather, and yet she did nothing, not even a loan, while our mother died and Father had nothing? While Owen—?" Annie could not go on. "Why?"

"I believe your aunt considered her power in withholding this knowledge, and the estate itself, as her only hope of controlling your father or enticing your brother to stay.

"Winston Hargrave ruined your father's reputation. Mackenzie could not find work within the empire. By the time your mother died, he was penniless, entirely at Eleanor's mercy for food and clothing—even housing—for you and Owen. She berated him as the cause of your mother's death and finally convinced him that he had as good as murdered her through their marriage." Mr. Sprague rubbed his forehead and ran his fingers through his thinning hair.

"She ground and ground away until your father had no way out of the box she and Winston had created. I believe it is not too much to say that Eleanor schemed toward Mackenzie and Owen the same way in which her father had schemed to keep her at his side." He sighed heavily and pulled back, folding his hands. "She had learned at the feet of a master—a master of misery. In her own sick way I believe she loved your father—or the idea of him."

"Loved?" Annie choked.

Mr. Sprague looked away. "She wanted to escape—as your mother had—the bondage and servitude her father had forced upon her. But Eleanor never developed the courage your mother displayed in leaving their father. Eleanor could not conceive how to build a life of her own. She could only imagine taking your mother's husband and children."

He stood and clasped his hands behind his back, looked fully into Annie's eyes, and crossed to the window. "When Helen died, Eleanor threatened to legally take you and Owen from your father if he refused to marry her or if he tried to leave England. He dared do neither. Mackenzie was without means or prospects, a man trapped and without hope."

Annie's head swam. *This must be what seeing a play upon the stage would be like.*

"She preferred to see Father die than leave her?" she whispered, for if she did not whisper, she knew she would scream.

"That is strong language—" Mr. Sprague returned to his chair—"but accurate, I believe. Though I do not think she anticipated his death. She thought she had made him subject to her. Because your father left no will, Eleanor was named legal guardian for you and for Owen. Though Owen was finally released from her guardianship, he was not of age to inherit."

Mr. Sprague narrowed his eyes in concentration. "I do not attempt to understand your aunt's transfer of affection to Owen. Affection, control—whatever twisted thing it was."

"Owen would have cared for me, provided for me. He made every plan for me to join him!"

"Yes. Yes, I know." Mr. Sprague straightened and drew a file from his drawer. "Eleanor Hargrave did not anticipate your brother's courage and foresight. In fact, before Owen left, he had me draw up a will." He passed a legal document across the desk to Annie. "It names you as beneficiary of all his worldly goods. However, your aunt is still your guardian until you are eighteen. In her present condition, she is not capable of exercising that guardianship, and since her affairs fall to me for the time being, I undertake that responsibility."

It was too much. Annie knew she had not comprehended all that Aunt Eleanor's vengeful control over her family had meant, but she felt she was drowning in words. "What does that mean for me?"

"It means, my dear, that you and I need to talk about your future and set upon a course that is both pleasing and wholesome for you—for your education, your social and spiritual growth, and your happiness. I regret very much that I was not able to act in the best interests of your dear parents or your brother, for whom I always held the greatest respect."

Tears of frustration sprang to Annie's eyes. She blinked and looked away. She would not cry.

Mr. Sprague came round the desk. "I will not make that mistake again, Miss Allen. While I am at liberty to act as your guardian, you will learn all you wish to know of me and the handling of your family's affairs, and I will do all in my power to prepare you to take your place in society."

"And if Aunt Eleanor recovers?" Annie held her breath, knotting her gloves.

Mr. Sprague sighed, massaging the bridge of his nose. "If a doctor testifies that she is fully recovered, she will resume your guardianship until your eighteenth birthday, at which time you will receive Owen's portion willed to you. At twenty-one you will inherit your own equal portion held in trust."

Annie wished that her aunt would die, would die that very day. The thought thrilled and frightened her.

As if reading her mind, Mr. Sprague counseled, "Do not absorb the bitter, spiteful character of your aunt, Elisabeth Anne. You can see the lonely, cold woman she has become. Wealth has not comforted her and will not mourn her when she is gone." He sat in the chair beside Annie and leaned forward, his words urgent. "Take instead your brother's legacy—the fine person that he was—and let that be the model for your life. You know that is what he would wish for you."

Annie murmured, "Yes," but hardly knew what she was agreeing to.

"If your uncle in America were still alive and his business stable, I would urge you to go there, but given the circumstances . . ." Mr. Sprague spread his hands, then abruptly began to detail the arrangements he had in mind.

Annie tried to separate his words from the jumble in her head. She pressed her fingers against her temples even as she shivered in the warm room.

Mr. Sprague stopped talking. "This is too much for one day, Miss Allen."

Annie nodded. It was the first thing that seemed perfectly clear.

"If you will allow me, I will set a course for your education and socialization. We can certainly amend the plan as we proceed. I would not so urge you forward at this very difficult time, except that I do not know how much time we have before your aunt recovers sufficiently to resume your guardianship. I would like to see your health and well-being firmly established before that happens."

Mr. Sprague rang the bell. "I believe that, once a plan is set in motion, she will not be so likely to squash it if there is some amount of public accountability. She is rather inclined to succumb to the criticism of her peers—something I believe can be arranged, if need be."

Annie only nodded and watched as first Gregory the butler reappeared and then her own Jamison. She sighed in relief. She believed, in some fevered part of her brain, that Mr. Sprague must have her best interests at heart, else why would he have divulged such a sordid tale of Aunt Eleanor?

It was all beyond her now, and without Owen or Miss Hopkins, there was no one else to turn to. Jamison seemed to trust him. She would have to trust that.

Mr. Sprague handed Annie a cup of hot tea, laced with sugar and something that burned but warmed her throat as it passed down. She felt a little sleepy but no longer shivered. She was content to let Jamison and Mr. Sprague talk. She needed, for a little while, to shut out all she'd learned and all she had seen yesterday. Annie leaned her head upon her hand and closed her eyes.

The clock bonged the hour when she opened them again. Mr. Sprague was still talking and scribbling away. Jamison nodded and pointed to the paper. Annie tried again to focus on his words.

"My daughter, Constance, has joined Red Cross," Mr. Sprague was saying. "If you've no objections, Elisabeth Anne, I shall have her call for you on her way to their next weekly meeting. It would do you good to socialize. You are rather younger than the age allowed . . . but I think by going with Constance it will smooth the way. Training is not difficult. It is all quite respectable and worthwhile, and I believe the girls have a lively time together. You might also like to join my family in our pew on Sunday."

Annie agreed and bid Mr. Sprague good-bye, but she could not think about his plan now. All the way home a mantra sang in her mind, over and over, to the rumbling of the wheels: *Aunt Eleanor knew. Owen could have waited. He need not have died. Aunt Eleanor knew. Owen could have waited. He need not have died.*

When Annie and Jamison reached home, Jayne, a kitchen maid in a rumpled apron, hurried up the stairs bearing a pitcher of hot water. "What do you think?" she sputtered. "Her ladyship's opened her eyes!"

Annie did not stop to remove her coat or hat, though Jamison repeatedly called after her, "Your coat, Miss Annie! Miss Annie!"

She took the stairs slowly at first, then determinedly. She pushed open the door to her aunt's bedchamber but, owing to the dimness of the shuttered room, could barely see the frail form wrapped in sheets. Annie pulled the drapes and pushed back the wooden shutters, scattering dust mites and splaying sunshine across the floor, the bed.

"Argggh," her aunt growled in protest.

Annie stood at the foot of the bed and stared but made no move to go near her. "I want to see what you look like, Aunt Eleanor."

Her aunt half raised a withered hand toward her slackened face. But the feeble action fueled Annie's anger, and she grabbed the mother-of-pearl looking glass from the dressing table, thrusting it before her aunt's face. "And I want you to see what you look like. You are no longer beautiful. Do you see, Aunt Eleanor? Do you see?" she demanded. "Though you were never so beautiful as Mother. And you were never loved."

Barbara, her aunt's maid, gasped, nearly dropping the linens she carried into the room.

Annie picked up a flannel from atop the washstand and tossed it to Barbara. "Scrub her, Barbara—if you can bear to touch her. Scrub her clean."

Alarm, mingled with something daring, almost smug, crossed her aunt's eyes.

But Annie did not care. No matter if the woman in the bed recovered from her stroke—Owen was dead and gone. He could not recover.

Annie vowed to daily hold a mirror before her aunt—more than a reflection of her face. She would cry foul before the world for all the evil Aunt Eleanor had done and, through jealousy, had failed to do. She would paint her the vicious, piteous, spiteful, laughable spinster she saw her to be before the society whose good opinion she craved.

Annie nearly smirked at the expression in her aunt's eyes. If all Aunt Eleanor feared from her was a good scrubbing, she had much to learn.

On her way from the room Annie passed her aunt's prized vanity mirror and was momentarily surprised to see Aunt Eleanor's haughty, young portrait staring from the glass. She had reached the hallway before her breath caught in her chest, before she realized that the hard and icy features reflected had been her own.

≋ CHAPTER TWENTY-NINE ≋

ANNIE COULD NOT SPEAK past the weight in her heart, not to the staff at Hargrave House, not even when Barbara asked if she would like to read to her aunt in the afternoons. And though Annie carried her aunt's breakfast tray of hot tea and thin gruel to her bedside each morning for three weeks, she turned her back on the dark and pleading orbs enlarging daily in the shriveled face.

What pity could Annie afford the woman who had never shown pity to her own family—her precious family whose lives and deaths could have been so eased and altered by the power of her goodwill?

Clipped discussion of her aunt's health was limited to Dr. Welbourne and Nurse Sise, employed by Mr. Sprague to carry out the doctor's detailed instructions. But as far as Annie could see, around-the-clock private nursing made no difference. Her aunt was dying, a little each day—and not fast enough to suit Annie.

"You'll want to forgive her, Miss Annie." Jamison spoke softly, matter-of-factly, one late afternoon as he lit the fire in the drawing room's gas grate. Even June could not relieve the cold and damp of the old house. "You'll want to forgive her for your own sake, before it is too late."

"No," Annie said. "I do not forgive her. I will not forgive her." She closed the piano, stood, and walked evenly from the dim and somber room. How could Jamison or Mr. Sprague or Barbara or Jayne or anyone imagine she could forgive the witch in the bed upstairs?

Had God not struck Eleanor Hargrave, Annie had no doubt the woman would be dangling Annie's life by a thread, just as she had dangled her mother's, her father's, and Owen's. "I hate her," Annie whispered to no one as she climbed the stairs to her room. "I cannot wait until she's dead. God in heaven, make her die soon."

The next morning Annie balanced her aunt's breakfast tray on one hip as she reached to turn the latch on the bedroom door. But Nurse Sise opened it wide from the other side. "Your aunt spoke today." The nurse smiled significantly and inclined her head. "That is a very good sign."

Annie's breath caught. Her hands trembled so that she nearly dropped the tea.

"You are overcome, my dear. Let me take that." Nurse Sise, the model of efficiency and kindness, relieved Annie of the tray, setting it squarely on the table beside the bed. "You've been through so much, Miss Elisabeth Anne. But not to worry; your aunt is sleeping peacefully now." She dusted her hands as if all was put to rights. "She had a rather restless night. Even so, just before dawn she distinctly said, 'No.'"

Annie stared at the nurse without blinking, her mind screaming, *No! No! No!*

Nurse Sise colored slightly at Annie's blatant stare, then sat in her ladder-back chair beside the bed. "I know that is not an entire sentence, but it is a beginning. I believe your aunt will recover far more than any of us had anticipated."

The nurse appeared hopeful to Annie, waiting, Annie knew, for her to sound pleased, to reassure her that her aunt's recovery was all Annie wanted as well. But Annie wanted no such thing.

A bell rang belowstairs. Nurse Sise hesitated, clearly uncertain in the face of Annie's unblinking stare. But she stood and smoothed her skirt. "Well, there is the breakfast bell. I shall be just belowstairs if you need me, Miss Elisabeth Anne."

Still Annie did not, could not, speak.

Nurse Sise, her brow momentarily wrinkled, walked quickly from the room.

Annie stared at her aunt's sleeping form and willed herself to breathe. *She could be dead. She could so easily be dead.*

And then she thought, *Why not? Why shouldn't she be dead?* Annie stepped nearer the headboard. Smells of camphor and witch hazel, of things that evoked sickrooms, pervaded her aunt's linens. Only the tea from the pot on the tray smelled of life and earth and daily routines.

Annie lifted the tea cozy and removed the lid. She picked up the steaming pot with a towel, then stepped closer to her aunt's face. *It would be so easy to drop it, to watch this scalding liquid burn and flood her eyes, pour across her crooked mouth. I could hold her down. I could burn away forever those hateful orifices. I could drown her as Owen drowned. I would be rid of her forever.*

She straightened, considering. *Who would accuse me? I could say that she startled me, that I was pouring her tea—to let it cool for her—and that she startled me. An accident.* Annie breathed and waited. She smiled. She drew one more short and ragged breath, then hefted the pot.

Aunt Eleanor's black eyes snapped open. Annie jumped. The swaddled pot wobbled in her hands. Fear and rage raced through Eleanor Hargrave's eyes as a steaming trickle of pungent, reddish-brown tea narrowly missed her neck. "No!" she gasped distinctly.

Annie barely caught the precarious pot. Hot tea sloshed, scalding her hand, just the way she had imagined scalding Aunt Eleanor, and she cried out.

In that moment Annie knew she was defeated. She saw her aunt look into her mind, comprehend her calculation, sense the evil intent in Annie—evil as familiar to her aunt as her own name. Annie gasped at the superiority of knowing in her aunt's expression, at the power it instantly bequeathed her.

Fear eclipsed Annie's fury as she knew, beyond a doubt, that Aunt Eleanor would recover and again reign supreme. And Annie knew she could not return to such a servile life—not now, not ever again.

She dropped the pot awkwardly onto the tray and stumbled from the room, groping her way to the staircase. The low wail she heard came not from the withered woman in the bed but from someplace deep inside herself.

Annie's temples throbbed, two beating drums. Her jaw and neck and shoulders ached; her limbs tingled. Her heart raced so she feared it might burst through her chest, speed toward the parlor, smash the bay window, and tear through the streets of London. She gripped the railing, forcing her feet to stop on the grand staircase landing. "I am mad," Annie whispered, silently laughing and crying at the realization.

Quietly, deliberately, as if the stairs might tear themselves from the wall and run away, Annie centered her foot on each one, climbing to her room at the top of the house. Quietly, deliberately, she closed the door and slid the bolt.

Annie's lips parted. From her deep center came a soft, low moan. The moan spread; the volume grew—a bleeding, mortal wound in the making. She grabbed her hair by its roots and jerked and jerked until tears sprang from her eyes. If only the pain of her scalp could distract her from the living, crawling, writhing pain in her chest. But it was not enough. There was not enough pain in all the world for that. And so she keened, beyond the power of her lungs, her anger and venom and loss—the grating, throbbing, screeching pain she had carried silently for weeks. She heard Jamison call her name, heard him pound the door, but she pushed back all thought until she listened only to the voice inside her head, the one that would not go away.

Alone. I'm alone. They're all dead. They're dead because of her. I'll be next. She will rise and walk and kill me next. She would not have hesitated had it been me in that bed. I should have done it. I should have . . .

❁ ❂

When Annie finally sat up, she saw that the light had changed. Her dampened pillow slip, her rumpled bed, the rose and yellow flowers stamped across her comforter, the pale-yellow wash of her walls turned gold, the heavy chintz of her drapes—all came into vivid focus.

Of course, she thought. *It's simple. Why did I not see it before?*

Annie unbolted the shutters and pushed wide the window. She heard but did not heed the firm but even knocking at her door. She pulled her desk chair across the floor to the window.

One step to the chair. One step to the window. One step to the street, Annie thought. *And I shall be free. I shall be with Owen and with Mother and Father. She cannot hurt me there, not ever again.*

"Elisabeth Anne," came a voice from beyond Annie's door. "Annie, listen to me. This is Mrs. Sprague, Betty Sprague. I want you to open the door. I have come to take you home with me."

Annie heard the strange voice and in the background the pleading of Jamison, but the voice in her head spoke louder and would not be stilled. *Owen is waiting. Mother is waiting. Father is waiting, waiting for me.* Annie stepped onto the seat of the chair.

"Annie, I know you miss Owen. I know you want to leave this house, and you should leave; you can leave. You may come home with me, with me and with Mr. Sprague and with our daughter, Constance. Constance needs a friend. She needs a sister. It was so long before I could have a child. I need another daughter, just like you. I need you, Annie. Open the door."

Owen is waiting. Mother is waiting. Father is—

"Open the door, Annie. Open it now. We'll pack your things and you will come home with me for as long as you like."

Owen is waiting. Moth—

"Open the door, Annie. Let me take you home, dear."

Owen is—

"Dear?" Annie asked.

"Yes, dear Annie!" The voice came again, firm but loving in a way Annie had not heard for so long that it hurt her heart to remember.

Annie stepped back. "What?"

"Open the door, dear Annie! Open the door, sweet child."

Annie stepped down from the chair. Her head swam, so she steadied herself against the chair's back. The moment she unbolted the door, arms swept her into an embrace so unexpected that Annie choked and coughed.

"It's all right, Annie. It's all right now. Everything will be all right," the woman crooned as if to reassure herself as much as Annie.

It was a lie, Annie knew. Things would never be all right. But just for a minute, for a few minutes, until she could catch her breath, Annie resolved that she would believe the laughing, tearful woman with the strong arms and the resolute voice.

≋ CHAPTER THIRTY ≋

"CALL ME CONNIE." The girl plopped before her looking glass, pulled tortoiseshell combs from her long chestnut plaits, and began to brush. "One, two, three, four, five, six, seven, eight, nine . . ."

"Mrs. Sprague—I mean, your mother—said I should call you Constance," Annie responded, standing in the center of the room, feeling stupidly out of place.

Connie sighed dramatically. "Only in front of Mother and Father—to humor them. Mother and Father are so old—older than any of the other girls' parents—and their ideas are terribly old-fashioned. None of my friends call me Constance. It's so . . . so stuffy." She stopped brushing and inclined her head significantly. "You do want to be my friend, don't you?"

"Yes," Annie mumbled, shrugging. "I suppose." But she did not know what she wanted. She only knew that she would allow herself to be cued and would reply with whatever lines seemed necessary.

"Good." Connie resumed her brushing. "Tomorrow we shall stroll through St. James. Father insists. He said the fresh air will do us both good. And then we are to take a carriage ride round the park. It seems entirely too warm for all of that to me—even Mother agrees—but he insists." She tossed her brush onto her dressing table at last and stood. "One thing you will learn about Father is that when he gets a bee in his bowler, nothing stands in his way."

Mr. Sprague knocked and spoke through the closed door from the hallway. "Lamps out, girls. Ten o'clock. Sleep well."

"See what I mean?" Connie whispered, then called more loudly, "Yes, Father!"

Annie folded her wrapper across the foot of the bed and climbed beneath the eiderdown. She turned her back on Connie. Never in her memory had Annie shared a room, let alone a bed, except for those few weeks in the dormitory in Southampton.

A sister was something she'd never thought to wish for. She'd wanted only Owen, needed only Owen. But there was something—not quite comforting, but something in knowing another human body lay alive and breathing close by—that helped stave off the pull of darkness. Annie sighed quietly. She could not decipher what that something was.

Annie had not walked or driven through St. James's Park since Owen had moved to Southampton over a year ago. Never had she taken formal tea in a grand hotel, never heard the magnificent choir in St. Paul's Cathedral, never attended evensong in Westminster Abbey, where she could not help but weep for the beauty of the young boys' voices. She'd never gone to a professional dressmaker's shop to choose fabric of her liking nor to a milliner's to model hat after hat, never had her hair coiffed by a lady's maid. First her mother, then Aunt Eleanor had made each decision about her simple wardrobe, her toilette, her rare comings and goings.

But in the weeks she spent with the Spragues, Annie did all those things with Connie and her mother. And after each outing, Mrs. Sprague arranged a treat to top the day—vanilla ice in a sweetshop or apple tart smothered in hot custard in a corner tea shop. Once they sat on the grassy bank of the Thames, just to picnic and watch the young men punt.

Annie began to think of herself as something of a puppy—one that Mrs. Sprague seemed intent on training. But training for what, and why she would bother, Annie could not decide, nor did she have heart to ponder the question thoroughly. She determined to plod along dutifully, knowing that, however sad she still felt inside, however impossible it was to summon the enthusiasm Mrs. Sprague determined she exhibit, this arrangement was better than suffocating in Hargrave House with Aunt Eleanor. Remembrance of her aunt sent shudders through her limbs.

One bleak morning just after a soaking rain, the three stopped in a nearly deserted Trafalgar Square, where Mrs. Sprague repeated, with all the deliberation of a tour guide, the history of Admiral Lord Nelson, who regally commanded the square from his stone column. Annie sighed, having heard tales of the admiral since she was a child, and Connie rolled her eyes. "Mother, we know," she whispered. "We read the empire's history every year! Can't we feed the birds? Just this once?"

Mrs. Sprague ignored her daughter's impudence. "You say that every time we come, Constance. It simply is not a proper pastime for young ladies of your standing."

"But it is such fun," Connie coaxed. "You did it as a child outside St. Paul's—you told me! You loved it, Mother! You know you want to do it too!"

Her mother, determined disapproval lurking about the corners of her mouth, placed a coin in each girl's palm.

"Come on!" Connie dragged Annie behind her.

"Walk, girls; please walk!" Mrs. Sprague insisted.

Connie pointedly slowed until they'd purchased packets of corn from a crippled peddler woman crouched on the curb.

"You must stand very still," Connie instructed, pulling Annie back into the midst of the square. "Spread your arms wide, hold your head high, and don't twitch."

Annie did as she was told. She felt silly standing like a human letter T and wondered if Connie meant to have a laugh at her expense. But not a minute passed before the cooing pigeons dropped, one by one, onto Annie's arms and shoulders, even atop her summer straw hat, happy to perch while Connie fed them from her hand.

"They tickle," Annie whispered, surprised. "Their little feet tickle my arms right through my shirtwaist!" She felt her eyes open wide. Mirth pulled at her lips, lifting their corners, until she hiccuped, then laughed aloud—the first spontaneous joyful sound to erupt from her throat in weeks.

So startling was the merriment, so infectious was her sudden awakening that Mrs. Sprague and Connie began to chuckle. All three giggled. Their giggles burst until their eyes filled. When Connie spewed an unladylike snort into the sudden late-morning sunshine, the flock of pigeons, startled and clearly insulted by such an indignity, rose in a gray-white beating of wings by tens and twenties, a great whooshing orchestra, into the sky. Annie laughed and laughed until she cried.

※ ※

Owen's July birthday came at last. For once Mrs. Sprague made no plans for the girls. Annie spent the morning at Bunhill Fields cemetery, tending the graves of her parents and Owen.

At least on her parents' graves, the flowers she and Owen had planted were blooming—as blue as the blue of her eyes, just as Owen had promised. But to Annie, Owen's grave looked sad and empty beside their lavish bouquets.

"In the spring, Owen, I promise. Just as soon as Mother and Father's flowers have gone to seed, I shall gather every tiny one, and in the spring I will plant them for you. By your next birthday your spot will be a garden too." She stood. "I'll not forget."

She passed the afternoon alone in the Spragues' back garden, rereading Owen's journal—the last months of the last year of his life. It was a family tradition—a new book begun on each birthday. She wished there were more and wondered what had become of all the journals of his life. They had each kept them since they were taught to read and write. Owen had written his entries daily—more faithfully than she had ever done.

Perhaps, Annie thought, all those books, those precious accounts of his precious days, lay at the bottom of the sea amid *Titanic*'s wreckage, or perhaps Owen had at some time sacrificed the words of his life in a huge bonfire. Annie could imagine Owen offering his journal's fertile ashes as a gift to the roses he loved.

By the time she finished reading, the sun had crossed the sky. Owen's birthday was nearly past, and Annie loved her brother again, all the more. When she'd first read of Lucy Snape, she'd felt indignant that Owen had kept such an important secret from her and miffed that he held another girl—a woman—in higher esteem than his sister.

But now Annie wondered if Owen had found Lucy before the ship went down, if he'd told Lucy of his affection for her. She pitied Lucy

Snape for not living, for never knowing the love her brother could have offered her.

In her compassion for Lucy and in reading again of Owen's concern for and brotherly claim on Michael Dunnagan, Annie found she despised the boy stowaway a little less. If Owen loved him, owned him as a brother and friend, if he had secured his future within their family, then perhaps, Annie thought, she should not altogether hate him. How she could do that without entirely forgiving Michael, she did not know.

❧ CHAPTER THIRTY-ONE ❧

UPON DISCOVERY of the treasure stitched inside the pockets of Owen's coat, Daniel planted every slip and root he could salvage. He planted a third of the seeds, storing the rest as security for another spring. But the fields that Owen had planned and drawn while aboard *Titanic*, the paths and routes and outlines for the gardens, Daniel undertook with a will that bowled Michael's brain. By August they began to see the slim promise of their plantings.

"Another lean winter, but we'll manage with what we've got," Daniel pronounced. "We'll begin working next year's ground and building the structures for Owen's plans now—every minute we can spare." He wiped his brow. "The lad was a genius. We'll follow in his wake."

It was almost like working for Owen—not that Daniel himself was like Owen, but because they were laying the wooden and stone structures and plowing the fields of Owen's dreams.

Some nights, as Michael lay on his cot inhaling the stars and honeysuckle through his bedroom window, he could feel Owen's excitement growing inside himself. The beating of his heart was Owen's beating heart, as though Owen lived inside his chest. Michael could not explain that, dared not try. But he felt Owen walking before him, behind him, beside him.

The sun and rain and occasional picnic trips to the nearby seaside strengthened Michael's lungs, his limbs, and his purpose. The earthy smell of the black and sandy New Jersey soil as it sifted through his fingers surged through Michael's nostrils and skin—by every means a tonic.

And Maggie's kitchen garden, ripe with variegated greens, bright-orange peppers, brilliant-red radishes, and finally glossy tomatoes, became for him an artist's tryst with the soil, the sun, and the sky.

August brought blue-white skies, violent thunderstorms, and long days of peach and corn harvesting. The hot weather also brought mosquitoes—flying, biting insects Michael had never known—to share their land and suck their blood.

"Their bite reminds you that you're living, Michael!" Daniel laughed at the boy's fitful swatting and frustration. "They tell you to be grateful for your life's blood, lad—for if you're not, they'll gladly relieve you of it!"

Michael might have grown tired of Daniel's glee at his expense had he not known his jest was kindly meant. He'd also learned that Daniel McKenica seldom wasted words, that one word spoken often doubled for two meanings.

So he wondered how it worked—this being grateful for your life when you knew it was at the expense of another. He knew by Daniel's own words that he did not see Michael's life as a trade but as a gift that should be gratefully received and dutifully, joyfully shared. By the end of summer, Michael alternately feared and dared to wonder if there could be some truth in that.

It was in the evenings, with the day's work behind, that a gentle melancholy sometimes settled over the threesome. Michael fell easily into their custom of sitting in the small parlor on the rare cool or rainy evening or, more often, sitting on the porch if the evening was fine. Daniel puffed his pipe, sometimes reading or rereading the weekly newspaper. Maggie mended or darned until the light failed. Then she leaned back, rested her head against the rocker, and hummed the old songs of Ireland.

The tunes brought an ache to Michael's heart for he did not know what—something he'd long forgotten, if he'd ever known it. At times they reminded him of the bagpiper on the stern of *Titanic* piping "Erin's Lament" as the ship pulled from her shores. And then he would think again of Owen, standing beside him. He thought mostly of Owen.

Maggie and Daniel talked of Sean, Maggie's husband. Though Michael saw her grow quiet at odd times throughout the day and lift her apron's hem to wipe stray tears, she just as often told Michael funny stories about her husband and their life together. All the years they'd lived in

America, Daniel had worked for them. Through those years he'd become a brother to Sean and Maggie; together they had formed a family.

One fine day when September waned, Maggie banned Daniel and Michael from the kitchen. They took their meals, morning and noon, on the porch steps.

"Whatever has come over you, woman?" Daniel demanded. "What's that you're hiding behind your back? What smells so goo—?"

"That's none of your nevermind, Daniel McKenica. You'll both be allowed in my kitchen when I say so, and not a moment before. Have you not work enough in the gardens? Do you need me to find some employment for your idle hands?" Maggie shook a wooden spoon in his face. "If you're finished blathering, I can surely find another job for you two to—"

"Come, Michael. She's got her dander up. We'd best put our feet to the road before she reads us her doomsday list."

Michael hurried to keep up with Daniel's rapidly retreating gait. "What sort of list is that, then?'"

"Ach. That, my boy, is a list that will keep our noses to the grindstone from now till doomsday—nary a breath nor break between!"

But Maggie's banishment lasted only until supper. When the two wary males returned from the fields, she bade them scrub at the pump outside the kitchen door till their skin glowed red. She left a pail of steaming water for each and hung clean trousers, shirts, stiff collars, and even neckties over the porch rail.

"What has the woman gone and done now?" Daniel fretted.

Michael swallowed his panic. *Has someone died?* He'd never been so smartly dressed, not even the day Owen made him change his shirt to eat in the third-class dining room aboard *Titanic*. But to wear a necktie—he'd no idea how to finagle the thing about his neck. What could Maggie Allen be thinking? And why was Daniel McKenica near laughing at his discomfort?

"Come round the front, the both of you." Maggie ordered. "Close your eyes, Michael."

"What did you say?"

"I said, close your eyes," Maggie repeated patiently.

"Do as you're told, lad. Things will go easier with you," Daniel warned, gruff in his nod.

Michael closed his eyes and, for good measure, covered them with both hands. He did not know if the pull of temptation was because he'd been forbidden to look or because he dreaded whatever unknown thing lay ahead.

"Daniel, hold the door! This way, Michael. Take my hand," Maggie crooned, leading him round the side of the house, up the front steps, and over the threshold.

"Why are we coming in the front door?" Michael asked. He'd rarely entered through the front since the day he'd fallen through it and into the world of Allen's Run Gardens.

"So many questions," Maggie chided good-naturedly.

The moment he stepped through the portal, Michael's nose gained control of his senses. Never in all his life, not even in the Christmases of his early childhood, could he remember having smelled anything so tantalizing, so utterly amazing. It was as though every hair on his body stood up and every bud on his tongue shouted, "Creation!"

Whatever his face showed was enough for Maggie. She laughed aloud and pulled Michael's hands from his eyes.

The three stood in the dark dining room—a room rarely opened even for airing—now bright with sixteen burning candles stuck in a blackberry pudding. A roasted goose, bigger than any Michael had ever seen, was circled with steaming apples, and a platter heaped in golden-brown St. Michael's bannock sat on the sideboard, surrounded by bowls of cabbage and carrots swimming in butter and an array of sweetmeats and nuts, barely squeezed into the space.

"Happy birthday, Michael! Happy Michaelmas!" Maggie hugged him.

Daniel, no longer in the least bewildered or vexed, clapped him on the back, a perfect partner to the conspiracy. "You can have a birthday every month if this be the bounty it brings!" He laughed.

"For me? All this for me?" Michael could not believe it.

"You were born on Michaelmas, were you not?" Maggie teased.

"I was! But how did you know?"

"You said you'd turn sixteen in September. I wagered a boy named Michael must have entered this world on Michaelmas."

"Named for the angel, I was—Mam said." Michael blushed.

"And not just an angel, the archangel—the angel above all angels!" Maggie laughed. "What better day to be born?"

"You two are stickier than the pudding I've a mind to plow into," Daniel fussed. "See what your lungs can do with those candles, my boy."

Michael was mesmerized by the beauty and wonder of the pudding set afire. "Nobody's ever made me such a feast, Maggie."

"I'm glad you like it, Michael. But you need to make a wish and blow out the candles."

"Before they burn down the house!" Daniel nearly shouted.

"A wish?" Michael had never heard of such a thing.

"Just in the quiet of your mind. A wish or a prayer," Maggie coached, "then blow them out."

"Blow them all out at once and the wish is bound to come true," Daniel added.

That made no sense to Michael. How could blowing out candles make something as important as a wish or a prayer come true? But he would not miss the chance.

"Please, God," he whispered so low no one else heard, "bring Annie here—for Owen's sake." Michael filled his lungs until he thought they'd burst. He blew and blew—not only the candles, but the very flowers that Maggie had so painstakingly arranged upon the pudding.

Daniel laughed till he cried; Maggie looked very nearly distressed before she pulled Michael away.

Never had a meal tasted so wonderfully good—not one he had earned nor one he had stolen. Michael ate and ate until he would not have been surprised to see the buttons pop from his trousers. At last he sat back, full, contented, and licked the goose grease from his fingers. Maggie gave him a reproving wag of her head but smiled just the same.

By the time the table was cleared and the dishes washed, the sun had pulled a blanket over its head. Frost was still far away, but the chill of a late-September evening drew them into the front parlor. Daniel built a fire. Maggie sank gratefully into her rocker, her sewing basket by her feet.

Michael stretched across the rug by the hearth, letting the heat from the fire seep into his skin and comfort his bones, and opened *The Call of the Wild*, the new Jack London novel Daniel and Maggie had given him—wonders for his heart and soul in one slim volume.

Daniel loaded his pipe and took up his newspaper. For once, Maggie chased neither him nor his smoke out of doors.

Michael shut his eyes, holding close the moment. When he opened them again, Maggie rocked slowly, back and forth, back and forth. Her needle plied a sock stretched taut across her darning egg, working it round and round.

"A letter came from Annie today," Maggie said, not dropping a stitch.

Michael stiffened. *Could a wish come so suddenly true?* he wondered and closed his book.

Daniel stopped puffing. "How is the lass?"

Maggie sighed. "Hard to tell. She wrote that she's been living with her family's solicitor and his wife. They have a daughter." She laid her darning in her lap. "She says they're friends. They go about London with the missus, and the girls go together to some Red Cross lessons or other."

"And what's wrong with that? It's good for the girl to have friends her own age."

"They're not her family, Daniel. We're her family."

"A family is those you're stuck with—like it or not."

"Daniel!"

"Well, maybe she likes them. Look at us. We're not a family by blood, but you're both as much of a family as I've ever had."

Maggie tilted her head, watching Daniel.

Daniel squirmed and, clearly trying to relieve himself of Maggie's attention, said, "Well, what about that aunt she's got, right there in London? Has she not been her guardian since Mackenzie died?"

"Eleanor Hargrave . . ." Maggie rocked back and forth more quickly, then stopped. "But there's something not right about it all. Mackenzie would not come to America because of her, though why, I never knew.

He did not love her. And Owen insisted Annie not stay in the woman's house. He wrote that he'd enrolled her in a girls' school in Southampton until he was certain that moving to America was a good and stable change for them both."

"Sounds very responsible." Daniel puffed again.

"But that's the quandary, don't you see? Why would Owen think their aunt, their mother's own sister, not a proper guardian for her? And why now, of all times, would Annie be living with her guardian's solicitor?"

"You're getting your detective mind going again, Margaret Faye. You'll be drawing a mystery where there is none."

"Annie said her aunt suffered a brain hemorrhage after they recovered Owen's body," Maggie mused.

Michael swallowed, and Maggie looked to him as though she regretted the reminder her words had surely given.

"There you are, then. The girl canna stay with an aunt who's likely bedridden or incapacitated."

"I don't know," Maggie said again. "Something's not right. Annie doesn't sound happy."

"Owen's dead," Michael answered after a time, as though a question had been posed. "He was her family—her true family. How can Annie be happy?" Michael remembered the love lights in Annie's eyes when she gazed at her older brother on Easter morning. "How can she ever be happy again?"

Maggie's brow creased. She studied Michael a long time, almost as though she'd not clearly seen him before. "Why don't you write to her, Michael?"

Michael felt the heat and shame run through his body, but he did not shrink from Maggie's gaze. "She'd not want to be hearing from me."

"I think she would. You and Annie knew and loved Owen best of all the people living, as near as I can tell. I think you're just the person to write to her."

Michael looked away.

"You can send your letter with mine. I'll write tomorrow."

"Maggie," Daniel cautioned, "are you certain you want to interfere?"

"Helping to heal hearts is not interfering. I know what I'm about."

Daniel ducked behind his paper.

"And I think, Michael Dunnagan," she said, "that it is well nigh time you called me Aunt Maggie." She smiled and, without looking at Daniel, said, "Don't you think so, Daniel?"

Daniel shot Michael a glance that held, pulled the pipe from his mouth, leaving its corners half-turned up, and blinked. He shook his paper again, raised it to a proper reading level, and said in feeble gruffness, "Suit yourself. It's as good a name as any."

≋ CHAPTER THIRTY-TWO ≋

ANNIE STAYED with the Spragues past her fifteenth birthday, past a sub-dued Christmas, and well into the bleak new year. A month before the anniversary of Owen's death, Annie made her announcement.

"No, Elisabeth Anne, I do not think it wise for you to return to Hargrave House." Mr. Sprague had never formed the habit, as had Mrs. Sprague and Connie, of calling her Annie. "You have done well here."

"And we love having you, dear," Mrs. Sprague insisted. "You know you are welcome to live with us—for as long as you wish."

"Why?" Connie probed. "Why do you want to go?"

"It isn't that I want to go. It's just that . . . just that I think I need to begin my life. It is time to begin my life."

"What do you call this?" Connie demanded.

"Constance!" Mrs. Sprague interrupted. "Allow Annie to explain."

"I'm not certain I can explain. But it is spring." Annie raised her eyes and shifted in her seat. "Father and Owen always turned the beds at Hargrave House in spring . . . and they pruned and planted."

"But they are not there, Annie dear," Mrs. Sprague offered patiently.

Annie sighed. "I know that, but I can do it."

"Turn the beds?" Mr. Sprague's brows rose.

"Garden? You?" Connie challenged.

"Yes, Owen taught me ever so much. I know I cannot do everything, but I can do some. I want to do it. I want to feel the soil; I need to feel . . ." Annie spread her hands helplessly, frustrated that they did not understand.

"Alive," Connie finished.

"Yes," Annie replied gratefully. "And I want to be close to them." She looked at her hands and said quietly, "I'll find them there. Father always said that life began in a garden."

Mr. and Mrs. Sprague exchanged glances over Annie's head. Mrs. Sprague reached for Annie's hand. "But you can't, darling. It's impossible. Why, a grown man alone could not . . ."

Annie's eyes welled and threatened to overflow. Owen would have understood.

"Wait, Betty." Mr. Sprague stopped his wife.

"But, Edwin, you know that it is out of the question for her to return to that house."

"Returning to the house is indeed out of the question. But as for the garden . . ." Mr. Sprague looked into Annie's eyes. "No, I think that is not out of the question. I think if anyone could grow and tend a garden, it is Annie Allen."

Annie looked up. He had used her name, just as she was.

Mr. Sprague smiled. "It might be just the thing, mightn't it?"

Annie nodded through sparkling tears.

"We shall hire someone to turn the beds for you, to do the hauling and heavy work. But you direct them. You plan and plant the gardens—as you wish."

Annie drew a quick, clean breath. "Yes! Yes."

"But I—" Mrs. Sprague began; her husband raised his hand.

"You must, however, continue to live here, with us. You may work in the gardens weekday afternoons and as long as you wish on Saturdays. But you must promise to apply yourself to your studies with your tutors weekday mornings. You must keep up your piano and voice lessons. And you will attend Red Cross meetings and outings with Constance, as well as services with us on Sundays. Is that understood?"

"Yes, sir," Annie said, relieved on all counts. "Thank you, Mr. Sprague."

He nodded. "Prepare a list for the gardener of all that you require. I shall see that he is able to keep you supplied."

That night Annie could not sleep for the anticipation building inside her. She closed her eyes and tried to remember in detail the gardens of Hargrave House. She was surprised to realize that, although she had played in and roamed those gardens for years, she could not picture each flower in its season.

Should she wait through this year, watch and record what emerged, or should she have the beds turned completely and begin anew? Such a daring contemplation thrilled her, but what she wanted most was to feel near Owen and Father, to remember them through their flowers and herbs, to rediscover their earthy spring scent in the upturned beds.

The downstairs clock bonged half past two. Annie tossed, then turned, and tossed again. She knew it was not only excitement for the new gardens, nor was it simply the thrill of grown-up responsibilities that stole her sleep. By returning to Hargrave House, even if she never stepped foot inside the front door, she knew she would not be able to avoid Aunt Eleanor forever.

She had not asked about her aunt in weeks, had not been directly told the current state of her health. She wanted to picture her aunt as helpless and bedridden, her piercing eyes closed, wanted to think of her power and control confined to her bedchamber. But Annie knew that was not the case.

She'd overheard Mr. and Mrs. Sprague two days before, when she stopped short to listen at the breakfast room door. "I visited Hargrave House yesterday," Mr. Sprague said. "She is able to sit in a wheeled chair now, able to respond to questions by nods and the shaking of her head."

"That is not the same as being able to direct a household or handle her financial affairs!" Mrs. Sprague insisted.

"No." He seemed to consider. "Her few words are not always clear. But Eleanor Hargrave is better able to reason than she is to communicate. It may be only a matter of time before she can and will insist on resuming some of her own affairs."

"But Annie—" Mrs. Sprague spoke quietly, urgently—"she would not take Annie, surely."

The silence was long. Annie stood outside the door, her ear pressed to it, her heart pounding in her chest.

"I cannot say what Eleanor Hargrave will do." Mr. Sprague sighed wearily. "I have never been able to predict the workings of that woman's mind. But I do not believe she holds Elisabeth Anne's best interests in her heart."

"Oh, Edwin—" Mrs. Sprague's voice caught.

"There, my dear. We shall keep her with us for as long as we are able. I will prolong the workings of the law for as long as humanly possible."

And that was what worried Annie. Even though she was only a few months from sixteen, Annie feared she would not be able to live with the Spragues until she could become independent. Sooner or later her aunt might insist upon her return, determined and within her legal rights to control Annie.

"If I must go back, it will be on my terms," Annie whispered to the dark. "Hargrave House is part mine—or will be. By working in the gardens, I stake my claim, my right. I will make certain that she knows she cannot trample me."

Even her vow made Annie cringe. It was one thing to whisper safely in the night, with no one to challenge her—with feisty Connie breathing nearby and stalwart Mr. and Mrs. Sprague sleeping just down the hallway. It would be quite another to stand up to Aunt Eleanor.

≋ CHAPTER THIRTY-THREE ≋

DANIEL AND MICHAEL split and hauled wood for the community all winter. The moment Michael learned that locals paid three dollars per tree for evergreens hauled into their parlors to decorate for Christmas, he insisted they plant a hundred saplings come spring.

"We'll call it Annie's Evergreen Garden! One season will bring enough to fetch Annie here and set her up in the best school—wherever that is!" But he was astonished and chagrined to learn that the trees, once planted, would not be ready to harvest and sell for another three to five years.

"Growing is a patient thing, lad," Daniel explained. "You must give all living things time to adjust to their new surroundings, their new soil, then time to grow, as well."

But Michael had worked almost a full year and was out of patience. By the first anniversary of *Titanic*'s sinking, Daniel had established nearly half of Owen's seeds. A third of his slips and roses thrived. More young plants from the Old World stock struggled; their futures loomed uncertain. Selling to the public was out of the question.

How can I bring Annie here when the business is barely surviving? Aunt Maggie and Daniel barely scraped together enough cash for the land taxes. There's not a farthing for ship's fare.

But bringing Annie to New Jersey was the only thing Owen had demanded. Michael felt feeble and useless, as though he'd betrayed his friend.

Still, Owen's words played through his mind: *"Everything I touch grows and thrives. And now I've touched you, Michael Dunnagan. So you've no choice but to grow and thrive as well."*

Owen believed in me. What would Owen do if he were here? Michael knew he would not stand by and say, *"Oh well, we'll have to wait five years to bring Annie across."*

He'd do something, surely! If he couldn't make the money one way, he'd make it another. Michael thought and thought. He pondered until his brain was sore. And in the end, the idea came from Annie herself.

"Her letter is brimming over with news and sketches of her garden plans," Maggie said of Annie's latest letter while she served the perch.

"Her garden plans?" Michael stopped chewing and paused with his fork in midair.

"Look here." Aunt Maggie spread the new letter before Daniel and Michael across the table. "She's like her brother, what with all the plans and grand notions. And a fine artist she is!" She clucked her tongue, approval in both dimples.

"What's this, then? It says *rose garden*." Michael set down his fork. "What's this she's drawn by the rose garden?"

"Let me see. She's labeled everything in great detail! Ah, that is a gazebo—a little wooden garden house for people to sit in. And see here, with the morning glories winding round the post—that's a birdhouse."

"Owen and I talked of building gazebos. But—'birdhouse'—you mean a regular house for birds? With rooms and all? Do people really make such things?"

"Why, yes! Of course they do—well, not with rooms; it's empty inside. A safe and dry place for a pair of birds to build their nest." Aunt Maggie laughed.

"Made of wood?" Michael demanded.

"Yes, yes, of course. You've never seen a birdhouse, Michael?"

Daniel interrupted Maggie's question. "Some folks fashion them from gooseneck gourds. Even paint the funny things to add a bit of whimsy."

"Would people with a spot of money buy such a thing?" Michael demanded again, a sudden spring in his chest.

"Why, yes," Maggie answered. "I suppose they would."

"That's it, then!" Michael slapped the table. "I'll build those houses—for birds, and bigger ones for people to sit in inside their gardens. There's stacks and stacks of lumber behind the barn!"

"All that lumber came from an old barn Sean tore down a couple years back," Aunt Maggie said.

Michael looked closely at Annie's picture. "See here! She's drawn a swing—one here hanging from a tree, but across the way is one in a frame—a double-sided thing. I'll make that, too!"

"Furniture for the lawn and garden," Daniel mused. "It's not a bad idea, that."

"Oh, Daniel! Not you too!" Maggie chided. "You're both daft. Haven't you enough work for five men, and here, such talk of adding more."

"We've got to do something to raise money for Annie's ticket!" Michael pleaded.

"It isn't just the ticket," Maggie patiently explained for the hundredth time. "We cannot bring her here when we don't know if we'll lose the land and house. Owen did not want that—you told me so yourself."

"We'll not lose the land!" Michael pounded the table. Maggie jumped and Daniel raised his eyebrows. Michael's color rose, but he would not take it back. "We'll make it work! Owen said that a man, once he's put his hand to the plow, is bound to accomplish what he's set about; there's no turning back. We'll do it—we will!"

Daniel pushed his spectacles to the top of his head. "Well, you heard the man, Maggie. You'd best pour us another cup of coffee. There's work to be done."

Daniel smiled and Maggie looked nearly vexed, but she poured the coffee.

※ ※

Michael took Annie's drawing from Maggie's letter and set to work that very night. Daniel showed him how to draw a pattern on old newspaper and how to measure and cut the wood for birdhouses. Michael cut and nailed and hammered; he sanded and wiped, then sanded again; some he stained and varnished, while others he painted.

Daniel and Michael worked full days in the fields and gardens. But Michael no longer joined his aunt and Daniel by the fire in the evenings. He worked on his birdhouses in the barn each night until he could no longer see. By the end of three weeks his eyes were itchy and red from sawdust. He'd stacked twenty-five birdhouses along the barn shelf, each one different from the last.

"You must call him in, Daniel," Maggie urged. "He's working himself into a dither."

"Leave the boy alone, Maggie. He's got a purpose. Have you ever seen him so glad and driven?"

"I know, but what if she does not want to come? What if Michael wears himself to the bone and Annie says no? He'll be devastated."

"She'd be a fool not to come," Daniel said as though that decided it.

"Well, she wouldn't be the first girl who—oh, Daniel, she sent his letter back unopened."

"Maggie, Maggie Allen." Daniel shook his head. "You've got to stop playing matchmaker."

"I'm not playing matchmaker, Daniel McKenica! I'm simply trying to help Michael! Annie has the Spragues, but Michael has only us."

"Let the boy be. Let nature take her course. It will all come right in the end."

"You didn't read her letter. She said not one word about Michael but sounds ever so happy now that she's tending the gardens her father started. Her spirits are lifting."

"It's natural. Gardening is in the Allen blood. It's good and gladsome, a healing thing. You know that. What did you expect?"

"I just don't want to see Michael hurt. It's almost as though he's falling in love with her, possessed with the idea of bringing her here." Maggie shook her head and sighed. "What am I saying? He's only sixteen years old, and he's never met her face to face! I am a goose, but I won't tell him she returned his letter!"

"Nay, lass. You're not a goose. You're a good and wise woman. Michael is living for and would die for Annie, though he may not say it in those words. He's in love with the idea of her, and I'm thinking 'tis not only to do with his promise to Owen. Whether or not she'll look his way is another thing. She's been raised in the golden mansion. It's hard to know if she'll find farming to her liking. But you must let things lie—don't vex yourself. They'll come out as they're meant to. Your fretting will not help them either way."

Maggie sighed. "Daniel McKenica, that's got to be the longest string of words I've ever heard tumble from your mouth. Sometimes I don't know whether to hug you or throw you out."

He raised his brows, picked up his paper, and smiled behind it.

Weary and thirsty, Michael stepped inside the kitchen door for a glass of milk, just in time to hear Aunt Maggie's and Daniel's every word. "I'm not in love with her—nor the idea of her," Michael swore beneath his breath. "Annie's a sister to me because I promised Owen. I promised him! And I won't fail him. I failed Megan Marie—I didn't keep watch; I didn't stand guard. But I'll not fail Annie."

≋ CHAPTER THIRTY-FOUR ≋

Annie loved receiving Aunt Maggie's warm and lively letters—until her most recent one.

Aunt Maggie knew about flower gardening, more than Annie herself. She understood the joy and beauty of flowers and herbs, considered the importance of cutting gardens planted purely for bouquets meant for tables and live wreaths, as well as those for drying. She appreciated the graceful layout of paths and sitting areas in a garden's design. She understood the significance of texture and fragrance, of hues and colors arranged, and of flowers and shrubs rotating through their seasons—beauty from a woman's point of view. There was no one in England with whom Annie knew to share such joys.

In her last letter Aunt Maggie had enclosed a sketch of Allen's Run Gardens in New Jersey. It was crude; Aunt Maggie was not artistic on paper. But Annie was surprised and delighted by the new layouts of winding paths amid themed gardens. In some places they mirrored the gardens of Hargrave House. Certainly more expansive. Some large areas were cultivated for rest and beauty, some for cutting, efficiency, and productivity. In a few spots Annie sensed a whimsy she'd not imagined from her aunt and uncle, and she had written, questioning the newer designs.

Aunt Maggie's responding letter rang with laughter, at least at first:

I should say not! Your uncle Sean was not the creative one of the Allen brothers. Your own da took the lion's share of that—even as a youngster before he left Ireland. Hardworking as the day is long, my Sean was, but you'd think he was more German than Irish in his long, straight rows and rigid, sharp corners. He ran our gardens as a well-oiled machine.

I'm sorry to say he hadn't the necessary strength once his heart gave way—nor did he always seem to know what it was our customers craved. But the gardens are changing. For the first time in many years, I hold hope for our gardens—hope for our home, hope that we will be able to offer to share it with you, sweet Annie, in another year's time—if you are ready and wanting to come.

Your brother designed the new gardens I sketched for you— at least many of them. Michael delivered the drawings Owen had placed in his charge, and Daniel and Michael have made them a reality.

When Michael landed on our doorstep, I did not know if he would live, let alone become the strapping young man and the great help that he is. He is doing all he can to stabilize our business and to raise money for your passage and living expenses. He promised Owen he would work to bring you here, you know.

You should know that I was the one who urged Michael to write you. He feared that you would not want to hear from him, but I assured him that his letters would do you good. I reminded him that the two of you share a natural love for gardening and a great love for Owen. I was certain you would want to hear from someone who loved your brother and who Owen held dear.

Perhaps I was wrong. Still, it was not necessary for you to return his letter.

I've come to love Michael as the son I've never borne, my dear. I hope, in time, that you will be able to forgive him for living. He did not take Owen's place; Owen insisted upon and secured Michael's safety—for him, for your future, for all of us. Michael would have given his life for Owen's had he known how.

Now tell me more of your own gardens, dear, and your Red Cross work. It brings me closer to you to think how you spend your days.

Know that I love you, my sweet niece, and look eagerly to the day I can welcome you with open arms.

Always,
Aunt Maggie

Annie felt the heat of shame spread across her cheeks. Immediately she wanted to argue with Aunt Maggie for pointing out her poor behavior, to force her aunt to pity her. But something quiet and insistent inside Annie recognized the ring of truth.

Owen would be astonished at my behavior. He would say I've grown arrogant and bitter, like . . . She pushed a tendril of hair, and the trickle of a tear, from her eye. She knew her feelings toward Michael were unfair. But it helped to have someone to blame. *Does Aunt Maggie never feel like blaming someone for Uncle Sean's dying?*

She reread the letter, then spread the map from Aunt Maggie's previous letter across her lap and read again the names of the new gardens: Annie's Evergreens, Elisabeth Anne Rose Garden, Owen Allen's Old World Flowers and Roses.

And now, in this new letter, there was the newspaper clipping. Aunt Maggie had enclosed a story from a New Jersey weekly about Michael and his lawn and garden furniture for Allen's Run Gardens. There were three photographs—two of birdhouses custom built to look like miniatures of the houses of wealthy patrons who had placed orders. The third photograph was of a tall young man, broad of shoulders, boasting an unruly shock of dark hair and a half grin, his arm draped over the railing of a gazebo he'd built—one that looked very much like the one set in the far corner of the Hargrave gardens.

He's grown strong and handsome enough. He smiles. Still, Annie thought, *his eyes are sad—the same sad and anxious eyes he wore that Easter Sunday and that day on the bow of* Titanic. *What made them so?*

Annie realized that Michael was not arrogant or crude or rude as she'd once thought, but tortured. After living a year with torture, she recognized it readily enough in others. She cringed to recall her childish behavior during her last days with Owen in Southampton. *How did Owen stand me? What did Michael think of me—rude and cruel as I was?*

Then came a ripple, a trickling current of pity for Michael. *Aunt Maggie's right. It's not Michael's fault that he lived and Owen died. If anyone was to "blame," it was Owen. If Owen had not saved Michael, he would have saved someone else at his own peril—anyone willing to be saved. He would not even consider that there was anything to forgive. I'm the one demanding Michael pay for the gift Owen gave him.*

"God, forgive me," Annie prayed. The image of Aunt Eleanor loomed before her. "No, Father! No! I don't want to be like her. I want a heart like Owen's." She choked on her sob.

Annie sat and thought long in the garden that afternoon. She knew that Owen had found his example for everyday living in Christ. But Annie didn't think she understood either of them enough to know how they would have addressed her situation. *What would they have done about Michael? About Aunt Eleanor?*

Annie had no clear answer for her questions of duty or love. She only knew Owen had loved Michael and had always treated their aunt respectfully. *He was never spiteful or insulting, though he did separate himself from her. He must have understood what Aunt Eleanor had done to Father's spirit, even without knowing all she'd schemed and all she'd withheld. Owen refused to succumb to her wiles and pleas and threats—even when he believed it would cost him his inheritance. And he moved me—once he could, and once he believed it necessary. But if he had truly known everything—all she had done and refused to do for Mother—would he have been able to forgive her?*

As much as Annie did not wish to see her aunt Eleanor, she loved the gardens. Her restoration—the work she'd done and the work she had ordered done—of the beds and borders felt like part achievement and part memorial to her loved ones. And restore them, she had. Fountains and curtains of roses filled the air with such fragrance that passersby stopped, breathed deeply, and lingered over the palette of color and light.

"Thank You, Lord," she whispered as she folded the letter, the map, and the clipping and tucked them into her pocket.

Annie took up her trowel and loosened the soil surrounding her favorite pink roses, roses her father had propagated. Annie had no idea of their botanical name, but she remembered that Father and Owen had always called them the Elisabeth Anne, in her honor. She could not help but smile to think that Michael was preparing a similar garden in America—a garden that promised beauty and a home for her, should she want it.

Annie blushed suddenly and knew she was blushing. She dug deeper into the soil. *I should write to him, but what shall I write? It would have seemed natural if I'd responded to his letter. But now what?*

She wished she knew how to propagate roses, how to combine the qualities and traits of more than one variety to create something new. She would love to create an Owen Allen for Michael's "Owen Allen's Old World Flowers and Roses."

Perhaps I can write Michael about that. I wonder if Owen told him how to propagate roses. But how can I? Annie groaned, throwing down the trowel. "It seems so contrived, so out of the blue! If only I had not returned his letter!"

CHAPTER THIRTY-FIVE

FOR THE SECOND YEAR Annie spent the morning of Owen's July birthday visiting his grave in Bunhill Fields. The gathered seeds she'd planted in the early spring had taken root and blossomed, as blue, if not as full, as those on her parents' graves. Annie circled Owen's plot, gently pinching the faded petals and pulling stray weeds, then sat back on her heels, wishing there were more she could do to add to the beauty of the grave.

"I do not feel as if I have reached the Celestial City, Owen," she said aloud. "Every day I'm still trudging uphill with that wretched load on my back." She glanced at the relief of Christian, weighed down by his heavy burden, on John Bunyan's stone and sighed. "How long does it take, I wonder?"

She spent the afternoon in the gardens at Hargrave House, alone except for the surreptitious visit of Jamison, who carried her a small flask of tea and a napkin hiding two orange-and-currant scones—the recipe Owen had loved best. Midafternoon she wrote in her journal:

> Owen would have been twenty-two and perhaps building a home
> for Lucy and Margaret Snape by now. I would have crossed and been
> living with Aunt Maggie and Mr. McKenica and with Michael.
> And perhaps, if Owen had lived, we would all be a family, the
> family he intended.

"A family," Annie said aloud. "I cannot even remember what that was like."

"Moping, are you?"

Annie hadn't heard Connie cross the garden path. "Connie, what are you doing here?"

"I know the date. I figured you'd be off by yourself, weeping your eyes out."

"You're too blunt."

"It's a simple statement, Annie Allen." Connie plopped on the bench beside her friend, then swept her arm across the gardens. "However, do not fear, for I have come to lift you from your doldrums!"

"Please, Connie. I don't wish to—"

"You don't wish to discuss it? Fine! Neither do I." Connie stood and grabbed both of Annie's hands, raising her to her feet. "I wish only to whisk you away from all this botanical loveliness—which, by the by, you have forged into a living, breathing mausoleum—and march you into the world of living, breathing people."

"Not today. I—"

"Yes! Today of all days. We're going to our Red Cross meeting—or have you forgotten your promise to Father? You are to practice rolling and applying your bandages and boiling eggs and brewing tea until Matron declares that you have passed and are capable of rolling lint for the remainder of your spinster days."

"Another day, Connie."

"Today!" Connie insisted and shook her friend's shoulders. "Don't you see? You've become morose. You're throwing away the very life God has given you by continually bemoaning your loss. Is that what your brother would have wanted for you?"

Annie pulled back.

"I don't believe he would have tolerated it, not for a moment! If he was half the man that you and Father have made him out to be, he would be fed up with your moping about this place!"

"Owen loved the gardens!"

"But he did not live for them! They lived for him! And anyway, I'm not speaking of gardens. The gardens are gorgeous, Annie—amazing! But life only begins in the garden, as you so dearly love to remind me; it must not end here! When you close that garden gate, you lock yourself in and shut out the rest of the world. It's time to venture forth, to explore new horizons."

"Stop talking like Shakespeare," Annie chided. Connie was right; despondency draped a comfortable cloak.

Connie smiled. "There now. I am delighted that you appreciate the likeness. Now put up your hair, and off we go."

"I feel like a sham and so made-up with my hair pinned high. You know they're going to realize sometime that I've been pretending to be your age, and then what a row we'll face!"

"They'll never know from me, and not from you unless you tell them, foolish child. With your hair pinned up, you could pass for seventeen, probably eighteen—if you would raise your chin and stop acting so mousy."

"I never act mousy, Connie Sprague! You take that back."

But Connie laughed. "Not that time, you didn't. Keep up that spark and they'll be convinced you're old enough to sit with the VADs. Besides, you take it all so seriously, Annie! Just as if we were real nurses in training. That alone makes you look eons older. And you can bandage better than any of us—especially those that come just for the tea and crumpets."

"And gossip," Annie added. "You can always tell who comes for the gossip."

"And gossip, my dear!" Connie echoed, laughing and linking her arm through Annie's. "We must never allow ourselves to forget our duty to tea, crumpets, and gossip!"

※ ※

Annie would have preferred to spend her sixteenth birthday alone in the splendor and sanctuary of her Hargrave House gardens. But on the morning of 22 August, Mrs. Sprague announced that they would attend a lecture in London.

"Does Father approve of our becoming suffragettes, Mother?" Connie asked.

Mrs. Sprague pulled a pale-gray veil over her hat and raised her chin but did not return Connie's merry gaze. "We are not suffragettes—not truly." She tugged her gloves securely. "While your father does not entirely approve of the image of the suffragette movement, he understands that nothing short of their current campaign will result in the emancipation of women. I believe your father to stand shoulder to shoulder among the most generous and enlightened men of our time."

She hesitated, then added more quietly, "He did not ask about our morning activities, Constance, and I did not mention our schedule for the day." She looked away as color spread across her cheek. "I have decided that you and Elisabeth Anne are old enough to take an interest in world affairs, especially as they affect the young women of our time."

The laughter in Connie's and Annie's eyes nearly burst their dams, but their mouths did not betray them.

"Straighten your brooch, Annie. As soon as the meeting adjourns, we shall pick up a box of sweets from Reilly's Sweets and Pastries Shop and take a picnic to St. James. We've a birthday to celebrate today!" Mrs. Sprague smiled.

"St. James is always lovely, Mrs. Sprague. But . . . this is Friday."

"Why, yes, of course it is Friday. Whatever does—?"

"The little digger goes to her gardens on Friday afternoons," Connie reminded her mother.

"Constance, do not call Annie a 'little—'"

"I don't mind the name, Mrs. Sprague; truly I don't. But I would love to have you and Constance come to my gardens for tea. Mrs. Woodward, Jamison's sister, promised to send me a box of Banbury cakes and scones for my birthday—orange and currant, and some lemon, too—and Barbara prepares the loveliest teas. She could easily build it round that box of sweets you mentioned. Jamison is so courtly—he would serve us, I know, just as in a grand hotel! And the gazebo is surrounded by roses in their second bloom! I'm dying for you to see it!"

"It's really quite something that she's done, Mother. You ought to see it." Connie sounded the sage.

"Why, it sounds delightful! Thank you, Annie. I have been curious about your gardens. As soon as the morning session ends, we'll go."

So happy was Annie in anticipation of serving tea in her garden—so eager was she to sit in the gazebo with two other women, all three in long skirts and hair piled properly (and at last, appropriately for Annie) high—that she barely heard the morning address.

Sixteen! Why, Mother ran away to marry Father soon after she turned sixteen!

Annie wondered what her mother could have been thinking. She could not imagine looking at a young man with the thought of marriage. *But Mother ran off with the family gardener!* Annie didn't know whether to giggle or be horrified by such an idea. *It would be like my running off with Michael!*

Annie felt herself blush furiously and turned her thoughts back to her mother. *I suppose Grandfather was livid, Mother was delighted—and frightened, surely—and Aunt Eleanor . . . Aunt Eleanor was angry and insanely jealous.*

She felt an unfamiliar pity for her aunt. The sensation was so odd, so out of character and confusing. Annie tried to force her attention to the stark and severe fashions of the women before her and to focus on the bold female speaker. Still, she could not scrape the image of a pitiable and younger Aunt Eleanor from her brain.

Annie felt the old pull of darkness, the pull she experienced each time she allowed her mind to wander to her aunt, but she pushed it away. *Today is a wonderfully happy day. I'm sixteen! I will not think about her today. I will not!*

Distracted by a sudden charge that tore through the room as the speaker posed her challenge to the audience, as though lightning had struck from the podium and run the length and width of each aisle, Annie looked up. Women jumped as one to their feet, shouting, cheering, waving banners on sticks, and chanting in unison, "Vote! Vote! Vote!"—Mrs. Sprague and Connie among them.

But Annie could not take it in. She stood with the others. She waved idly, as if a window before her needed polishing, but wondered, *If women win the vote, what will that mean to me? To Aunt Eleanor? Will it give me more legal rights and protection from her, or will Aunt Eleanor gain a stronger hold?* Annie shuddered at the thought as she followed Mrs. Sprague and Connie into the street.

Whyever am I worried? Aunt Eleanor is not fit to do anything anymore! I am quite safe with the Spragues. As soon as I turn eighteen—just two more years—I shall inherit Owen's legacy and be free to travel to America if I want. Aunt Eleanor can no longer hurt me.

The freedom of such a thought grew inside Annie until she dared to smile. She no longer had eyes or ears for the excitement of the suffragettes. She could think only of the possibilities her future might hold—a future free of Aunt Eleanor. And perhaps, if she could learn to pity her aunt, then she would also be free of her bitterness toward the broken woman.

I know what it is to be jealous, and I know how, if left unchecked, it can eat through you as it has Aunt Eleanor, and for that I do pity her. Whatever she was before, she is not now. She's lost everything and everyone dear to her in any way. And so have I. But I'm still able to love Connie and Mr. and Mrs. Sprague. I can still love Aunt Maggie and . . . and I can like Michael and Daniel McKenica, she qualified her thoughts but smiled just the same. *All of life is before me.*

Annie stopped in her tracks and repeated the thought: *All of life is before me!*

She could barely keep from running down the street to Hargrave House.

"We could take a taxi, Annie dear, if you are in such a hurry." Mrs. Sprague tried to catch her breath. "Remember you are a lady now. Please slow your steps!"

"Oh, I am sorry, Mrs. Sprague. I'm so terribly excited! I was thinking, back in the hall, that my mother and father married soon after my mother turned sixteen."

"Oh?" Connie tilted her head to intone sarcastically, "Do you have plans of which we have not been informed?"

Annie laughed. "You know I don't! I'm just happy today. For the first time in a long while, I realize that I am standing on the threshold of my future!" She threw her arms wide, then suddenly embarrassed, leaned toward her companions confidentially. "And somehow, I feel the gardens have been part of rebuilding me and getting me ready for today. Does that sound silly?"

"Not silly at all, my dear." Mrs. Sprague smiled and stroked Annie's cheek. "It is just what Mr. Sprague and I have hoped for you. You have come a very long way, and we are so proud of you, dear Annie."

Annie knew she was too old to stand in the street and clap her hands. But that was exactly what she felt like doing.

They passed Bunhill Fields. "Not stopping today?" Connie whispered.

"Not today." Annie smiled. "I'll go soon but not today."

"Good for you!" Connie squeezed her hand.

Mrs. Sprague spared no expense at Reilly's Sweets and Pastries Shop: a jar of lemon curd and one of strawberry to go with Mrs. Woodward's scones, a crock of Devonshire cream and one of currant jam, chewy nougats, marzipan, and toffees to Annie's heart's content.

"We shall all have toothaches in the morning!" Mrs. Sprague laughed and the girls joined her, delighted with the conspiracy, the camaraderie.

Their arms were happily laden as they made their way down the cobbled walk. Briefly Annie thought, *Perhaps I'll cut a bouquet for Aunt Eleanor. Surely she must remember this is my sixteenth birthday. Owen's flowers will please her.*

Once they turned the corner, the day dimmed just slightly—a gray cloud passing.

"What is that smoke?" Mrs. Sprague asked.

"Where? I smell something foul but can't see where it's coming from." Connie wrinkled her nose.

Annie stopped and stared in the direction of Hargrave House, beyond the house. She narrowed her eyes, tried to comprehend what lay ahead. Her heart stopped. Her throat constricted and she gasped for air. *No. No. No!* Annie dropped her packages to the cobblestones without realizing what she'd done and began to run.

"Annie! Annie, wait!" Mrs. Sprague called after her.

"No—oh, don't let it be!" Connie whispered and, thrusting her load of packages into her mother's arms, tore down the street after Annie.

"Girls!" Mrs. Sprague cried.

But Annie could not stop. She stumbled as she ran. Her feet took on lead, and she felt as if her lifeblood drained through her heart and torso and limbs, through her feet and into the street below.

So heavy was the weight in Annie's chest that by the time she reached the rear garden gate of Hargrave House, she could not breathe.

The garden—the entire length and breadth—was plowed under: every tree and bulb and shrub and rose, every spike of lavender and trail of ivy, had been ripped from the ground and was in that moment piled onto a heaped and growing bonfire at the far end of the garden.

Orange flames roared high, a violent rending of the day. The stench of tar and kerosene poured into the flames spread a dark plume across a blackening sky as five muscled workmen threw her joys and dreams—from the most delicately carved trellis and intricately painted birdhouse to the lowliest flower—onto the roaring heap.

A rushing fire and wind whirled, as a tornado, through Annie's brain. Animal rage came from someplace beyond her ken—an intense keening from her bowels and heart and throat, from every muscle and sinew and nerve crawling within her.

She struggled and tore against Connie's strong, relentless arms—arms that tugged her from the ashes and mud she clung to. But Annie would not be moved. She screamed and wept and heaved in gulps until she could scream no more.

Connie and Mrs. Sprague pulled her again and again from the ground she would not leave, urging her to "let us take you home."

At last Annie stopped fighting.

Mrs. Sprague and Connie lifted her, one on each side.

And Annie glimpsed Aunt Eleanor, sitting on the high terrace, straight-backed, in her wheeled chair. A palsied smile pasted on her lips. She did not need to speak clearly—did not need to speak at all—to direct the inferno.

CHAPTER THIRTY-SIX

MICHAEL FELT THE URGENCY in the whispers and wrinkled brows that passed between Maggie and Daniel over the kitchen stove at noon. He'd not intended to eavesdrop, but their concerns were his concerns, their worries his worries. When he heard Annie's name slip from Maggie's lips, he lost all pretense of not listening.

"What's the matter with Annie?" Michael demanded, standing in his stocking feet by the kitchen door.

"What have you heard?" Daniel tried to look gruff but failed miserably.

"Only her name. But there's something not right. What's happened to Annie?" Michael demanded more fiercely.

Maggie placed her hand on Daniel's arm. "She's in hospital, in London." Michael felt the color drain from his face.

"A letter's come from Mr. Sprague, the family solicitor." Aunt Maggie twisted her apron ties round her finger. "It's that woman—Eleanor Hargrave—"

"Annie's aunt?"

Maggie lifted her chin. "I'll never call her that again. She does not deserve the title." Anger and pain warred across her features. "She's had all the Allen gardens torn from the ground—the ones Mackenzie dug by hand and those Owen added to all the years of his life, the gardens that have been Annie's healing with her love and daily tending all these months. She burned the gardens, that—" But Maggie stopped short, her mouth spread grim, and great salt tears streamed her cheeks. Daniel drew her to him and held her as she shook and sobbed. "It's all she had of Owen—of either of them! Dear God! I should have insisted she come, poor or not!"

Michael stood in the doorway, one muddied boot in his hand. He tried to picture the destruction of a garden the size Owen had described, a beautiful, breathtaking garden long developed and loved by each member of the family, one that held the variety Annie had sketched and so happily detailed in her long letters to Aunt Maggie.

And then he tried to picture Annie, what such theft and rapacious destruction would do to her heart. It was not hard to conjure the image. He felt her pain in the pit of his stomach—a pain not unlike what he'd felt at the stealing of Megan Marie when he was but a boy. He recognized the cruel, queer nature of this woman intent on crushing a tender heart; he'd seen its likeness in his uncle Tom's face, in the perverse pleasure he'd gained in tormenting, blaming, and beating Michael until the blood flowed from his mouth.

The room swayed before Michael at the memory. Fury swelled inside him for Annie's sake. He wanted—needed—to smash something; he wanted—needed—to rescue Annie. "How bad is she?"

It was a time before Maggie spoke. "Mrs. Sprague told her husband that Annie screamed for the longest time that day—the day they came upon the garden. It was Annie's sixteenth birthday." Maggie's voice broke.

Daniel finished because Maggie could not. "He said she's not spoken since. She refuses to eat. Simply lies there in hospital."

Michael could not stand the heat, the closeness of the kitchen. He was gone before the door slammed behind him.

Two hours later Michael sat in the potting shed, painstakingly printing small letters across tiny, handmade packets.

"What are you about, Michael?" Daniel pushed wide the door.

"I'm sending Annie a garden."

"A garden? Not the last of Owen's seeds?"

"They're her seeds if they belong to anyone. Owen would want her to have them."

"Aye, he would. But not this way." He laid his hand over Michael's.

Michael pulled back. "I knew you would say that. It's why I'm not asking you." Daniel's brows rose, but Michael pressed on. "Owen entrusted these seeds to my care. He made me promise to get Annie here—and what have I done? I've left her to the torment of that witch of a woman!"

"That's not your doing, Michael."

"It's my lack of doing!" Michael pounded the table with his fist. "I've failed her! Do you understand? I failed Annie!"

Daniel spoke low but with all the intensity of Michael's shout. "You've not failed her. You've been working yourself as hard as five grown men to bring her here, as have I to keep Maggie Allen afloat. It has not been the time for Annie to come—not yet.

"If you send the last of these seeds before we can reap the seeds from this year's crop, we stand to lose everything. You'll grow an old man before you make these gardens profitable—as I am now. And the truth is that if we don't catch up the mortgage, the bank will foreclose. If the gardens fail, what do you have to bring her to, Michael? Did you think of that?" Daniel grabbed the front of Michael's shirt with his fist and yanked him to his feet. "Or are you so intent on bludgeoning your way through your plan that you canna see the big picture—the possibility that looms just ahead for the first time for any of us?"

Michael glared in return.

Daniel reddened and dropped Michael's shirtfront as if his hand had been branded by a steaming poker. "You raise the ire in me, Michael Dunnagan."

Michael sat back, breathing heavily. "What can I do, then? I can't leave her there!"

Daniel pushed his hand through his thinning hair. "We'll do just what we've been doing—"

"But—"

"And once we reap the seeds from this year's harvest, we'll make packets for Annie, if you've a mind to—if you think she'll want them for next spring, if you think she'll be staying to plant a garden there." Daniel leaned forward until his finger poked Michael's chest to punctuate his words. "But if I were you, I'd build twelve gazebos and sell them at the best price you can fetch. Then I'd write her and tell her things are just what they are—hand to mouth—and ask her if she doesn't want to come anyway."

Michael blinked. "But the best schools—what about sending her to the best schools?"

"What difference will the name of a school make if her spirit is broken or if we lose this land? Don't send her seeds that her crazy, jealous aunt can steal away from her; give her the hope and friendship she needs to keep her heart beating!" Daniel backed toward the shed door. "You and Maggie talk and talk as if the lass needs a diamond tiara! If she were my woman, I'd get her here come hell or high water; then I'd love and labor for her every day I breathed." Daniel slammed the door.

Michael dropped his pen. The sheer tumble of words from Daniel's mouth toppled his nerve. Never would he have imagined Daniel McKenica in love with a woman, slaving for a woman. *But isn't that just what he does for Maggie Allen from the sun's rising to its setting?*

Absorbing such an idea took Michael a long time. But he urged his brain to concentrate on Annie, not the heart of Daniel McKenica laid bare. *How can I help Annie from so far away? How can I give her hope until I can bring her here?*

Michael sat in the shed, staring at the small seed packets until the mid-September sun crossed the sky. Annie had not answered his first letter. He knew from Aunt Maggie that she'd not wanted anything to do with him, and that was nearly a year ago. But that was also when she had the garden—the garden that brought her closer to Owen. Now there was only Owen's grave. *And what comfort is there in a grave and a stone? She needs a bit of Owen, a bit that no one else possesses—a bit that cannot be burned or taken from her, something to know and hold, to live inside her until she can do her own living again.* Michael hardly knew where such a thought came from. It seemed unlikely that it was his own. But he held it close as the sun set, and by the time the stars came out, he knew that it was so.

Michael struck a match to light the lantern. He tucked the seed packets into a storage hole of the chest. Someday he would give them to Annie, but not today.

In the kitchen he found a note from Daniel on the table saying that he'd sent Maggie to bed to nurse her sick headache and that she was not to be disturbed. Michael ladled a bowl of cabbage soup from the back of the stove—surely prepared by Daniel from its odd mix of flavors.

Daniel had taken to the front porch to smoke his pipe. Michael pondered the love between Daniel and Maggie—he'd always thought of them as brother and sister, but they knew and cared for each other as though one was part of the other's body. Michael wondered if it was always that way—and if Sean Allen, Maggie's husband, had been equal part of that union. He suspected that he had, and he wondered if they knew how rare such caring was—even he, with no experience in loving, knew it was rare.

Long past midnight, Michael sealed his letter. His eyes felt gritty, too heavy to read it all again. He'd written and rewritten it five times, hoping the grammar and spelling were sufficient, hoping it said what he meant it to say. It was long and, he feared, rambling. He'd bared his heart as plainly as Daniel McKenica had bared his. Michael ran his hand over the address and whispered a prayer to the Sweet Jesus—not for himself, but for the one person he had bound himself to in this life—then blew out the lamp.

CHAPTER THIRTY-SEVEN

MRS. SPRAGUE placed a basket of fragrant Banbury cakes from the widow Woodward on Annie's bedside table. She arranged Jamison's second bouquet of heather in a glass vase beside the cakes and laid the foreign-stamped, handmade envelope by its side. She pulled the drapes to partially block the late-afternoon sun from Annie's sensitive eyes.

The hospital had sent Annie home to the Spragues near the end of September, saying that she was not responding and they had no cure for melancholia. In the days that followed, Connie had coaxed just enough broth and tea between her friend's lips to keep her alive, but Annie lay, a gray and sullen shadow of her former self.

"What was the name of your handsome young gardener in the New World?" Connie teased. "Michael Dunnagan, was it not?"

Annie did not answer.

"At any rate, I see a letter has come from someone by that name. I'm thinking that if you're no longer interested in him—simply as a friend, of course—I might be. I've always fancied those lovely Irish brogues and silver tongues blessed with the blarney." Connie exaggerated the last word and danced the envelope before Annie's face.

The tea bell jingled in the hallway. Connie's lips turned down into a pout. "Oh, blast! I must wait until after tea to open this deliciously fat letter!" She made an elaborate showing of returning the envelope to Annie's bedside table. "But I warn you, Annie Allen, that if you have not opened and read it by the time I return, I shall be forced to read it for you—just to make certain the cad has addressed you appropriately."

Annie closed her eyes, too tired to endure Connie's teasing. She waited until she heard Connie's footsteps on the stairs before she opened them.

Annie glanced at the envelope. She saw his name and recognized Michael's handwriting from the letter she had returned last year.

She wondered why Michael had written again, after all this time. *Could it be that something has happened to Aunt Maggie? Oh, God, no! That would be too much!*

Ten minutes ticked by before Annie reached for the envelope. The letter felt truly thicker, by far, than the one she'd returned. Annie's curiosity, mingled with fear for Aunt Maggie's health, gave her the necessary strength to break the seal, to pull and lift the letter's pages.

Dear Miss Annie,

Aunt Maggie told me of the burning of your garden, and that your great sadness has stolen your reason for living.

Annie felt her cheeks warm at such presumption, but she continued reading.

Long ago I lost my parents and my little sister, the person most dear in my life. I could not help that my mam and da died of the fever. But I should have—could have—saved Megan Marie, if only I'd not let go of her hand. I failed her, and I cannot take it back.

I do not mean that you are responsible for the death of your gardens, Miss Annie, or that you could have seen such a thing on the horizon. What I mean to say is that, after Megan Marie was stolen away, I begged for a name, a way to find her, but to no avail. And when all hope was gone, for the longest time I knew no reason to go on either. I cradled no hope in my chest and no belief that there could be any good in the world—until I met your brother, Owen.

Owen opened to me a way of living beyond my ken. I've no way of knowing if I was the only stowaway aboard Titanic, *but I do know this: I deserved no grace, no seat in a lifeboat that fateful night. And none would have been given me, not that night nor for all my life to come, had it not been for the gift of Owen Allen.*

I wish I'd saved your brother. But I did not save him, could not see how to do it. Yet he saved me. And again, when I thought that dying was the only ending of the pain of his loss, Aunt Maggie and Daniel McKenica pushed wide that door to the possibility of a greater life.

I know your gardens meant more than soil and flowers and roses, Miss Annie. Your losing them was like losing Owen again, like my losing my sister—Megan Marie was all in all for me. Both end in despair. But there is a place beyond despair. Owen showed me—he showed me by how he lived and the way he worked to bring life to all around him.

Come to America, Miss Annie. I've no promises for a grand, high life here. It is hard work, from the first birdsong to the rising of the moon, but there is love and joy and life in this home of Aunt Maggie's. One person lives for the others, and we are not alone.

By next summer I will have earned enough for your passage and for a year's schooling for you, beyond the needs of Aunt Maggie and Daniel.

I'm saving you the last of Owen's original seeds—the ones he packaged with his own hands. You can plant them yourself in this New Jersey soil, just as Owen would have planted them.

There is something you should know—something about Owen that no one else knows: About a year after Titanic *foundered, I read a story in a newspaper—a paper that came as packing in a shipment of seedlings. The story was written about a man named Colonel Gracie, a survivor of* Titanic, *and his accounting of all that happened that night. I'm tucking the part I saved in this letter for you to hold and to keep. It is the only thing of value that I own, and now it is yours.*

Read it now, before you read more of this letter.

Annie picked up the yellowed and crudely torn paper that had fallen from the envelope onto her coverlet. Part of the story was circled in pencil. The writer of the story reported Colonel Gracie as having said, "A man swam alongside of our overturned Collapsible B and wanted to get on. We were already overloaded and in danger of foundering. Someone near his end cried out, 'Don't climb on; you'll swamp us.' And the man, a strong swimmer, pulled away, saying, 'It's all right, boys. Good luck and God bless you.'"

Annie's heart beat faster. She turned the paper over, but there was no more. She picked up Michael's letter.

Some believed the man was Captain Smith, the master of Titanic. *But I know better. It was just the sort of thing Owen would have said. He said it to me time and again, and to Lucy Snape, the lady he loved and hoped to marry. He said it to the woman he urged to rescue me in the lifeboat. He lived that same generosity each moment I knew him and surely in his last.*

Don't you see, Miss Annie? Owen not only prepared a life for us—for you in America—he went ahead to make a place for you and for me. He saved my doomed and wretched life and sent me to a home and a family. He showed us how to live a bigger story than our own, to keep going, keep living and encouraging others to live until our last breath.

Whenever you doubt that, whenever you despair of life, hold this paper in your hands, read Owen's last message to you and me, to the men in the midst of the sea, and know that he wishes us luck and life and the blessings of the Sweet Jesus.

I am waiting for you, Miss Annie. I promised Owen that I would do all I could to bring you to America, to bring you to this Allen home—your home. It is a vow I live to keep. Please get well. Please come home.

Michael Dunnagan

Annie held the newspaper clipping—a sign and message from Owen himself—close to her heart. The tears that had dried over a month ago came again, only this time softly—a healing summer rain.

She folded the clipping and letter, returned them to their envelope, and slid the envelope beneath her pillow. How odd, she thought, that such a gift—the clipping, the friendship, the real hope and promise of a future—should come from the one she'd so wanted to blame for losing Owen.

"God, forgive me," she whispered. "Thank You, Father. . . . Thank you, Michael."

For the first time since the burning, Annie slept peacefully, through the afternoon and all the long night. No one disturbed her.

When morning light swept the room, she placed her feet on the floor, stood, and washed her face. Even before the maid brought tea to her room, Annie had penned her first letter to Michael.

The next few days her steps were tentative, her naps long, and her cheeks pale. But Annie Allen had risen from the grave and determined, at last, to walk free, out of the dungeon of despair.

≋ CHAPTER THIRTY-EIGHT ≋

MICHAEL BUILT and sold his twelve gazebos in New Jersey—two a month—by working into the wee hours of each morning after long days in the fields.

Far away in London, Annie worked each day to regain her strength.

Letters flowed back and forth across the Atlantic with the regularity of the changing tides. Understanding and respect grew between the two young people whose early lives had been so different, but who were bound in their love for Owen and in the growing of the gardens they loved. If something besides friendship grew alongside, ever so tenderly and tentatively, neither owned, neither wrote, neither spoke of it.

By spring Annie knew she would accept Michael's offer to travel to America, though she told only the Spragues. But she determined not to arrive on the Allens' New Jersey doorstep poor or a burden to that hardworking family. She would finish her schooling and wait for her eighteenth birthday, at which time she would inherit Owen's legacy, then travel with enough money to arrive safely in good weather. She would have the resources to pay the mortgage and help build the business that Owen had dreamed of and for which Aunt Maggie, Daniel McKenica, and Michael had all loved and labored. When she turned twenty-one, Mr. Sprague would deposit and forward her inheritance held in trust. The plan, she was certain, would have pleased Owen. It pleased her.

Annie's waking thoughts were bound and bent to New Jersey. She chose not to write Michael or Aunt Maggie of her coming inheritance; she wanted that gift to be a surprise. But she did write that she would be ready to sail as soon after her eighteenth birthday as possible—just over a year away.

Even Mr. and Mrs. Sprague blessed her plan once they saw the bloom the letters from America brought to Annie's cheek. Connie admitted she would miss her but vowed her heart beat glad hopes for her friend.

In the meantime, Connie schemed to convince her father to take them all to Europe for Annie's seventeenth birthday. "We absolutely must get her out of London, Father. We do not want her reminded of last year! It must be something stupendous, a trip she will love and never forget!"

Mr. Sprague was not swayed by his only daughter's dramatic gestures or by her insistence that nothing less than a holiday in Europe could possibly distract Annie from last year's sorrow. He was confident of Annie's full recovery. But he had long planned to conduct his own daughter on a tour of the Continent before she wed—had, in fact, begun planning it. He believed Annie's companionship for Constance would make a nice addition to their group. And Eleanor Hargrave, though not his favorite client, had asked him to personally oversee the transfer of substantial funds to a distant relative in Germany—an annual transaction he usually relegated to a junior partner. Perhaps he could accomplish both purposes in one trip.

He considered a week in Paris, a week in the south of France, perhaps a week or two in Italy—certainly Rome—then a week in Berlin and another along the German coast—perhaps even take in Denmark before they returned. Six or seven weeks—he would certainly need to return to his firm's offices by then. July and August would be the best time to travel, he believed; in addition to the prospects of pleasant weather, they could celebrate Annie's birthday and take advantage of the bank holiday.

Mr. Sprague took note of a minor newspaper article published at the end of June concerning the assassination of the archduke Franz Ferdinand and his wife, Sophie, in Sarajevo. It didn't trouble him unduly; he considered the Balkan states a continual tempest in a teapot that had little to do with the empire, no matter their close political connections.

"Still," he mused to himself, "it may be the better part of wisdom to spend our holiday before that web of related European monarchs stir their simmering pot of resentments."

Annie and the Spragues sailed from Dover on 14 July. Annie penned a letter to Michael, feeling a bit selfish to write of such an extravagant trip when they were working so very hard, partly for her benefit, but she felt her New Jersey family would be glad for her.

Michael always had a way of cheering her on, though Annie thought he was rather more protective than his place allowed. Still, there was something in his concern she enjoyed—from a distance. *He isn't Owen, after all, to think he has any say about my life. He's not my brother by any means,* she thought, and something about that thought pleased her.

She wrote:

The North Sea is lovely and lay fairly calm our day of sailing. I confess to having been afraid. I have tried very hard not to show it, for the kindness of Mr. and Mrs. Sprague in inviting me. Still, I could not help but think of all that you and Owen and those hundreds of poor souls faced out on the Atlantic two years ago. But this was a journey made in daylight and good weather; for that I am thankful. I do hope this experience will help me grow braver before sailing to America. Mr. Sprague says that travel broadens the mind and fortifies the soul. I hope to prove him true.

We sailed up the mouth of the Elbe River until we landed in Hamburg. Such lovely painted window boxes bursting with flowers—everywhere! How the Germans love color—in their flowers, certainly, but even in the painting of their houses. Each garden is meticulous—not a weed to be seen! I do believe you could sift their soil between your fingers and watch it fly away. Such beauty makes me long for Owen and Father's gardens at Hargrave House—and mine.

Truly, I must push those memories from my brain or I am consumed with bitterness toward Aunt Eleanor. I must not allow memories of her meanness to spoil this opportunity. She has spoiled so much already.

We took tea on land the second afternoon—only they call it "coffee"—the first coffee I have ever tasted. It is rather more bitter than tea. But perhaps you know that. I hear they fancy coffee in America.

In Germany there is no such thing as crumpets or Banbury cakes. They prefer gigantic cakes with mounds of whipping cream and syrupy fruit tarts and flans. Their noon meal is rich in sausages and hearty black and brown breads—more root vegetables and not so many greens as we grow in England. I do not think I could sustain such a diet for long, but eating is quite as much an adventure for the tongue as touring is for the soul!

You will notice, of course, that I am beginning at the end of our planned trip. Mr. Sprague changed our itinerary at the last moment. He said the change is merely a precaution due to the political climate. Despite the sensationalists, none of us believes there will truly be a war. The European powers will surely resolve their differences peacefully. This is, after all, the twentieth century.

I shall write again when we reach the capital.

Please give my love to Aunt Maggie, and let me know how your gardens grow.

Respectfully yours,
Annie

❧ ❧

Near the end of the second week, they entered Berlin. Mr. and Mrs. Sprague were pleased with the well-appointed rooms they were able to secure on short notice. They had no trouble procuring seats for the foremost German opera of the season.

"It is as though the city is emptying of tourists, Edwin, and the streets are filling with locals. You do not imagine there is something we don't know, do you?"

Mr. Sprague assured his wife that things were quite as they should be, though when alone he did his best to ascertain daily the political news. He was not pleased with the strengthening of the alliance between Austria-Hungary and Germany. He registered the furtive glances among shopkeepers, the growing groups of men clustered outside the nearest telegraph and newspaper offices, and the squared shoulders of the daily-growing number of military uniforms in the streets. He completed

Eleanor Hargrave's financial transaction on the second morning, before the ladies had risen for the day, and was relieved to wash his hands of the matter.

The little party of tourists kept to their schedule, but after two days of touring in the summer heat, each was keenly aware of the growing and anxious crowds in the streets, especially those surrounding government buildings. The cafés along Unter den Linden and just outside the Tiergarten were jam-packed, morning to night, with noisy natives, tense and argumentative as if waiting for a gloved challenge to be thrown upon the ground. Men shifted from foot to foot, impatiently waiting at newsstands for the next delivery, quick to drop their coins, then hustle away, devouring the latest paper.

Mr. Sprague regretted that he spoke so little German—enough to order a proper meal and exchange pleasantries on the stairs, at best. He'd never felt so in need of a newspaper written by locals yet so unable to read one.

"There is a change in our itinerary, ladies. We shall make our way to Paris tomorrow morning," he said after being knocked squarely in the shoulder by a rude passerby. "I cannot ascertain precisely what is about to happen, but I must see you ladies safely away."

"But, Father!" Connie said. "We've still so much to see and do here! Tomorrow is Sunday—not so many trains will be running. Truly, I think the tension is simply their excitable German temperament—so much life!"

"I quite agree with you, Edwin. We shall be packed and ready to leave immediately after breakfast." Mrs. Sprague caught her husband's eye and nodded approvingly.

But the next morning the atmosphere in the hotel was charged with a new electricity. Hotel patrons and employees alike spoke rapidly. Annie's arms prickled as she sensed cold glances directed their way, though she could not imagine why anyone would think ill of them.

"There's a rumor," a bold American journalist confided to Mr. Sprague from the table behind them, "that the kaiser's not gone to the Hohenzollern for the holiday, as planned. He's still in Berlin, waiting for some word from Austria—this thing could blow wide open, if you catch my meaning." He raised his brows sarcastically. "I guess even royal yachts must wait for matters of state."

Annie could not hear what more was said, for Mr. Sprague turned his back to the women and spoke quietly with the journalist for some minutes. When he turned again, Annie knew something was dreadfully wrong—never had she seen him so pale nor so agitated.

Moments later the hotel waiter sloshed steaming coffee across Mrs. Sprague's serviette, scalding her fingers. *"Entschuldigen Sie, bitte!"* He bowed, but a smirk belied his apology, no matter that tears sprang to a startled Mrs. Sprague's eyes.

Mr. Sprague stood, furious beyond the ability to speak, and gently wrapped his wife's reddened hand in a water-soaked serviette. Though Connie's and Annie's mouths were still crammed with toast points, he threw several coins to the table, not waiting for the bill, and drew his family away. "Pack your hand luggage, ladies. I shall send the bellman for our trunks in ten minutes."

"But, Father—" Connie began.

Mr. Sprague took his daughter firmly by the arm and ushered their small group to the door. "Not another word, Constance," he insisted quietly, more severely than Annie had ever heard him speak. "Whatever you value most, you must wear on your person beneath your clothing—jewelry, money, whatever that might be."

Connie's eyes grew wide; Annie knew her own stood as mirrored images.

"Yes, Father," Connie replied. Never had Annie heard her friend so meek.

By the time the four left their hotel, the press of the growing crowd intently combing the streets of Berlin nearly forced the travelers apart. Groups of men and women shouted; opposing groups shouted urgently in return. But Annie could not tell what they were saying. She knew only that her party was fortunate to procure a carriage.

The railway station overflowed with passengers waiting for trains that had not come or ran late. Would-be passengers waved paper money, demanding to purchase tickets from sellers who shrugged helplessly and closed their stalls, clearly having no more tickets to sell at any price. Hustlers offered tickets for five times their price.

The air was punctuated by the piercing whistles of trains and grayed by great clouds of steam continually released from the iron horses begging to bolt from their gates.

Mr. Sprague dickered with two hustlers alternately in excellent French and pitiable German. "We shall not be able to sit together," he announced when he rejoined the ladies, pulling tickets from his vest pocket. The lines in his forehead deepened. "I was unable to procure a sleeper. We shall sit through the night."

"You take charge of Annie, Edwin. Constance and I will sit together."

"There are three tickets and one, Betty—seated in separate compartments of the train. I was fortunate to get them. You must keep the girls with you. Do not leave the train until Paris—it is a direct route. No matter what happens, do not leave the train." He punctuated each word.

"Oh, Edwin!"

Annie found the rising tension and display of affection between Mr. and Mrs. Sprague unnerving. She was keenly aware that except for her, the Spragues would have been able to sit together. But she didn't have the courage to offer her seat to Mr. Sprague.

"I will find you at the train depot in Paris." Mr. Sprague spoke quietly and then, even lower, to his wife, "Wait for me there only until you can get a train to Calais. If we are separated, you must use the gold in the lining of—the gold you have—to get the three of you out of Germany and home to Britain, by whatever means you can."

"Father?" For the first time Connie looked truly worried.

"Things are falling apart here. Our paper currency will be useless on the Continent. We must get home—and right away. Once Germany joins forces with Austria, France will certainly mobilize against them— and Belgium will be caught in their midst. You know what that means for England. Do not speak to anyone unless it is imperative. Our British accents are not an asset at the moment." Mr. Sprague kissed his wife and held his daughter close. He hugged Annie and conducted them safely to their seats, then stowed their hand luggage above their heads. Mr. Sprague cradled his wife's injured hand once again, stroked Connie's cheek, and smiled feebly at Annie. He climbed down and was gone.

Mrs. Sprague sat rigid against her seat, her chin lifted, her veil lowered, and stared straight ahead. Connie followed her example, as best she could. But Annie, suddenly frantic to call him back, leaned from the window, searching the crowd for Mr. Sprague's hat, desperate to keep it in view as long as possible. She watched him weave through the growing number of uniforms and mass of people, until he disappeared in the long line of cars.

CHAPTER THIRTY-NINE

CURIOUS, MICHAEL WATCHED as Mr. Hook, deacon and local telegraph operator, whispered a full three minutes into the ear of Reverend Tenney, delaying the Wednesday-evening prayer service in Swainton's Asbury Meeting House.

Half the congregation leaned forward in their seats. When his words ran out, Mr. Hook handed a telegram to the reverend and sat, red faced, in his accustomed pew.

Reverend Tenney stood longer than usual, longer by far than it would have taken him to read any normal telegram. At last he took the pulpit, gripped its sides, and searched the eyes of his congregation. He seemed about to speak but bowed his head.

Whispered questions spread through the pews of the small church. Mrs. Hook, the organist, coughed, then began to play strains of the opening hymn, "A Mighty Fortress Is Our God."

By the time the organ finished its call to worship, it appeared that Reverend Tenney had regained his composure. He straightened and held the paper in midair. "Mr. Hook has delivered a telegram from one of our parishioners visiting New York." He hesitated. "It says that the New York papers report Austria-Hungary has declared themselves at war with Serbia."

Murmurs of disbelief fluttered through the congregation.

"War?"

"Serbia's no more than a spot on the map! They'll run right over her!"

"But war? What does it mean?"

The minister raised his hand again for order. "It means we must pray—we must all pray very hard for the leaders of these countries, that God will grant them wisdom and discernment and mercy."

"Tell 'em the rest—the worst, Reverend!" Mr. Hook called from his pew.

The reverend's lips formed a grim line; he waited for silence in the church. "It appears that the nations of Europe are mobilizing, supplying their armies, and moving them into position near their borders—most notably Germany, Belgium, and France."

"All the countries?" The words passed from lips to lips.

"Those closest to Germany's borders in particular," the reverend answered.

"But my Harry's in Belgium," a woman whimpered.

"My sister and her family still live in Alsace," another whispered. "That's just between. What can they be thinking?"

Reverend Tenney spoke again. "This telegram quotes excerpts from a newspaper article stating that Germany has been building her military for quite some time and that her navy intends to rival that of Britain." He searched the eyes of his congregation once more as if wanting to pour understanding into them. "We must wait—and pray for reason and peace."

Maggie Allen sat stone faced and pale between Michael and Daniel McKenica. Daniel reached for her hand.

Michael's heart constricted in the walls of his chest. "Annie." *Annie's in Germany.*

≋ CHAPTER FORTY ≋

PORTERS AND CONDUCTORS pushed their way through the crowded train, punching tickets, stowing bags and kits above and beneath every available seat, in every conceivable crevice, and shouting orders that neither Annie, Connie, nor Mrs. Sprague understood. The women kept their tickets readily available but alternately pretended to sleep or read so they would not be compelled to communicate with other passengers and forced to display either their nationality or their near ignorance of the language.

The hours stretched long into the humid night and crept through the next hot morning. The passenger train stopped innumerable times, or so it seemed to Annie, to take on civilians as well as more and more men in uniform. She'd never ridden a train so packed or with as many stops.

Each time a train carrying military personnel approached, the passenger train was forced onto the nearest side track to wait until the military train had passed—sometimes twenty minutes, sometimes as long as an hour. And each time, no matter how long the delay, the Germans—military and civilians alike—packed aboard the passenger train cheered and hurrahed the men of their passing army.

After the third such detour, Mrs. Sprague sighed so loudly Connie gently elbowed her. "Mother, we must not draw attention to ourselves."

Annie turned her face to the window, pretending not to notice.

When at last she could wait no longer, Annie pulled Connie from her seat and the girls made their way to the water closet, excusing themselves in feeble German through the stifling corridor packed with soldiers in gray-green uniforms, toe to heel, and those who sat side by side, their kits stashed between their legs.

Some soldiers stepped aside for the young women to pass, either averting their gazes or nodding respectfully, but a few eyed Connie and Annie in ways Annie had never been eyed by a man. She felt her cheeks flame; how she wished she were a little child, able to climb into Mrs. Sprague's lap and hide her face.

Back in her seat, Annie massaged her throat and knew her traveling companions must be as dry and parched as she.

"I'm dying for a drink to break this heat!" Connie commiserated. Mrs. Sprague nodded in sympathy.

But none of the ladies ventured to the dining car to purchase a cup of tea or a glass of lemonade.

By the time they neared the French border, Annie had lost track of the names of the towns they'd passed.

"If only your father could have stayed with us," Mrs. Sprague whispered.

"Father's resourceful," Connie responded, but Annie heard no confidence in her assertion. "He promised to meet us in Paris."

"If this train arrives in Paris! I cannot imagine these German soldiers are headed directly for the capital city of France!" Mrs. Sprague seemed to alarm herself with those words and immediately took hold. "All will come about as it should. We must keep our wits and our peace within."

It was sound advice, and Annie might have taken it to heart—if the train had not lurched suddenly to a grinding stop.

Connie lowered the window, leaning as far out as she could, to see around the bend in the track. "They're emptying the train."

"We cannot have arrived in Paris yet—this is nothing like it!" Mrs. Sprague exclaimed.

Connie straightened her hat. "No, Mother. I don't know where we are, except in the middle of the countryside."

Soldiers in full uniform, their firearms and kits tightly stowed, ordered civilians from the train, communicating clearly, even though the women could understand few of the words.

Mrs. Sprague took charge. "Gather your things, girls, before they reach us. Out—out the door, quickly."

Annie tripped, stumbling to her knees as she climbed down from the train. Stones by the track tore through her stocking and gravel grazed her hand. The moment she stood, she sensed the wet blood trickle from her scraped knee.

"Move! Move along!" a boy soldier, very near her age, shouted in broken English from behind her.

Flustered, Annie dropped her bag and bent quickly to retrieve it, but the soldier kicked it sharply away with the toe of his polished and heeled boot, barely missing her hand.

Connie jerked Annie to her feet, pulling her away. "Leave it! It doesn't matter!"

"But . . . our luggage?"

"They do not seem interested in returning trunks, Annie. Keep going!"

For the next hour the three travelers walked quickly beside the tracks, placing one foot in front of the other, careful not to stumble or dawdle, never daring to look back. They knew the German soldiers followed them, making sure the discharged passengers continued their straight and narrow march to the French border—in sight at last.

"Where do you think Father is?" Connie whispered.

"Your father will find a way; he will find us," Mrs. Sprague insisted.

"He wasn't on the train, was he?" Annie worried.

"I hope he was, my dear. With all my heart, I hope he was."

CHAPTER FORTY-ONE

FOR THE THREE REMAINING WEEKS of August, Maggie burned the morning porridge, and for those three weeks Michael did not notice; Daniel did not care. No word came from Annie—a sharp break in her twice-weekly cycle of letters to Michael or Maggie or both.

News from Germany alternately boasted of and justified its grim rape of Belgium and invasion of France in the battles of Lorraine, Ardennes, the Sambre, Le Cateau, and Guise—halting within thirty miles of Paris.

Michael swore like his uncle Tom the night his hammer pounded his thumb instead of the nail he had intended on the gazebo railing. When he smashed his thumb a second time within the hour, he not only swore but kicked the half-finished gazebo in two, then in quarters and eighths—he kicked and smashed until he had shattered a full week's work.

"You'll not bring the mail by laying low your work, Michael." Daniel stood in the dim lamplight of the barn.

"It's the only honest piece of work I've done these twenty-one days." Michael threw the hammer aside, spent at last, and slumped against the barn's supporting beam.

"Aye," Daniel sighed. "It's a hard thing, not knowing. But we can't give up hope. The best you can do for Annie is to build these gazebos; work your heart out to bring her here."

"The best thing I can do for Annie is to go to England and join up! The best thing I can do for Annie is to kill the Huns that started this idiotic war and find her!" Michael fairly screamed. "I've got to find her!"

"I understand your heart's as splintered as this gazebo you've smashed.

I understand that all the rage of the French army is nothing to compare with what's grinding in your bones. But joining up will keep you in your regiment, not out searching for Annie. And getting yourself killed will not save Annie."

"Neither will standing here like the coward that I am." Michael spoke low.

"It's not cowardly to build a life for the ones we love. If the time comes that America calls her own to go, that will be different. But if you go to England now and join with them—"

"Or Canada—I could go to Canada." Michael stood, the light of that new idea flashing through his mind.

"Canada, England, Ireland—it won't matter! You'll lose your hopes of American citizenship if you run off to join through another country. And then you'd be an ocean apart from Annie for years and years! You must wait until America calls—and she will, surely, when—"

"When President Wilson stops sleeping at the helm!"

"When he knows he has the support of the people behind him. German Americans are leaving by droves to join the kaiser's army—I heard it from Tom Hook himself, just in from Philadelphia. But it can't last. The tide will turn. If Germany is hell-bent to rule the world, she'll not leave America out of the fray forever. And when she strikes, the president will be forced to declare war."

Michael stood. "I can't wait for that, Daniel! I can't leave Annie stranded in Europe alone. I'll not fail her. I did not act in time for . . . for my own sister when she needed me, and . . . and then it was too late. I may already be too late for Annie, but I'll not risk her a minute longer!"

Michael was grateful when Daniel stepped back, when he held up his hand in a sign that he would say no more, and walked out.

He packed his bag at first light, determined to catch an afternoon train and make his way to New York. He knew how to stow away if necessary—he'd surely done it before—and though he'd vowed he would never sail again, he determined to do exactly that.

Maggie had just tucked her Bible into the corner of his bag when Daniel returned from the post office, a letter in hand.

Dear Aunt Maggie,

By now you must have heard the frightful news from this side of the world.

As you might have surmised, the Spragues and I arrived in Berlin shortly before the kaiser declared war against Serbia. We had hoped—indeed, tried—to escape the madness and make our way to Paris by train, but the railways were bombarded by like-minded tourists frantic to leave the country. The entire city, it seemed, had taken to the streets—a veritable mob awaiting the kaiser's proclamation.

Miraculously, Mr. Sprague purchased tickets, but we were separated from him at the last possible moment. Our train—painstakingly slow—neared but never crossed the German-French border. Trains in both countries were commandeered, used for soldiers bound for their front lines.

Mrs. Sprague, Connie, and I have returned to London after a fortnight spent trudging our way northwestward through the rough and mucky fields of France—and I mean, quite literally, "the fields."

Connie tried to keep our hearts light by saying adventurers would pay a hundred pounds for such an experience—sleeping in fields and barns and haymows. But we were a weary, footsore, miserable group for both the terror of the war and not knowing what had become of Mr. Sprague.

Still, the French people were generous in every way, even when they had little to share—farmers, on occasion, offered us rides in hay carts drawn by their stalwart workhorses, and kindly women took pity on our blistered feet, driving us short distances in their little wagons bound for market. I never before knew the intense pleasures of cool well water and humble brown bread. We sailed, at last, from Calais to Dover. I blessed those white cliffs as we neared home. We reached London two days ago and have slept straight through until this morning. How very precious and rare are a clean bed, a hot meal, and a cup of tea laced with sugar!

Mr. Sprague telegraphed yesterday that he is in Le Havre and hopes to return to England within the week. Sailing schedules and timetables mean nothing in the midst of this chaos, but we are wonderfully relieved to know that he is safe and well. As you can imagine, it has been an anxious time for Mrs. Sprague, though I fear there is worse to come for everyone.

The world has gone mad, and I cannot imagine where this might end. Men and boys of all ages are queuing at the recruitment offices, eager, they boast, to "clean the kaiser's clock." They shout that they will "hammer the Hun" and return home before the leaves fall.

Well, September hovers at the door, and I read daily of Germany's advance through little Belgium and poor France. Russia has invaded East Prussia, and Austria-Hungary has invaded Russian Poland.

The leaves are ready to turn, and the girls of the Red Cross came yesterday to talk of knitting mufflers for our boys in arms, just in case. We're all anxious to do something useful, and of course nothing is.

Please give my regards to Mr. McKenica and Michael. Write to me, dearest Aunt Maggie, of gardens and harvests and birds migrating sanely through their seasons.

All my love,
Annie

"Will you wait, then?" Maggie asked softly as Michael finished reading the letter. "Wait and see. Annie is safe."

"Safe for now. What if Germany invades England? It's just over the North Sea."

"Aye," Daniel said. "I think Annie should come now—to America."

"But wouldn't it be safer to wait until this is over? This can't last long." Maggie's brow wrinkled more. "Surely they'll come to their senses!"

Daniel shook his head. "Germany's built her military for years, waiting for such an opportunity. There'll be no holding her back. She's joined with Austria and struck her blow. She will surely plow ahead."

"Until we stop her!" Michael set the letter on the table. "Until we all stand up and say, 'No more!'"

"But it doesn't have to be you, Michael," Maggie pleaded.

"It has to be all of us, Maggie," Daniel answered for him. "We must stand as one, or one by one, the nations will fall to the kaiser."

"Then you agree I should go?" Michael dared to hope.

"I would go myself if they'd take me. It's not what I want, but it's right—or will be when the time comes . . . when President Wilson declares war."

"But—"

"Let us both wait until then, Michael. And let us send for Annie now."

Michael hesitated, then nodded. It was decided; Annie coming to safety and to America was what he wanted.

But once Annie came, could he—would he—enlist should President Wilson finally call?

≋ CHAPTER FORTY-TWO ≋

In late September Annie and Connie passed their Red Cross examinations with flying colors and earned their First Aid Certificates. By mid-December they had each earned their Home Nursing Certificates, as had every girl of similar station in their circle.

"We can officially brew beef tea and bandage broken limbs!" Connie crowed. "In addition to keeping current on all the London gossip."

"And poach eggs," Annie amended with a pretentious twinkle. "You mustn't forget that we are now fully capable of poaching eggs, changing and smoothing bed linens, and dressing all sorts of cuts and scrapes."

"And that is quite enough for young ladies to know of such things." Mrs. Sprague looked over her spectacles at the girls as she knit.

"No, Mother, actually . . . it is not," Connie responded.

Mr. Sprague lifted his eyes from his newspaper and Mrs. Sprague dropped her knitting, so rare was a maternal contradiction from their outspoken daughter.

"Constance?" Mr. Sprague inquired, the shade of a warning in his question.

"I am sorry, Mother—truly. It is just that the training we've received in our weekly Red Cross meetings is not enough—not enough for proper nursing."

"Nursing?" Mrs. Sprague spoke the word as if she could not comprehend its meaning.

Annie bit her lip and held her breath. She knew Connie's plans, and she knew the Spragues would not approve.

"Yes, I have spoken with Matron about further training. I shall be twenty-three February next—the required age to apply for overseas service through the Voluntary Aid Detachment. I want—I intend—to go to the front."

"That is absurd!" Mrs. Sprague retorted, picking up her knitting as though the juvenile discussion was closed. "Edwin! You will not allow it!"

Mr. Sprague pulled his spectacles from his nose and studied his daughter closely. "I certainly hope the war will be over before 1916! In any case, I do not wish you to go, Constance."

"But, Father—"

Mr. Sprague held up his hand for silence, interrupting his daughter's tirade before it began. "I said that I do not wish you to go. I did not say, however, that I would forbid it."

"Edwin!" Mrs. Sprague tried to laugh. "It is out of the question! She could be killed."

"We could all be killed, Mother—sitting in our drawing rooms. The Germans are racing the French and Belgians to the North Sea and the channel now by way of their trenches. The moment they cross, we might all be eating sausages and sauerkraut for the rest of our lives." And then, quietly but firmly, "If I were a boy, you would not flinch."

"But you are not; you are our daughter!"

"Is not equal treatment between men and women what we seek when we seek the vote?"

"Not this! Not in war!"

"I'll not be fighting; I shall be nursing our own British soldiers."

"You cannot let her go, Edwin. I forbid it!"

"I shall be twenty-two in February, Mother. After training, I intend to volunteer in the hospitals here in London if they will have me—and I think they will. The number of casualties is astonishing, and the hospitals are overflowing. I shall apply for foreign service as soon as they allow. I shan't need your permission."

Mrs. Sprague looked as if she might burst. "Constance!"

"Ladies," Mr. Sprague intervened.

"Father—you do understand, don't you? It is my patriotic duty! The duty of our family."

"I understand your point of view, Constance. I respect and commend your call to duty and charity, though I must ask if it is daring and adventure you crave in—"

"Father!"

"My apologies," he sighed and bowed his head wearily. "Tell me about the training."

The training details Connie offered were truthful and straightforward, but Annie knew her friend couched them in terms as delicate as possible, for her mother's sake. Even so, the reality of nursing, bathing, and caring intimately for dirty, wounded, traumatized men was not lost on Mrs. Sprague's imagination; it was etched in her face.

"Edwin, please . . ." Mrs. Sprague looked as though she might weep.

"The war may be over in twelve months, Betty. And Constance is correct; she does not need our permission."

Connie raised her chin. "Thank you."

"But I do ask you to consider a proposition."

"Terms, Father, as in a legal contract?" Connie half smiled.

"Rather." Her father returned the smile. "Take the training in the new year—take all the training you need. Then nurse here in London for two years. Our hospitals are desperate for nursing volunteers."

"Two years! But—"

Mr. Sprague held up his hand again. "If after those two years you are still determined to go abroad, your mother and I will not stand in your way. I will give you my blessing."

"One year," Connie countered. "The necessary training, and if I pass the examinations, one year of nursing in London."

Mr. Sprague studied his daughter. "Before you apply for an overseas position."

Connie hesitated only briefly before accepting the offer. "One year of nursing in London before I apply for an overseas position."

They shook hands.

Mrs. Sprague looked about to erupt, but Mr. Sprague placed his hand on her forearm. "It stands at least a year and a half away, my dear. We shall see what transpires in that time."

"And what about me?" Annie softly raised her question, kneading her thumb into her opposite hand.

The Spragues turned as one toward Annie. They seemed to have forgotten her.

"You, my dear?" Mr. Sprague asked.

"Yes, may I take the training as well?" Annie pushed back her shoulders and lifted her head a little higher, trying her best to look confident, steady, mature.

"But you are only seventeen!" Mrs. Sprague gasped.

"It is the minimum age required for VAD training. But it doesn't matter; they all think I'm the same age as Connie—as Constance."

"Why?" Mr. Sprague asked. "You are leaving for America in August. Your family is expecting you."

"Yes," Annie replied. "But what if the war is not over by then?"

"It must be!" Mrs. Sprague all but jumped from her chair.

"I pray that it is. I pray that everyone comes home safely and that I can go to America and spend my life puttering in Allen's Run Gardens and helping Aunt Maggie design wreaths and dry herbs for sale, as planned. But what if it is not? What if this war goes on and on? The need for nurses will surely grow." Annie hesitated. "I don't imagine that I would apply for foreign service." She glanced apologetically at Connie. "Our experience in France was more than I am eager to repeat, and I know that was nothing to compare with what France must be now.

"If the war ends before I'm needed, I shall simply be better trained to make my way in the world. But if it doesn't end, and if I am needed, I would be trained to volunteer here in London."

Annie leaned forward. "I do not want to sit inside the house and wait. Because of Aunt Eleanor, I have gone an entire year without my gardens. I'll not be allowed to plan for and work in them this spring, and I cannot focus on what I do not have. What else would I do for nearly a year?"

"Have you forgotten your studies, my dear?" Mrs. Sprague's patience was wearing thin.

"Mother, she has no tutor," Connie interrupted. "Mr. Lounsbury has enlisted. He leaves for training next week. He told me as I passed him this morning, on my way to post office, just as he came out of the recruitment office."

"But he has a contract!" Mrs. Sprague sputtered.

"He had to go—all the men are going." Connie looked away. "He said he's planning to speak with you tomorrow, Father." And then more quietly, "He'd been given the white feather."

Annie gasped. "You did not tell me that! Mr. Lounsbury is no coward!"

Mr. Sprague sighed and massaged the bridge of his nose as though a headache lodged there. "No, he is no coward. Contract or no, he must do his duty for God and king. We all must."

Mrs. Sprague paled and looked for all the world to Annie as if she had been plopped down into a foreign country, right in the midst of her own drawing room. She placed her knitting squarely in her bag, rose, and walked from the room without saying good night.

※ ※

Annie had not imagined that convincing Mr. Sprague would be so easy. An hour later, as the girls prepared for bed, she congratulated Connie on her excellent speech and powers of persuasion.

Connie threw her hairbrush onto the dressing table. "It was too easy. Father would not have given in so quickly were he not wrestling with the matter himself."

"What do you mean?" Annie felt a prick up her spine, fearing she knew exactly what Connie meant. "He's too old to fight—too old to be conscripted! They would not allow him to enlist, would they?"

"If the war goes on too long, they may be forced to extend the ages of conscription. And even if that does not reach Father's age . . ." Connie shrugged, a frown pursing her lips. "I know Father; he will find a way to do something. I'm simply not certain what he has in mind. But I do know that Mother is not going to like it."

CHAPTER FORTY-THREE

HEADLINES OF THE WAR in Europe and the list of countries that had now joined the fray tainted Michael's third Michaelmas birthday with Aunt Maggie and Daniel but strengthened his hope for Annie's early arrival in New Jersey.

Daniel's suggestion made perfect sense to Michael—Annie should come now, before the war spread across the channel, before England found herself at the kaiser's mercy.

When Annie blatantly disagreed, Michael threw her letter to the table and his hands in the air. *How can I protect Annie when she doesn't think she needs my protection, when she thinks my plan a poor one, when she chooses to stick to her own timetable?*

Even Daniel shook his head.

But Maggie clucked her tongue. "It makes perfect sense for Annie to finish her training before she comes! You men think you can work out every situation with your sage advice and your snap decisions. You're spoiled for real women—the both of you—and I'm to blame! You've foolishly taken my good nature for granted. Not all women will let you go stomping your bluster about and having your way so freely."

Michael had no idea what she meant. But he and Daniel hustled out the back door.

Whatever the reason—and Michael dared not ask—Maggie spent less time in the kitchen fussing over their meals, less time darning their socks or sitting by the parlor fire through the evenings. She took to moonlit walks and spent more time at the church through the long autumn.

"What is she doing over there every evening?" Michael wanted to know.

"I think she's in the cemetery, talkin' things over with Sean." Daniel puffed on his pipe.

"But . . . how . . . ?"

"That's one of the ways of women you need to understand—when they've something on their minds, they must talk it out, whether anyone be listening or no."

"What do you suppose she's talkin' over?" Michael was not interested in Maggie changing. He liked her fine, just the way she was, though he'd like to see the frequent sadness leave her eyes.

"Maybe about what she should do next, or what she should do with two old bachelors living under her roof."

"You don't think she's fixin' to pitch us, do you?" That had never occurred to Michael.

"Maybe she's thinking of marrying and what she'd do with us if she did." Daniel tamped his pipe. "We'd be a mite in the way of a new man."

"Why would she be thinking of marrying?"

Daniel shrugged. "It's more'n two years since Sean died. Maggie's a good woman—a fine-looking woman yet and young enough."

"She's old!" Michael wanted to shout some sense to someone—anyone who might listen.

Daniel stiffened and puffed. "She's not old, Michael. She's a rare bird—a heart of gold, a head for business, and a sweet companion. She'd make a fine wife for any man."

Michael stared at Daniel as if he didn't know him.

Daniel stopped rocking, grunted, then took himself down the steps, out to the street, and headed toward the church.

Michael was only mildly surprised when Daniel began following Maggie out the door and down the lane after supper during late October, through November and most of December.

He wondered how long Daniel had loved Maggie—or known he loved her, for surely he did. Michael saw it in the way Daniel rose early and built the fire in the cookstove each morning before Maggie made her way to the kitchen, in the way he served her favorite cuts of meat or fish or fowl as he carved at the table, and when he fished the choicest pieces of stew from the pot to set on her plate. He saw it in the way Daniel pulled the buggy close to the overhang of the porch after rainy-day rides so Maggie would not have to run through the downpour, and the tender way he helped her up the steps to the house or the church or the post office.

But does Aunt Maggie love Daniel? Michael wondered. *Surely they're longtime friends. But they seem so natural, so comfortable together. Has Aunt Maggie seen Daniel as a friend for so long that she cannot imagine him as a man to share her bed?* Michael felt his own neck flame at such a question. Still, he wondered.

On the twenty-third of December, Michael, at Maggie's instigation and Daniel's direction, cut one of the small evergreens from Annie's Evergreen Garden and shaved its uneven branches.

Tall enough to stand proudly on the parlor table, the little tree filled the room with Christmas fragrance. Maggie searched the drawers for candles as Daniel and Michael clamped small tin candleholders and wired glittering pinecones and sweet gum balls to the tree's branches.

When they'd placed a punched tin star on top of the tree and lit the candles in the darkened room, the three stood back.

"Oh, it's lovely, isn't it? Thank you, gentlemen!" Aunt Maggie clasped her hands with the delight of a child, and instantly Michael remembered Megan Marie. He'd not thought of her for weeks, and he wondered how that could be.

"Aye," Daniel said. "She is lovely."

Michael noticed Daniel wasn't looking at the tree at all, but at Maggie. And Michael had to agree; she looked something like an angel, fresh in the yellow glow of the tree lights.

Maggie caught the twinkle in Daniel's eye and blushed. She laughed, then looked away, but not before the candlelight danced between them.

On Christmas Eve, Maggie cooked a goose, roasted apples and onions, and concocted a savory sage-and-onion stuffing with the magic of herbs dried from last summer's garden. Parsnips, potatoes, squash, and the summer's canned green beans rounded out the meal.

"We'll have our Christmas pudding tomorrow," Maggie said. "We'll enjoy it more when we're not so very stuffed."

Michael was stuffed, to be sure, and more than glad to stretch long on the hearth rug by the fire.

But Maggie prodded him with the toe of her shoe. "Up, then, and wash and comb your curly locks, Michael Dunnagan. We leave for church in half an hour."

"Just twenty minutes' sleep, Aunt Maggie. There, you're a sainted aunt, then. You wouldn't drive a poor, hardworking orphan out into the bitter cold, now, would you?"

Maggie tapped her toe and dug her fist into her hip, but Michael rushed on. "The sky says it's begging to snow. We could all stay home by this good, warm fire if you like," he pleaded.

"If the Sweet Jesus could leave the peace of heaven and come down to earth and eat and sleep with sinners . . ." Aunt Maggie was clearly winding up for a sermon, and Michael covered his ears with a chair pillow.

She pulled the pillow away. "If He could suffer and die and rise again so the likes of us can spend eternity with Him in the heavens above, then we can surely pull our weary bones off the floor and march to the church for a hymn and a prayer and a bit of thanksgiving on the eve of His birth, Michael Dunnagan! A bit of snow never hurt a soul!" Maggie prodded him again, this time more severely.

Washed and brushed and bundled against the cold, Michael hefted onto the church doors the evergreen wreaths he and Daniel had fashioned. Maggie tied each wreath with a bow of bright-scarlet ribbon, pulling their long and festive tails nearly to the threshold, then stood back to admire them.

Daniel helped to light the outside church lanterns and guide horses and buggies to their appointed spots, far enough from the motorcars to avoid the spooking backfire of unreliable engines.

Michael's breath caught as he stepped into the little white church, reverently aglow in the wash of its wall lanterns, filled with the music of its organ pipes and choir echoing, *"Gloria, gloria, gloria—in excelsis Deo."* He did not need to know the exact meaning of the words to understand that the melody, the phrasing, the bellowed low and high bell tones of the organ, combined with the bright and shimmering eyes of the ten-member choir—their mouths all formed in perfect Os—re-created the songs of the angels on that first Christmas night.

Michael had learned by heart all the words of the carols sung in the church services of the past two Christmases. They were the most glorious songs he'd ever heard. There were days when he had worked alone in the fields throughout the year that he'd fairly shouted the words—perfect expressions of joy and thanksgiving for all he had been given.

That he, Michael Timothy Dunnagan, was alive, well, loved by a real family, and standing in the vestibule of a church to hear such a thing was, to him, the greatest miracle of all. *If only you could see this, Annie!* Michael realized with surprise that it was the first time he'd not directed such a wish toward Owen or even toward his long-lost Megan Marie.

When the invitation came for silent prayers, Michael knelt at the altar rail and prayed earnestly, *Sweet Jesus, You already know my prayer is for Annie's keeping through this war, for her safe and merciful passage across the sea. Until that time comes, show her Your tender care as You've shown it me. Lift her heart this Christmastide; remind her of Your great love for her, the love Owen gave her, and the love that awaits her here . . . of Aunt Maggie and . . . and of me.* Michael shifted uncomfortably on his knees. *I don't know why You've blessed me with this grand life, Sweet Jesus. I know it should be Owen kneeling here, not me. So make me worthy of this gift. Show me what You'd have me do, how You'd have me live. And if Owen is there with You now, wish him a merry Christmas for me, if You will, sir. Tell him I've not given up on getting Annie here, but that she's a mite stubborn.*

Michael wondered through the sermon about his feelings for Annie. It was not the same protective love he'd felt all his life for sweet Megan Marie, no longer bound up in guilt or regret. It was not even the same he'd felt when he'd promised Owen to do all in his power to bring her to America.

Something held him back from saying just what it had become, as if he had no right to name the wonder, no right to feel such things for a young woman so highborn as Annie. And yet, as the pastor told again the story of the Lord of lords having come to earth as the babe of a peasant woman, His first night spent in the hay-filled manger of a stable, Michael's heart lifted. If God in heaven did not think it wrong or mean to be poor, then perhaps Annie would not look at him as a Belfast gutter rat but see him as a man who would willingly lay down his life for her and love and protect her till the day he died.

After the service, Michael pulled the carriage round to the front of the church and waited for Maggie and Daniel, but they did not come through the door. He saw Reverend Tenney's wife snuff the candles in the windows and the reverend himself lower the gas lamps. Together they locked the door, nodded to Michael, and headed off into the dark toward their home across the way. Still, Maggie and Daniel did not come.

Michael tied the horse and walked round the back of the church. At the far end of the cemetery, just beneath the drape of an old fir tree, Daniel and Maggie stood, lit by the lamp of Daniel's lantern, before the stone of Sean Allen. Michael watched as the couple—for he'd gradually come to think of them in that way—knelt on the ground, their own hands clasped and placed atop the stone. Michael felt he was spying, eavesdropping on something intimate and sacred, and turned to go. He was halfway to the buggy when he heard his name.

"Michael!" Daniel called, and Michael turned again, surprised by the laughter in Daniel's voice and the returning song in Maggie's. "We've something glad to tell you!"

❧ ❦

Michael stood beside Daniel McKenica as he pledged his vows to Maggie Allen in the front parlor of Allen's Run Gardens on Christmas Day—a fitting and happily solemn ceremony for that blessed day. Reverend and Mrs. Tenney stayed for tea and to share the celebration. It was the first wedding Michael could remember attending, and it held all the joy and intimacy he could imagine. He only wished Annie were there to share it. He wished Annie could be there to share it all.

❧ ❦

Unmindful of the muddy, rat-infested trenches that snaked through the fields of Belgium and France just across the channel, Christmas erupted in the shops and squares of London with as much levity, color, and excess as it had in holiday seasons past.

Bells of the great cathedrals pealed through the dusk and into the night, and church choirs sang in many-part harmony their Christmas cantatas. Butchers and bakers hired extra workers to match their flurry of orders. Hawkers of chestnuts, holly, and evergreen wreaths and swags shouted their wares from snowy street corners, while others peddled from door to door. But Christmas at the Spragues' was a quiet affair.

"It simply is not comely to celebrate when so many are in mourning," Mrs. Sprague said, looking over their very ordinary Boxing Day tea.

"No," Connie agreed. "And I've no heart for it. I don't understand how anyone can celebrate this year."

"It is a needed diversion," Mr. Sprague said, "and a reminder of hope. Let us not begrudge Christmas."

"Hope is past for some, Father."

"Hope is eternal, thank God—even in the midst of war. Just ask those boys in the trenches."

"It is the trenches I'm thinking of," Connie replied. "I cannot love our warm and dry and well-fed Christmas when our fellows are freezing, squatting in trenches and tunnels amid dead bodies, two feet of water, and human waste."

"Oh, Constance." Mrs. Sprague sighed but did not censure her daughter.

"Owen loved Christmas," Annie remembered aloud, "and I with him. But it doesn't seem the same anymore—especially this year." She laid aside her spoon, weary of pretending to eat. If she didn't take her thoughts off Owen, she knew she would weep. *What,* she wondered, *is Michael doing this day?* Her heart quickened. *Oh dear—that's not helping either.* She sighed, determined to change the subject. "Did you hear that Bernice's older brother went missing at Ypres?"

"Gilbert? When?" Connie paled.

"None of the family has heard from him since the middle of November. They didn't want to believe that . . . They wanted to . . ." Annie looked down, unable to say the words aloud. "But I saw Bernice this morning outside the chemist's. She said her father and mother received a telegram Christmas morning from the BEF. Mr. Langford is still hoping that Gilbert will turn up among the wounded or as a war prisoner, but Bernice doesn't believe it. She said Gil would never miss his Christmas pudding—even in a bundle through the mail. She's certain that if he were alive, he would have found a way to let them know in time for Christmas."

Mrs. Sprague shook her head. "So many young ones. I cannot take it in." She returned her cup to its saucer, her tea untouched. "We should send round a box of baked goods and sweets for the children and some of the orchard fruit your client sent us, Edwin. There is far more than we can use before it spoils. May we use the car tomorrow, dear, to deliver?"

"We should deliver the car," Mr. Sprague said, staring moodily into the fire.

"Give the Langfords our car? But, Edwin, isn't that extreme?"

"Not the Langfords, my dear," he responded testily. "We should contribute our car to the war effort. There is a call for large touring cars and lorries to be used as ambulances."

"Father! It would be just the thing!" Connie clapped her hands.

"It is little enough," he said.

"We can make do—" Mrs. Sprague nodded once—"just as we did in all the years before we owned an automobile."

"Father," Connie begged, "teach me to drive before you send the car. Please."

"And me," Annie piped up. "Teach me, too, please."

"The idea!" Mrs. Sprague fussed.

But Mr. Sprague studied his daughter and Annie for several moments before answering. "Yes, you should both learn to drive."

"Edwin!"

"If they find themselves nursing abroad, I want our girls to know how to drive an ambulance. It will do neither them nor their wounded any good to have all the touring cars in the world donated if someone does not know how to drive the machine out of a battle zone."

He stood. "Few enough soldiers have had the experience of driving.

I intend to see that Constance and Annie are as prepared for this war as I can make them."

Mr. Sprague was as good as his word. He left his offices early on Monday and gave Constance her first lesson. Both returned for tea winter-pale, their hair, coats, and hats disheveled. Mrs. Sprague smiled behind her teacup; Annie did not dare.

Annie's turn came the day following with all-too-similar results. But by the end of the second week of January, both girls could fuel, crank, and start the car, drive round the block, and were proficient in the theory of changing a tire, if not in the practice.

Mr. Sprague pronounced them reasonably safe drivers, if they did not have to go too far or too quickly or through streets with more than one pedestrian. On 19 January, Mr. Sprague donated his family's touring car to the war effort. The Spragues and Annie celebrated both events with sherry and brandied pudding that very night—the night of the first zeppelin raid.

CHAPTER FORTY-FOUR

ANNIE PENNED Michael's address. Her hand cramped from writing, but it was only in letter writing that she found sanity.

They swept like great gray ghosts through the night—long, finned cylinders the shape of gigantic cigars, floating between clouds, bearing deadly New Year gifts from the kaiser to the people of England.

The first one came 19 January and dropped its bombs east of London, over Great Yarmouth all the way to King's Lynn and Snettisham in Norfolk.

But I'd gone to bed early, and of course we saw none of it here in London. Some in Great Yarmouth said they heard the gigantic airship approach and that the zeppelin engine sounded like a distant express train. But everyone in the region, for miles and miles, heard the dropped bombs, one after the other, so close together—grating, horrific booms and crashes, they said, and an explosion that lit the night sky once a gas line was hit.

Four people were killed instantly and sixteen injured—all civilians, several of them women and children.

I've come to fear moonless nights, Michael—I never did before. The Germans are able to glide through our skies undetected and do what they will. How long until they reach London?

Mr. Sprague said there is talk of stationing searchlights throughout London, and perhaps other cities will follow. Mr. Peterson, the postmaster, said our bullets are no good—that they do not penetrate the shells of the zeppelins and we cannot shoot high enough. Mr. Sprague reddened when I told him that and said, "We shall see."

We observe blackout now, as soon as it is at all dark. No lamps are lit in the streets, and all the shops close early. No one wants to be made a target. Our patrollers say that even the smallest spark can be seen from the skies. No one dares light so much as the tip of a cigarette in the streets.

The police have posted warnings and instructions about what we are to do in the event of a zeppelin raid. We must all keep water and sand handy—for fires, you see. And they are adamant that people not go into the street but stay inside. Yet the entire populace flocks to the street each time there is a warning siren of any kind or an explosion! It is as though we are irresistibly drawn, fascinated by the very threat of those majestic death ships bearing our own destruction!

I do not mind so much about the blackouts or the curfews. But I do mind the waiting—forever waiting for the next round of shelling—the strain of not knowing, of lying awake in the night, anxious for a morning that may not come.

Outwardly we keep the British stiff upper lip; but, Michael, inwardly I cower.

I do not want to die young. I have not yet lived—not truly. Sometimes I fear that I will not live through this war, that I will join Owen and Father and Mother very soon. And other times I long to join them, to joy in that glad reunion and end this wracking of my nerves. Oh, God, forgive me! I have grown morose and I did not mean to.

I trust all is well with Aunt Maggie and Uncle Daniel, that they are happy in their new life together. Please give them my love. I envy you there—safe together.

Annie

❧ ❦

Michael ripped a clump of his hair by its roots. He wrote, begging Annie to come to America immediately, begging her not to wait until she turned eighteen.

But in February, newspapers reported Germany's new policy of unrestricted submarine warfare against its enemies—torpedo attacks, without warning, on enemy merchant and passenger craft.

Michael wrote again, this time urging Annie to wait. The risk was too great. He shuddered, unable to think of Annie being blown into the frigid Atlantic water, then unable to think of anything but that. Nightmares and memories of *Titanic* and Owen and Annie swam in circles and cyclones in his head.

In late April, Annie wrote:

Yes, let us wait, then, and see how things progress. Mr. Sprague feels certain that the Germans will not decrease their submarine attacks until Britain releases our blockade in the North Sea. He is equally certain that Britain means to keep the Germans from being resupplied in this way, hoping to force an early end to the war. Our newspapers say that the people of Germany are nearly starving; I cannot help but pity them. Desperate people—on both sides—do such desperate things.

I do want so very much to come, to be with you all, and to be free of this war. And yet Mr. Sprague is concerned for my safety and the wisdom of crossing the Atlantic now. He seems to age daily, to bear the weight of things I do not know. He and Mrs. Sprague have been so very good to me; I could not leave against his wishes.

Do not worry for me, Michael. I have grown somewhat used to the new zigzagging aeroplanes raging over our heads on dark nights. It is the stealth of the great zeppelins and not knowing when they will come that unnerves us all.

By way of more cheerful news, I am getting on in my voluntary aid studies—I should not like to leave England before my training is finished. I feel so glad to be doing something needful at last— something quite outside myself.

Matron has us spend as much time in the hospital wards as the sisters will allow. And although I am only doing simple things, they are useful, and my hands help free the sisters—the real nurses—to assist the doctors and to relieve the suffering of our poor, wounded soldiers. My heart bleeds for them, Michael.

The villains have unleashed a new evil in the second battle in Ypres, something none of the sisters or doctors here have ever before seen—a kind of poisonous gas. It blisters and blues faces and eats away at the lungs in great lesions. It blinds the eyes—sometimes temporarily and sometimes permanently. It is as if the men have bronchitis; they gasp for breath as their lungs fill with fluid until, though terrified for suffocation, they quite literally drown. It is hideous, and I cannot conceive the creature that would curse another mortal so.

We have all been making masks by the dozens and hundreds to send to our soldiers in Belgium and France. They are homely little things—simple butter muslin over cotton wool pads, with tapes to tie behind the head—but if they help at all, it will be worthwhile.

I have done something I think rather brave—though Connie says it is very foolish. I've written my aunt Eleanor, imploring her to turn the unused rooms in Hargrave House into a temporary hospital for the wounded and convalescing. There is great need for additional medical facilities here in London. She has not responded, but I can hope that my letter pricks her conscience. That great, empty house is such a waste.

Even with every practical reason to wait here until the war's end, I confess that I long to come to you and Aunt Maggie, Michael. It seems ludicrous that we've never officially met, never been properly introduced. And yet I feel as though we are lifelong friends—nearly the family Owen wished us to be. I pray this war will end soon, that we shall all find ourselves safely together on one shore.

Michael's stomach churned. His pulse pounded, just behind his eyes. He could not help her, could not spare her the indignities and atrocities she described.

What if German troops breach the Allies' faltering lines in Belgium and France? What if they take possession of the Continent's channel ports, cut supply and reinforcement lines between Britain and France, and eventually leap to England's shores, to Annie?

≋ CHAPTER FORTY-FIVE ≋

"THAT'S DONE IT." Mr. Hook slapped the Philadelphia paper across the Swainton post office counter. "Surely President Wilson will declare war now."

Michael's skin pricked and his ears shot up as he bundled the day's mail. "What's happened?"

"The Germans have gone and sunk *Lusitania*—that British liner—with 1,198 civilians dead in the water, 128 of them US citizens." Mr. Hook shook his head. "Americans will never stand for it! Give that paper to Daniel. He'll be wanting to read it."

Every step of the way home, Michael read and reread the report of the 7 May German U-boat attack. From New York, *Lusitania* had been bound for Liverpool.

Visions of thousands of body parts blown beyond recognition and floating on the ocean's surface turned Michael's stomach, raising the bile in his throat. The next five nights he dreamed again of *Titanic*, of the freezing, screaming, dying humanity struggling for their last breath in the icy Atlantic.

For weeks, after work Michael haunted the post office, the telegraph, or the train station, eager for word that President Wilson had at last called up American troops to aid the Allies, but no word came. A severe warning was issued, and offers for mediation between the battling countries—but no declaration of war.

≋ ≋

"Where have you been?" Maggie asked when Michael walked in the kitchen door late one evening. "Supper was ready an hour past. Daniel and I have eaten." Maggie sounded more concerned than vexed. She set the last washed bowl in the cupboard.

"I stopped to see Reverend Tenney." Michael hung his coat and cap on the hook by the door.

Maggie cocked her head. "Oh?"

"He's a brother over Avalon way—a brother with a lumber business."

"Do you need more lumber for the gazebos already? Isn't there another pile behind the barn?"

"It's not lumber I'm wanting, Aunt Maggie. It's learning to drive."

"To drive?"

"Aye."

"Is this because Annie knows how to drive and you cannot stand that a slip of a lass might know something you don't?" Maggie placed her hands on her hips and lifted her chin, clearly ready to expound on the pigheaded ways of men. "Haven't you enough work with the fields coming on?"

"It is something to do with Annie, but not that." Michael did not flinch. "I want Annie to know everything she can, everything she stands the chance to learn."

Maggie dropped her hands to her sides. "I'm sorry, Michael. I know you do. But why, then? Why do you need to learn to drive? We've no automobile, as near as I can see, and no hopes of buying one this side of a miracle."

Daniel walked in from the parlor and leaned against the doorpost. "So you're thinking of going, then?"

"I am," Michael said.

"Going where?" Maggie colored, clearly annoyed that the men spoke a language she was not privy to.

"To Annie, lass; to Annie," Daniel whispered and bent to kiss the back of his wife's neck.

Maggie's eyes flashed panic. She drew a sharp breath. But before she could speak, Michael cut her off.

"I'll work the fields by day and take my driving lesson by night—the days are long now. When Mr. Tenney is satisfied that I drive safely, I'll deliver lumber for the yard in the afternoons for the remainder of the summer—then the deal is square."

"But—" Maggie began, but Michael rushed on.

"When our fields are harvested and the wood for deliveries is split and the Christmas trees delivered, if President Wilson calls for troops, I'll go and do my bit. But if America hasn't joined the fight by then, I'll go to London and Annie in the new year. I'll help there, in the hospital work, if they'll let me. I'll watch over Annie and do all I can to protect her."

"They'll send you to France, Michael. They're sending everyone to France," Maggie argued.

Michael shook his head. "Surely, with all the men going off to fight, they need ambulance drivers and orderlies to fetch and carry the wounded returned to England."

"The English will not take kindly to an able-bodied Paddy slumming the streets safe at home when their own men are dying on the fields of France," Daniel warned.

"Daniel!" Maggie sputtered, shocked.

"He will hear that and worse. He'd best be knowing it."

Michael nodded. "I do know it, and I thank you for the plain telling. If I must go, I'll seek out a private corps. Annie wrote that private citizens are shipping to France on their own—outside the military and outside the Red Cross—to nurse and doctor and create hospitals in houses and churches and halls. They need ambulance drivers—ones who can drive and repair their cars, as well.

"If I help without joining the military, there is nothing to risk my American citizenship. I've thought it through from every side, and I mean to go. I won't leave Annie to face this war alone. I should have gone long ago."

"We all thought the war could not last," Maggie whispered. "Can't you wait for Annie to come here?"

Michael shook his head. "It's too dangerous. I'll not have her cross!"

"The danger goes both ways!" Maggie insisted.

"It's done. I've decided." Michael stood firm, but Maggie's crumpled features softened his heart. "I'm only taking driving lessons for now. It's months yet before I'll go—a good seven or eight at the least. I'll be here until the new year, unless President Wilson calls for troops. And who knows? The war might take a turn and end tomorrow! But I've got to plan this out or I'll go mad with worry. If I still lived in Ireland or England, I'd be bound to go to war—gone already, Aunt Maggie."

"But you don't live there anymore, Michael. You live here. You're safe here." Maggie did not seem to notice the tears streaking her face.

Michael opened his arms, pulled her to his chest, and wiped them away. "If Owen had lived, he would have gone back to watch over Annie—and more; he would have surely done his part, Aunt Maggie. I must do mine." He held her close as her shoulders dropped. "If the fiends are not stopped in France . . . I can't leave Annie there and do nothing." Michael sighed. "I'll come back to you both; I swear it. And when the war is over, I'll bring Annie home."

❋ CHAPTER FORTY-SIX ❋

THREE THINGS HELPED to settle the question in Annie's mind: the first was the sinking of *Lusitania* in early May—she would not knowingly risk the same fate as Owen's in the cold Atlantic.

The second was that the zeppelins returned to Britain's shores in May and early June—this time targeting London.

Mrs. Sprague, her nerves frazzled and frayed from the bombing and the growing independence of her only daughter, took to her bed with blinding headaches. Mr. Sprague spent long hours and sometimes several days absent from home, involved in war work that he was not at liberty to discuss. Each week he seemed more bent and gray to Annie than the last. The Spragues had become family to her. She could not leave them at such a time.

The third and deciding factor came in the unexpected form of Michael's letter and his promise to sail to England in the new year if the war did not end before.

She would wait until the war ended to travel to America and prayed that would not be long.

Annie was astonished by Michael's bold plan, frightened by the prospect of his week at sea, and thrilled—much to her surprise—by his determination to be near her for the duration of the war.

"It's wildly romantic, don't you think?" Connie baited. She spread her hands as though posting newspaper headlines: "'Gallant Knight Charges across Sea to Rescue Fair Damsel in Distress!'"

"It's nothing of the sort," Annie asserted. "It is simply that he promised Owen to watch over me—after a fashion—in a brotherly sort of way." *Then why am I feeling anything but sisterly toward him now? If my heart races any faster, it will fly out my chest!*

"Ta-ta," Connie teased. "Brotherly, indeed!"

Annie smiled. She didn't mind Connie's teasing. She owned—to herself—that it was more than justified. But she'd never tell Connie how the mere idea of Michael again in England stopped her breath.

Through the next weeks Annie found herself staring long into the mirror at night, never seeing her own reflection. She caught herself smiling, self-consciously, over the smallest things, her mind an ocean away. Two long evenings she played with her hair, first pinning it high in one fashion and then taking it down to pin it in another, determined to find the style that drew attention to her best features and wondering what Michael would think of her when he first saw her. She sometimes imagined conversations with Michael and afterward alternately laughed or chastised herself for silliness. She watched the letter flap for the post with the same anticipation as the pigeons waiting outside the kitchen door for breadcrumbs and suet. Letters became food for her heart.

Anticipating Michael's arrival helped the months pass more quickly for both girls. Despite their long and busy hours volunteering at the hospital and collecting funds for the Red Cross, they longed for something brighter—some activity beyond war and work. The curfew kept them from going out at night with friends, and the gradually increased rationing made rare afternoon socializing less entertaining. But Michael, Annie confessed—if only to herself—was more than a distraction; he was quickly becoming her main event.

Letters raced back and forth between them. Annie assured Michael of her pleasure in his coming in the new year. Mr. and Mrs. Sprague said he would be most welcome to stay with them indefinitely.

Delighted, Annie planned and revised Michael's welcome-dinner menu over and over, estimating just how much sugar and butter she must hoard to create the feast she envisioned. She was revising the menu yet again, in light of stricter sugar and beef rationing, when the summons came in July, the afternoon of Owen's birthday.

"Your aunt Eleanor would like to speak with you, Annie," Mr. Sprague said after returning from his monthly meeting with his most difficult client.

Annie felt the blood drain suddenly from her face and limbs. "Aunt Eleanor wants to see me? Why?"

Mr. Sprague spread his hands. "Let us go into the garden."

Once outside, Mr. Sprague pulled two wooden chairs close. "Your aunt has a birthday proposition for you, something she wishes you to consider."

"A proposition?" Annie could only repeat his words. She would gladly never lay eyes on her aunt again. The idea that she would offer a birthday surprise prickled Annie's skin.

"She would not tell me. She insists on seeing you in person, the day before your eighteenth birthday."

"A month away." Annie shook her head, slowly at first and then firmly—an involuntary reaction to the storm of cruel and hurtful memories raised by the image of her aunt. "I cannot. I am sorry, Mr. Sprague, to disobey if you wish this, but I cannot see her." Annie began to tremble and her voice rose. "I will never go to see her again. I will never let her have power over my hopes or plans or life. I cannot—"

"Annie, I am not asking you to see her. I am only delivering the message of my client. No one will compel you to go to her. And I understand that you do not wish it."

"Then why tell me when you know—?"

"Because she said that she has an offer to make—something to do with your commitment to the war effort."

"The war effort?" Annie could not imagine her aunt taking an interest in anything but her own creature comforts. "What does she care of that?"

Wearily, Mr. Sprague sat back. She was instantly sorry for the burden she and Aunt Eleanor had added to his life. "I believe she has had you followed or at least observed. She knows that you have attended Red Cross meetings with Constance and that you trained with the VADs. She either knows or has surmised that you have not been forthcoming with those in charge of the program concerning your age." Mr. Sprague waved the confusion away. "I have no idea why she would care, but she seems to think that knowledge gives her power of some kind."

"Do you think she will report me? What good could it do her? And it does not matter; I was seventeen when my training began."

"Unless you apply to nurse abroad," Mr. Sprague observed, then studied Annie. "I had not thought of that until Eleanor brought the subject to my attention. I assumed, from our discussion in December, that you had no desire to leave London, but I realize that may no longer be correct."

"I have considered it, for Connie's sake, but decided against it. I do not wish to go abroad. I want only to go to New Jersey, and I must wait for that." Annie shuddered. "I wish she had told you what it is she wants."

Mr. Sprague shook his head. "She said that she will only make her offer to you in person and only make it once. I told her—if you agree to see her—that I, as your legal guardian at this time, must be present."

"And she agreed?"

"Oh, she did not like it, but I will not permit that woman to hurt you further, Annie. I would not have allowed the gardens if I had had any idea she would have . . ."

But he did not finish, and Annie, unable to listen, turned away.

"As I said, you do not need to see her. She cannot touch your inheritance from Owen or your trust from your grandfather. . . . There is, however, one other thing—something I have not told you."

Annie looked up.

"Your aunt's health—"

"Has she suffered another stroke?" Annie could not stop the spring in her pulse.

"Cancer." Mr. Sprague waited for his words to sink in. "She does not have long. I spoke with her physician, and he estimates another six months at most."

Annie sat quietly. She would not outwardly rejoice, but she could not mourn. *Would that she had died when Owen died!* "What could she possibly want with me?"

"I wonder if she is seeking to make peace or restitution before she passes away."

Annie stood. "She cannot make restitution—not for all the wickedness she's done." She felt her throat constrict, her nostrils narrow, as though there were not enough oxygen in the open air. "Aunt Eleanor has never apologized for anything!"

Mr. Sprague's brow furrowed as Annie, more anxious than she had been since the burning of her gardens, walked the length of the garden and back, then walked it again. At last she slowed and sat down, her agitation partly spent.

If only Owen were here. She sighed, tugging a loose thread in her cuff. *He would know what to do. . . .*

Annie took in the slump of Mr. Sprague's shoulders, the resignation in his posture. "Do you think I should see her, then?"

"Not for her sake, my dear. But—" he hesitated—"perhaps for your own."

"Mine?" *Has he gone mad?*

"Do you remember when I cautioned you—the day we first met in my office, after Owen's funeral?"

Annie stared at him, replaying the scene in her mind. "You told me not to become bitter as Aunt Eleanor had." She looked away. "I have not forgotten."

Mr. Sprague nodded. "I advised you to take Owen's example as your own, to live the life of forgiveness and generosity that he so exemplified."

Annie studied her hands. "I have tried, Mr. Sprague. I forgave Michael Dunnagan . . . for living when Owen died. We've even become friends—the very best of friends, I think—and correspondents. I have forgiven Owen for leaving me here alone and for saving others rather than himself." She looked up. "But I do not know how to forgive Aunt Eleanor. In some way or other she has been at least partially responsible for the death of every member of my family. I hate her."

"Nor has she changed, at least as far as I am able to discern." He leaned toward Annie, taking her hands in his own. "But I must ask you, does your hate make you happy, my dear, or does it continually eat through you, a cancer of its own making? Does the constant fueling of that angry fire not exhaust you and take away from living the wonderful life you've been given?"

Annie shook her head tiredly, biting her lip.

"Is it what Owen would have wanted for you? Is it why he made provision for you—to sustain turmoil?"

The tears behind Annie's eyes threatened to spill, but she held them back. "No." She pulled her hands away and clasped them before her. "He would have wanted me to forgive her—for my sake, for Christ's sake, and for his. I know that."

"It may be that the only way you can be entirely free of your aunt—free of the hatred and fear you carry for her—is to see her face to face and tell her that you are no longer afraid of her. Then forgive her if you are able."

Mr. Sprague leaned forward. "She will be gone soon, Annie. She will never be able to hurt you or your loved ones again—unless you continue to carry this burden of hurt and anger. You will have to lay it down if you hope to be free."

But Annie turned away. Mr. Sprague's words churned memories of her morning with Owen, before the tomb of John Bunyan. She saw again the relief on Bunyan's stone—the heavy burden that weighed Christian down—and felt a deep-down weariness in her bones and the weight of her own load so aptly pictured.

Minutes passed as Annie stared into the hearts of the pale-yellow roses in full bloom, the blue phlox and creeping thyme that spilled over the walkway. She had come so far in the last year. She did not want to risk losing that progress by facing her aunt.

But if I don't, if Aunt Eleanor dies before I confront her, will I ever be truly free? Which burden is heavier? Please, Lord . . . oh, please be with me in this.

Annie stood at last and brushed her skirt. She looked at Mr. Sprague, hefting in her mind again and again the weight of her decision. At length she breathed deeply. "Please tell Aunt Eleanor that I will see her—as long as you are beside me, Mr. Sprague."

🙢 🙠

The meeting was set for Saturday afternoon, 21 August, the day before Annie's eighteenth birthday. As they drove the streets to Hargrave House, Mr. Sprague prayed for the girl he had come to love as a second daughter.

As they stepped from the taxi, he prayed for Eleanor Hargrave, that the bitter woman would use wisdom, discretion, and unaccustomed kindness in her speech and actions toward Annie.

As they ascended the great front steps of the family home, and as he lifted the heavy door knocker, Mr. Sprague prayed this visit was not a grave mistake. He never knew what to expect from Eleanor Hargrave, but history gave him every reason to mistrust her. He would remain at Annie's side throughout the interview.

Old Jamison, looking even more bent and weary than the last time Edwin Sprague had been to visit, showed them to Eleanor's first-floor drawing room. It had been converted into a spacious and comfortable bedchamber and sitting room.

Eleanor Hargrave lay, blue-veined and thin, against a daybed, covered in layers of cotton and silk coverlets, despite the warm summer day.

Once they were seated, Eleanor lifted her eyes in acknowledgment. "I have decided to open Hargrave House as a hospital, a convalescent center for our wounded soldiers returning from France."

Mr. Sprague blinked, certain he had not heard correctly. He sensed Annie's loss of equilibrium in the chair beside him.

"This decision will affect the girl, as my surviving Hargrave heir. This house and its contents will—" Edwin Sprague noticed that she nearly choked—"one day pass to her."

The silence in the room lay thick. At last Annie whispered, "It is a splendid idea, Aunt Eleanor, the very thing I have wished for."

Eleanor did not acknowledge Annie. "If there are no objections . . ." She waited.

Mr. Sprague and Annie exchanged surprised looks. "It is an arrangement," Mr. Sprague replied with as much composure as he could muster, "which Elisabeth Anne has expressed a desire for on more than one occasion."

"We are agreed, and it is settled. A modernized kitchen and laundry will be installed immediately. I'll have the appropriate government and medical authorities contacted. You should be ready to receive your first patients within a fortnight, Elisabeth Anne."

"My—my patients?"

Aunt Eleanor's thin lip lifted. "You have completed your VAD training, have you not?"

"Why, yes, but—"

"You cannot expect me to administrate a project of this magnitude given my current state of health." Aunt Eleanor sounded offended.

"Of course not," Mr. Sprague intervened. "There will be no difficulty in procuring an experienced hospital administrator of the highest order. But Annie is not yet eighteen. She cannot be expected to—"

"Elisabeth Anne, not eighteen?" Aunt Eleanor feigned surprise. "I understood from the matron of her hospital that she is twenty-three—or very nearly. Tomorrow, I believe." Her smile fell away.

"What is this about, Eleanor?" Mr. Sprague frowned.

"It is about the future of Hargrave House and the patriotic responsibility of our family in wartime. To those ends, I wish to speak with my niece alone. You may wait in the hallway, Edwin."

Annie's fingers gripped Mr. Sprague's arm.

He covered her hand protectively. "That is not our agreement."

"Those are my conditions." Eleanor Hargrave lifted her chin, staring her challenge to Edwin Sprague.

"In that event, we wish you good day." Mr. Sprague stood and waited for Annie to do the same.

But Annie, sitting rigidly in the chair, did not move.

Mr. Sprague knew the spell cast by her aunt was a long one, and Annie's feet seemed frozen to the floor. "Elisabeth Anne," he said quietly, "let us go." He waited, then urged, "Annie?"

Eleanor Hargrave's piercing eyes and presence had clearly mesmerized her niece. *She has the eyes of a snake. I must get Annie out of here before Eleanor overcomes her with her cruel and perverted logic. I wish to God that I'd not brought her here!*

In fleeting expressions Edwin Sprague saw Annie resisting, considering, and finally succumbing to her aunt.

"I will stay. I will hear what Aunt Eleanor has to say."

"I do not think it wise to—"

"Wait in the hallway, Edwin. We shall not be long." Eleanor Hargrave closed her eyes, awaiting obedience to her commands.

Mr. Sprague touched Annie's shoulder. "Are you certain?"

Annie visibly shivered but nodded. "I'll join you in a moment."

Every nerve in Edwin Sprague's body shouted misgivings, but he closed the door behind him and waited. He pulled the handkerchief from his pocket, wiped his brow, and cursed himself for bringing Annie to Hargrave House.

In less than ten minutes Annie emerged, pale but dry-eyed, her back straight.

Mr. Sprague followed her through the great hallway. When they reached the foyer, he pulled the heavy door open quickly, glad at last to whisk Annie from the drear old house.

But Annie placed her hand on his arm. "Please have my things sent round. Thank you for all you have done for me. Please thank Mrs. Sprague and Connie. I shall write them, of course—"

"What—what are you saying? What did she say to you?" Edwin Sprague felt as though a cat ran its claws down the back of his neck.

Annie looked up; her lower lip barely trembled. "It does not matter—truly. There is something I must do, and I must live here to do it."

"My dear—whatever she said to you—"

"This is my decision, Mr. Sprague."

"And I am your guardian for at least another day. I'll not leave you in this house!"

A momentary fear flashed through Annie's eyes, but she regained—by force, Edwin thought—some small amount of composure. "You have been a wonderful guardian, Mr. Sprague, and I am glad and grateful for all you have given me. But I must do this."

"Do what?"

"Open a hospital in the house—the second and third floors."

"Elisabeth Anne—"

"For our wounded. There are not enough hospitals in the city. Citizens are opening their country homes by the score, but more are needed here in London, where there are more doctors available." Annie's words sounded rote, even though he knew she believed them.

"Annie, my dear, the administration of a hospital, even a small one in such a house as this, is too great a burden for you!"

Annie nodded. "It is her condition for . . ."

"For what? Whatever is she thinking? You are far too young!"

"I will have help. But I will run it." Annie faltered. "Aunt Eleanor knows I have posed as being older for some time. And you were right about her investigations—she knows about Aunt Maggie and Uncle Daniel being married. She knows every detail of their mortgage and financial obligations. She knows about Michael and Owen and . . . and everything that has happened in your home and business for months, including your war work."

Edwin Sprague felt an unfamiliar dizziness but forcibly steadied himself. "None of that has anything to do with you, Annie. If she is trying to frighten you or blackmail you in some way, you must not let her. Do not stay in this house, I implore you."

Annie placed her hand on her guardian's sleeve. "Be careful, Mr. Sprague, and trust me that this is best and will be best. It will only be for a few months at most. She does not wish to die alone."

"And blackmail is her way of keeping you here?" he all but shouted.

"It will open another hospital; it will spare us all embarrassment and . . . and difficulty." Annie squeezed his arm.

Still he waited, unable, it seemed, to decide what to do.

"I will not go home with you, Mr. Sprague."

"Someone must stay here with you. Perhaps Constance can—"

"No!" Annie's eyes widened in alarm. "Connie must not come—not ever. Jamison is here . . . and Barbara. Please, Mr. Sprague, do as I ask."

"I do not like this, Annie. I do not think it wise. Come home with us, if only until your birthday tomorrow. Let us talk over and reconsider whatever she has proposed. If you do that, I will accept your decision— whatever it is."

"I'm sorry. Please send my things round as soon as possible. I'm taking Owen's room, opposite Aunt Eleanor's." Annie gently pushed a dumbfounded Mr. Sprague through the door before he heard the lock turn and click into place.

≋ CHAPTER FORTY-SEVEN ≋

AFTER *TITANIC*, Michael had vowed he would never sail again. Yet he booked passage to Southampton on an ocean liner. He'd vowed he would never again set foot in the steerage hole of any seagoing vessel, not even one resting in the docks. Yet he set his bag squarely on the third-class bunk and stowed his few belongings in the ship cabin's cupboard.

He would have kept his vows, but for Annie. He latched the cupboard door and leaned against it. "What have you done? Why will you not answer me, Annie Allen?"

It was just over six months since he or Aunt Maggie had heard from Annie. She'd not responded to their birthday letters or to the book Michael had mailed her. She'd not written, even at Christmas.

Michael could think of nothing he'd put in his letters that might have offended her. She had responded straightaway, delighted, when he'd written in June that he was coming in the new year. She had replied that Mr. and Mrs. Sprague had kindly offered him a room, that they might spend every day together and all live as a family for the duration of the war.

Michael, albeit pleased and flattered, had refused, feeling the impropriety of such an arrangement, even if Annie did not. He could not imagine living in the same house with her day after day and keeping his distance; he could no longer think of her as a sister.

By the time I escort you to America, Annie Allen, I hope—I pray—it will be with a ring on your finger and the promise of marriage on your lips. Michael knew it was a bold thought—a bold and secret plan. But his love for Annie had made him bold.

In November, Mr. Sprague had responded immediately to Aunt Maggie's letter begging for news of Annie. The man had been genuinely astonished that Annie had not written her family in New Jersey. He'd explained, as best he could, that Annie had returned to Hargrave House at her aunt Eleanor's insistence and was running a hospital for the British wounded.

The small New Jersey family could not believe such a tale, and so Maggie had written again, and Mr. Sprague replied in more detail.

I see Elisabeth Anne from a distance once a month—if that—when I attend her aunt's affairs at Hargrave House. She is thin and grave in her countenance, though it is little wonder. The cases sent to Hargrave House are particularly gruesome—not at all the life I would choose for any young woman.

Still, Annie refuses to see or speak with me alone. Much as I wish to, and though I am greatly concerned for her welfare, I cannot force her to return to us or hinder her from her chosen course.

"It isn't right." Aunt Maggie had shaken her head, her brow wrinkled. "Annie loved living with the Spragues, and she would never have returned to that woman's home on her own! There is something he's not telling us."

"Perhaps he doesn't know." Daniel frowned. "It's not like the girl to drop everyone—you, Michael, the Spragues—like hot tinder."

But it had settled things in all their minds. Michael must go to England and talk to Annie. He must convince her to return to the Spragues or come with him to America. German torpedoes could not be more destructive to their Annie than Eleanor Hargrave—they were united in that belief.

So Michael left by the Swainton train late in the last week of February.

The barns were stacked with wood that Daniel would deliver to neighbors and longtime customers throughout the winter. Michael had made a special arrangement with Mr. Hook for the loan of a truck and driver once a week for heavier deliveries farther away.

He had finished all the gazebos and birdhouses he could, provided all he could, done all he could—but he hated to leave the couple he had come to love as dearly as the parents he'd been born to. Still, he loved Annie more.

Michael ran his hands through the unruly curls of his freshly cut and pomaded hair, alternately pulling it by its roots and smoothing it with his fingers as he rationalized her silence. If Mr. Sprague had not seen Annie himself, Michael would have feared that a zeppelin's bomb had fallen on her head. He could think of nothing less that would account for Annie's silence.

At length Michael sighed and unbuttoned Owen's overcoat—the coat he'd grown into—and hung it on the hook nearest the door. Almost four years of Maggie Allen's home cooking and of gardening and building in the bright New Jersey sunshine had added a foot to his height and two stone to his weight. He would be hard pressed to fill the coat's pockets, still sewn inside, and have room for all of him.

Michael sat on the bunk, remembering the day Owen found him in the gardens of Southampton, homeless and nearly starved, his legs the size of kitchen kindling. Not since that day had he needed to steal scraps from meals others had eaten and thrown away.

That a life could grow and so change through one man's blessing and legacy in four short years was a miracle beyond Michael's imagination; he shook his head at the wonder of it.

Michael leaned forward, elbows on his knees. "Help me, Sweet Jesus," he prayed, "to be the blessing to someone in this life that Owen was to me. Help me find Annie, to protect and shield her. Do not let me fail in this, I beg You. You've given me a family. Help me not to lose it.

"Protect me from what You will, and give me courage to do what You will. Thank You, Sweet Jesus, for letting me live, for the joy of Aunt Maggie and Uncle Daniel. Bless them; give them the comfort of each other and of You. Amen."

Michael spent as much time as he could in the ship's library, reading the volumes available to passengers. He had no heart for walking the promenade, no wish to stare at the miles and miles of endless ocean. He forced, as best he could, the persistent images of icebergs and torpedoes from his mind, and concentrated, as much as he dared, on meeting Annie face to face.

For weeks Michael had tried to imagine how she'd grown and

changed in the four years since he last saw her standing on the docks of Southampton, a young girl searching the crowds aboard *Titanic* for her brother's face and finding only Michael. He could not deny that, miserable and hopeless waif though he was, he'd been attracted to her violet-blue eyes and the soft, golden ringlets round her face. Such a longing was safe then, in its way, he had reasoned, for she was beyond his hope or reach.

Now he dared hope, dared take the dream of marriage from his mind and turn it over and over. He would not push Annie—not even confess his love for her, at least not until she seemed ready to receive it. But to be fair, he knew he must tell her before they sailed to America. If she did not want him, then he would serve her as a brother all his days, as he'd promised Owen, as Daniel had served Maggie and Sean.

Michael sighed. He hoped to be more to her than that.

When the ship slipped through Southampton's harbor nearly a week later, the calendar had turned to March. Michael leaned over the rail, eager to search out the docks, the streets he remembered. But the harbor teemed with ships of all sizes, and the streets of town, at least those he could see, were flooded with men in uniform—lines of soldiers and sailors, their kits stowed at their feet, cigarettes in their hands, ready and waiting to be shipped out. If his ticket had not verified this port of call as Southampton, he would have thought himself in some far-off place—for surely this looked nothing like the site of *Titanic*'s sailing four years past.

Michael strained his eyes against the sun. The deck of a ship nearby appeared to be covered with bunks—stretchers and stretchers of men in row upon row. He squinted and identified scores of British Expeditionary Force uniforms among the men on stretchers—many torn, some with only pants or shirts of a piece. Some uniforms he did not recognize at all. As he came within earshot of the dock, he heard languages he did not know interspersed among the wide variety of British accents, men of every class and county.

Michael's chest tightened. For weeks all he'd contemplated was his hope of wooing Annie. He'd barely considered the odd dread of walking again the land in which he'd been nothing but an outcast. But here he was at last, and even those anticipated joys and dreads paled in the light of the drama, the bedlam before him, these thousands upon thousands of men.

He'd just stepped from the ship when a young woman in faded Red Cross uniform and cape slipped her arm through his and tickled a white feather beneath his chin. "And why are you not in uniform, a fine strapping bloke like you?"

"I've only just come," Michael stammered, surprised as he heard himself slip easily into the heavy brogue he'd believed tamed.

"Well, Paddy, these boys have only just come from doing their duty." She pointed to a steady stream of stretchers borne from ships.

Michael watched in horror as some of the crudely bandaged wounded—and some whose bandages had been reduced to blood-soaked, filthy rags—were carried before him and placed in rows along the docks, in the cold and open air, to await transportation and further treatment. Men stared vacantly, some with half their faces blown away, many with blisters and pus festering their eyes, their cheeks and chins, their hands and arms.

One sober-faced stretcher bearer turned aside, gagged from the stench of gangrene, wiped his mouth with his sleeve, and passed without slowing a step.

"Where are they from?" Michael asked, unable to imagine a place that produced such horrors.

"Over there." The stretcher bearer cocked his head toward the channel and France and all that lay beyond.

The persistent nurse swished the feather across Michael's cheek. "Don't wait too long, Paddy. You'll not want the English and French to do all your fighting for you." She arched her brow, tucked the feather in the buttonhole of Michael's coat, and sauntered away in search of new victims.

Michael fingered the feather in his buttonhole, the place designed to hold a flower—a thing of beauty and grace. For just a moment he remembered the millions of flowers he and Owen had helped place aboard *Titanic* the night before she sailed, the hundreds of Bealing's buttonholes presented to passengers, and the curtain of flowers that had rained down upon this very dock at the moment of sailing.

Michael remembered, with a pain he could not describe, all that had gone before. He viewed the scene on the dock before him as from a great distance. He realized that just as certainly as *Titanic*'s curtain of flowers had closed the stage on that long-ago part of life—English life painted in luxury, beauty, and grace—these ships, loaded as they were with crumpled human cargo, had raised the curtain on another stage, a nightmare awash in blood and death and terrors more horrific than he knew to imagine.

How long Michael stood staring, he did not know. At length he was pushed along by the sheer volume of soldiers and the din of need surrounding him.

He exchanged his American dollars for pounds and shillings but found there was no space on the London-bound train, at least not for two hours. Military took precedence in travel. Michael searched out the pub where nearly four years ago he had slipped in through a window and licked the last drops from dirty glasses. This time he placed his coins on the counter crowded by men in uniform, and he ordered a pint. He pulled from his pocket a wrapper of fish-and-chips, hot and greasy, that he'd purchased next door.

It was a taste woven of childhood longing and memory; the reality was not so dear as he'd imagined. He wondered if there was something sweeter about food that was stolen or forbidden, or if the unattainable took on a sweetness of its own. He wondered what Aunt Maggie might cook for supper that night.

With time to spare, Michael sought out Annie's old school and watched girls in the schoolyard turning ropes, skipping to singsong rhymes. His heart quickened in the anticipation of meeting the young woman who had opened her mind and heart to him through letters, rather than the girl he'd spied upon from afar. Michael made his way to the town hall gardens, where Owen had first stumbled over a young boy's near-skeletal form, all wrapped up in tarps against the cold.

The gardens had matured, and Michael marveled at the landscape bones Owen had laid and the beauty his plantings had grown into. He sat on the wooden bench, now weathered gray but still situated in a particular circle of evergreen ground cover. He ran his fingers beneath its seat and found the names carved there—Owen and Annie Allen—within a neat oval. And farther out, Michael found his own name, crudely carved by a young boy longing for the family he'd seen in Owen and his sister.

Michael shook his head. *I wanted to be in their circle, Sweet Jesus, not take Owen's place, not push him aside. God, forgive me. After seeing those lads come off the ship, I'm afraid. Reading Annie's letters and the newspapers in America, it was all so different. But I'm here now, and if I have been spared to give my body, my eyes, my life for this time, Sweet Jesus, as they have—or in Owen's place, or for the sake of this land he loved—so be it. Give me the courage and generosity Owen lived each moment until his last. Give me that courage, Sweet Jesus, for I've none of my own.*

The train to London stopped again and again; Michael thought it would never reach Waterloo station. So eager was he to see Annie, so afraid was he to meet her face to face, that he jumped off the train, then had to run back to retrieve the bag he'd forgotten.

Breathe, man; breathe! he chanted in his mind as he deciphered the city map posted in the center of the station, then purchased tokens for the Underground. At Charing Cross he studied the map again but finally gave up and asked the help of a stranger.

Michael hopped the tram the leery Londoner pointed out and kept careful track of the stops and crossings. He pulled the cord and stepped off one street early, just to give himself time to steady his pounding pulse, run a comb through his tangled hair, and straighten his coat. At last he strode down the street, through the gate, and up the walk to the Spragues' front door. He checked the number twice, pocketed the address from Annie's last letter, and pulled the bell.

CHAPTER FORTY-EIGHT

CONNIE TURNED HER HEAD from side to side and rolled her shoulders to her ears, listening appreciatively to the gentle cracking sounds her body made. *Thank You, Lord, that I have this bone-weary body—my neck, my back, my shoulders and arms—to feel this pain. Thank You for the strain in my legs and for varicose veins and for my aching arches—thank You that I have two legs and two feet!*

Long night shifts in the mortal-wound ward of London General effected more thanksgiving in Connie than all her years of Sundays spent in church.

Connie climbed the stairs to her room, threw her woolen cape and starched cap over the vanity stool, and collapsed across her bed. She did not bother to remove her black shoes or stockings or to wash her face. She did not care that she had crumpled her once-white collar, cuffs, and apron. The entire uniform was stained with blood and vomit; it would have to be washed and blued.

"Will you be wanting tea, miss?" Tilly's bright voice spoke through the doorway. But Connie was too tired to form the words to reply. Tea could wait until she had slept—for hours, if only her mother would leave her alone and not fuss about the lateness of her working schedule or the state of her hair or hands or the dark circles beneath her eyes—all of which was as much the uniform of a VAD as was her clothing.

Thank You that Mother and Father are out. I don't think I could stand another round of interrogation.

"Miss?"

"Not now, Tilly. Please, just let me sleep."

"Yes, miss, as you say." Tilly pulled the door closed and Connie fell immediately asleep.

It seemed no time at all had passed when Tilly tapped again on her bedchamber door. "Begging your pardon, Miss Constance. . . . Miss Constance?"

Connie turned over in bed, pulling the pillow over her ears. *Perhaps if I don't answer, she'll go away!* But it was no use.

"Miss Constance?" Tilly stood by the bed, anxiously wringing her hands.

"What is it, Tilly?"

"A visitor, miss—and Mr. and Mrs. Sprague have gone out."

"I am not up to seeing anyone. Ask whoever it is to leave their card. Tell them I've worked through the night at hospital."

"But, miss—"

"There's a war on, Tilly! I'm certain they will understand."

"I tried to tell him to go away and come again tomorrow, when the mister and missus are here, but he says he's come for Miss Annie—all the way from America—and says he won't leave till he's talked with Mr. or Mrs. Sprague. Whatever shall I tell him, miss?" she asked. "I don't know what I'm to say."

Connie stared at the ceiling. *It can't be.* "Did he give his name?"

"Michael Dunnagan, miss."

Connie sprang from her bed, then stopped abruptly in the center of the room, desperate to clear her head. She needed a moment to think, but Tilly kept standing there, infernally wringing her hands.

Connie crept through her door, knelt by the upstairs banister, and peeked, hoping to catch a glimpse of the fabled Irish waif turned American gardener and the author of the silver-tongued letters that she had teased Annie about for months.

Why Annie had not written the dashing young Irishman that she'd left the Sprague household, Connie could hardly imagine. What she would tell Michael about Annie's whereabouts, she could imagine less.

At that moment the dark-haired stranger turned and found Connie staring through the rails of the banister. Connie felt her face flame to the roots of her unkempt hair. Undone by the blue lights in the bright eyes that stared through her, she stood, lifted her chin, and walked down the stairs with as much dignity as she could retrieve in her crooked stockings and a stained and crumpled VAD uniform.

All Michael saw was another Englishwoman in uniform. Every humiliation, every limitation of his poor Belfast childhood cast a wide divide between his spit-polished brogans and the now-familiar and chastising uniform of this highborn lady—even though she looked rather like she had been to the war herself.

The young woman stopped short on the bottom step, tilted her head, placed her hand on her hip, and quipped, "Not who you're looking for, Mr. Dunnagan?"

Michael stammered apologies. "No, mum! I mean, I beg your pardon, mum. I'm looking for Annie Allen."

The haughty line of the woman's mouth melted into a lopsided smile. "No doubt." She stepped down and reached out her hand to him. "I am Connie Sprague, Annie's friend."

Michael inclined his head and took Connie's hand. "How do you do, miss? I'm Michael Dunnagan, from New—"

"Jersey!" Connie finished. "Annie told us all about you."

"She's here, then?" Hope sprang, a thing alive, in Michael's face. "Annie's here!"

"No," Connie countered. "You did know that? This is not some horrid surprise, is it?"

"No, Miss Sprague, I mean—"

"Please, call me Connie. I'm as good as Annie's sister."

"Thank you, Miss—Connie," Michael stammered, not used to speaking to young women, especially young Englishwomen. "I wrote Miss Annie in the early summer, telling her I was coming—that I was hoping to come in the new year. She was expecting me; she said that Mr. and Mrs. Sprague were expecting me."

"But Father wrote Annie's aunt that she's gone—I am quite certain."

"Yes, mum. But we thought—Aunt Maggie and I thought—that I should come and talk with Annie, that I should urge her to come home with me."

"Urge her to cross the Atlantic? Now? You can't be serious!" Connie shook her head. "You've come all this way—by ship—when it's not safe to travel." She hesitated. "Oh, you should not have come!"

Michael stood firm.

"No, I don't mean you should not have come to England, but you should have waited; you should have written Father directly before you came." Connie frowned, clearly flustered and short for words. "I don't know how to tell you this, Michael." She stopped again. "Annie left—just before her birthday. We've heard no word from her since . . ."

Michael nodded.

But Connie rushed on. "And—oh, this is beastly—we don't know what has become of her."

Michael felt a great chasm in the floor open wide, though his brogans remained planted to the tiles. "Mr. Sprague wrote that he has seen her and that she is well," he argued.

"Yes, that was so—originally."

"Originally?"

"Father thinks that Miss Hargrave may have in some way coerced Annie to leave her house."

"Then where—?"

"To leave London."

Michael felt the world spinning. He looked down and found Connie's hand on his arm, guiding him into a drawing room off the foyer, pushing him gently to a chair. From a great distance he heard her talking about her father and Annie's aunt Eleanor.

He tried to concentrate on Connie's details of the birthday conference and the plan to set up hospital and convalescent wards in Hargrave House, and of Eleanor Hargrave's insistence that Annie run the entire operation, despite her youth and inexperience. He'd heard all of that before from Mr. Sprague's letters.

"But Annie has disappeared."

Michael reflexively reached for a mass of his own dark curls and pulled hard, as if that could make the entire crazy picture right itself. "She can't—"

"She's simply gone missing." Connie's hands spread wide. She stood and began to pace. "Her aunt Eleanor was true to her word about fixing up the house. The moment Annie moved in, so did a lorry full of workmen—as if they'd been waiting in the wings. They worked night and day, and no expense was spared; they finished the hospital renovations in less than a fortnight.

"Two days later a team of doctors and nurses arrived and then the first group of patients—all BEF casualties and convalescents at first, just as her aunt had promised." Connie sat down. "Only, gradually, the cases became more and more severe. Men whose faces or limbs or both had been blown away, gangrene victims needing amputations, gas victims—everything! They should never have been placed in a private home, even if it is a hospital ward, even if they have one of the best surgeons anywhere!"

Michael sucked in his breath, remembering the half men—more breathing corpses than wounded men—carried from the ships on stretchers, lining the docks of Southampton.

"Our hospitals are overflowing, so large private homes are in demand. But Annie is too young to manage such a hospital. She was run off her feet from morning till night—and the most gruesome cases you could ever imagine. Father had seen Annie, though he was not permitted to speak to her. He said she's lost weight—and she had none to lose. After the incoming cases grew so much worse, her nerves frayed. She began having nightmares."

Michael blinked hard, about to speak, but Connie rushed on.

"She could not bear it. I know because I forced myself through the back door one day. She had refused to see me. She did not answer my letters. She would not take my telephone calls." Connie leaned forward. "I was terribly frightened for her. I didn't know what else to do."

"But you saw her?"

"I did." Connie frowned. "She looked as though she had aged ten years and could barely keep on her feet. She told me what I've told you and said that, if she could get away, she would meet me in two days at her brother's grave in Bunhill Fields cemetery." She seemed to realize that might sound odd to a stranger. "She would often go there, to sit and—"

But Michael waved her explanation away. "Owen's grave." The image formed a clamp round his heart, but he was not unfamiliar with Annie's ways. "And then you saw her? What did she say? Did she say why she—?"

"That's just it—she never came. I waited for two hours, in case she'd had trouble getting away. But she did not come, and she sent no word." Connie sat back. "So I went to the house again, and Jamison, her old butler and friend, answered the kitchen door."

"And so?"

"And so, Jamison said that she had gone—left just hours before, in the middle of the night—and that Miss Hargrave would only say that she's gone to do her duty and that he was to speak of it to no one."

"Her duty?" Michael nearly pleaded. "What does that mean?"

But Connie was already shaking her head, tears trickling down her cheeks. "I've no idea, Michael. I've no idea. But I'm terribly frightened for her. This was a week ago, and no one has heard anything from her. It is not in character for Annie. She isn't brave in the sense of running off for new adventures. She loves the tried and true. She loves being home and settled." Connie leaned forward again. "She was mad with joy that you were coming to London. She wanted nothing more in all the world than to go to you and her aunt Maggie in America. She was desperate for the war to end so she could do just that. She would never have run off on her own."

"The police—the constable—" Michael stammered, unable to make his mouth do his will.

"Father has tried everything—everyone, everywhere—to find what has happened. He's at Hargrave House now, since early this morning, with the magistrate and an investigator, demanding an explanation."

Michael stood, not knowing what to say, to think, to do, frantic to do something.

The front door opened and closed. Connie sprang to her feet. "Father!"

The slump-shouldered man standing in the foyer looked far older than the man Annie had described in her letters, and Michael wondered if there was some mistake.

"What did the witch say, Father?" Connie demanded. "What did you learn?"

Mr. Sprague, gray faced and weary, glanced up. He did not seem to see the stricken young man standing behind his daughter. "She's dead. Eleanor Hargrave is dead."

"I don't care about Eleanor Hargrave! Father, where is Annie?" Connie begged. "Did she tell what has happened to Annie!"

"France," Mr. Sprague replied quietly, his voice ragged and hollow. "She has gone to the front . . . to nurse in France."

≋ CHAPTER FORTY-NINE ≋

PALE-FACED NURSES, sick from the sea-tossed ship's zigzagging attempts to avoid German torpedoes, held tight their cloaks and kits against the fierce February wind as they made their way along the docks in Boulogne.

Already Annie knew to avoid Matron Artrip—a younger, vigorous form of her aunt Eleanor and a veritable sergeant major all rolled into sister's garb.

"None of the girls like her," whispered Liz, a VAD who looked every bit as young as Annie but who vowed to Matron that she was "twenty-three, Sister—minimum requisite age," even though she'd been unable to look Sister Artrip in the face when she'd said it.

Annie could not imagine why anyone so young and timid would volunteer to nurse overseas when she could easily have gained a post in one of the London hospitals or wealthy homes turned convalescent centers. She certainly would not, had she any choice. But her contract with her aunt stipulated she nurse in France for the duration of the war.

Annie saw no reprieve, not even if her aunt died—as she prayed every day she might—for Aunt Eleanor had set in meticulous motion guardians to carry out her threats should Annie violate the terms of their agreement. For the sake of Aunt Maggie and Michael, dearest Michael, for Mr. Sprague—indeed for all the Spragues—Annie would follow those terms to the letter.

Aunt Eleanor was privy to the loans Uncle Sean had taken out on Allen's Run Gardens. Somehow she had procured a dominant share in the bank that held those loans and their overdue mortgage. Her aunt's pleasure in detailing the plans of her threatened foreclosure sickened Annie. *Oh, why did I not anticipate her? Why did I not arrange for Mr. Sprague to send the funds to Aunt Maggie before I ever set foot in Aunt Eleanor's house?* Annie closed her eyes. *Why should I be shocked by her venom? It is not new. Her joy lies in the manipulation, the destruction of all whose happiness and generosity stand in contrast to her meanness.*

Mr. Sprague's financial dealings with Aunt Eleanor's distant relatives in Germany had been at her aunt's behest and carried out for years before the war. But when Mr. Sprague had challenged Eleanor Hargrave concerning Annie's welfare and future in the two years following Owen's death, she had openly hired another solicitor for some of her affairs. That solicitor had, her aunt told her, recently hired a "colleague" to create a distinct and incriminating paper trail between Mr. Sprague and not only her legitimate distant German relatives, but the German military as well—the latter recipients unknown to Mr. Sprague.

She had made it perfectly clear to Annie that her imminent death would eliminate the one person who could vouch that Edwin Sprague had no inkling of his connection with the enemy government. There was enough, Aunt Eleanor had vowed, to ruin Edwin Sprague and his family.

She'd laughed at Annie's horror and insistence that Mr. Sprague was a good and innocent man, a true British patriot.

"It matters not," Eleanor Hargrave had purred. "He will stand in the dock until the end of the war. Suspicion and a ruined reputation alone will prevent him from practicing law in the empire—ever."

Aunt Eleanor had cast a grimy lens over Mrs. Sprague and her support of the suffragette movement and hinted that no one would marry Constance, the daughter of treasonous and modernist parents. The woman had left no stone unturned in her devilish and spiteful imagination.

Annie's heart sank, but she never doubted her aunt's determination or ability to carry out her threats. She'd known her too long.

The price of her aunt's silence and inaction—both in America and Britain—was Annie's contract to nurse near the battlefields of France for the duration of the war, to leave her inheritance untouched until her return, and to abruptly end all communication with family and friends.

Cruel though the terms were, Annie dared not test her bluff. The cost was too great, the stakes for her loved ones too high.

Annie closed her eyes as she waited in line. Her disappearance would hurt the Spragues and Aunt Maggie and Michael, in turn. She choked back a sob at the thought of losing Michael when she'd only gained the desire to truly know and be with him, the secret hope that he might love her in return. But if she stayed, they would all be hurt more; they would all lose everything dear to them.

The train to Revigny was quiet, packed with soldiers returning to the front from their all-too-short fortnight of leave. The dread mixed with quiet determination lining their faces did nothing to calm the shooting pains in Annie's stomach. She swallowed, her tongue thick, her throat dry.

Barbara—Babs, one of the bolder girls—smiled at a soldier staring from across the aisle; he did not smile in return. Not even the fresh young Englishwomen in spotless VAD cloaks kindled lights in their eyes. Annie looked away.

Revigny was the end of the line—the last stop before the long lorry trip to Verdun along the only road left open.

"They call it *la Voie Sacrée*—the Sacred Way. Verdun is a veritable hellhole and gorge of French blood," Andee, the only volunteer American among them, confided with the intensity of a master storyteller. "It is a point of greatest honor—all France is bent and driven to recapture it from the *Boche*."

Annie had heard the same rumor in London, and more: Germany, determined to take advantage of France's patriotic spirit, continued to lure the enemy to Verdun and to their knees by the thousands, with the sole intention of bleeding the French army white.

The engine's long whistle announced their arrival in the gathering dusk, well before the train lurched to a stop. Matron stepped confidently from the train, but even her rigid face paled at the sea of men and the stench of their blood-soaked bandages and unwashed bodies.

Annie and the other young women followed tentatively, stumbling over broken cobbles. Not one of the freshly recruited and voluntarily trained young Englishwomen had encountered in close proximity so many filthy, broken soldiers straight from the battlefield.

Lines of black-powder burns creased the natural contours of male faces, their eyes hooded and weary beyond their years. Rows upon rows of stretchers burdened with men, and what was left of men, waited for the cars to empty of soldiers so they might take their place and return to Calais or Boulogne or any port that would send them finally to England and respite care.

The VADs stood, mesmerized, horrified, and rooted to the muddy ground.

"Come along, girls!" Matron shouted above the din. "We are bound for that parade of lorries—step smartly!"

But the lorries were loaded and heaped with ammunition and equipment bound for Verdun. "Nothing supersedes the resupply of our men in Verdun—not the wounded, not the dying, and certainly not you, Sister, with your gaggle of VADs!" shouted the driver of the last lorry. Matron drew herself up and prepared to launch an attack, but he waved her away and gunned his motor that she might not be heard.

The girls stifled giggles. Annie knew better and studied her feet as Matron returned to the clustered group, her face red and her eyes nearly bulging from their sockets.

The stationmaster shrugged. "The young ladies must wait until morning for the lorries to return. Only then may they be transported to their field section."

Matron shouted at the little man. "You cannot expect these girls to sleep in the station with soldiers roaming hither and yon!"

He shrugged again and pointed to a wooden café across the square, brightly lit and boasting a Union Jack. Annie caught the words *La Cantine de Dames Anglaises.*"

Matron led her gaggle away in a huff.

"Welcome to *Café Gratuit*!" sang two young Englishwomen from an open window above a long outdoor counter. They called with all the cheeriness of French mademoiselles, bundled though they were against the cold in layers of woollies and mufflers.

"Tea," Matron ordered. "Serve them tea." She turned to her charges. "We shall spend the night here in the canteen. There are no accommodations. Remember your orders. Be ready to board the lorries first thing." And then, to the relief of all, Matron stalked away into the gathering gloom.

"Well, she's rather frightful, isn't she?" one of the sprightly young women observed critically.

"At least she's gone!" Andee exclaimed.

"Don't speak so loudly," Marge begged. "She's got eyes in the back of her head and invisible ears plastered to our foreheads; I'm sure of it!"

Andee scoffed but stole a glance toward Matron's retreating form.

Annie turned her head, wishing only to remain anonymous.

"My name is Kimberly, and this is my sister, Karen," the young canteen worker offered. "Do come round the back, and we shall let you in. At least you'll have a place to sit down. You'll need to keep your wraps. It's frightfully cold!"

The moment the girls were settled, Karen and Kimberly began filling a round of mugs with tepid tea. "It's been ages since we've had a group of girls here—always soldiers, don't you know."

"And that's a problem?" Marge asked, laughing as she shivered. "We've a shortage of eligible men in England this year!"

"There's no shortage of men here!" Karen raised her brows significantly. "Not if you don't mind being proposed to twenty times a day." She laughed as she pulled a twisted paper from her uniform pocket. "Here, share our sugar ration—we've been saving for a celebration."

The girls accepted appreciatively. Annie had stirred sugar in her tea in England that morning, but it seemed ages ago.

"But are they sincere proposals? That's what I want to know!" Babs begged.

"Oh, they're sincere enough in the moment," Kimberly answered. "But then they're off to the front to do their 'sacred duty,' and who knows if we'll ever see them again!"

"Don't be callous!" Karen admonished. "Poor blighters. This canteen and the women who run it are the loves of their lives—their short lives, many of them."

"Is it really as bad as they say—up in Verdun?" Liz asked nervously.

Karen and Kimberly exchanged a glance.

The VADs drew back. Annie swallowed. She had already nursed survivors of Verdun.

"Let's not talk of that now," Karen said. "Enjoy your time here. Anything we can get you, we will." She forced a smile and returned to her post behind the counter.

Babs tugged Kimberly's sleeve. "Tell us."

Kimberly glanced over her shoulder at her sister, waited until her attention was captured by a flirtatious French officer, and lowered her voice to the group. "This road—the French call it the Sacred Way. It is the only road into or out of Verdun. Thousands of soldiers go in every day. Not so many return." She cast another glance at her sister, but Karen was still pouring coffee. She whispered, "They mean to recapture and hold Verdun, no matter what the cost." She looked away, then studied the girls and repeated, "No matter what the cost."

Andee whispered to the girls, "I told you so."

⁂

Annie stretched toward the ceiling every hour or two; her back and legs cramped from sitting at the canteen tables on hard wooden benches through the long, cold night.

"At least we're allowed inside." Judy kept her stiff upper lip, no matter that it shivered. "The men have to sleep out in the cold."

"I don't know how they manage," Evelyn said near midnight. "It's absolutely freezing out there."

Annie didn't know either. She was so cold that she could barely bend her fingers; she longed for a hot bath, a hair wash, and a steaming cup of tea.

The girls tried to sleep sitting back to back or used their forearms crossed on the table for a pillow.

Gray morning came at last, bearing none of the niceties Annie had wished for.

Kimberly appeared in the doorway, rested and chipper. "We shall open in another hour. You girls will want to use the facilities before we open the window to serve—too many observers, if you know what I mean."

The queue filed through quickly. "Nothing like cold water to shorten a lady's trip to the lavatory!" Andee quipped.

Kimberly poured an early round of tea for the girls. "You're a quiet one," she said to Annie. "What is your name, love?"

Annie's spine stiffened. "Elisabeth," she said. "Elisabeth Hargrave." The name her aunt had insisted upon still came none too easily.

"You'll want to post your cards before the lorries return," Karen announced to the group, who stared blankly at the sisters. "Your post-cards—to your families."

"But we've only just arrived," Marge said. "There's nothing to write yet."

"Not even!" Babs echoed.

Karen and Kimberly exchanged their secret-code glances.

"Just the same," Karen replied before she turned to her duties, "let your families know you're here—in Revigny, in France."

It was a sober reminder of all that lay ahead, and the girls obediently penned tiny letters onto cards, intent on cramming in every detail they might for loved ones beyond the channel, now a world away.

"You've no one to write to, Elisabeth?" Kimberly chided good-naturedly as she collected the cards. "No one at all?"

Annie drew in her breath, squared her shoulders, and turned away. "No one."

Before the lorries roared to life at seven thirty and pulled their long train over the rough and shell-holed road toward Verdun, the VADs posed, smiling, for a group photograph.

"We post them on the canteen walls so the soldiers can see them as they pass our serving window," Kimberly said, snapping the photograph. "It's a happy reminder for the blokes of what they're fighting to preserve— a little smile of encouragement away from home."

"Your smiles will mean more than your words to those poor soldiers in hospital," Karen advised. "Men with no faces or shrapnel in their neck need to see that you see them as men—as human beings—and not their deformity. Remember that. It may be the best thing you can do for them."

≋ CHAPTER FIFTY ≋

OVER THE NEXT FEW WEEKS Mr. Sprague sifted the contents of Eleanor Hargrave's will, her papers, her house, with a fine-toothed comb. Through private investigation, the government, the war office, and by offering payment for information, he did his best to trace Annie's whereabouts—in France, in England, on every British front.

Michael and Connie combed street after street, site after site of London and even Southampton as they waited for Mr. Sprague to receive word. They searched every place that either of them had ever known Annie to visit in the belief that Eleanor Hargrave might have lied with her dying breath—in the hope that Annie was tucked away somewhere they had not looked.

Newspapers were hawked on every street corner, all with the devastating war news of the slaughter at Verdun. Connie pulled a sickened Michael away, reminding him that any thought given to the war was a thought stolen from finding Annie.

Mr. Sprague rubbed his temples after weeks of fruitless searching. "It comes down to the fact that she has gone. If the stories are to be believed, of her own free will, asserting that she is twenty-three years old, and thereby absolving every government worker of responsibility in any form."

"But we know that's rot!" Connie exploded.

"Please, Constance," her mother began, "do not use slang."

"It only matters that we find her and bring her home," Michael insisted.

Mr. Sprague looked up. "Yes. If there is a way. But if she is truly in France . . ." He shook his head. "The conditions there are horrible. They desperately need every nurse, every doctor, every man or woman able to fight or fetch or carry. They will not send her home because we ask."

"She sent her to die," Connie said quietly.

"Constance!" her mother admonished, but without conviction.

"Mother, we know it's true. We should say it. I don't know what that woman said to compel Annie to go, but she sent her to the place of greatest danger and instilled every ounce of fear possible in her mind by having her nurse the worst of the wounded here before going! Annie needed to be in peak mental and physical form for the rigors of nursing in battle zones in France—Eleanor Hargrave made sure she was a wreck! It was a long and devious plan! Annie never wanted to go overseas and could not have known how to go without someone setting it all in motion." Connie looked at Michael. "You know that, don't you?"

Michael nodded, the pain of weeks of fear and worry lining his face.

"There is nothing for us to do but pray," Mrs. Sprague said.

Michael stood and stared at the three Spragues as if they had all lost their minds. "That is not all there is to do. We've done all we can here. Now I must go and find her."

"You've no hope of finding her, son," Mr. Sprague argued half-heartedly. "My sources say she is not listed in any of the British hospitals. If she is working with a French field hospital somewhere in the area of the front . . ." He threw his hands up. "We don't even know which front, and where is but a guess!"

"But you said France—"

"I have sent word to every French field hospital of which we have any record. There is no Annie Allen or Elisabeth Anne Allen listed." Mr. Sprague ran his fingers through his thinning hair. "That information came from Eleanor Hargrave in her last moments—how reliable can we expect it to be? She could be anywhere on the Continent. With the funds Eleanor had at her disposal, she could have had Annie sent anywhere in the world!"

"I will find her, and I will bring her back." Michael stood his ground. "What can you do, Mr. Sprague, to get me to France?"

"Short of enlisting, I do not believe—"

"Then I'll believe for us both!" Michael leaned across Mr. Sprague's desk, within a breath of his face. "Get me there as an ambulance driver. It will allow me to search the field hospitals, the churches, the schools, the halls—anywhere they might have set up a medical facility. I can drive. I learned before I came!"

"You must understand," Mr. Sprague explained wearily, patiently, "no one will allow you to run willy-nilly through the hills and dales of France unmolested! If you go out of uniform, you will be shot as a spy. If you go in uniform, you will have to follow orders that will not allow you the freedom you seek."

"Father, listen to—"

"You cannot have it both ways!" Mr. Sprague's temper rose.

"Then talk to those government officials you know," Michael insisted. "Get me to the Red Cross or a private, citizen-led convalescent home in a way that allows me the needed freedom."

"I do not have the rank and pull you seem to think, young man."

"Then use whatever you have," Michael shouted. "I beg you!"

"Edwin." Mrs. Sprague gently laid her hand upon her husband's arm. "What about that young American who gave the speech to raise funds for medical volunteers—the ones who drive those American Model T cars he was so very fond of?"

"The American Ambulance Field Service." He shook his head. "They've virtually become part of the French military."

"I heard about him, Father—A. Piatt Andrew, a powerhouse of a man in the face of all our blasted bureaucracy and red tape!"

"Constance, do not swear in this house!" Her mother fumed.

Connie ignored her. "Where was he stationed, Father?"

"Alsace." Her mother spoke authoritatively, surprising everyone. "He was setting up his ambulance service in Alsace at the time. Do you remember how he said those little cars could fly up and down the steep Vosges mountains—how they make better ambulances than our large touring cars? So very odd."

They all turned to look at her.

"Tin Lizzies," Connie said.

"Yes, Tin Lizzies, he called them—funny little name. He was working in Alsace. But he said there were field service sections in many places and more spreading all the time."

Mr. Sprague studied his wife's face, his brow wrinkled in thought.

Mrs. Sprague cocked her head and smiled. "I imagine that a sizable financial donation and the pledge of a qualified Irish-American driver would be of some assistance in helping Mr. Andrew respond agreeably to our request."

Mr. Sprague frowned and turned to Michael, who vigorously nodded.

Mr. Sprague considered, nodding slowly in return. He stood and pressed his wife's fingers to his lips. "I'll wire Sir—I'll wire my colleague in Dover. He will know where Mr. Andrew may be reached."

❧ CHAPTER FIFTY-ONE ❧

MR. SPRAGUE'S SOURCES revealed that sixteen units of VADs had departed from England's shores in the space of two days—the two days in which they first believed Annie had disappeared. Ships had departed from Folkestone, Dover, Plymouth, and Southampton. There was no Annie Allen, nor an Elisabeth Anne Allen, listed among the passengers.

Michael scribbled, as best he could on the wave-tossed ferry, a letter to Aunt Maggie and Uncle Daniel, telling them all he knew of Annie and all he hoped might come from his joining A. Piatt Andrew in the American Ambulance Field Service in Paris.

Before she died, Annie's aunt Eleanor told the authorities that her niece had gone to do her sacred duty at the front. The Spragues and I can only believe that means she sent her to nurse in France. But which front? There is no record of her going anywhere.

Within the AAFS I will have the greatest freedom of movement between field hospitals and private hospitals. Mr. Andrew has agreed to give me every opportunity to search for Annie within the limitations of the ambulance service as long as I perform adequately in the role of driver.

I report tomorrow to the American Military Hospital in Paris and then go for training. I'm hoping for my assignment within the month.

All of this I owe to the kindness and connections of Mr. Sprague. I do not understand his work in this war, but I am grateful that he holds whatever position of authority he does. I would have no hope of finding Annie without him.

I've left some of my belongings with the Spragues. Mr. Andrew
advised Mr. Sprague that ambulance drivers must travel lightly.
Do not lose heart, Aunt Maggie. I will find our Annie.
Keep Owen's bridal roses wrapped until April, Uncle Daniel, then
tend them with care. We'll be needing those blooms by and by for
Annie's welcome-home bouquet.

I love you both.
Michael

A. Piatt Andrew, head of the American Ambulance Field Service, drummed his fingers across Michael's file. "You are searching for a needle in a haystack. You know that, don't you, young man?"

"She's a bright needle, sir. I'll find her—I will, sir." Michael stood at attention.

Andrew sighed. If he did not owe his benefactors so many favors, he would never have taken on this bold Irishman or his harebrained venture. He leaned back in his chair. "They tell me you can take a Ford apart and put her back together again."

"From the ground up, sir. In record time." Michael lifted his chin.

Andrew stood and, turning his back on the cocky young man, looked out the window at his fleet of ambulances, a row of well-oiled Fords, precious Tin Lizzies, ready for deployment. The man was not so different from himself, Andrew conceded—brazen, confident, determined—and his driving and mechanic experience exceeded that of most of his new recruits.

"You have your assignment?"

"Yes, sir! The Vosges."

"There is a field hospital west of Guebwiller." Andrew did not turn to look at Michael again. "See that you report there in two days."

"Yes, sir!"

"Dismissed."

"Sir!" Michael turned to go.

"Dunnagan! Take care of the old girl."

"Her name is Annie Allen, sir," Michael contradicted.

"Her name, Dunnagan, is Tin Lizzie."

≫ ≪

In three months Michael knew every back road and narrow mule trail through the forests of Alsace. His nose grazed his knees more times than he could count maneuvering up and down the steep, slippery mountains of the Vosges through forests so dense and green he could not see the winding road behind him—a far cry from the flat fields of New Jersey and the seaside of Belfast.

He hated passing the nearly starving, frostbitten, and battered French soldiers, hated leaving them to trudge painfully up the steep mountain passes. He could have so easily picked them up, offered them a running board, or simply let them hang on and relieve the strain of lifting one weary foot in front of the other—at least one or two of them. But it was not permitted. He would lose his job and every opportunity of searching for Annie.

The French soldiers, good-naturedly called the *poilus*—the hairy ones—understood the rules, and though their eyes begged, their arms waved in grateful recognition and Godspeed to the men who trucked their jaunty little American ambulances to the snowy mountain peaks, retrieved their wounded French comrades, and sped them down again to casualty stations, field hospitals, and railheads bound for civilization.

Michael took every assignment he could beg or trade—the farther afield the better. In each encampment, field hospital, convalescent center, every private home and small community, he stopped, pulled Annie's photograph from his coat pocket, and asked in broken French if they knew her, if they had seen her. Always the answer was *"Non, mon pote. Je regrette"* or a simple shake of the head and shrugging of shoulders.

All the while the great guns blasted faraway Verdun; Michael heard them rumbling softly in the distance. The earth trembled beneath the mountains, a constant reminder to the feet of soldiers, Red Cross workers, ambulance drivers, and the French poor who refused to leave their homes that their blighted lives could be worse. They could be one hundred miles north.

Michael wrote twice-monthly letters to the Spragues and Aunt Maggie and Uncle Daniel, urging them to pray, to take heart, reassuring them that he had only begun to search for their precious Annie.

By the middle of June, he began writing daily letters directly to A. Piatt Andrew, requesting reassignment anywhere in France—anywhere he had not yet searched for his Annie.

※ ※

In Paris, Andrew grew exasperated with the growing pile of communication from the bold—and probably crazy, he decided—young Irishman. Reports, however, declared him the most daring and competent of drivers, with enough rescues to his name to earn a string of medals—if medals ever came to the American Ambulance Field Service. The courage Dunnagan inspired in his other drivers was no small thing.

But Andrew grieved bigger troubles. Funds donated by Americans sympathetic to and supportive of their emergency work in France never reached him. He desperately needed someone with political clout or substantial wealth to intervene for the sake of the ambulance service and the French they served. He could not be bothered with Michael Dunnagan and his fanatical search for a girl he barely knew, no matter what the young man's connections.

Andrew tossed Michael's latest letter—received that morning—into the trash bin, unopened; he knew what it said.

≋ CHAPTER FIFTY-TWO ≋

ANNIE HAD NEVER KNOWN such bitter, relentless, bone-chilling cold as the remaining winter of 1916.

Wind-blasted tents were as common as old châteaus in housing medical personnel and patients year-round. Hot water bottles froze long before morning. Annie and the other VADs slept in woollies and nightclothes, then wrapped themselves in their VAD cloaks, topped by whatever blankets they could lay claim to.

But Annie bit her tongue each time complaints sprang to her lips. She knew the men fighting suffered worse. Frostbite and cramping rheumatism competed for the greatest misery among soldiers in the winter trenches with rats the size of cats and the need to sleep standing up. Weight fell from their bones through shivering as much as lack of rations. Puttees wound tight around their calves never dried. Shoes and socks, soaked and frozen in the mud and icy slosh, did little to protect their feet.

And spring brought its own agonies. Neither Annie nor her tentmates were prepared for the plague of lice presented by the French wounded with the spring thaw. The persistent parasites found the long, thick hair of the VADs—despite the nurses' tidy, upswept buns—especially warm and comforting, the perfect place to thrive and multiply.

Night after night the young women fine-tooth-combed their long tresses to rid themselves of the itchy, nasty vermin. Night after night they scrubbed and, if someone from home had mailed bluing bottles, soaked their bloodied aprons, cuffs, and caps white in small basins of tepid water.

"I hate this war. I hate it!" Judy fumed. "What I wouldn't give for a good hair wash and a steaming-hot bath!"

Annie closed her eyes. *Me, too!*

Andee grunted. "That's just where you'd be when the shelling started up again—quite a picture for the visiting *Boche*!"

"Andee!" Babs shouted. "That's bold, even for you."

"What is that supposed to mean—bold, even for me?" Andee retorted. "Crying about a hot bath is bold when there's no chance in—"

"Girls!" Evelyn pushed wide the tent flap. "I can hear you fussing across the lane. The surgeons are snickering their heads off at you—the ones that aren't fed up!"

"Our nerves are frayed," Marge admitted. "We've been at each other's throats all morning."

"Well, you'd best take it down a notch or two. You'll have Matron over here next."

"I do wish they'd stop," Liz whispered to Annie. "They make it worse with their shouting and bickering."

But Annie did not know if it could be worse. At least their noise broke the tension of waiting for the next round of shells. "I can't always tell the difference," she said.

"What do you mean?"

Annie blinked, surprised the other girl had heard. "I'm sorry, Liz—I suppose I mean that one sort of bickering is with words and one is with shells."

"Well, it's not the same at all, you know," Liz huffed.

※ ※

The bombardment of Verdun continued, day and night. Whatever breath the Germans had taken because of winter blizzards was long gone. The only gift to the French war effort was the spring-thawed mud that sucked German tanks and lorries into great holes and craters blasted by their own guns. The German army moved forward slowly but unsupplied.

VADs, doctors, orderlies, and ambulance drivers worked round the clock in shifts, and still they could not keep up with the ever-increasing number of wounded.

Missing a shift was tantamount to desertion and permissible only if one lay unconscious or was suddenly killed by stray shrapnel. If ambulances poured in with great numbers of casualties or extraordinarily gruesome shells of men, sleep and timetables were forgotten; there was work to be done.

By June, Annie was an old hand at cutting away blood-soaked or burned uniforms of unconscious soldiers. More pitiable were those soldiers who lay conscious, screaming in pain beyond bearing. Annie did not look away while cleansing wounds of men who'd lain too long in the field before a stretcher bearer could reach them—men with wounds so putrid that the pus puddled thick and the stench of gangrene filled the marquee tent until it reeked.

Gently Annie sponged the eyes of men whose hair and faces and torsos had been set afire by the German flamethrowers. She learned the pressure points of arteries left exposed when limbs were blown away. And she, more than all the nurses, smiled softly into the eyes of men who no longer looked like men—men who had been gassed or whose noses or mouths were burned or blown away. "Lost souls," the girls called them— men forever disfigured, unless they were lucky enough to be fitted for prosthetic limbs or sent to the tin-noses shop for artificial restructuring.

"Even then," Babs whispered, "they're not the same. Something inside them is gone—something that all the suturing and pasting in the world cannot bring back."

Annie knew it was so. And yet looking at these men was an odd sort of comfort to her. She saw, in plain view, the ugliness thrust upon them through no fault of their own—the physical results of the evil of violence, one man pitted against another. She had known such evil from her aunt Eleanor, and yet Annie's wounds could not be seen from the outside.

But Aunt Eleanor's soul, reeking, putrid, and gangrenous from spite and wounds imagined, was hidden from the world, covered by a respectable, if empty, outer shell. Annie shuddered to think of the state of her aunt's heart.

The other girls cringed and wondered aloud at the way Matron openly and unjustly criticized Annie. It was common knowledge that Matron consistently assigned Annie the most grueling shifts and cases. Still, Annie dared not complain.

In July, German zeppelins—overblown slivers of gray against a new-moon sky—dropped their bombs across the trenches, fields, and French forces of Verdun. Whether aimed directly at the field hospital or not, the surgical marquee tent in Annie's section was blown to bits, along with two of their best surgeons, a VAD nurse, and two orderlies.

Explosion after explosion lit the night. Metal, glass, bones, and limbs shattered and severed, flying upward, shooting their own shrapnel through the tents. Patients unable to walk or lift themselves screamed for help, prayed aloud for help or merciful death, and clamped tight their eyes and mouths, certain the end had come.

When at last the shelling abated, gray-and-yellow morning dawned through smoke. Matron and the remaining VADs stumbled through rubble, pulling the injured and dead from the tents and debris. All day and into the night they toiled, fetching and carrying, dragging and lifting bodies, scrubbing new wounds and old, bringing as much comfort as they could to their remaining patients. Before they'd finished, another load of ambulances brought their newly maimed.

At the end of the second day, while the shelling of Verdun continued to rattle their nerves and instruments, Matron and Annie found themselves momentarily alone with a patient in the surgery, both having assisted in the removal of shrapnel from the man's chest. Matron swabbed the skin around the sutured wound. Annie spoke softly, gently urging the man awake, assuring him that all was well, all would be well.

When at last the orderlies had come and carried the man away, Annie, who'd not slept for two days, collected the instruments and blood-soaked bandages and sponges. She felt, rather than saw, Matron's cold eyes upon her and wished the woman would just go away. Shaken from the relentless bombardment, the days of toil without sleep, and the boring of Matron's eyes, Annie's fingers fumbled. She dropped her tray of instruments and sent them clattering into the dust.

Despite her determination to maintain control, Annie began to shake, to dig her nails into the palms of her hands to keep tears of nervous exhaustion from rolling down her cheeks. She breathed as steadily as she could, bent down, and retrieved her tray. By the time she'd found every instrument and begun the sterilization process once more, she had collected herself. *I'll not give her the satisfaction of looking up.*

At length Matron pulled her bloodied apron from her shoulders and rolled down her sleeves. "Whatever could such a slip of a girl have done to incur the wrath of Eleanor Hargrave?"

Annie felt the blood drain from her face. She stopped her work, straightened, confirmed at last in her suspicion that Matron Artrip was her aunt's puppet and assigned monitor. No wonder she'd been cornered and hounded. No wonder she'd been given the worst tasks. The woman was her aunt's paid spy.

Annie breathed deeply and turned to face Matron. "I was born."

Matron blinked and walked out.

The operating theatre whirled for Annie; she steadied herself against the instrument table.

Scrubbing down the table at last gave her a sensation of freedom, a symbolic scrubbing away of her doubts.

Her answer to Matron had been truthful. Annie had only to look in the mirror to see the reflected image of her mother at eighteen—her mother, happily married and with child. Aunt Eleanor, trapped at home and rejected, the overlooked older sister, had forged a chained life from her jealousy and venom and made a lethal weapon of her power and money.

And when she had destroyed her own family simply because they lived and were happy—Annie's mother, father, and brother—there was only Annie and those who had been kind to her, those who might even love her.

Annie beat the table with her rag. Bottling the tears that threatened to flow, she vowed, beneath her breath, "I will abide by your terms, Aunt Eleanor, for the sake of those I love. But there is a timeline. This war will end, and I and all those I love will go free."

CHAPTER FIFTY-THREE

Seated across the desk from A. Piatt Andrew, Anne Harriman Vanderbilt drummed manicured nails on the arm of her chair. She would wait as long as it took.

The opportunity for a woman to tour the Verdun sector, no matter how great her fortune and influence, did not come every day.

Andrew's secretary stood, blinking and clearly tense, awaiting his supervisor's decision.

"He left his post; there is little to decide," Andrew maintained.

"Yes, sir," the young secretary replied. "But what shall I do with him, sir?" And then more quietly, "He's one of our best drivers and mechanics."

"Crazy Michael Dunnagan is the last thing I need this morning," Andrew said, not quite under his breath, and ran his fingers through his hair. He stood, tugged his jacket into place, and cleared his throat as if ready to make a proclamation.

The door flew open before he opened his mouth.

A dashing young man, brushed and combed, red faced, with striking blue eyes and broad shoulders, marched in, twisting his cap between his fingers, and began a tirade about having applied repeatedly for immediate transfer to a new sector.

Andrew's color heightened. His attempts to get a word in edgewise failed so miserably that Anne was tempted to laugh. It was the first time she had witnessed Andrew in anything less than total control of a situation.

"I'll go anywhere, sir—Verdun, if you'll let me. She's not in the Vosges area. I've asked everyone—everywhere! No one's seen her."

The young Irishman, or Irish-American, as Anne learned, begged only for permission and the requisite papers to search for a missing young

305

nurse, someone named Annie. Having received no response to his daily letters, he had come to deliver his urgent request in person.

But Andrew, Anne saw, clearly embarrassed by the upstart, would go hard on the fellow. Anne realized, too, that the driver was a man determined.

Graciously, simply, Anne relieved them both. "Mr. Andrew, I believe I would like this young man for my driver."

"Your driver?" Andrew stared. "But Rogers is your designated driver. Dunnagan has no formal education, and our drivers are typically from the best sch—"

"Your secretary said he is one of the best drivers and best mechanics, both, did he not?"

The secretary arched his brows and gave a small nod out of Andrew's line of vision.

A vein in Andrew's neck throbbed visibly.

"Is that not correct, Mr. Andrew?" Anne Vanderbilt persisted.

"Michael Dunnagan—" Andrew protested, but Anne cut him off.

"I would appreciate the best protection and precautions you might afford. I really do care more about my safety than I do any discussion of the classics. And it would give Mr. Dunnagan the opportunity to view each of the hospitals and their medical personnel in the Verdun area." She flicked a stray piece of lint from her skirt. She smiled. "I do like a good love story," she said, at which Michael Dunnagan blushed brightly. "I daresay you might consider his transfer while we are away."

A. Piatt Andrew looked as though he might burst a rivet. Anne knew he was a man who did not like to be crossed. She also knew he dared not cross her.

"Bring me the papers," Andrew ordered his secretary.

Anne studied her driver and smiled.

※ ※

It was the first week of August before Mrs. Vanderbilt, disguised in a nurse's white Red Cross uniform to protect her from advances—both by the enemy and by solicitous French soldiers—accompanied Andrew on their tour of the Verdun front. If Andrew was still angry with their driver, Michael Dunnagan, he hid it well.

Anne Vanderbilt found the young Irishman intriguing and the story of his desperate search for Annie Allen pitiable but charming.

Their first stop was Revigny, the beginning of the Sacred Way. Like every French soldier, they sought the comfort of the *Café Gratuit* or *La Cantine de Dames Anglaises*.

When Anne Vanderbilt reached over the counter to accept the offered cup of coffee and two cigarettes, Karen's eyes widened. Anne followed the young woman's gaze and winced. There was not a nurse in France with painted fingernails. The eyes of the women met.

"You won't give me away, will you, dear?" Anne asked.

"That depends on your game . . . my dear," Karen replied.

But a word of explanation from Andrew, well known to the ladies of the canteen, gave Anne a ticket to hospitality.

"Any friend of Mr. Andrew's is a friend of ours. Would you like to come inside and see our operation?" Kimberly pushed between her sister and Mrs. Vanderbilt. "Men," she said significantly to Andrew, "are not allowed."

"I am honored!" Anne sang.

Kimberly whispered to her sister in Anne's hearing, "She may be a bit of a toff, but I think she's all right, don't you?"

Karen shrugged and continued to offer coffee and cigarettes through the canteen window to the passing troops.

Kimberly gave Anne the grand, one-minute tour of their volunteer operation.

"And who are all these young nurses?" Anne pointed to the groups of pushpinned photographs hanging on the wall beside the door.

"All the VADs who pass through and the Red Cross workers—and the sisters, if they'll deign to have their photographs taken. It's our little way of honoring them. Those ladies don't get the recognition they deserve, you know, and some—like the soldiers—never make it home again. We're bound to watch our own."

Anne nodded, unsettled once again by the determined service and willing sacrifice of so many.

"Ours is an operation of cheer and comfort—nothing more, nothing grand like the nurses do. But if it helps those poor men go back and fight again, if it cheers them even a little—torn from their homes and loved ones as they are—well, then, it's worth it, isn't it?"

"Yes, yes it is," Anne answered. "And who posts your picture, Kimberly? Yours and Karen's?"

"No one, that I can think." Kimberly blushed. "It's such a little thing we do."

Anne laid her hand on Kimberly's arm. "Kindness is never a little thing." Kimberly's blush deepened, and she smiled.

"I wonder . . ." Anne paused at the door. "There is a young man—our driver—who has been searching everywhere for a young nurse—"

"Aren't they all?" Kimberly quipped.

Anne smiled. "Might he come in for just a moment and look at your photographs to see if she passed through here?"

Kimberly glanced nervously at her sister's back by the open window. "Well, I don't know. We're really not supposed to let anyone in here—not soldiers, certainly."

"He isn't a soldier; he's an ambulance driver and a very good one."

"One of Mr. Andrew's? An American?"

"One of his best—an impeccable record." Anne thought it unnecessary to mention Michael's Irish roots.

"Well, if you're here with him, and if it's only for a moment, I suppose . . ."

"That's wonderful! I'll call him and we'll return right away!"

Karen bristled when Anne Vanderbilt appeared at the side door and openly fumed when she came back and boldly walked in with an ambulance driver in tow.

"See, just here, Michael. Kimberly said that these are all the nurses—well, nearly all, I suppose—who have come through the canteen on their way to . . ." She turned to Kimberly and Karen. "On their way to where? Verdun? Did they all go to Verdun?"

"Not all," Karen answered, taking a step toward Michael.

Anne ignored her cold stare and gracefully, quickly, stepped between

Michael and the sisters. "Is she here, Michael? Do you think any of these nurses look like her?" She pushed him closer to the photographs.

But he needed no urging. He squinted into the grainy black-and-white images, searching each one for any likeness of Annie. He shook his head. "I can't tell. I've never seen Annie in uniform. I don't know if I'm looking at her and not seeing her."

He sounded so miserable that Anne slapped his arm. "Give me your photograph."

"What?" He pulled back, gripped Annie's photograph, and looked as though nothing in all the world could make him turn it loose.

"Give me your photograph, or show it to these young ladies. They may remember her."

Michael laid Annie's picture on the counter before them. "She's pretty and young and kindness itself. Her name is Annie Allen."

Kimberly shook her head slowly, then stopped and studied the photograph again. It was the image of a girl—perhaps sixteen or seventeen—with an older girl and, presumably, their mother and father. "I don't remember anyone by that name. Why are you looking for her?"

"She is family," Michael said. "I've bound myself to find her."

Kimberly frowned but hesitated. "There was a girl who looked something like this, but . . ."

"Is her photograph here?" Michael held his breath.

Kimberly searched the wall and pointed to a group of VADs. "We snapped this one in February." She pointed to the girl who had called herself ". . . Elisabeth something or other."

"Elisabeth Anne Allen!" Michael nearly shouted. "That is her name!"

"No," Karen answered, barely looking at the photograph. "There was no one here by that name. We ask all their names. We would remember."

"But neither of you could have been on duty every minute of every day!" Anne protested.

"We are the only ones with a camera."

Michael's face fell.

"She rather looks like her, don't you think, Karen? What was her surname?"

"I don't remember, and neither do you."

Kimberly glanced at her sister.

"Did this lot go to Verdun?" Michael asked as calmly as he could.

"We don't know where they were sent," Karen insisted.

Neither Anne nor Michael missed the almost-imperceptible nod that Kimberly gave.

※ ※

That night Kimberly turned her back on her sister, not caring that she snubbed her only confidante in France. "You should have told them."

"It wasn't the right name; you know that."

"No, but they—"

"He said she was family," Karen interrupted, "and Elisabeth said she has no family—no one at all; don't you remember? She said her name is Hargrave."

"But they both seemed so nice—and isn't he a handsome devil?" Kimberly pouted.

"The American woman tricked you into letting that Irisher in. Think of it, Kimberly. She was English and from a good and cultured family—sometime, somewhere. He was northern Irish if I've ever heard it! None of it fits. If Elisabeth truly changed her name, she must have had a reason. For all we know, she's running away from this very bloke. We dare not give her away!"

Kimberly punched her pillow, fluffed it as best she could, and rolled onto her side. *Irish or not,* she thought, *he seemed more a man to run to than away from.* Aloud she said, "I don't know. I hope we've done the proper thing."

≋ CHAPTER FIFTY-FOUR ≋

MICHAEL PULLED THE STEERING WHEEL hard left, swerving from the road and into the field just in time to miss a crater-size pothole.

Anne Vanderbilt squealed in the seat beside him, grabbed the door-frame for balance, and just as quickly composed herself.

Michael bit his lip. *Feisty lady! And she's kept up—day after day, hospital after hospital. If only we don't get a load of German shrapnel on our heads!*

Indeed, Anne had accompanied Andrew and Michael on a tour of every château and shop and deserted school turned hospital and nearly every surgical marquee tent wilting in the August heat. They'd spent the second half of a long night of artillery attack in the rubble of a dim, dank cellar, surrounded by soldiers and patients, certain the world would end for them that night.

It was the first time Michael had seen a lady in her sleeping cap and robe since he'd left Aunt Maggie in New Jersey. It had the odd effect of making him pine keenly for home, despite the immediate whistle of how-itzers and the sky lit by exploding rockets. They reminded him of the dis-tress rockets shot up from *Titanic*. For the first time Michael entertained thoughts of quitting, giving up this mad search for his "bright needle" and going home to Aunt Maggie and Uncle Daniel.

There were only two field hospitals left to tour in the sector; Michael's hopes of finding Annie in Verdun waned.

By late afternoon of the following day, he had walked through half the new wards and shown Annie's photograph to everyone with eyes that could still see. Every head that was able shook a familiar no.

"Please, Sisters." Michael stopped two VADs just coming from mess. He called every woman in white uniform "Sister." Better to ingratiate himself to all by using the title freely than to risk offending one who truly carried that high rank. "Please, I'm searching for someone. Her name is Annie Allen—Elisabeth Anne Allen." He pulled the tattered and creased photograph from his vest pocket.

"Judy, look! Why, it's Elisabeth, isn't it?" one woman asked the other. She handed the picture back to Michael. "But her name isn't Allen; it's Hargrave. At least it surely looks like her."

"Elisabeth Hargrave." Michael's jaw dropped. He forcibly closed his mouth but thought the earth might spin off its axis. *No wonder she's on no lists! I've been looking for the wrong name!* "Is she here?" The words sounded as though they came from someplace far away, a voice not his own.

The young women pointed to a tent thirty feet away. "Over there— the surgical tent. Elisabeth's on duty—or just finishing her shift."

Annie stepped through the flap of the tent into the fierce August heat. She wiped her brow with the sleeve of her uniform and squinted into the late-afternoon sun. Rolling down her sleeves, she straightened her cuffs.

"Elisabeth!" Judy beckoned her.

Annie turned and walked toward the small group. *Why are they staring?*

They stood just in the face of the sun; Annie lifted her hand to shade her eyes. The broad-shouldered and uniformed ambulance driver standing beside Judy and Marge removed his cap slowly but gawked boldly, openly. Annie straightened and swiped at her hair. Undone by the young man's blatant stare, she felt compelled to drop her eyes. Unaccountably, she could not.

As she neared the group, she took in the man's startling blue eyes, the unruly mass of dark curls atop his head, and the sharp dimpling in his cheeks. Her brow wrinkled, but her heart quickened its beat until it pounded in her ears.

"It cannot be," she whispered. But she had seen that lopsided grin—a lifetime ago, in a newspaper clipping, amid birdhouses and gazebos. And before that, she'd seen those blue eyes high aboard a great ship about to sail, and even before that, on a street corner one Easter morning.

Michael? Is it you? Why . . . How is it you are here? But words refused to come. Her breath caught. *Oh—you're handsome—and I'm a mess!* She wanted to run to him but made herself walk toward the uniformed driver, her eyes caught in his. Annie's knees trembled.

She stumbled, catching her heel in her skirt. Her hands shot out, her left palm breaking her fall onto the gravel. Pain shot through her arm and heat up her neck.

The young man was beside her before she raised her eyes. He pulled her to her feet, his arm firmly about her waist, then dropped his hand from her side as though it had been set afire—and surely, his reddened face looked to Annie as though it had.

Standing so close that she felt his breath upon her ear, he opened her palm and examined the scrape with the diligence of a surgeon. She looked into his face, so near, and saw the muscles flex in his jaw. But he did not meet her eyes. She saw, as if from a distance, his larger hand holding hers, felt his strong fingers entwine with hers.

"Annie." The young man's voice broke. "Annie," he said again, cradling her hand.

Annie could not hold the tears welling in her eyes. She could not stop them from coursing over her cheeks. "How did you find me?" she whispered at last, swiping her face, rubbing her wet fingers over her bloodied apron.

But all she could think was, *Why did you come? Did you come just for me? Thank You, God! Oh, thank You!*

Slowly, reverently, he lifted her dirtied fingers to his lips. He held them there and closed his eyes, as though he breathed a prayer over them.

"Ahem." Marge coughed, tapping Annie on the arm. "I say, 'Ahem!'" She tugged Annie back to consciousness. "You two had best leave off. Matron's sprinting down the avenue as we speak."

Annie pulled her hand away. She brushed away her tears again and lifted her chin to face him. "We musn't let her know. I'll explain later. Do this for me."

"Oh, what a scrape!" Marge exclaimed loudly. "You've got to see to that straightaway, Elisabeth! Here, let me help you."

"What has happened? What is going on here?" Matron demanded.

"Matron—Elisabeth's taken a tumble, that's all." Marge stepped between Annie and Michael. "This gentleman saw her fall and came to give us a hand. But never you mind; we'll see to her."

Matron looked from one girl to the other, barely scanned the bleeding scrape in Annie's palm, and narrowed her eyes at the beet-faced ambulance driver. "Very well. See that you do." She half turned. "And you." She nodded toward Michael. "Drivers are billeted over there." She pointed across the way, to the far end of the camp.

"Yes, Sister." Michael tipped his cap. "Thank you, mum."

Matron raised herself, looked as if she was about to say something more, then turned and stormed away.

"She's not fond of the Irish," Judy whispered, leaning near him. "But never mind her. Let's get Elisabeth cleaned up, and you two tell us what in blazes is going on!"

"I'll help her. Show me where I can wash her wound." Michael lifted Annie's hand protectively and squared his shoulders.

All three girls looked up.

"Round the mess tent. There's water there." Annie nodded the way. She whispered to Marge and Judy, "Please, oh, please, don't say anything to anyone."

The girls lit with the delight of new suspense. "You can count on us," Marge whispered back. "Just be sure you tell us—" she looked at Michael—"everything!"

Annie smiled despite her wish to remain serious, then allowed Michael to guide her behind the mess tent. "Where did you come from? How did you get here?" she begged, but Michael led her on.

"Wait. Wait here," he ordered gently.

He poured water from the standing supply keg into a basin and unpinned a clean rag from the line of washed linen. "Give me your hand."

Carefully he dipped Annie's injured hand into the water. He picked the surface gravel from her bleeding palm and wiped the grit from the surrounding area. He swirled the dirty water in the basin, tossed it away, and filled the basin again.

Annie watched his face, the line of his jaw and the long dimple that creased his cheek, now very near her hair. She stood close enough to know that he swallowed, that his breath drew shallow, that his nerves remained tensed.

She'd stood beside, even bathed, wounded men for months. Never had she wanted with everything in her to stand closer still.

"You'll need to keep this clean," Michael ordered again, still holding her injured hand beneath the water. "The bleeding's stopped."

Dutifully, Annie nodded. She could not hide her smile. She nestled closer.

Michael stopped his washing. He glanced at her from the corner of his eye, smiled in return, but did not face her.

"Michael?" *Why won't he look at me? He looks positively petrified!*

Annie slipped her free hand into the water and, holding her breath, clasped the top of Michael's hands. She watched the miracle of his hands unfold and wrap her fingers.

"You're a treasure hard to find," he whispered in her ear, exploring her wrists and the slender spaces between each finger. "I swear I'll never lose you again, Annie Allen."

Annie's heart caught. She felt it swell and swell until she thought it might burst. She leaned her hair against his face, catching the stray tear that trickled from the corner of his eye.

Michael pressed his face against the top of Annie's head and closed his eyes.

A minute passed, and unaccountably, she giggled. And then she laughed—for the first time since setting foot on French soil. Annie felt her eyes widen at her foreign outburst. But she laughed again. She pulled her hand away, cupped water from the basin, and splashed him fully in the face, delighted with her own impudence.

Michael gasped and stepped back.

But she did it again and again, teasing until he splashed her in return.

They were both soaked when Michael grabbed her by the wrists, the blue lights dancing in his eyes. "Enough of that, Miss Allen!" Worry lines melted from his face. He pulled her into his arms.

Willingly she came; willingly he kissed her.

≋ CHAPTER FIFTY-FIVE ≋

OVER THE NEXT TWO DAYS Matron had a difficult time keeping track of Annie. When the girl was scheduled for duty, she reported promptly, as always. But after her shift, Matron was hard pressed to locate her.

"She must be dead on her feet. Elisabeth picked up an extra shift in the night for one of the girls, Matron." Marge had looked her in the eye when she'd said it, but Matron was certain she was lying.

Doubtful, Matron peeked in the tent Elisabeth shared with the other VADs, but seeing the form of a girl beneath the sheet, she walked away.

When Elisabeth did not appear at mess, Matron demanded an explanation. Judy whispered that it was "Elisabeth's time, poor thing, and she cannot eat a morsel."

≋

Michael learned enough from Annie not to write the Spragues or Aunt Maggie and Uncle Daniel, nor to mention his great find to Mrs. Vanderbilt or A. Piatt Andrew, though he was determined to convince Andrew to reassign him to the Verdun sector.

"I'll desert if he won't transfer me."

Annie spread her hands. "It's not that simple, Michael!"

Michael squared his jaw. "I was charged by Owen with your care and deliverance to America. I lost you once. I searched until I found you. I love you, Annie Allen, with everything that is in me. I won't lose you again."

❧ ❦

"I sense you are no longer telling me everything, Michael Dunnagan," Anne Vanderbilt observed on the morning of their second full day at the field hospital.

Michael did not answer but continued to grease the engine of his Ford.

"Is there something I should know?"

Michael straightened. Carefully he wiped the grease from his fingers. "There is something you would like to know. There is something you deserve to know. But I'm not at liberty to say." Every line in his face begged for understanding.

Anne Vanderbilt was not used to guessing games, and she would have been vexed were it not for those magnificent blue eyes. She tilted her head. "You've found her."

Michael looked away.

"There's more to the story," she guessed. "The girl's in trouble, isn't she?" Anne could not keep the edge from her voice.

"Not in the way you're thinking." Michael's face hardened. "She's not that kind of girl."

"I'm sorry." Anne softened. "I should have known better. You love her, don't you?"

Michael did not answer, but his silence told Anne Vanderbilt all she needed to know.

"What can I do to help?"

"Get Mr. Andrew to assign me here—to Verdun, to this hospital. But I beg you, Mrs. Vanderbilt, don't let him know that I've found Annie. She doesn't even go by that name."

Anne sighed. *What good it will do, I cannot tell. The chances of either Michael or his lady living through this awful shelling are not high.* But she knew that she owed Michael this. She'd brought him this far; she had been instrumental in accomplishing his purpose, and now she must help him complete it.

"I can do that. But you won't like the way I do it." Michael blinked. "I trust you, Mrs. Vanderbilt. And I thank you for helping me. God bless you, mum." He extended his hand.

She looked down at his greasy nails, smiled, and pressed his large, strong hand in her small one. "God bless you, Michael Dunnagan."

※ ※

"What has he done?" Andrew threw down his dinner serviette. "Has the cad insulted you?"

Mrs. Anne Harriman Vanderbilt straightened her spine. "Mr. Andrew, I am not accustomed to being questioned. I am accustomed to having my wishes granted." She looked over the table of ambulance drivers at mess. "I rather like that young man." She pointed appreciatively to an athletic and flirtatious young driver intent on catching the eye of a table of pretty VADs.

Andrew blinked. He held Anne Vanderbilt in the highest esteem. Such a request seemed entirely out of character for her. "It would mean a reassignment."

She shrugged. "Should that concern me?"

"No, of course not. But it will mean leaving Dunnagan here."

She shrugged again.

Andrew frowned. He did not like Dunnagan; that was true. But they had come this far looking for his girl; shouldn't they finish the job?

"I shall be packed and ready in half an hour." Anne Vanderbilt rose and walked from the mess.

"As though she owns us," Andrew whispered under his breath. He rubbed the back of his neck. "I suppose we're lucky if she thinks she does."

CHAPTER FIFTY-SIX

ANNIE NEVER KNEW that love could so change a person, but Elisabeth Hargrave, the reserved young nurse with the sad violet eyes, had disappeared. In her place, in the midst of the most horrific days of the Battle of Verdun, blossomed a vibrant young woman.

Wounded men in the wards feasted their eyes on her bright cheeks and soft, honey-gold hair. Surgeons looked twice at the nurse who could not hide the spring in her step or the smile that played round her lips.

VADs were forbidden to socialize with soldiers or medical personnel or the few stragglers of men left from the deserted town—men in any form. Dating was forbidden, dancing forbidden, walking out forbidden, sitting together in mess forbidden.

Neither Annie nor Michael knew when they stole a kiss or a brief embrace behind the mess tent if they would be caught or if it would be their last.

They and half the VADs—at least the ones who were not mad with envy—did all they could to hide the romance, but it was like a fire set on a hill. By mid-September even Matron suspected and called Elisabeth Hargrave to her tent, demanding an explanation.

"My brother, who died on *Titanic*, left my welfare in Michael's hands. When I disappeared from London—when Aunt Eleanor sent me to France for the duration of the war—he came looking for me. I did not contact him." The facts were simple. Annie did not know if Matron believed her, what use she would make of those facts, or what forces those truths might set in motion. But Annie was jubilant in Michael's pursuit, and there was no way to hide it, no use in denying it.

Matron tapped her pencil against the edge of her makeshift desk. "You know I am bound to report this."

"It has nothing to do with my work, Sister." Annie had never dared speak up for herself. But silence had not served her well.

"No. And your labor is needed, impertinent though you may be." Matron frowned. "Do you know that your aunt's last solicitor sent me a letter, written in her own hand, to be delivered upon her death?"

Annie felt herself pale. "No, I did not."

Matron continued to tap her pencil. "Your aunt left instructions for me to put you in harm's way."

Annie felt her eyes grow wide.

"I asked you once why she hated you so, and you replied, 'Because—'"

"Because I was born," Annie finished.

"I believe you." Matron cocked her head. "She paid me handsomely. And there are others I report to in this situation."

Annie held her breath.

"But I find, as inconvenient as it seems, that I cannot carry out those orders. I thought I could—when I believed all she wrote me." Matron shook her head. "I no longer believe the things she wrote about you. In any case, I cannot do it."

She stood and took a moment to frame her words. "Do not flaunt your relationship with this young man. Do not write to these Spragues your aunt referred to in my letter or whatever relatives you have in America. Do not repeat what we have said here. I have the power to change my mind and the influence to have your Irishman reassigned. I do not have the power to stop others your aunt arranged to watch over your affairs, nor do I know who they are."

"Thank you, Sister." Annie could not believe such unexpected mercy.

"Do not thank me. None of us are likely to leave Verdun alive."

※ ※

Michael wrote to Aunt Maggie:

*The French fight like demons for every centimeter of ground, and
I say, "God bless them!"
Through the autumn they gained an upper hand, despite their*

terrible losses—wounded men, dead men, missing men by the scores and hundreds and thousands.

Rules of shift orders and leave in the field hospitals and ambulance service mean nothing. Neither I, nor any other ambulance driver or stretcher bearer, nor any of the medical staff proper expect to sleep through the night.

I miss your fine dinners, Aunt Maggie, and the aroma of Uncle Daniel's pipe by the fire of an evening. I miss the rattle of his newspaper and the way you push your hair from your eyes after a long day.

And yet, I tell you, these are the best days of my life, with more to come. Someday I'll explain. For now, know that I love you with all that is in me. Know that I will come home to you at war's end.

Your Michael

※ ❈

Michael pretended to have developed a wartime attraction to Elisabeth Hargrave, the shy English nurse—all from a discreet distance. Each clandestine meeting was no more than a handful of fleeting moments behind the mess tent or a rare passing in the dark between shifts—long enough for him to squeeze her hand or for her to push the tumbled locks from his eyes.

Michael held tight to the joy of living each precarious day near Annie, but his fear for her safety grew with the passing of those days of increased shelling from the enemy. He could not reconcile his joy of being with her with his responsibility and inability to protect her. She must leave this place, he knew, but how?

As Christmas approached, he laid his plans and forged a ring from scrap metal.

It was not the ring or proposal he'd so long and diligently planned. It was not the vision he'd carried while digging, planting, and hoeing the gardens of Owen's roses in New Jersey, singing Christmas carols at the top of his lungs. It was not the image he'd held close while barreling through battle zones to retrieve wounded during the last year.

But it was wartime, and there was no end in sight. He needed to see that she was safe—away from battle zones—if only she would agree. A promise, hope for brighter days—any days—might carry them through. And when the war was over, they would go home to New Jersey together.

How he would manage a proposal, let alone a wooing in the intimate setting Annie so deserved, he had no clue. But he knelt and laid bare his heart's petition to the One whose example he followed, the One who knew above all others how to woo a Bride.

Three days before Christmas, Michael believed the answer came when Mack, the tentmate whose bunk lay opposite, dropped his news after a long and grueling transport from Revigny.

"They're sending a civilian up to do a Christmas Eve Communion for the field hospital." Mack pulled his boots from his feet, wrapped his toes in rags for added warmth, and wound himself in his tarp. "All against regulation, but the brother of one of the doctors. Just goes to show whose country pulls rank in this stinking war."

"Not French, then?" Michael wondered.

"And not a priest—a proper Protestant vicar, from Lincoln. Came to check on his younger brother, wounded at the Somme, but too late. Decided he'd best stop here for a visit with his older brother before something happens to him." Mack rolled over. "They'll probably both be shot to bloo—" he mumbled into his coat. "I'm to fetch him from Revigny tomorrow." Mack pulled the tarp over his head. "Close that tent flap. Let me pretend it's dark."

Michael pulled the flap tight and shook his head. He knew what it meant to lose a sibling. The fear of losing another reminded him of Owen, stirring again his sense of the urgent. *A vicar, a proper English vicar.* He repeated the words over and over in his brain, a mantra of growing proportions. "I've need of your help, Mack—and perhaps we can ask for that of Liz and Evelyn."

Mack pushed the tarp away. "Evelyn?" Just saying her name lit a small fire in Mack's eyes. "What now, Dunnagan?"

"Can you arrange a quiet moment for me with the vicar before you release him to the officers' tent?"

"In exchange for . . . a quiet moment with Evelyn?" Mack was fully awake.

"That'll be her saying yea or nay. I'll not urge based on friendship." Michael held his breath.

Mack stared him down. "What do you want with the vicar?"

"A wedding." Michael's grin spread from ear to ear. "A secret, surprise Christmas Day wedding for Annie and me. You and Evelyn and Liz and that bloke she likes come and stand with us."

"You're crazy—bonkers! Didn't ya notice there's a war on?" Mack turned away. "Stupid Paddy."

"Bonkers I am—bonkers in love!" Michael gazed stupidly into the half-light, scheming, dreaming. He pulled Mack's shoulder until he faced him. "But will you do it, then? And you'll stand with me?"

Mack groaned, punched his makeshift pillow, and shook his head. Grinning, he turned his back on Michael again and mumbled, "Just make sure she tosses Evelyn the bouquet."

CHAPTER FIFTY-SEVEN

ON CHRISTMAS DAY the officers and surgeons ate dinner first, then the sisters, and later the VADs. Last of all came the ambulance drivers, stretcher bearers, and all those besides. It was a cheerful day, compared to others. The mess was warm, if not tempting. The Germans were quiet and, Michael prayed, deep in their cups.

After the vicar served Communion to the surgeons and staff, he went through the tent wards. Michael recognized the holy hush that had fallen over the ranks. It was the same quiet as before Communion served by Reverend Tenney in the meeting house in Swainton. It was the same pervading peace that followed.

Michael saw the vicar as a good man, with the added bonus of being a civilian not bound by military regulations. At least no one had specifically forbidden him to perform marriages in battle zones. Younger than Michael had imagined; still, the vicar was married—a man who surely understood the pain and longing of love. Michael had not actually told the vicar that he'd not yet proposed to Annie in words face to face, but he was certain of her answer—more certain of her than of the ultimate ending of the war. Memories of Aunt Maggie and Daniel's Christmas Day wedding hallowed his preparations.

As soon as he'd spoken with and received a blessing and pledge of secrecy from the vicar, Michael set arrangements in motion with Liz and Evelyn. They would give Annie his letter after Communion, then accompany her to the vicar's tent—against regulations, he knew, but for the best of causes, and the vicar would be there, after all.

By then, nothing could mar the day, nothing more would require her attention, and the vicar's brother would be on hospital duty—no interference there. Thanks to Mack, the night would belong to the newly married couple. Mack had persuaded the vicar to trade his tent for Michael's bunk—a wartime wedding gift. Michael thought they might name their firstborn after the man—or at least after Mack.

On the morrow, Michael would walk with Annie, hand in hand, to Matron. She would be furious, likely dismiss Annie on the spot. Michael figured his bride would surely be sent home within the month, and he would follow as soon as he could. Even if he had to wait out the war, Annie would be safe from the battle zone and out from under the thumb of Matron Artrip. Everything would work out fine.

※ ※

The blessing of shared Communion and the peace she found when partaking of the one bread and one cup was a gift so rare that Annie had almost forgotten its beauty. That her Lord loved her and had died for her was beyond comprehension. "Owen understood this mystery better than I," she whispered. "Bless him for that, Lord. Thank You for the life You lived, the life that Owen lived, and this life that You've given me with all there is to come. Help me to sacrifice as lovingly, as willingly as You have done for the world, as Owen did for Michael and me. Bless our love, heavenly Father. Give me patience. Help me stay the course, and please, oh, please, bring an end to this war."

She'd barely risen from her knees to her cot when Liz eagerly pulled her to her feet and shoved a clean apron in her hands. "I know you've nothing proper to wear, but take my fresh apron. I blued it yesterday. It will do." Liz clapped her hands like a child.

"Whatever for? Is this a Christmas gift?"

Evelyn pushed Liz aside. "Don't pay her any mind. But you will want to do something with your hair, and I'd suggest a good nail scrubbing. You know how the muck gets under our nails."

"What are you two going on about?" Annie wondered if they'd been in the coffee or, perhaps worse, discovered Christmas spirits sold on the black market.

"She gave it to you, didn't she?" Evelyn turned to Liz. "Well, did you? Did you give it to her?"

"Gave me what?"

Liz slapped her own cheek. "Oh, here it is! Read it quickly—over here, by the lantern." She passed Annie a paper, folded and refolded, addressed in Michael's hand.

Fingers near trembling, Annie smoothed the creases one by one. "He's arranged a meeting time and place. The perfect Christmas gift! I was beginning to fear he'd not taken any notice of the day!" Her breath caught and her heart danced at his words:

My dearest Annie,

When first I promised Owen to watch over you, I did so with duty and gratitude to the best friend I'd ever known. But I have found in your love more life and joy than I have ever hoped or dreamed—more than any man has a right to claim this side of heaven. I love you, Annie Allen. I love you with all that is in me. I will love you always. Come with Liz and Evelyn. We've a surprise waiting.

All my love,
Michael

Annie bit her lip, smoothed again the paper he'd written upon, and smiled at the girls. "What have the three of you been up to?"

Liz and Evelyn exchanged tentative glances.

"I still think we should tell her," Evelyn admonished.

"But he said not to say a word—it would spoil the surprise!" Liz wrung her fingers.

"But it could be a shock," Evelyn began. "What if she doesn't—?"

"Never mind! If he wants to surprise me, let him. He must have conspired and troubled to do it. I don't want to spoil it." Annie tucked the missive in her pocket.

"Oh, it's most definitely a surprise!" Evelyn quipped.

Liz poked her friend in the ribs.

"Now, help me with my hair," Annie ordered. "It's not every Christmas Day a girl gets a date with a handsome ambulance driver in a French battle zone!" She laughed, and even to her, her happiness rang like the sound of bells.

A half hour later Liz pronounced her friend presentable. The three girls wrapped themselves in another layer against the cold and peeked through their tent flap into the last light of day. The first stars were just beginning to shine, and the moonrise cast a glow across the crusted snow. They needed no lantern to guide their way but picked their steps gingerly along the shoveled trail, shushing each other with good-natured jabs and giggles. Annie could not guess why her friends were in such high spirits, but it gave welcome relief from the normal tension and tedium of camp life. She began to suspect that Michael had prepared a party of some sort. Perhaps he'd found some secret store of sweets or perhaps there was a letter from Aunt Maggie. She gladly joined in their small parade.

When they reached the vicar's tent, Annie had second thoughts. "We're not to be here, surely!" She stopped the girls, arms linked on either side, in their tracks. "Matron will hold us accountable!"

"We've worked it all out. If necessary, we'll say we've been to confession," Liz assured her.

"But he's not a priest! He doesn't give absolution!" Annie knew that much.

"And we're not asking—we're simply confessing!"

"Confessing what?" Annie demanded.

But Evelyn pushed her through the tent flap, and when Annie saw Michael standing there, the love light risen brighter than the moonrise in his eyes, she forgot about confessions and absolutions altogether. She barely realized that Mack and T. C. and the vicar stood behind him.

When Michael pulled her gently from her friends, she came willingly, her heart beating a joyful staccato in her chest. When he pushed back the hood of her cape, she felt the warmth of his palms upon her face.

"Merry Christmas, Annie."

"Merry Christmas, Michael." It was only a word, a name, but it meant everything.

Turning away from the group huddled near the far side of the tent, Michael pulled her to a camp chair in the corner, kneeling before her. "I'd hoped to ask you in the gazebo I built in the midst of Allen's Run Gardens," he whispered, her hands cupped in his, "outside our future home. I'd planned to bend my knee and offer you a bridal bouquet of Owen's white double roses, lobelia the very blue of your eyes, and that trailing English ivy you love. But summer is gone, and we are not in New Jersey."

She felt his fingers massaging hers. The staccato in her chest drummed into a powerful beating.

"Even so, marry me, Annie. Marry me now—today—and let me take you home."

Annie felt her eyelids open and close without rhythm. She opened her mouth, but no words came out. She closed it.

"Annie?" Michael squeezed her hands. "The vicar has said he'll marry us—marry us today. Here, now."

Still Annie sat, stunned and unable to take in the group across the tent, the five huddled expectantly in lamplight.

"You do love me . . ." Michael paled slightly, then colored. "Don't you?"

Annie shook the stupor from her brain. "Of course I love you. I love you with all of my heart. You know that." She whispered so low that she knew Michael was forced to press his face close to hers to hear. "But don't ask me now. We cannot marry now—you know we cannot. Not while I'm under Aunt Eleanor's contract, not while I'm serving with the VADs." She drew a trembling breath, willing the cobwebs away. "I can't leave France—not until after the war."

"But the war could go on a long time yet. And she's dead!" Michael pulled Annie's face up, forcing her eyes to meet his. "The witch is dead—she can't touch you if you're sent away from here, away with me. Matron can dismiss you for going against regulations, and I'll follow as soon as I'm able. At least you'll be safe!"

Annie blinked back tears, frustrated by his simplicity, desperate in the warmth of his love. "We're not the only ones, Michael." She wrapped his face with her fingers in return. "My darling Michael. We must be patient—for Aunt Maggie, for the Spragues, for all our life ahead. We would never know who spied on us, who might carry out her terrible plans."

"What if this is our life? All our life?" Michael pressed.

"I cannot bear that thought! Oh, Michael. Dear God in heaven, I cannot bear that thought!" Annie clutched his arms, digging her nails through his coat.

Michael's lips kissed away the tears that found her face. "I'm sorry, Annie. I'm sorry. 'Twas a foolish thing to say." He pushed stray wisps of hair from her eyes and held her close. "The war will end. The war will end, and God be pleased, we'll both go free."

The vicar coughed discreetly and spoke from the far side of his tent. "I take it there is to be no wedding this night?"

Annie looked up to see their friends anxiously waiting, awkwardly watching, Evelyn gripping with two hands a bouquet of hand-sewn flannel roses.

The vicar stepped tentatively forward. "Is there anything I can do?"

Annie shook her head and tried to smile while wiping her eyes with the backs of her hands. She wished for all the world that she might melt into Michael's beating heart, the one she'd heard so clearly . . . or was it her own?

"There'll come a day, Annie Allen," Michael whispered gently, lightly, into her ear, "when I ask you and you'll be ready. I'll not let you off a second time."

She held him close. "Ask me when we stand in the gardens of home—holding that bouquet in your hands. I want to stand in your beautiful gazebo to take our vows. I look forward to that day, to all our future, without threats, without shadows."

Michael pulled Annie to her feet. "You mean you fancy something better than flint-bandage roses and our boots beneath a lumpy army cot in a charitable vicar's tent?" He smiled sheepishly. "What about a secret wedding now and a real one later?"

She took in the forlorn scene before her and smiled at his tease, though she could not bring herself to laugh. "You know I would love to spend this wedding night here with you." She traced the long dimple in his cheek with her finger.

He caught her hand and kissed her palm, pressing it against his heart. "We'll wait."

Annie and Michael stood before the vicar, surrounded by their friends, and pledged to love their life long and marry at war's end, before Reverend Tenney in the gardens of Allen's Run. Michael vowed to pick the bouquet himself.

As for the flint-bandage roses, Mack pinned the flowers in Evelyn's hair. She wore them beneath her nursing veil for two days, until Matron saw the bunch pinned beneath and confiscated them for the wounded.

≋ CHAPTER FIFTY-EIGHT ≋

THE COLD SET IN with a vengeance. Annie's hot water bottle, tucked between blankets and woollies, began to freeze again.

Firewood was still plentiful, for the trees in the hills and valleys and forests surrounding Verdun had long been blasted to kindling. But it was not enough to keep warm.

"If only we can make it through till the snow cripples things," Liz said, "it will all slow down again."

"Not this year," Andee replied. "This is the big push, the final push."

"You can't know that," Liz complained. "We've thought it before—every Christmas is to be our last, but it simply goes on and on and on. There's never any end in sight!"

"There is this time," Evelyn contradicted, and because of that rarity, everyone turned to listen. "The Germans are at the end of their tether. It cannot last much longer."

"I hope you're right," Judy said. "And if you're not, this will be my last month in any case. Well, I hope it will. I'm going home."

"What?" Babs exclaimed, half-joking. "And leave us here to face the enemy alone?"

Judy's eyes filled. She pulled a creased and recreased letter from her pocket. "Dave's been wounded—seriously."

"Judy!"

"His unit was nearly wiped out at the Somme. Dave is one of the lucky ones." But she began to cry.

Annie sat beside her friend, wrapping an arm about her shoulders. She waited for Judy to calm, knowing *wounded* carried many a prognosis and that those who lived often carried losses into their futures.

"He's been sent back to England to convalesce." Judy stood. "I don't care what they say. I'll go, no matter what, if Dave needs me."

"Of course you should," Annie said. "You should go straightaway. I would leave today—in a moment, if I could."

The girls turned with arched brows toward Annie, whom they'd come to refer to as Steadfast Elisabeth and who rarely spoke in their group.

"God willing," Evelyn whispered, drawing their attention away, "we shall all go home soon."

※ ※

The sirens began at two the next morning. They rose until they screamed, then wailed and wailed. The shelling of the hospital began at 2:06 and rained like fire from heaven—no one knew how long.

Every man and woman claiming two legs to walk sprang from bed, pulling on boots and cloaks as they ran to duty.

In the light of the explosions, Michael cranked his ambulance to life and pulled into the line forming outside the ward tents.

"Évacuiez-vous! Évacuiez-vous!" Word raced from tent to tent and throughout the encampment.

"Careful!" Matron ordered. "Lift them carefully."

"Vite, vite!" the surgeon cried, pushing her aside. "Nothing will matter if we don't get these men out of here."

Every VAD scrambled to the work of orderlies, helping to lift patients and collect bandages and medicines that had now become priceless, irreplaceable in the quantities desperately needed.

"Annie!" Michael shouted into the din, tearing through the tents.

An explosion blasted the ground next to the surgical tent. Metal pans, operating instruments, glass beakers, and rocks shot through the air . . . and blew Michael thirty feet from the site.

"Get to your ambulance, driver! Get these men out of here!"

Michael did not know where the command came from. He must obey, but he could not go without finding Annie. "Annie! Annie, answer me!" he cried and prayed and cried again.

Another explosion flooded the camp in crackling light.

"Go!" the surgeon shouted.

"She's already with the wounded—in the ambulance with Mack! She's on her way!" Liz pushed Michael toward the little group of ambulances as she ran back for a last load of supplies.

He stumbled to his loaded and cranked Ford, revved the engine, and followed the line headed toward the river and the road away from Verdun. He searched ahead and behind, saw Liz disappear into the ambulance behind him, and prayed that Annie had found space in one of the lorries ahead. He prayed she was safe, that she was truly with Mack, and that he would find her in Revigny.

"No headlights! Headlights forbidden!" The word swept down the line.

"Thank You, Sweet Jesus!" Michael prayed. They were nothing but marking pins for those blasted German shells.

Without so much as a match head or spark to light his way, Michael crept through the dark. With his ambulance less than two meters from the ambulance before him, his knuckles gripped white around the wheel of his Tin Lizzie.

The shelling of the hospital area and fields, just to the south, continued. Michael knew that reinforcements had recently dug new trenches in the targeted area. How the Germans knew, he could not guess. That the shelling was intended for the fresh men, he did not doubt, nor did it make a whit of difference that the hospital was leveled in the process.

Flashes of rifle fire through tunnels of barbed wire in no-man's-land and shells exploding over trenches in the distance oriented his improvised and precarious route over fields and crumbling roads.

Piteous moans from the throats of the gassed and blinded, and from shrapnel-carved and bleeding men crammed into the back of his worse-for-wear bouncing ambulance, serenaded each meter. He hit a rut in the road; some cursed, screaming obscenities; some were silenced. Michael pitied them all but drove on, silently begging, *Where is Annie? Sweet Jesus, be with my precious Annie!*

And then, above the engines and the moans, Michael heard the hateful whine, heard it draw closer and closer. Sweat beaded his forehead; still he drove.

Just rounding a curve, Michael saw the gray cylinder fall slowly against the faint-mooned sky. He saw it impact the road two cars ahead. He heard the deafening explosion in some faraway part of his brain, felt the heat of the inferno rush against his cheeks, knew the wheel of his ambulance was yanked from his death grip as he flew toward heaven.

PART THREE

ANNIE'S EYES would not open. She felt, rather than saw, that both her arms lay in casts. She could not feel her legs, and in a sudden panic to think what that might mean, she tried to lift her head. It would not do her bidding.

"She's awake!" Annie heard the elated voice of a woman—a voice she knew from somewhere but could not immediately place.

"Oh, you've come back to us, Elisabeth!" Liz and Marge chattered above her head.

"You gave us quite a scare," Liz whispered. "But you'll be all right . . . You'll be all right!"

"Wha–what happened?" Annie could not think for the pain in her head. Before she blinked, she caught the anxious exchange between the two above her.

"It was the shelling—do you remember? Poor thing, you've been out of it for ages. January's nearly over! Shrapnel lodged in your neck and spine, but the surgeon's done wonders," Liz assured.

"Shelling?" Annie tried to focus. "The evacuation . . . I remember."

"Good. You've a few more to go—surgeries, I mean. But you'll get better now." Marge smiled. "Oh, I'm so glad."

"Where is everyone? Did we all make it?"

"We'll talk later," Liz said. "We have to go, but I'll be back just as soon as I can. I'm seeing Marge and Judy off at the station."

"Where are you going?" Annie asked sleepily.

"Home—home to my Jake," Marge said. "He's got a fortnight's leave at last, and they've granted me one week. I can't wait to see him!"

"And Judy's going for good. Dave's recovering in Lincoln; they're getting married the minute he's released from hospital! Isn't it romantic?" Liz enthused, but Marge frowned and slightly shook her head.

"It's wonderful," Annie said, but she couldn't stop the ringing in her head. She felt certain there was something she should ask but could not form her thoughts into words.

"Rest easy. I'll see you in a few days." Liz stroked Annie's brow.

Annie murmured, and the two girls stepped away from her line of vision. Their footsteps had reached the door of the ward when Annie thought of Michael. She opened her mouth to ask for him, but the heavy sleeping draught once again did its work.

※ ※

Marge and Liz walked slowly toward the railway station.

"I hate it," Marge said. "I don't know how we'll ever manage to tell her."

"I don't want to be the one to do it," Liz insisted quietly.

"You nearly did! Don't be talking to her about romance or weddings! You know how she loved him!" Marge hefted her case. "She mustn't be told everything too soon. It could set her back."

Liz nodded. "I'll be careful. I promise."

"Dear God," Marge moaned, "how I hate this war!"

※ ※

Doctors came and went. Nurses checked vital signs of the woman whose chart read *Elisabeth Hargrave, VAD*. Orderlies shifted her to flat boards as VADs unknown to Annie changed her linens.

She asked for Michael again and again but was told he was not at the hospital. She begged for someone to search the records for ambulance drivers, and two nurses agreed to ask, but no one gave her that vital information.

Annie's head and neck hurt so that, heavily sedated, she slept nearly round the clock. Recurring nightmares—images of exploding lorries and white double roses, the sensation that she was flying upside down and backward, all downhill to a trench of English ivy—raced over and over through Annie's mind as she slept.

Two more surgeries followed. By late February, despite pain in neck and spine, Annie was able to sit up in bed for ten minutes at a time and take solid nourishment when spoon-fed by a VAD. By early March, when Annie's arms and wrists mended, she began to feed herself and to stay awake for longer stretches of time. Without the medication she began to think more clearly and to demand more forcefully answers to her questions about Michael.

Annie asked for her friends, Liz, Evelyn, Andee, and the other girls, but was told that they had been reassigned and so could not come. The orderly she asked did not know where they were stationed. No word was left.

March faded into a blustery April. Annie's pain deepened with the torrent of spring rains. She feared the worst for Michael. She could not believe he would have forgotten or deserted her. It was not possible.

Because they'd never let Aunt Maggie know that Michael had found her, Annie dared not write to her.

Annie felt nothing below her rib cage. Even so, with the use of two wooden canes, she began to awkwardly limp short distances in the ward and then the hallways. There was talk of sending her back to England to convalesce. But for some reason, they kept her on in the ward. Annie had no doubt that somewhere along the line her name had met with resistance from one of Aunt Eleanor's minions. She could guess no other reason for filling a needed ward in France. *A prisoner in Paris.* If it were not further evidence of the extent of her dead aunt's power, Annie might have smiled.

On May Day, Annie dreamed of gardens and sunshine. She opened her eyes to a small bouquet of lily of the valley placed in the center of the ward. She closed them again, inhaling and savoring that dear, familiar fragrance. When she reopened her eyes, she found a young woman sporting a smile above her.

"There you are! You look ever so much better than the last time I saw you!" Liz stood back, tipping her head. "Are you feeling well?"

"Liz? Liz!" Annie struggled to sit up, feeling a flush of pleasure rise in her cheeks. "Where have you been?"

"We were all sent out for a bit of recovery, after the shelling. And then they unexpectedly sent some of us home on leave—far overdue, my parents said!"

Annie nodded. "I remember the explosions—at least some of it."

Liz shook her head. "Oh, it was frightful! You probably blacked out straightaway. But we're right as rain now—at least that's true for most of us." She leaned forward. "Babs has had a bad time of it. I don't think she'll ever be able to use her right arm again."

"No?"

"No. No more nursing for her, either. She's home in England. But she's met the most wonderful man, so that's all right. They'll be married come June."

"Married?" Annie's familiar fear for Michael nearly crushed her chest.

"Elisabeth? What is it? You look as though you've seen a ghost."

"Michael," Annie whispered. She clutched Liz's arm. "Liz, where is Michael?"

≋ CHAPTER SIXTY ≋

REVEREND TENNEY walked into the post office just as Maggie McKenica peered into her box. He saw her run a hand round its edges, stop, straighten slowly, then close the door.

"Why do you torture yourself, Maggie darling?" Daniel whispered to his thinning wife.

Reverend Tenney turned away when the flood threatened Maggie's eyes, then watched from the window as Daniel gently pressed his hand into her back and guided her out the door and down the post office steps, away from the prying, pitying eyes of their small community.

He stepped up to Daniel once Maggie was seated in their buggy. "Have you heard anything, Daniel? Anything at all?"

Daniel looked at Maggie, but she turned away. He lifted the black purse from her lap and pulled from it a worn letter, the envelope post-marked 9 May 1917. He handed it to Reverend Tenney, who searched Daniel's eyes as he carefully unfolded it.

The letterhead was from A. Piatt Andrew, of the newly renamed American Field Service, in France, but was dated 31 December. It was almost the same "missing, presumed dead" letter Reverend Tenney had read two days before at the home of a grieving family in Cape May Court House. In this case, the writer had forwarded Michael's will, hastily scribbled in his own hand and barely visible in stubbed pencil:

*In the event of my death, I leave the whole of my property and effects
to Maggie and Daniel McKenica, Swainton, New Jersey—*

my family—in the hopes that they will use it to provide for
Annie Allen—my sister by Owen's charge and my friend by
God's grace.

Michael Dunnagan
American Ambulance Field Service

Reverend Tenney could not swallow the lump in his throat. He started to speak, then rasped and tried again. "I am so sorry. So very sorry."

Daniel nodded and silently took the letter.

"If you and Maggie wish there to be a service . . ." Reverend Tenney paused.

"Do not be so fast to bury my Michael, Reverend Tenney!" Maggie's Irish brogue sounded thicker than it had in years. "He is not dead!"

"But the letter—"

"The letter is a scrap of paper that says they don't know where he's got to, nothing more. Were Michael dead I would know it in my bones. He'll come home to us yet—by and by. You wait. You wait and see." Maggie bore steely eyes and a tearstained face. Her chin quivered, but Reverend Tenney was certain no warrior had ever manifested a more fearsome countenance.

He removed his hat and meekly, respectfully, bowed his head. "Forgive me, Maggie McKenica. Forgive my lack of faith. I look forward to our Michael's glad homecoming." But he could not smile.

Maggie nodded curtly, then looked away. She dried her tears and lifted her chin. Daniel flicked the reins and drove his wife home.

≋ CHAPTER SIXTY-ONE ≋

CAROL FONDREY pushed wide the chintz curtains of the sickroom. *"Bonjour, ma chère!"* She brushed the tousled hair from Annie's forehead. "It is June, *ma petite,* and the roses are in full bloom. I insist you rise and that we walk into the gardens. It will do us both a world of good."

Annie turned her face to the wall, the only indication she knew to show her displeasure. Complete sentences no longer formed in her brain. Words spoken required too much effort and more energy than she could muster. She did not know why that was or why the woman spoke in two languages—beginning in French, then English, then lapsing again into French—all in the space of a sentence. Annie did not understand all that the woman said, despite her years of schoolgirl French and the knowledge that she had nursed French soldiers for months and months in Verdun. She knew she should be curious about such lapses in memory, but she was not.

The woman, there each time Annie opened her eyes, was not to be resisted. Annie allowed herself to be pulled to a sitting position. The woman tied a dressing gown round Annie's waist and, wrapping an arm around her shoulders, led her out the kitchen door and into a large garden.

Annie's heart began to race. She did not want to walk in the gardens. She wanted nothing to do with gardens, never again. She closed her eyes and turned her head, groping for the door latch.

But the older woman pulled Annie's hands away and guided her gently but firmly to a wicker chair in the sunshine. She lowered Annie into the timeworn seat and tucked a lap rug round her knees.

"Du thé, ma chère. I know how the English love the tea." The woman poured a steaming amber stream from a Limoges pot. She poured another stream, this one pungent and reddish brown, into the center of the cup

and stirred. "You will drink this, my pet. You will drink this and all the world will seem as it should—in time, in time."

Annie could not seem to curl her finger through the slim handle or grasp the cup. The woman closed her warm hands around Annie's, helping her to lift the delicate china to her lips. Annie trembled. The woman's smile was kind, her touch soft, knowing, but Annie did not want to be touched. She could not, must not trust her, must trust no one.

The woman pulled her hands slowly away once Annie had taken a sip of the fragrant tea. "There, there, *ma chère. Ca va mieux, non?*"

Annie's eyes met the woman's. The delicately painted cup slipped through her numbed fingers, spilling the amber tea across Annie's dressing gown, splashing it over her feet. The lovely Limoges cup crashed loudly onto the flagstones, a dozen painted puzzle pieces.

CHAPTER SIXTY-TWO

JEAN CLAUDE DUBOIS drew a deep breath. With all his might and to the consternation of his arthritic bones, he pulled the half-burned brush from the roughly hewn cave's entrance. He hefted his half-filled skin of wine, tucked his last bit of cheese into his tattered pocket, and mumbling to distract himself from the stabbing pain in his knees, crawled through.

Once he turned the corner, the darkness was complete, but the cave opened wide and he could almost stand. Jean Claude probed the rough, wet wall beside him until he found the shelf that held his tin box and the stub of candle he'd melted and stuck in a broken crock. The striking of the match against the stone made him wince, as always. It took three tries before the stubborn little wick caught the flame.

If the man was still there, he would share his bounty. If he had crawled out or died in the night, what was that to Jean Claude? He did not want to share his food or wine, there was so little to be found. But he did not want *le bon Dieu* to strike him from any hope of heaven. He did not want to spend eternity away from his precious Giselle.

Que cet homme est une malédiction. Why could the man not have died or been carried away like the others in the great crash? Why did he have to land in front of my cave instead of where the soldiers could find him and drag him away to be repaired or piled with the others for the burial detail?

At first, Jean Claude thought the man might provide companionship. He might get well and thank him, might find him food and drink, might come back from his day's work to share an evening bottle of wine. They would laugh and drink and talk of the days that had been. But days became weeks and weeks rolled into months and the man did not truly recover. He became a nuisance and a drain on Jean Claude's meager pantry.

Jean Claude shrugged. Once he had farmed and raised chickens. He had gathered eggs from his henhouse. Once he had cut wood for his neighbors. But his chickens were requisitioned by the army, and wood had been plentiful for months—trees blasted into firewood, free for the gathering.

His neighbors had gone when the town was told to evacuate—only a few weary firemen and the blood-gorged rats that feasted on corpses remained. There was nothing left for Jean Claude to do but pick the pockets of the dead and gather what he might.

He had no more bread, nor any hope of begging or stealing any. He must do what he had promised Giselle he would never do. He must leave their land and follow *la Voie Sacrée* to Bar-le-Duc, to her sister's home, and beg her to take him in. He must do that or die in his cave.

But what to do with the man? He could not push him all the way to Bar-le-Duc in a garden cart. He could not leave him in the cave to die. *Le bon Dieu* would know and curse him; he would have no hope of reaching his sweet Giselle. Jean Claude sighed.

He held the flickering light of the candle stub over the man's blackened and bearded face. The man moaned, tried to open his eyes, but fell asleep again.

For the first four months there had been little moaning, even though the man's legs were painfully contorted and Jean Claude knew his ribs were broken—how many places he could not guess. When he had tried to set the bones, there had been flickering of the eyelids and words whimpered that Jean Claude did not understand.

The man swallowed the tiny morsels Jean Claude fed him. He was thinner but more alive than before. Jean Claude sighed again. *Que faire?*

He pulled the cork from his wineskin and forced a tiny stream of the dry, red wine between the man's crusted lips and then a stream of water as he had done every day of the six long months. He lifted the man's head by his matted hair and massaged his throat, encouraging him to wake and swallow.

Jean Claude wound his fingers through the man's tattered jacket and dragged him slowly through the rough cave, over the rocks and rubble, and into the morning sunshine. Long ago he had traded the man's uniform for food. Jean Claude could not see that it mattered. The man would not soon be driving ambulances again, even if he lived. If the army found him and restored him, they would gladly give him a new uniform before they sent him out to die on the battlefield. Jean Claude shook his head and mumbled. He had long decided it was a crazy world, a crazier war.

By the time Jean Claude rolled the moaning man onto his garden cart, he was wet with sweat. He found that pushing his garden cart up the rocky hill to the road was the most taxing thing. The blackened, broken man kept falling off one end.

Twice Jean Claude stumbled and lost his balance. In trying to steady himself, he tipped the cart and the man; all three tumbled down the hill, landing in a heap. The man cried out in pain. After the second tumble, Jean Claude was not certain that the man still breathed. That worried him more.

Should he bury the man in the ditch beside the road? Should he drag him up the hill again and leave him in the hope that someone would find him? What if a lorry rolled over him in the dark?

Jean Claude shook his head. He knew Giselle would have cried, "*Un tel sot!* You cannot leave a man by the road!" And then she would have kissed his forehead and his cheek and his mouth, and all would be well. But Giselle was not there, and all was not well.

When at last he reached the road with the cart and the broken man, Jean Claude sat, exhausted. He leaned against the wheel of the cart and buried his head in his hands.

If he waited, he was certain a military lorry would drive by. But what would he say? He could not confess that he had hidden the sleeping man for six months and fed him nothing but red wine and dried bread soaked in the broth of chickens stolen from the army camp.

They would not credit him with having saved the man's life. They would say, "Why did you hide in the cave and steal from your own army when we ordered you to evacuate?"

They would not understand that he could not leave the grave of his

Giselle. Who would tend it? He would not go now but that there was no more wine, no food in his pantry, and the army had no more chickens. No matter which way Jean Claude turned the matter in his mind, there was nothing but trouble for him in this.

At length Jean Claude heard the faraway hum of a motor, like the drone of a bee. In the distance he saw a small dust cloud rising. Jean Claude stood. He dared not be found with the man.

He hated to leave his garden cart. It would have come in handy in bargaining for work and food with Giselle's sister. But he had no choice; there was no time. Jean Claude scurried, as best his old joints and bones allowed, down the rocky embankment. He tore his pants in another tumble, scrambled to his feet, then ran, stumbling again, toward his hiding place. The motor on the road above squealed to a stop, shooting up bits of rock and dirt, just as Jean Claude pulled the brush from the cave's entrance. He heard the door of the vehicle slam as he crawled inside, pulling the brush behind him.

Jean Claude scrambled round the corner, crouched, and waited in the dark. How long he waited, he did not know. He sat on his buttocks on the cold ground and told Giselle and *le bon Dieu* all about it.

He confessed that he should never have stolen the chickens, even if he did feed the broken man with their broth. He confessed that he should never have taken the man's papers with the photograph of the pretty girls and their parents, or the tiny aluminum plate with raised letters that hung about his neck. They were such pretty things. He would have liked to give them to Giselle, when he reached heaven.

He knew now that he'd done wrong. He buried the stolen treasures in the cave so that *le bon Dieu* could do with them as He pleased. Then, too tired to confess more, he curled up on the floor of the cave and slept.

Dusk had gathered when at last Jean Claude peeked round the corner of the cave. He stretched, crawled out, rubbed life into his old knees so he might stand, then carefully pushed brush across the entrance.

Hearing nothing but the sweep of a bat in search of an evening roost, Jean Claude climbed slowly up the hill to the road, searching first one way and then the other.

The truck had gone. The broken man had gone. But his cart remained.

"Mon bon Dieu! Je vous en remercie! Merci!" Jean Claude cried, laughing quietly. With his sleeve he swiped tears from his weather-lined cheeks and happily shrugged, wondering aloud over *"les façons mystérieuses du bon Dieu."*

His heart lifted, Jean Claude, by the light of a full moon rising, set his feet square on *la Voie Sacrée* and his face toward Bar-le-Duc.

CHAPTER SIXTY-THREE

"THERE IS NOTHING more I can do." Carol Fondrey spread her hands helplessly across the breakfast table before her son. "She will not respond to me—to me! Never have I been so . . . incapable!"

Phillippe Fondrey had rarely seen his mother distraught. She was not accustomed to exasperation. He smiled behind his mustache to think of anyone daring to ignore her, especially, as she had called her, "a slip of a girl."

"Do not be impatient, *Maman*. Perhaps she cannot speak. This war does many things to many people." The dark-eyed soldier waved his hand as though it did not matter.

But it mattered to Carol Fondrey. She squared her shoulders and lifted her chin. "The matron from the hospital said she was in a terrible lorry accident during the shelling of a field hospital evacuation from Verdun. But she spoke while in the hospital in Paris. They said she spoke until, in one day, she spoke no more. Someone—perhaps a friend—tucked a letter into her pocket suggesting that her inability or unwillingness to speak has something to do with a broken heart." Carol pressed her hand to her heart, a habit since the loss of her younger son. "But I do not know what, and if I do not know, how can I help her? You must speak with her, Phillippe. You must seek her out."

"*Moi?* Why not leave her alone? She will gather her wits in her own time." Phillippe frowned. "And I am home on leave, *Maman*. I wish to rest, to walk in our gardens, to sip champagne—*avec ma chère maman*." He tickled her fingers.

But his flirtation, normally the delight of his mother's heart, had no effect. "You can do all of those things—as you seek her out."

Phillippe sighed. He did not wish to argue with his mother on his first day at home. He stood and tossed his serviette on the table. "I am not a nursemaid, *Maman*. She is your project for the war effort. I have my own, and they are not going well."

But later that morning, as Phillippe strolled through his mother's magnificent gardens, an artist's palette of color oddly untouched by the long war's misery, he caught somewhere the humming of a sad tune he'd not heard since childhood, a mournful but oddly comforting nursery lullaby.

The gardens covered two acres and were divided into "rooms" walled by an open maze of tall hedges, privets, yews, and age-old English boxwood. Phillippe could not be certain from which direction the humming came, but he followed the winding trails and sharp corners until he believed himself nearby. Gently he pulled apart a flowering hedge, creating enough space to see but not be seen.

On the other side of the hedge in the center of a small garden of blue hydrangea sat a young woman in a simple white frock beside a slowly gurgling fountain. She had pulled down her golden hair and was brushing its heavy coils in long, rhythmic strokes, maintaining a slow accompaniment to her humming.

This must be his *maman's* "slip of a girl," though he would not have described her in that way. That she could speak, regardless of what his mother believed, he knew by her tuneful humming. That his breath caught and his heart stumbled in its beating at her open and innocent beauty, he could not deny.

Phillippe Fondrey, decorated with the highest honors of France for his stalwart bravery and heroics on the battlefield, noted by his comrades for his confidence with the ladies, stepped back from the flowering hedge. Beads of perspiration dotted his forehead. His hands, usually steady as the timbers in his mother's ceilings, trembled.

He rode hard across the hills of his estate that morning to push the image of the young Englishwoman from his thoughts. He spent the afternoon increasing the revenue of the only remaining tavern in town.

Twilight settled over the green hills when at last he returned to his mother's estate. Phillippe lifted the saddle from his stallion, fed and watered him, then slowly brushed his coat until it shone in the stable's lamplight.

Over dinner that night he met the young woman formally, through his mother's introduction. After dinner the three sat by a fire in the open garden, his mother's favorite outdoor room. Carol nursed the last of the evening's wine as she probed her son for stories of his wartime exploits. But Phillippe had no stomach to speak of war.

"Elisabeth nursed our men in Verdun," Carol told her son as though Annie were not there. "You were there, my son, *ce n'est pas vrai*?"

Phillippe nodded, holding Annie's eyes for the first time.

"It was a horrific time, *certainement*," Carol encouraged.

"Non, Maman," Phillippe said quietly, still looking at Annie. "It was worse."

The connection was not lost on Carol. When nothing more seemed forthcoming, she sighed aloud. *"Excusez-moi, s'il vous plaît,"* she murmured, touching her forehead lightly in apology. "I nurse the headache. Too much sun this afternoon, too much wine this evening, I fear." She rose and kissed her son's cheek. "If you need anything this evening, *ma chère*—" she pressed Annie's shoulder gently—"simply ring the bell. Angele will come."

Annie smiled faintly.

When his mother had gone, Phillippe swirled the last of his brandy and stared into his glass.

Annie rose, inclined her head as if to go indoors, and picked up her cane.

"*Pardonnez-moi*, mademoiselle. You will sit with me, *s'il vous plaît*."

But Annie bowed apologetically and made as if to go.

Phillippe did not rise. "Indulge me, mademoiselle. You have deceived *ma mère*. I do not understand why." He waited, but the girl, still standing, said nothing. "Is it that you wish to stay here? To live in my mother's château for the duration of the war?"

Even in the firelight he could see the young woman's color deepen.

"Make no mistake. I do not wish to send you away."

Annie sank slowly into the chair. Her chest heaved.

"Your companionship is good for her. You are a project she has needed for some time." He watched her carefully. Still she did not speak. "You should know that my younger brother, Bertrand, my mother's pet, was killed tragically at the Marne, the first year of the war."

Annie blinked.

"She has needed someone to look after, someone to care for, someone she can, through her attentions, restore." Phillippe set his snifter on the low table between them. "It is helpful, when we lose someone we love so desperately, to give of ourselves to others. It eases the terrible pain. Do you not agree, Mademoiselle Hargrave?"

Annie sat for a full minute with her hands folded, until at last she raised her eyes to his. She breathed deeply and said quietly, her first words to another in weeks, "*Non*, Monsieur Fondrey. Nothing . . . nothing in this world eases the pain."

Phillippe's eyes widened, but he did not move for fear of breaking the delicate spell.

Annie grasped the arms of her chair, pulling herself to her feet. She steadied herself on the chair's rail, wrapped her cardigan more tightly round her shoulders, and leaning heavily on her cane, limped into the house.

Carol, hidden in the shadows of the kitchen's garden window, wiped stray tears from her cheeks and smiled.

※ ※

The night was rent with the animal-like keening of Annie for her Michael. The first tears she had cried of anything but frustration since the shelling, the first she had opened her mouth wide since the day Liz told her of the horrible explosions, of the dead and missing.

Annie moaned that she had not gone to America when Michael and Aunt Maggie had begged her, regardless of the risk, regardless of her loyalties to the Spragues.

She cried that she had stepped foot in Aunt Eleanor's house the day before her eighteenth birthday—a lifetime ago—the day her life was laid out like a chess game.

She screamed that she had not married Michael in secret when he'd asked her, despite her aunt's threats to those she loved and the rules for VADs.

She keened, high and piercing and long into the wee hours of the morning, that she had not died with him in the exploding inferno of lorries and ambulances and shells and craters.

How she would walk through life without Michael, Annie did not know. And for that mystery she cried again.

Twice Carol Fondrey believed she could stand no more and rushed to the girl's room to hold her, to comfort her. But Phillippe slept in a chair, guarding Annie's bedchamber door the long night through. He shook his head. "The dam has burst, *Maman*. You must allow the waters to flow."

It was nearly dawn when Annie quieted. Outside her door, the stalwart soldier listened to the silence for another half hour. Just as the cock crowed, he stood, stretched, and took to his bed until noon.

Two days later he introduced Annie to his mother's gardener and to a garden space in need of gentle restoration. Together they toiled through the mornings: Phillippe on his knees, his mother choosing flowers and herbs and directing the gardener, and Annie in a chair, trowel in hand, giving new life to straggling planters. By the middle of the second week, the sun and fresh air, the gift of Phillippe's kindness, and their mutual toil had planted a faint bloom in Annie's cheeks. A small light, not before seen by the Fondreys, found its way to her blue eyes.

Phillippe Fondrey remained at his mother's château for two weeks more, the most refreshing leave he'd enjoyed through the long war. When he left again for the front, he had secured the permission of his "*petite* Elise," as he called Annie, to write often, and her promised return of the favor. This pledge Phillippe sealed late the last evening as the two walked in the château's gardens, when he lifted Annie's fingers to his lips.

CHAPTER SIXTY-FOUR

CONNIE TOOK THE TEAPOT from her mother's trembling hands and poured.

For weeks she had tried to convince her distraught parents to get away. A trip to the Lake District—even in the dead of winter—would be just the thing, if only her father would agree. But the war raged on, and he had refused, saying that he could not leave London.

Maggie McKenica's letter changed that.

"It is too much," Mrs. Sprague cried. "I cannot celebrate Christmas with the children missing. First Annie and then Michael!

"Surely, if he were alive, if he'd found her, they would both have written. It's been nearly a year since we've heard from him! But that McKenica woman is so certain. Her letters make Michael seem so much alive and Annie with him!"

"Stop torturing yourself with that woman's letters," her husband urged. "She is not able to accept the realities of this war, but that does not mean you must be drawn into her fantasies. We must let them go. We all must get on with our lives!"

Late that night Mr. Sprague knocked softly on his daughter's door.

"I am sorry you heard me speak so harshly, my dear. I am concerned for your mother. It is entirely too great, this loss. For her sake, for the sake and hope of keeping your mother's sanity, I beg you not to mention either of them again." He hesitated. "And I must ask something more."

"Anything, Father."

"I must ask you to go through the post, each day, and take away any letters from Maggie McKenica—before your mother sees them. Will you do that, Constance?"

Connie agreed. She loved her mother, perhaps more than any other being on earth. She'd seen the toll the year had taken. Connie would watch and hide the letters from America. She would not speak the names of Annie or Michael aloud in the house again.

But it would not keep her from searching the hospital wards of London each day as she had done this last year. Nothing would keep her from that.

CHAPTER SIXTY-FIVE

DR. NARVETT watched the quiet young man, still weak from malnutrition and recovering from leg surgeries, poke his finger into the potting soil and gently drop a seed into the tiny well. He saw him tilt his head as though trying to understand what he'd done, then sprinkle the seed with a fine layer of soil.

The doctor stroked his chin, pulling the end of his goatee. He'd not taught the silent young man to plant. He did it instinctively. It was the first sign of memory or native intelligence, indeed the first voluntary movement he had seen in the patient. The doctor shook his head and smiled; the young man would make a perfect test case for his theory.

For months, Dr. Narvett had badgered the hospital board, urging them to adopt a gardening program. "Having patients plant and tend a vegetable garden on the hospital grounds will not only help to provide food for the staff and patients alike—of which we are in great need—but it will create the most ideal therapy for these physically and emotionally scarred war veterans!

"Every Frenchman," he'd propounded, "knows that gardening is good for the body and better for the soul. It is too bad that modern medicine has lost sight of the elementary!"

By mid-February Dr. Narvett had secured the approval needed. During the first days of March he instructed twenty patients in the potting of vegetable seeds and carefully set planting trays in the newly built cold frame. They searched the black soil daily for sprouts.

But it was the young man who intrigued Dr. Narvett in his classes of war-worn veterans—military and civilian alike. Whether the lesson concerned the care and use of tools or the proper amount of water to pour as rain over seedlings, the young man seemed to know exactly what to do before he'd been told or shown. It was the first light of purpose Dr. Narvett had seen in the patient's eyes.

"And what is your name, my son?" Dr. Narvett asked each day as casually as if he were petting a dog. The young man did not reply. He did not seem to hear or understand the question.

By mid-April the sprouts were ready to plant in the ground. The patient worked with a will. When his allotment of plants was finished, he sat beside the slower patients and, guiding their hands, helped them plant their sprouts.

Dr. Narvett and his wife walked between the garden rows as the patients worked, watching their progress.

"Why have you not sent this one to England? His body has healed." Glenda nodded toward her husband's patient of special interest.

"Ah, his body. But not his mind. He would be wheeled into a corner and forgotten there. See what progress he makes in the garden? See how he helps those who are weaker?"

"You will drive yourself mad with that one," she observed, standing with one hand on her hip. "Can you not see he is unable to connect two thoughts?" She shook her head. "Whatever happened to him has removed his ability to speak, to reason. He will do no more than plant seedlings."

"You judge harshly, my dear," Dr. Narvett replied quietly.

"And you, Armand, are a dreamer," his wife teased, nipping his earlobe. "And I love you for it."

"I love you," the patient repeated in a monotone, never lifting his head.

The doctor and his wife gaped first at the patient and then at each other.

Dr. Narvett nodded. *"Très bien. C'est un début."*

❧ CHAPTER SIXTY-SIX ❧

THE LILACS OF 1918 were the most fragrant, the most brilliant that Annie could remember.

"You must press these petals and send them to Phillippe, *ma chère.*" Carol smiled. "He will find their fragrance reminds him of home, of life, and of you, Elise."

Annie smiled. She had grown used to the pet name the Fondreys had given her. She had grown used to life in the beautiful old château, to song-bird mornings in the gardens, and to the pleasure of sharing Phillippe's letters with his mother by the fire on chilly evenings or outside once the days grew warm. She'd grown as fond of Carol as of Phillippe in their different ways and wondered if this might be what a family was like. She could barely remember.

Through the long winter Annie had confided to Carol her love for and loss of Michael and of her brother, Owen. Saying the words aloud somehow helped Annie to shape them, to mold them into a story she could grasp, tragic though it was.

She did not explain the misery caused by her aunt in England or the loving-kindness of the Spragues and her relatives in America.

Annie had learned through a letter from Liz that Matron Artrip was killed when the lorry of nurses crashed and rolled over and over, down the hill that night—the crash Annie could not clearly remember. Though she suspected that her long hospital stay in Paris and her convalescence in France were part of her Aunt Eleanor's far-extended web, she could not guess who might be directing those affairs now. She could not imagine Carol or Phillippe Fondrey capable of such deviousness. She prayed that her aunt's minions had either forgotten or lost track of their charge. But she could not be certain.

Aunt Eleanor was dead, Owen was dead, and Michael—but still the Spragues and Aunt Maggie lived. For love of them, she would remain where she was. With Michael gone, there was no reason to evade or even wish to shorten her contract to remain in France until the war's end.

Now that the Americans—the Yanks—had come with their fresh troops and invigorating spirit, the war would end soon. At least that was what everyone in the village predicted. And when it was over, Annie would at last be free. Free for what purpose, she could not guess.

Carol had listened to Annie with an aching heart, hoping that the pouring out of such sadness would allow the young woman to release the ghosts of the men she had loved, to put those dead finally to rest. She hoped that by the time Phillippe returned—her dear Phillippe, who desperately needed love and restoration of his own—Elisabeth Hargrave would be not only fully healed in body but ready to embrace the living.

Carol sighed. She had her own losses and their ghosts to count in the night. *It has been a long, long war. It will be good to fill these rooms with children again and with laughter.* She smiled. *I sound the old woman, do I not?*

"*Eh bien.*" She shrugged. "I am, perhaps. I have need of patience."

By late summer Annie was able to do without her cane. She resumed the morning and evening constitutionals of her adolescence, walking daily the perimeter of the Fondrey estate. She'd regained the weight lost in her months at Verdun. Fresh air and exercise had put roses in her cheeks and, by mid-September, vitality in her step. Annie knew she should offer her nursing services to aid the war effort and not hide behind the walls of the grand old château. There was no denying the need in the field was great. But it seemed the VADs had forgotten her. So she did not offer to go, and Carol did not press her.

Phillippe came home on three days' leave the last week in September.

His first embrace, his first kiss was not for his mother, but she laughed and said she did not mind. Nor did she seem to mind that the young couple left her alone to stroll through the gardens, long after the sun sank into the fields beyond the walls, the harvest moon rising to replace it.

On the last day of Phillippe's leave, the three sat at the long, candlelit table of the dining room. "This is the day of Michaelmas, the great feast your people celebrate in Britain, *non*?" Carol commented over dinner.

Annie could not swallow the marrow she had placed in her mouth. A sudden tear escaped.

"*Ma pauvre* Elise, you are sad." Phillippe grasped her hand. "Do not worry. I will not be away long. It is the last push. We will be victorious yet—I hope before Christmas. At Christmas we will celebrate as we have not celebrated since before the war—a new year for our new life." He brushed her fingers with his lips.

Annie blinked and looked away until the moment passed. She could not say what was in her heart, what the reminder of the holy day meant to her.

What could she say when Phillippe carried such hope, such confidence in his eyes? She must not let him return to the front with anything less than joy in his heart. That she owed both him and his mother this, she was certain. And perhaps, in time, she could love him in the way he believed she did.

Before Phillippe left for the railway station, he pushed a stray tendril from Annie's eyes and held her face between the palms of his hands. "You will be here when the war is over? You will wait for me, *ma petite* Elise?"

"I will be here, Phillippe, when the war is over."

"I will await your answer—until then. You will consider me?"

Annie buried her head in the wool of his coat. "Yes, Phillippe, but you must allow me time to think."

He folded her in his arms. "Then I will wait for this war to end. Do not make me wait longer."

≋ CHAPTER SIXTY-SEVEN ≋

DR. NARVETT handed the letter to his wife and pulled back the drapery. He could see the hospital grounds and gardens from his office window.

"Ah," she said. *"C'est enfin arrivé."* She read the notification of her husband's transfer to Paris with apparent satisfaction. But when she looked up, she frowned. *"Tu n'en es pas content,* Armand?"

Joyful? Happy? he wondered. *Is the directorship of such a hospital not the position I have worked so diligently to achieve? Is it not the very thing for which I am most eminently suited?* But when he spoke, he spoke quietly. "No, in all irony I do not think that after all I am joyful. Not now." He dropped the drapery.

"You do not wish to leave Vittel?"

He solemnly shook his head. "I did not expect to see what I have seen here. I did not expect to do what I have done here."

"It is that young man—the one with the blue eyes and the dark locks. You think you have achieved something with him."

"I know I have achieved something!" he corrected. "It not only concerns the gardening; it is the remembering. It is as though the gardens create the peace and tranquility—the open field, if you will—for the mind to grow . . . and for these men to remember. That man is one among thousands in need of healing."

"He does not even remember his name! You have taught him to plant peas—to harvest salad for the table!" She tugged his coat sleeve. "What is this compared to the research you will do in Paris? *N'importe,* Armand! Do not throw away this opportunity for such daydreams!"

He pulled her gently to the window and pushed it wide. The late-afternoon sun cast long shadows down the empty garden rows—empty except for Dr. Narvett's special patient, his test case, seated along the garden's edge. *"Ecoute, ma chère,"* he whispered, pointing to the young man.

Glenda sighed, clearly weary of the conversation. She leaned from the window and tilted her ear in the patient's direction.

From the gardener patient's lips came a broken, tuneful ditty.

She could not make out the smattering of words, could not place the tune, until she hummed along. *"Les chants de Noël*—they are the carols of Christmas he sings!"

Dr. Narvett nodded. He'd captured her attention. *"Et regarde*, just there." He pointed across the garden to a small building on a pole.

"It is a model of the hospital, *non*? Why have I not noticed it before?"

Dr. Narvett smiled broadly at his wife. "I set it up today. Our patient made it—with his own hands and no instruction from me. It is perfect."

"But how?"

"I found him searching through the wood scraps behind the potting shed. Once I saw him shaping a house for the birds—yes, that is what it is—I offered him my tools. And that is what he produced."

"Ah," she whispered. *"Il est artiste."*

"And best of all—" Armand smiled slyly at his wife—"I know his name."

"Non, c'est pas possible!"

Armand laughed. "You are correct, my love; it is not *possible*. It is *Michael.*"

"You are guessing." Playfully she slapped his chest.

He shrugged his shoulders, still laughing.

"And how do you know this?"

"It is because of our harvest feast last week. Some of the staff and I spoke of the harvest feasts celebrated round the world, and Sister Bunnell mentioned the feast of Michaelmas and how her family always roasted golden a fine goose. The fellow's head jerked up and he shouted—but wait; I will show you." He pushed the window wider still and leaned out. "Say, there! What is your name, my son?"

The young man stood and turned. He tipped his imaginary hat to Dr. Narvett and bowed. "I am Michael."

"And how do you know that, my boy?" Dr. Narvett called again.

"Because Mam named me for the archangel himself—the angel above all angels!"

"Your mam named you well, Michael!" Dr. Narvett pulled back, closed the window, and smiled at his beautiful, incredulous wife. "It is a beginning."

"Oui." She nodded, new respect shining in her eyes. *"C'est un début."*

❧ CHAPTER SIXTY-EIGHT ❧

On 8 November, a nervous Matthias Erzberger, representing Germany, met with an all-but-cocky Marshal Ferdinand Foch, representing France, in a railway carriage deep in the forest of Compiègne.

Enemies at war, the two men and their delegations hammered out the details of an armistice, ending the Great War with the stroke of a pen. Cessation of hostilities was set for the eleventh hour of the eleventh day of the eleventh month.

Whole cities chanted the countdown. Across the globe, church bells pealed at eleven. Men, women, and children danced in the streets and byways, screaming, crying for joy, for an end to the terrible toil of war.

The populace of defeated countries lifted their hands and voices in the hope that armistice meant relief and peace of some sort; what sort, they could not afford to question. And when they had slept—victorious and defeated alike—they began the celebration again.

Annie refused Carol's repeated invitations to join the villagers' morning revelry, the town's first public dancing and singing since the war began.

"I need to be alone, Carol—just quiet, for a time. Please understand."

"Ah." Carol nodded wisely. "You wish to be alone with your thoughts—with your love." She smiled and tilted her head. "Soon Phillippe will return—by Christmas, I think." She stroked Annie's cheek. "And then you will dance."

Annie pressed her friend's arm. "Have a wonderful time, Carol."

"*Un moment.*" Carol raised her finger to her cheek in a sly smile, then crooked it, beckoning. "*Viens!*" She towed Annie through the corridor and up the stairs to her room. "I was saving this *pour Noël*!" she whispered. "But if today is not Christmas—the peace on earth—then when it will be, I do not know!

"Sit here, Elise!" Gently she pushed Annie to the seat at her dressing table. She rummaged secretively, half-laughing, through her wardrobe and finally lifted a brown paper package from the top shelf. She tore the paper away and pulled a bolt of creamy silk from its wrappings, hefted the bolt high into the air, and let the fabric flow across her bed, a perfect, rippling waterfall.

"*Voilà!*" She laughed, delighted. "It is the last of the wedding silk from the DuBock silk mill—the finest in France! They closed when the war took the last son to fight, but Maud—the great matriarch of that family—is my dearest friend. We were children together!" She held the featherlight fabric to her shoulder to better display. "*Une telle beauté*, such lavish beauty, *n'est-ce pas?*"

"It is lovely," Annie said, "truly lovely!"

"*C'est pour toi, ma petite* Elise." Carol smiled softly and twirled Annie round to face the mirror. She draped the cloud of ivory perfection across Annie's shoulders. "Do you not see? It is the perfect wedding gown! We will send for the best seamstress in Paris. Maud will know the one! I shall write her tomorrow!"

"It is too beautiful," Annie whispered. "I can't—"

"Nothing, *ma chère*, is too beautiful for the love of my son," Carol whispered fiercely and whisked the fabric away before her own tears spoiled it.

Annie stood and hugged her friend, who laughed at herself and said, "This is not a day for crying. It is a day to sing!"

Together the women folded the faintly shimmering silk. Carol wrapped it lovingly in the brown paper and reverently handed it to Annie. "I will be away through the day and late into the night, *ma chère*," she warned. "Such victory does not come to our village more than once in a lifetime."

"I am well. I will be well." Annie smiled and followed her friend to the hallway.

When the heavy door of the château closed behind Carol and the last servant had gone to join the revelry, Annie closed her eyes and breathed deeply. She listened and found in the silence the greatest peace of all.

Annie walked up the marbled stairs to her room. She sat before the long, low desk beneath her window, allowing the autumn late-morning sun to warm her face, to seep deep into her bones. She drew linen writing paper from the desk drawer and a pen from its holder. She cleaned the nib, then dipped the tip into the inkwell and paused, her pen in midair. She must think clearly and word carefully all that she would say. There were letters to write—long-overdue letters.

Annie's letter from France was a double-edged sword in Maggie Allen McKenica's heart. It brought joy and resolution but confirmed the worst of her fears.

Thank You, Lord in heaven, that Annie is safe. But why, Sweet Jesus? Why would You give me the joy of his life and let it be snatched away? Why not let me go to my grave barren rather than to have planted such joy in my heart as that lad brought? Was he not the son no other could have been to me? Is she not the daughter I have waited all my life to hold?

While the rest of Swainton and Cape May County celebrated the armistice, and the town and majority of middle-aged mothers rejoiced in the promise of their sons' homecoming from the Great War, Maggie's faith wrestled with her God who gave and her God who took away.

She pounded her fists and cried her tears behind the sheds in the gardens. She lay prostrate on Sean's grave on moonless nights. She slept in Daniel's arms.

By the end of two weeks she remembered that He was also the God who had sustained her through a young, arranged marriage, a trip on unknown seas to a new world, and a farm with a mortgage all their own. He was the God who had comforted her through years of barrenness and the death of her good husband Sean and then the death of Owen—the miracle lad who never came. He was the God who brought her instead Michael, the blessed son she had never borne. He was the God of her astonishing late-in-life marriage to Daniel, a man as good as any ten.

This God, she decided, who had held her when Michael came to live with them, was the same God who held her when Michael sailed away. He had comforted her when Annie hoped to come and when Annie disappeared and when the war dragged on. She had a long history with this God.

At the end of a very long month Maggie found her knees and vowed, "Though He slay me, yet will I trust Him." She sat back on her heels and whispered, "What is next, Lord? Show me Your path and give me the strength, the grace, to walk in it. But do not leave me, Lord. Stay close, for I must lean hard."

Maggie wrote Annie, repeating her offer of a home, if ever her dear niece wanted or needed it. And gripping her pen, Maggie wished Annie and Phillippe well in their forthcoming marriage, praying that would bring her joy.

Someday, when you are ready, dearest Annie, I hope that you and Phillippe will bring your children to visit Daniel and me. We shall walk together in Owen and Michael's gardens and the very special one Michael named for you. The pink and white double roses will bloom there again come June, the English boxwood will grow in its own slow way, the ivy will trail and spread, and the blue lobelia will be waiting.

All my love,
Aunt Maggie

≋ CHAPTER SIXTY-NINE ≋

WHEN CONNIE RECEIVED Annie's letter to her family, she wept. She wept for joy and relief that Annie was alive and safe. She wept for sadness that Michael was gone. She wept in fury that Annie had not let her or her parents know in nearly three years where she was or even that she was alive. And she wept for her parents' sake, for the terrible toll Annie's disappearance had taken on them, like the loss of a second late-in-life daughter. But she continued to read.

I do not expect any of you or Aunt Maggie to forgive me for the sorrow and anxiety my disappearance has surely caused you. Please believe me when I say that if I had been able to write, to let even one of you know of my existence or whereabouts, I would have done so—a thousand times.

One day I shall explain and hope you will believe I chose the only course I could, the only course Aunt Eleanor left to me. You were and are my family and were so very generous when I needed such kindness most, when I had nowhere to turn. I owe you everything.

I have missed you all terribly—words too feeble.

After the lorry accident, and after I learned of Michael's death, I was sent to the home of Madame Carol Fondrey to convalesce. She has been most kind to me and has treated me as a daughter in every way.

Her son Phillippe, an officer in the French army, has made me an offer of marriage. I am considering his proposal. I realize that I must build my life somewhere, as all the world builds upon the ashes of this war. And I am grateful to them both. He wishes to marry in the spring; his mother is even now making plans.

If this should come to pass, I shall have no great need of the inheritance left me by Grandfather Hargrave and Owen. In any case, before I wed, I should like to ask, Mr. Sprague, that you sell Hargrave House—if it remains—and liquidate my assets as quickly as possible. I never wish to see it again.

Please divide the final sum, giving half to Aunt Maggie and Uncle Daniel for payment of their mortgage and loans and for the prospering of Allen's Run Gardens, and retaining half for me. Please subtract from my portion your fees, plus a quarter of the remains to be used as a gift for you and Mrs. Sprague and Connie—some investment or enjoyment that will bring help and happiness. I know this plan would have pleased Owen. It pleases me. You may forward the necessary papers to this address.

If, perchance, Aunt Eleanor found a way to disinherit me after all, please do not fret. I will not, save for the gifts I cannot give.

Do you remember, Connie and Mrs. Sprague, when we fed the pigeons in Trafalgar Square? Oh, that we were girls once more, Connie; that we could turn back the clock and begin again.

But if I have learned anything, it is that time is not to be regained. The tide of our lives moves quickly; if we do not conform to its continuous ebb and flow, we will be washed away as surely as if we were sands upon the driven shore.

Forgive me—I feel old and tired tonight but curiously free.

I am at last forever free of Aunt Eleanor and all the Hargraves' troubled past, but at such terrible cost. Michael told me of her death. If only he had not come for me, he might . . . And yet, I confide, those weeks with him in Verdun were the most precious of my life. I will not know such joy again.

Know that I love you all dearly. I shall come to you soon, perhaps with Phillippe. I want you to know him, for you and his mother will be our family.

Your devoted Annie

Connie folded Annie's letter and tucked it into her pocket. She sighed. It all seemed so final. *She is not happy about this marriage. She's trying to please, to be dutiful again. Perhaps she is wise. Our generation of men is gone—an entire generation lost to the stupidity and brutality of war. Spinsters and widows abound in Britain and France—everywhere. Does it matter if we're happy? What right have we to happiness now?*

Connie sat up. "What insanity am I thinking?" she said aloud. "Marriage to someone you don't love is a stupid idea, Annie Allen! Your most stupid idea yet—and you've had a few, if I might be so bold!"

Connie did not know what she would write her parents. When she had signed on to take extra hospital shifts through the holidays, they had at last consented to go on extended holiday for the Christmas season. She hoped they would stay away at least until spring. Her mother so desperately needed the change, and her father had aged so that she was certain Annie would not easily recognize him. She was not about to interrupt their much-needed and well-deserved rest with news of Annie's ridiculous marriage scheme. And yet wouldn't the news of Annie's safety be a tonic for them? Shouldn't she forward to her father Annie's request for the liquidation of her assets? Dared she withhold a letter written to them all?

Connie creased the letter again and again. She determined to think her course of action through carefully. Once she expressed her relief and thanksgiving to Annie for her safety, she would do all in her power to set the young woman straight.

※ ❦

Dr. Narvett packed the last of his books and nailed closed the crate. He'd delayed as long as possible. The hospital board in Paris would not wait past the first of April. Already Glenda had opened their new apartment. She had expected him in Paris for Christmas, and he'd disappointed her. She demanded he come before Easter. Good wife that she was, he must not disappoint her again.

He closed his empty desk drawers, removed his certificates from the wall, and set the remaining half-filled boxes in the hallway for the movers. He would follow them on the morning train.

He had transferred his records to the new chief of staff and spent two days walking him through the wards, detailing special cases—unnecessarily, he knew. But these men were *ses enfants de temps de guerre*—his wartime children—and he hated to leave them before he felt they had reached their full potential.

That night he said his good-byes to staff and patients alike. When he came to Michael's ward, he sat beside him on his hospital cot. "*Tout est arrangé, Michel.* You will go to England within the month. There is a convalescent center in London where I think you will have good opportunity to continue your progress."

"Thank you, Doctor," Michael responded, but without enthusiasm.

"Do not be discouraged, my son. The mind is a tricky member. It seems to work best when we tax it least. Let it open itself to you."

"I remembered a name today." Michael looked at the doctor and frowned. "Owen."

"Owen? Who is Owen?" Dr. Narvett probed.

Michael looked at his shoes. "I don't know."

"Yet." Dr. Narvett smiled.

Michael nodded. "Yet."

Dr. Narvett pressed Michael's shoulder. "I would have liked to have known you before the war, my son."

Michael grinned lopsidedly. "I would have liked to have known me too, Doctor."

"A good sense of humor." Dr. Narvett laughed, reaching for Michael's hand. "Keep it always. It will help you through many, many days." He stood. "So for now—good-bye, *Michel.* Someday, when you remember more, you contact me. This is my address in Paris." He tucked the paper in Michael's shirt pocket and stood to go.

Michael began to speak but could not seem to command the words.

"*Oui,*" Dr. Narvett returned. "I understand." He pressed Michael's shoulder once more, then walked away.

CHAPTER SEVENTY

MICHAEL DID NOT LIKE the railway-carriage journey to the channel port. He liked even less the choppy channel crossing and the hospital ship, full of sour-smelling sick and wounded men and pasty-faced nurses. It was as though he had experienced everything before but could not remember when or where.

The convalescent home was early-spring dreary, the late snow outside the windows covered in black soot. Michael hated most of all the smell and dirt of the black coke used to warm the house, but he could not think why.

By the middle of April, Michael wished he might never taste porridge or beef broth again. He longed for the fresh peas of spring that wound up white trellises and mingled with fragrant sweet peas in Dr. Narvett's hospital garden, and for a salad of lettuce and radishes and tender dandelion greens—the kind Uncle Daniel grew. And then he wondered, *What are dandelion greens and where have I tasted such a thing? And who is Uncle Daniel?*

Each day brought new memories, new pieces of a great puzzle. *If only,* he thought, *I could lay the borders—the pieces might make sense!*

In late April, Michael began to help the groundskeeper dig and rake the garden. The fresh air and exercise became a balm; Michael could barely wait for the morning light to begin a new day. While digging, Michael found that he remembered all the words to his Christmas carols, stanza by stanza. He sang at the top of his lungs, no matter that the groundskeeper thought him a fool.

When Michael stooped and turned his spade, he found two worms struggling in the rain-wet earth. He cocked his head as if to listen and suddenly remembered two men struggling for coins and pints in a squalid flat.

As he removed his boots that night, memories of hobnails, his uncle Tom's sharp boot thrust flush against his ribs, and the crack of a leather belt singeing his back flashed before him. No one touched him, but Michael experienced the excruciating pain just the same.

That night began a series of dreams: a railway-carriage ride over miles and miles of countryside he'd never seen; a small girl's hand tucked into his own, her eyes blue like his own; peppermint sticks, a pair, separated by the hands of a trickster in a tall black hat; flashes of gold coins dropped into the palm of a beefy hand; and his Megan Marie, her eyes puffed from crying, her coal-colored ringlets damp and mangled, and her bow-shaped lips screaming, over and over, "Michael! Michael!"

New images swept through his brain, faster and faster: a giant ship listing, its whistles blasting long and loud, then exploding into a million stars in the night; cold such as he'd never known and ragged cries torn from his own throat of "Owen, Owen, Owen!"; a newly mounded grave beside a smiling, nearly silver-haired woman named Maggie; a girl—just the back of her long and lovely golden hair—always running, running, running away.

Michael flailed his arms, jerking free of the tangled, sweat-wet sheets wound tight about his neck. His heart drummed loud and erratic against the walls of his chest, pulsed in his eyes and in the space of his brain; he could not draw his breath, and he could not swallow the huge and aching gourd in his throat.

The evening orderly rushed in. The groundskeeper was roused to help, and even the matron herself tried to sedate him. But Michael pushed them all away. He could not separate the voices in his head from the din of yammering outside him. Even so, the pieces of the great puzzle, in all their stark colors, slid slowly, locking into place.

Sweet Jesus, how could I have forgotten her? Where? Where are you, Annie? Help me find her, Sweet Jesus. Help me find her!

CHAPTER SEVENTY-ONE

"INFLUENZA—there is no doubt. He must be moved to London General. If we leave him here, every man will be infected by morning. Even now it may be too late."

Michael heard but could not differentiate the voices above his pounding, aching head—a sledgehammer's thrust upon thrust, just behind his eyes. He saw the swarm of masked medical personnel moving in and out of the room as if they all dragged through warm treacle toffee. He wanted to shout at them to leave him alone, to let him go, tell them that he desperately needed to find Annie, and why didn't they understand?

But his body ached as though he'd been run over by the exploding lorries at Verdun, even as he alternately shivered and sweat, and his nose kept pouring something bright—something red. He coughed and coughed; his mouth spewed vomit. It would not form the words he needed. Even his brain, though it knew what he meant, what he wanted, betrayed him.

He knew he was being lifted and moved, and he had no power to stop it. *How will Annie find me?*

The dreams rushed, flashes of memory and nightmare fought and twisted, on and on, without end. After two days of thrashing, he fell into semidarkness against his pillow, certain only that he would drown in the putrid vomit of his own hell.

≋ ≋

Connie was grateful when her parents agreed to stay the spring in the Lake District. Her father had written that her mother's health had greatly improved and that he, for the first time since they were newly married, was digging a spring garden.

Connie was glad she'd not written to them of Annie or of her late-May marriage plans. *It would prove a distraction from their happiness.*

After she had begged Annie to reconsider her plans to marry a man she was less than head over heels in love with, she'd written enthusiastically in response to Annie's second letter proposing her and Phillippe's plans to visit London and the Spragues near the end of their monthlong wedding trip. She might not think Annie's decision a wise one, but she did not wish to alienate her friend. *Goodness knows there are too few of us left.*

Connie explained to Annie that she felt that would be time enough to share the news with her recuperating parents. She hoped Annie would understand. Either way, Connie intended to protect their holiday.

Nor did Connie tell her parents that she was working in the influenza wards. Indeed, she'd not known when they went away before Christmas that she would be reassigned.

But the pandemic was impossible. Military personnel and civilians alike were struck by the thousands. Patients slept on blankets on the hospital floor, each waiting for the man in the cot above him to die that he might be placed in his bed. Medical personnel fell ill by the hundreds, leaving each section desperate for help. Though the number of new cases had slowed, there was no end in sight.

As she walked to and from the hospital, Connie passed young girls—those untouched by the disease—chanting ditties as they turned jumping ropes:

"I had a little bird;
His name was Enza.
I opened up the window
And in flew Enza!"

Connie shook her head and wished for all their sakes that the girls' parents would censor them. But she would not wish the girls inside. Their chance of survival depended on fresh air.

Today Connie had already served twelve hours in a new ward with no time for a cup of tea, let alone a biscuit. The arches in her feet screamed, as though a thousand tiny pitchforks prodded them over an open flame; the pain in her lower back made her cringe. Her uniform was spattered in blood and smeared with vomit. She had washed enough men and changed enough sheets and scrubbed enough bedpans to last a lifetime.

She prayed that the tram would still be running when she finished her fourteen-hour shift. She could not think of walking the sixteen blocks home.

Connie had just stripped and changed the linens from a newly emptied cot. The skin of the patient who'd died had darkened so that his family did not recognize the body. She was returning with fresh blankets when she heard the new man behind the screen whimper, "Annie!"

Connie's heart leaped in her chest. Her breath stopped. "It can't be," she whispered. "It can't be." She steadied herself. Having been disappointed so many times, she knew better than to hope, to believe. She rounded the linen screen run around each cot, the hospital's attempt to isolate the deadly breathing of each man.

He was so changed, so thin and pale compared to the handsome young man she remembered. His eyes stared at the ceiling, but glassy as they were, she was certain he saw nothing. She waved her hand in front of his face. He did not blink but continued to moan softly, to whimper, "Annie, Annie."

Connie blinked back tears. From habit or simply because she did not know what else to do, she lifted his chart from the foot of the bed and read *Michael*. No last name, no details of rank or birth date—simply *Michael*.

Connie swallowed the fire in her throat. She read the details, the date of admission on the chart. He was not newly admitted but newly moved. Two weeks had passed since his admission. It was, in her experience, a miracle that he was still alive. That he would regain consciousness or be alive tomorrow, she could not hope.

Violating every rule, she sat on his cot, took his hand in hers, and wiped the sweat from his brow. She wrung a cloth and sponged his forehead, his cheeks, his mouth, his neck. She filled the cloth again and moistened his lips. She whispered, "I am here, Michael."

When Connie left, two hours past midnight, she penciled *Dunnagan* on Michael's chart and wrote her own name as nearest relation.

All the way home she wondered if she should write to Annie. But Annie and Phillippe's wedding was scheduled for the last Saturday in May. What if Michael did not live? What if she wrote Annie and Annie canceled her wedding only to have Michael die in her arms? Annie had suffered so much. How could she drag her through more?

When Connie reached home, she was too bone weary to walk up the steps to her room. She dropped in the winged chair of her father's library.

The maid, upon hearing Connie's step, pulled on her dressing gown and brought up from the kitchen a pot of tea and a tray of cold sandwiches. But Connie never knew, and Tilly, after building up the fire, crept away.

≋ CHAPTER SEVENTY-TWO ≋

ONE BRIGHT MORNING in mid-May, Annie stepped onto the dressmaker's platform temporarily set in the middle of her room. She turned slowly as Madame Desmettre critically viewed the hem, the flow, the lines of the wedding gown she had uniquely designed and sewn, every tiny stitch by hand.

"*C'est magnifique!*" Madame Desmettre smiled at last. "And you, Mademoiselle Hargrave, are beautiful—so very beautiful. It is the perfect wedding gown for the perfect wedding!"

Carol clapped her hands. "Oh! Maud was correct! She knew you would do as no one could, Deborah! It is all I hoped!" She held out her hands to Annie. "And you, my dear, do you not love it?"

Annie placed her hands willingly in Carol's and smiled her thanks to Madame Desmettre. "It is more lovely than any gown I could imagine."

"And do you not already feel the bride?" Carol teased, turning Annie to view her own reflection in the oval mirror.

The young woman staring back at Annie was indeed beautiful. The flowing silken gown created the perfect sculpture of her form. The sheer and delicate veil fell from a mobcap design in an icy waterfall over her upswept hair. Her shoulders and the hollow of her throat formed an exquisite backdrop for the sparkling necklace—large diamonds interspersed with midsize sapphires. Diamonds and smaller sapphires dangled from her earlobes, setting the blue of her eyes alight.

She looked a perfect Parisian fashion plate. But she looked nothing like Annie Allen.

Annie hoped that Carol Fondrey did not think her less exuberant than she. She did not want to hurt or disappoint her delighted friend.

Behind the screen Annie carefully stepped from the gown. A

housemaid knocked timidly on her door and brought in the morning post on a silver tray.

"J'en suis jalouse!" Carol pretended to pout. "Not one letter for me today, and yet for you there are two—one from America and one from your soon-to-be and soon-to-be-here husband!"

But Annie wondered. Already Phillippe had been delayed twice. He'd not been granted leave at Christmas.

Wars, he had written, *may conclude, but peacekeeping efforts labor on.*

Annie had forced herself to write Phillippe of her disappointment and shared that disappointment with Carol on Christmas morning. But when Easter came and Phillippe did not, Annie looked in the mirror and knew better than to belie her relief, a relief she did not wholly understand.

When Annie walked round the screen, tying the sash of her dressing gown, Carol playfully waved the letters before her.

"A mother is never so lucky as the bride!" Carol laughed happily and linked her arm through Madame Desmettre's as they made for the door. Turning, she whispered coyly, "I can guess which you will open first!" The women laughed as if old friends and closed the door behind them.

But Carol was wrong.

When Annie finished reading Aunt Maggie's letter, she held it to her heart and sat on the edge of her bed.

Gradually the morning light gave way; patches of sunlight crossed the floor.

At last she walked to her dressing table. Annie stared long into the mirror. She turned her head one way and then the other as she pulled the diamond-and-sapphire earrings away. She leaned forward to unfasten the exquisitely designed necklace—an early wedding gift from Phillippe. She placed the valuable jewels in their blue velvet box, arranging them carefully across the satin lining.

She raised her head and viewed the unadorned woman reflected before her. She wondered who Annie Allen truly was, what it would mean to find out—to put care and concern for herself above that of others, just once—and if Phillippe would understand such a quest. Would such searching be selfish?

What do You require of me, Lord?

She shook her head at the absurdity of her quandary. She did not, could never love Phillippe as she had loved Michael. That much she must face. But she cared for him, and who would not? Phillippe was a good and kind man, fully deserving of a wife's undivided love and affection; she could not bear to hurt him, nor his dear mother, her generous friend.

Which is worse: Marry him and carry forward a pretense with the hope that I will one day love him enough, be enough for him—for them? Or tell them I am sorry, but that I love a ghost more? Would they forgive me? Could I forgive myself for not being his happiness? Can I forgive myself for pledging my love to anyone other than Michael? How has it come to this? Where do the borders between sacrificial love end and loving and owning the life I've been given begin?

Is this presumption, to think that their happiness depends upon me? I can't be salvation for them. Only Christ can be that.

Is that what I tried to be for the Spragues, for Aunt Maggie and Michael, in shielding them from Aunt Eleanor? And yet, I had to protect them—didn't I?

Was that truly the sort of sacrifice Owen gave in helping to save others rather than trying to save himself? What is the difference between a willing sacrifice and a coercion—a blackmail—even on behalf of those I love?

The questions were so hard, the ramifications so deep, that they made her head hurt. *But perhaps,* she mused, *if Phillippe is delayed anyway, if we must postpone the wedding for a month, I could write Aunt Maggie. . . . I could—*

Carol rapped madly on the door of Annie's bedchamber. "Elise! Elisabeth!" Unable to wait for an answer, she pushed it open and cried, "*Ma chère!* A telegram from Phillippe—*il arrive en train le lendemain!*"

CHAPTER SEVENTY-THREE

CONNIE DID NOT WRITE to her parents of Michael. She didn't expect him to live, and she could not burden them with false hope. They'd return to London in a heartbeat; of that she was certain.

She did not write Annie, though she debated that decision hourly. *So many secrets,* she worried. *So many, and the burden too heavy.*

Connie spent every spare minute by Michael's bedside, though he did not know. She told the hospital staff that Michael Dunnagan was her Irish cousin, thought lost in the war, and that he was closer than any brother; she was all he had in the world.

The matron, having been pestered every day for a week and finally threatened with Connie deserting her post, for which she was desperately needed, relented at last and permanently assigned her to Michael's ward.

Connie did not know whether to pray that Michael would simply fall asleep forever or to hope for his recovery. She'd seen patients affected mentally and nervously beyond repair from bad cases of the influenza. She could not pray for such a life for Michael.

For nearly another week his only sign of intelligence was a constant murmuring for Annie. Each time Connie heard him, she brushed the damp curls from his brow, traced the slight dimple in each cheek, and whispered, "I am here, my love. I am here." Content, he returned to sleep.

If he awoke, she'd no idea what she would do, what she would tell him. She would cross that bridge when she came to it, if she came to it.

Early one morning, as Connie finished reading Michael's temperature, he opened his eyes. She studied him for his glassy, nonseeing probe of the ceiling, but he looked directly at her. He breathed, his chest slowly rising and falling. His voice cracked, but he whispered, "Connie."

She stared and gasped, too startled to speak.

"Connie?" he whispered again.

"Yes! Yes, Michael! I'm here!" Tears streamed down her face.

His brow furrowed. "Why are you crying?"

Connie laughed and cried and laughed some more.

That night Connie wrestled with her pen and writing paper. Twice she penned a letter to Annie, telling her of Michael. Twice she tore it in two and threw it into the grate.

Annie will likely be married by the time my letter reaches France. What good will learning of Michael do her? Might it not do more harm than good— play the mischief in her marriage to Phillippe?

Connie rationalized, aloud and in silence. *Michael will need someone to comfort him when he learns Annie has married another. Why not me? Perhaps, in time, he might . . .* But she dared not finish the thought, not even in the privacy of her mind.

Just after midnight, she turned down the lamp and climbed into bed. But a pricking conscience made a poor pillow.

Michael was moved ten days later, back to the convalescent home. Connie visited each morning and evening, before and after her shift. She had come to love smoothing the black curls from his forehead, stroking the soft indentations of his temples.

She brought him the duffel of his belongings, the things he'd left with her parents when he'd sailed for France in search of Annie three years before, and helped him sort through those treasures of home.

Though his hands still trembled in weakness, Michael grasped Aunt Maggie's Bible and held it to his lips.

Connie helped him hold a spoon and then a fork until he was steady enough to feed himself. At last he worked the buttons of his own clothing and, in a few days, walked the hallway, back and forth.

Each day, as he gained strength, he asked Connie about Annie— where she was, why she had not come to visit him. "Before I could open my eyes—at the hospital—I heard her. I know she was here!"

Connie did not have the heart to tell him that hers was the voice he had heard; hers were the hands that had soothed his brow and washed his face; hers were the lips that had kissed him good night.

She could not bring herself to tell him that Annie, believing him dead, had married another. Even to her, knowing Annie's good, if feeble, intentions, it smacked of betrayal after all Michael had done, after his pursuing, unfailing love.

※ ※

Michael was already packing his duffel when Connie stopped in the first week of June.

"Where are you going?" she demanded, but her eyes told him that she already knew.

"To find Annie." He stood and searched her face. "I don't know why you won't tell me where she is. I appreciate all that you've done for me, but you know why I'm here—why I came to England, why I charged over to France."

Connie sat down heavily on the cot between them. "I do know. It's why I've not wanted to tell you."

Michael stared at her, sat down beside her, took her hands in his own. "Tell me. Where is she? What's happened to Annie?"

He saw that she struggled to begin.

"We thought . . ." Connie met his eyes. "Annie thought you were dead—that you'd died in the shelling." She looked away.

Michael held his breath.

"And she was injured."

Michael pressed Connie's hands. "Annie's—"

"Oh, she's all right now." Connie's color deepened. "But she was badly injured in the lorry crash—after the bombing. She was nursed at a hospital in Paris and later by a woman and her son in the countryside."

Connie pulled her hands from Michael's, stood, and began to pace as though she could not bear to look at him. "She needed to begin a new life, you see."

"A new life?" Michael repeated the words.

"Yes," she said, looking back at him, clasping and unclasping her hands. Feebly she shook her head. "After the war—we all had to begin again."

Michael did not understand the pleading in Connie's face. But a weight beyond his own began to descend upon his chest and suck the breath from his lungs. Michael stood, steadying himself against the iron rail at the head of his cot. "What do you mean, 'begin again'?"

"She's married," Connie said at last. She raised her chin as though the telling was a battle she must face. "Annie married Phillippe Fondrey—the son of the Frenchwoman who nursed her."

"What? What did you say?" Michael narrowed his eyes, trying to focus on what she had said. But her words were impossible.

"Michael—"

Michael stepped back against the wall, shaking his head from side to side. "No. I don't believe you." He tried to sort the words that had spilled from her mouth, tried to comprehend why she would tell such a cruel and horrid lie. But the suffocating, leaden weight dropped like a stone-sharpened ax—a grinding, pounding ax that ripped his body from neck to groin.

Married! My Annie's married another! The phrase flashed over and over through his battered brain, ready to explode like the lights on a short-circuited marquee.

"I didn't want to tell you—not like this." Connie reached for him.

But Michael pushed her away, turned his back, and covered his face with his hands.

If the words had not come from Connie Sprague—Connie, who had nursed and visited him daily, who had supported his pursuit of Annie Allen through the battlefields of France—Michael would have called the speaker a liar and a thief. Only a liar would say that his Annie had married another. Only a thief would steal his heart, his life, his dreams.

But she would not take it back. And in the end, he knew Connie spoke the truth. He knew because hope and life had failed him before. He knew because his dream was greater than he had a right to dare to dream. He knew, most of all, because Annie, his loving Annie, had not come.

☙ CHAPTER SEVENTY-FOUR ☙

MICHAEL PENNED a letter to Aunt Maggie two days later. He would not be in England for her reply, but he trusted that she and Uncle Daniel would want him, though he failed to bring their Annie home. It was a long letter, but he did not want to tell the story in person. He never wanted to tell it again, once he set foot in America.

> *And that is the tale of my wanderings, Aunt Maggie. Had it not been for Dr. Narvett and Connie Sprague, I do not know what might have become of me or if I would ever have been able to let you know. I am sad and sorry for the grief I have caused you. The grief this war has brought us all is beyond my imagination or ken.*
>
> *That I cannot bring our Annie home—for you, for me, for Owen—is the greatest defeat I have known this side of childhood. The war and all that I've seen is nothing to compare.*
>
> *I ask you, Uncle Daniel, to do something for me before I come. Tear Owen's white double roses from the ground—the ones I planted for Annie. They were to be for her bridal bouquet. I know I never said that; I never dared. But it was a hope I carried every day. I cannot face them now. The roots can be planted elsewhere, if you want to propagate them for sale. I don't care—but not in Annie's garden. Please.*
>
> *I sail on 13 June and am scheduled to arrive in New York on the afternoon of 20 June. Do not trouble to make the trip. I shall take the train to Philadelphia and on to Swainton.*
>
> *Your loving son,*
Michael

The afternoon before Michael left England, he visited Bunhill Fields and Owen's grave. He smiled in spite of himself at the meager bouquet of yellow roses in his grasp.

Blue flowers, the same form of lobelia he'd planted in New Jersey from Owen's seeds, just the color of Annie's eyes, spread over the whole of his friend's resting place and that of his father and mother. He did not know the little flower's botanical name, but he knew he should not have been surprised. "Owen's Thumb," he said. "That's what I'll call you pretties from now on."

He sat on the bench nearest his friend's grave and told him the story— the long, long story. He told Owen that he was sorry he'd not brought Annie to America as he'd vowed, sorry that he had lost her and failed her.

Michael ran his hands over Owen's stone and, standing, took in the nearby gravestone of John Bunyan. He saw on one side the relief of a man burdened by a terrible weight, and he understood the image; he felt that weight in his own life.

On the other side he saw that the man had dropped his burden, having found and laid hold of the cross. "I don't know if I can let go," Michael whispered. "I wish I could. I wish I could."

❦ ❦

Connie saw Michael off at Victoria station. He thanked her for the box lunch she had packed for him, for all she'd done—before the war for Annie and during and after the war for him. He kissed her cheek, held her close, and was gone.

Long after the train pulled from the station, Connie stood alone on the platform, her hand pressed to her cheek.

❦ ❦

That night, over tepid tea, Connie absently sorted the day's mail.

A letter from France, in Annie's hand, had been posted from a port Connie could not quite make out and rerouted twice. Rather the worse for wear, it had arrived on the Spragues' doormat three weeks after its posting. Connie shook her head and fussed aloud at the state of the British mail since the war's end.

She contemplated the date on the letter and the fact that the return address gave Annie's maiden name. Silently she swallowed, noting that the nasty bile of a false friend did not go down easily. She moistened her lips and squared her shoulders. A sudden ache sprang between her temples as she slit the letter's seal.

Dearest Mr. and Mrs. Sprague and Connie,

I hardly know how to begin. I have disappointed dear Phillippe and his precious mother. I pray that you will not be disappointed in my breaking of my contract with him. But it has come to me that my acceptance of his proposal was, like so many things, an acceptance of what life offered or demanded of me. It was not my heart's choice— simply a following of the stream as it flowed toward the sea, a path of least resistance, one meant to appease and please others. As though pleasing others fulfilled a proper laying down of one's life—the kind of sacrifice our Lord gave for us, the kind of sacrifice Owen gave for Michael and for me. For the first time I realize that it does not. There is a marked difference between sacrificial love and the destruction of God-given boundaries of the soul.

I do not regret my desire to protect those I love. I did so with a pure heart. But I've sought forgiveness for believing that the salvation of my loved ones was up to me. And because I must, for my own sake, I've forgiven Aunt Eleanor for being only herself. Darkness was everything she knew. How I pity that. She died in her grasping and meanness. I pray God's mercy upon her.

At last I understand what it means to lay my burden—my own unique burden of sadness, bitterness, loss, and lost opportunities—at the foot of the cross and to look up with hope. At last I understand what Owen tried so hard to tell me—that joy and freedom may only be found in the source of absolute love and truth—in Christ!

For the first time I have paused and am choosing where my feet will take me—a journey of free will without fear, guilt, or coercion. I do not know what of life lies ahead, only that it does. And I am happy in anticipation. Can I write that with any

≋ CHAPTER /EVENTY-FIVE ≋

THE CROSSING took seven full days. "A slow boat to China," some called it, then added, laughing, "or New York." Michael did not mind. He had a great many memories to sort through and new ones to process.

The first days at sea reminded him of his days with Owen. *All the ways he saved me—from starvation and the elements in Southampton, from my own stupidity aboard* Titanic, *from drowning when he forced me into a lifeboat.* Michael shook his head at the wonder of it all. *Owen saved me for a hope and a future when he forced my arms into his own coat, a coat too big and sewn full of dreams—dreams of a charge and purpose, an occupation, a family.*

What was it he said? Michael tried to remember, standing at the ship's rail after two days at sea. *Ah, I remember. He said, "What are we without our dreams?"*

Michael sighed. *I do not know, Owen. What are we . . . without our dreams?*

That night Michael rummaged through the duffel he'd left with the Spragues before he sailed to France. He pulled Aunt Maggie's Bible from the bottom, leaned his forehead against it, then thumbed absently through it.

What would you do, Owen, if it were you sitting here? Off to America with no Annie?

Michael sat a long time before he realized that was exactly what Owen had done. He had sailed to an unknown land and unknown family with all the plans and hopes and dreams in the world. He had planned to carve a life around helping and prospering those he loved. And he had planned to bring Annie to America only when it was safe—because all he really wanted for Annie was what was best for her.

Can I want that? Truly? Only what is best for Annie? What if leaving her in France—leaving her to this marriage—what if that is best for Annie, better than the life and love I could give her?

Michael nearly choked. He did not want to believe that anything in this world could be better for Annie.

Even Owen's plans changed. In the blink of an eye he saved me, a gutter rat—a feeble friend he'd known only days. He gave away his dreams to a near stranger. He laid down his life for me, for Lucy Snape, and he secured a promise for Annie's future—Annie's best.

Michael shook his head and continued to flip through Aunt Maggie's Bible. *Owen was a better man than I can ever be; of that I am certain.*

Each time he flipped the pages, they seemed to slow in the same place. Michael thumbed again, carefully, and stopped when he found a slip of paper stuck close into the binding. It was Aunt Maggie's handwriting, a short note that began with a Scripture citation: John 15:11-14.

Curious, Michael traced his finger down the column until he found the passage:

These things have I spoken unto you, that my joy might remain in you, and that your joy might be full. This is my commandment, That ye love one another, as I have loved you. Greater love hath no man than this, that a man lay down his life for his friends. Ye are my friends, if ye do whatsoever I command you.

Michael swallowed. It was exactly what Owen had done, laid down his life for his friends, though they did not deserve it. Michael turned the scrap of paper and saw that Aunt Maggie had written, *These four have done this for me: Sean, Daniel, Owen, Michael.*

Michael sat until the light from his porthole faded. He could not believe Aunt Maggie had included him with those good men. He knew that each of them had done all the good they could, whenever they could, to whomever they could. Each had sacrificed and counted it only gain.

He knew from Daniel that Sean had loved Maggie with all his heart and Daniel as his brother. He knew that Sean Allen had tried his best to save his brother, Mackenzie, and his children from Eleanor Hargrave; he knew that Daniel had served Maggie and Sean all the days of his adult life and would love and serve Maggie till he died. Owen he knew best of all. Owen had taught him, by example, all he knew about love and kindness, about manliness and strength and sacrifice. No greater gift, no greater legacy could there be than his.

Michael read the passage again. *This is where they learned it. And so might I.*

Such knowledge was not new to Michael, but it felt new. It felt like a thread, a towline, a possibility.

He slept peacefully through the night for the first time in longer than he could remember. The next morning he stood at the ship's railing and watched the sun cast its pale-pink wash across the heavens, even before it rose from the sea.

"I do not know what my future holds, Sweet Jesus," he prayed, "but I beg Your forgiveness for my sins and shames, and I trust You—with all the failures of my past, with the uncertainties of this day, and with all my days to come. Make of me what You will, and make me a blessing to those in my path.

"I trust to You my precious Annie, Sweet Jesus, and all that is best for her. I trust to You her heart, her husband's heart, their love, and the children that will be born of that love."

Michael did not wipe away the tears that fell, but there was no need. There were only he and God to see.

When the great ship sailed into New York's harbor, Michael stood on deck. This time he carried no dread of customs or officials, no fear of being sent back. He knew he should be grateful to call this free land home. In time, he knew he would be again.

The hardest moment came when he stood in line and could not help but watch as men met their waiting wives and families with loving embraces, lingering kisses, small children running into the arms of their young parents. It was Michael's lost dream in a picture, in a moment.

He turned away, breathed deeply, and checked the train schedules to Philadelphia. With less than an hour to go, he thought he'd best make his way to the station. Michael hefted his bag and duffel.

As he pushed through the gate, he caught sight of Aunt Maggie and Uncle Daniel scanning the crowds, two not-quite-elderly, anxious halves to a whole—dear faces, faces that he loved. He had not expected them to travel to New York but was pleased they had come.

Michael forced himself to smile for their sakes, pushing down the dry lump in his throat, a grating reminder that he would have no half to make him whole; there would be no one else for him.

They spotted him suddenly. Their faces lit and they waved, Aunt Maggie jumping up and down, wildly pumping her arm and calling something he could not hear, pointing to something he could not see.

The afternoon sun broke through the clouds, and Michael shielded his eyes to better see them. In the shade of his palm, he thought he saw flowers bobbing over Aunt Maggie's head. He blinked and looked again.

From between the older couple stepped a slender young woman in a white summer dress, her golden hair twisted and swept high beneath a fetching, broad-brimmed hat and veil.

Michael's heart began to pound.

The young woman lifted the simple white netting, found Michael's eyes, and smiled, two dimples calling his name.

Running, stumbling toward her, Michael could not take his eyes from the face he loved for fear she would vanish. He raced up the platform, swept her high in his arms, and swung her round and round.

Annie laughed aloud just before she pulled his face to hers, just before she kissed him, her tear-filled eyes the color of the blue lobelia she carried, tucked into a bouquet of Owen's white double roses and trailing English ivy.

TITANIC has long fascinated me—the ship, her builders, the romance of the era, but especially her passengers and staff and the family members left behind.

I've wondered about the individuals, the hopes and dreams cut short of those who drowned that fateful night. And those who lived—how did they go on living, knowing they'd been miraculously, magnanimously saved in lifeboats while hundreds died around them?

The first time I saw a copy of the ship's manifest, I found details of a young man, Owen George Allum, a gardener who'd sailed third class from Southampton. Later, in a *Titanic* exhibit, I saw his name again and learned that he had drowned. A little research led me to his family, his intended destination, even the items found in his pockets once his body was recovered. And from that I wove a short story, "The Legacy of Owen Allen," which eventually grew into the full-length manuscript *Promise Me This*.

Based on those beginnings, I fleshed out the fictional character of Owen Allen. It was easy to imagine that he would save others and charge them with the care of his loved ones while sacrificing his own life—for isn't that what Jesus did for us? As I wrote, I fell in love with our Savior all over again and saw parallel after parallel between His gift and Owen's story.

But Michael, the recipient of that unmerited act of grace, has his own story: the charge he accepts to care for Annie and for Owen's family in America is our story—a picture of the charge that the Lord gives us to "love one another." We've learned through His gift of love and saving grace that there is no greater gift to receive or give than this: "that a man lay down his life for his friends."

The portion of the tale I did not fully see was Annie's story—the sister left behind—until, after two weeks spent researching in England and France, I remember sitting on a bench before the tomb of John Bunyan in Bunhill Fields, London, journaling, very early on the last morning of my stay. I contemplated the relief on each side of his tomb, taken from his book *The Pilgrim's Progress*—on one side, Christian, weary and bent, burdened by the load on his back; on the other, Christian, relieved of his burden and grasping the cross in joyous victory. In that moment Annie's story poured into my mind. I couldn't write fast enough, and I couldn't keep the tears of joy and gratitude from raining down my cheeks.

I think I might have frightened the groundskeeper that morning—what was he to do with the weeping American woman before the tomb of a centuries-dead author? I never knew his name, but I have much to thank him for by way of his kindness and patience, and for showing me another centuries-old grave I very much wanted to see. But that is another story.

The next year, with the help of my husband, son, and daughter, I returned to France and added Germany, knowing what I needed to see and experience to finish the story—for the survivors of *Titanic* were destined to face the horrors of World War I in their very near future.

And what better place to set Allen's Run Gardens, including Owen's garden of Old World roses, than in New Jersey—our own Garden State? When you can, take a stroll through Leaming's Run Gardens in Swainton, just outside Cape May Court House, New Jersey, and think of Annie and Michael.

I hope you've enjoyed *Promise Me This* as much as I enjoyed writing it. Stop by my website, www.cathygohlke.com, for more insights into the story, recipes from my characters, and news of upcoming books. I'd love to hear from you.

ABOUT THE AUTHOR

CATHY GOHLKE is the two-time Christy Award–winning author of *William Henry Is a Fine Name* and *I Have Seen Him in the Watchfires*, which also won the American Christian Fiction Writers' Book of the Year award and was listed by *Library Journal* as one of the Best Books of 2008.

Cathy has worked as a school librarian, drama director, and director of children's and education ministries. When not traipsing the hills and dales of historic sites, she, her husband, and their dog, Reilly, make their home on the banks of the Laurel Run in Elkton, Maryland. Visit her website at www.cathygohlke.com.

DISCUSSION QUESTIONS

1. Do you think there was a defining moment, a turning point in Eleanor Hargrave's life? Standing at that crossroads, what difference would another choice have made for her and her family?

2. Mackenzie and Owen Allen, father and son, were offered the same opportunity at different times: to join the family business in New Jersey. What do their different responses tell us about them?

3. Annie complained when Owen urged her to read *The Pilgrim's Progress* and asked if he could not have found her something "amusing." What value did Owen see in reading the book, and what lesson in showing her the tomb? How did this affect Annie throughout the story?

4. Do you see a parallel between Owen's gift to Michael and Christ's gift to us? If so, please explain.

5. Michael knew Owen only a short time. Why did he grieve so deeply for him? What did Michael eventually learn from Owen's example?

6. Do you see a parallel between Michael's and Annie's responses to Owen's gift of life and our response to Christ's gift to us? If so, discuss both their positive and negative responses. Relate those to our own responses.

7. Why did Michael reach out to Annie again after she had made it clear she wanted nothing to do with him? How did his letter after the burning of her gardens change her attitude toward him?

8. After all Annie had been through and with the joy of Michael's coming to England before her, why did she succumb to Aunt Eleanor's blackmail scheme to send her to France during the war? Do you think she made the right choice?

9. Discuss Michael's pursuit of Annie through the battlefields of France. Was there ever a time you thought he might give up the search? Can you think of a biblical parallel to his determination to find her?

10. Annie came to love Michael with all her heart. Why did she agree to marry Phillippe so soon after she thought Michael dead? What do you think changed her mind?

11. Michael did all he could to fulfill his promise to Owen to bring Annie to America. Why did he finally surrender his pursuit? Is there ever a time we should relinquish a vow we have made?

12. Owen, Michael, Annie, the Spragues, Maggie, and Daniel all showed great love in different ways. Which character do you most identify with and why?